Storm Dancer

Storm Dancer

Rayne Hall

STORM DANCER
Copyright: ©2011-2013 Rayne Hall
Cover by Paul Davies and Erica Syverson © Rayne Hall
Scimitar Press (2013 CreateSpace Edition)

ISBN: 978-1-4825-6722-9

British spellings.

Contents

Contents cont'd...

CHAPTER 1

The Summons

Even in the shade of the graffiti-carved olive tree, the air sang with heat. Dahoud listened to the hum of voices in the tavern garden, the murmured gossip about royals and rebels. If patrons noticed him, they would only see a young clerk sitting among the lord-satrap's followers, a harmless bureaucrat. Dahoud planned to stay harmless.

The tavern bustled with women - whiteseers hanging about in the hope of earning a copper, traders celebrating deals, bellydancers clinking finger cymbals—women who neither backed away from him nor screamed.

The youngest of the entertainers wound her way between the benches towards their table, the tassels on her slender hips bouncing, the rows of copper rings on her sash tinkling with every snaky twist. Since she seemed nervous, as if it was her first show, he sent her an encouraging smile. Ignoring him, she shimmied to Lord Govan.

The djinn slithered inside Dahoud, stirring a stream of fury, whipping his blood into a hot storm. *Would she dare to disregard the Black Besieger? What lesson would he teach to punish her insolence?*

Dahoud stared past her sweat-glistening torso, the urge to subdue her washing over him in a boiling wave. For three years, he had battled against the djinn's temptations. To indulge in fantasies would batter his defences and breach his resistance. He focused on the flavours on his tongue, the tart citron juice and the sage-spiced mutton, on the tender texture of the meat.

Govan clasped the dancer's wrist and drew her close. "Come, honey-flower, let's see your blossoms."

She tried to pull herself from his grip. Panic painted her face. Against a lesser man's groping, she might defend herself with slaps and screams, but this was the lord-satrap. She was too young to know how to slip out of such a situation, and none of her older colleagues on the far side of the garden noticed her plight. The other clerks at the table laughed.

"My Lord," Dahoud said. "She doesn't want your attentions."

"She's only a bellydancer." Contempt oiled Govan's voice. Still, he released the girl's hand, slapped her on the rump, and watched her scurry towards the safety of the musicians. "These performers are advertised as genuine Darrians. I have a mind to have them arrested for fraud. I suspect ..." He ran the tip of his finger along his eating bowl. "They're mere Samilis."

Dahoud, himself a Samili, refused to react to the jab. Govan was not only satrap of the province, but Dahoud's employer, as well as the father of the lovely Esha.

"Samilis are everywhere these days." Peering down his nose, Govan swirled the wine in his beaker. "Not that I have anything against Samilis. Given the right kind of education, their race can develop remarkable intelligence, practically equal to that of Quislakis. They can make valuable contributions to society." He stroked the purple fringe of his armband, insignia of his rank. "Provided they respect their betters."

The other clerks at the table bobbed their chins in eager agreement.

Dahoud the Black Besieger would not have tolerated taunts from this pompous peacock, but Dahoud the council clerk had to bow. Submission was the price for guarding his secret.

At the entry arch, a short man in the yellow tunic and turban of a royal rider was consulting with the tavern keeper.

"Is that messenger looking for you, my Lord?" Dahoud asked.

Govan shifted into his official pose and summoned the man with a flick of his sandalwood fan. The courier walked on bowed legs as if he still had a mount between his thighs. Conversations halted, glances followed him, and whiteseers peered, anticipating business.

Lord Govan put on his official smile to receive the leather-wrapped parcel.

"Forgive me, my Lord," the herald said. "The message I carry is for Dahoud, the clerk."

Govan's hand pulled back and his smile vanished.

Dahoud's stomach went cold: The Queen or her Consort would not write to an ordinary clerk. After three years of respite, his anonymity was breached. He stripped off the camel-skin wrap and broke the scroll's seal. The ends of the purple ribbon dropped into the mutton sauce.

The High Lord Kirral, Consort to the Great Luminous Queen, greets Dahoud, council clerk in the satrapy of Idjlara: Present yourself at the palace without delay. The Queendom needs the Black Besieger. K.

The expansive curves of the signature "K" claimed more space on the parchment than the message.

In his bowl, the uneaten mutton was going cold, whitish grease separating from the sauce. A large fly drifted belly-up in the liquid, its legs clawing for a hold in the air. The memories of siege warfare wrapped around Dahoud, those sour-sweet odours of fear and faeces, of disease and burning flesh.

At twenty-five, he had a conscience heavier than a brick-carrier's tray and more curses on his head than a camel had fleas. He had left the legion to cut himself off temptation, to deprive the djinn of fodder. After a siege, rape was legal, a soldier's right, practically expected of him, part of the job. By returning to war, he would forfeit his victories over his craving. The djinn would again be his master.

Yet he ached to wear the general's cloak again, to silence sneering bureaucrats, to make women take notice. He lusted for that power the way a heavy drinker, deprived of his solace, ached for a sip of wine. The yearning to wield a sword ached in his arms, his chest throbbed with the urge to command, and his loins flamed with the dark desire. He felt the panting breaths of women and their hot resisting bodies, smelled the scent of female fright and sweating fury.

"Why is the Consort writing to you?" Govan leant forward to grab the document. "You're out of your depth with royal matters. I'll read and explain."

"Why should I want your counsel?" Dahoud tucked the rolled parchment into his belt.

"Don't get pert, Samili!" Govan barked. "Give me that letter."

"The Consort summons." Dahoud rose. "Good afternoon, my Lord.

Don't expect me back soon."

He strode to the exit, his mind reeling like a spindle. Could he deny that he was the Black Besieger? Refuse a royal order? Lead an army without stimulating the djinn?

On a low stone wall near the entrance gate, a row of whiteseers perched like hungry birds. Whiteseers had glimpses of futures others could not even imagine. One of them slid off the wall and sauntered in his direction. A coating of pale clay covered her sharp-boned triangular face and her long hair, and painted black and blue rings adorned her clay-whitened arms.

"Your hands," she demanded.

"I need to know what will happen if—"

"Give your copper to a soothsayer," she snapped. "We white ones only give advice. We can see the future; we can see several futures for everyone, but we won't tell you all we see."

"Advice is all I want."

"That's what they all say. Yet everyone asks for more. I give one piece of advice, the best I can give to help a client. They always demand that I tell them what I see. Well, I won't." Nevertheless, she grabbed the copper ring from Dahoud's fingers and threaded it on her neck-thong. Her tunic smelled of old sweat and mouldy wool.

She grasped his hands to pinch their flesh, her long nails tickling. Her white paint contrasted with Dahoud's bronze tan. When she felt the pulse and lifted his hand to her face to listen and sniff, he could have sworn he saw her blanch under the white clay as her closed eyes stared into his past. She sagged forward and stayed in a silent slouch.

At last she straightened, her eyes wide, her mouth open, but no words burst forth. So she had seen what he had done, and worse, what he might do once more.

'I assure you, I'll never again..."

"I can't read if you chatter." She frowned at his hands. "My advice: Get stronger arms."

He flexed his biceps, startled. "My arms *are* strong! I do trickriding, I wrestle, I lift weights." Every night, Dahoud exercised until his muscles screamed, to block out his cravings and punish his body for its desires.

The seer's mouth curled with contempt, making more clay crumble. "You're not listening. I didn't say *strong*. I said *stronger*." She pinched his biceps. "Much stronger."

"What difference can arm muscles make?"

"I told you to give your copper to a soothsayer." She ambled off, leaving a cloud of unwashed stink and crumbles of clay.

Dahoud hurried to the stable to ready his horse. He had to persuade the Consort not to send the Black Besieger back to war.

~

At the entrance to the royal audience hall, green-uniformed guards confiscated Dahoud's dagger-belt. The door thudded shut behind him.

Light seeped through slitted windows, painting stripes on the carpet. Rows of whitewood benches stood empty, as if waiting for spectators to stream in and take their seats. The Consort Kirral sat on an elevated divan, a jewel-encrusted white turban on his head, his moustache shaped into a pair of pointed blades. The steep platform bearing the divan forced visitors to gaze upwards, a technique Dahoud himself had often used to intimidate callers.

"Highness, you summoned me."

Grape-green eyes peered from under dark bushy brows. Kirral cracked a saltnut between his teeth and spat the empty shell on the carpet at Dahoud's feet. Dahoud permitted himself no response. Standing as straight as a soldier before his commanding officer, he inhaled deeply of the stale incense and old breath that lay in the air, and waited.

A mural of the Queen, a white full-moon face under an ornamental headdress, dominated the room, reminding audience-seekers that she was the true ruler of Quislak—even if she took little interest in politics. She left the day-to-day government to her Consort, who in turn delegated most work to his head-wife.

"Would you like some saltnuts, young man?" Kirral's voice had the soft scraping tone of a sword grinding against a whetstone.

To take the nuts from the Consort's outstretched hand, Dahoud had to walk up to the platform and look up, the way a lapdog accepted morsels. Kirral grinned, and his slippered feet wiggled in anticipation.

If the Consort gained pleasure from humiliating visitors, pride was a waste of time. "Thank you, Highness."

"The Koskarans ransack our settlements, rob our caravans, slaughter our people." Kirral twisted a saltnut between his fingers, as if assessing its value. "Are you the man who subdued those savages four years ago?"

"I am." Dahoud glanced at the statues lining the cedar-panelled walls. He had looted many of those marble deities from temples in conquered lands, including Koskara. Now they queued at floor level, paying homage to Quislak's nine Mighty Ones, who stood haughtily on a brocaded dais. "If my experience may be of use, I'll gladly advise the general in charge."

Kirral cracked another nut. "I want you to squash those rebels to pulp."

"You need a different man, Highness."

"I need the Black Besieger, and I will get him." Kirral stroked the parchment scrolls at his side with a lover's caress. "My favourite reading matter: personal dossiers. These are from your employers, past and present. You were the youngest general in the Queendom's history, the first ethnic Samili to rise to that rank. Then you threw your career into the dust." Kirral's eyes focused like a hawk's before the kill. "Why?"

"Personal reasons."

"Your personal reasons entertain me," Kirral said. "During a fine game of Siege last night, I asked my good friend Paniour why the Black Besieger quit. I learnt that he had a sudden attack of conscience. Not about battlefield deaths, but the treatment of captives."

Dahoud stayed silent.

"To fool the world that the Black Besieger no longer existed, you spread rumours about his death. His supposed demise occurred not on the battlefield, but at the hands of an enraged woman. How imaginative." Kirral cackled like a spotted hyena. "Paniour tells me you imagined yourself possessed by a djinn. A mythical creature from nomad lore."

Dahoud knew better than to insist on the gruesome truth of demonic possession. "It was a figure of speech."

Kirral's bushy brows rose to his turban rim and stayed there. "For two years, all traces of you vanished as if you had indeed died. What did you do before Govan took you on?"

"Labour." The kind of work a Samili could get: digging latrines, dragging a builder's brick-loads like a sweating donkey, stirring a dyer's pots of boiling piss.

"Watching you would have been educational. A leopard may dress as a rabbit, but he will find the garments too small."

Dahoud said nothing.

"Last year, one of Satrap Govan's regular reports held an interesting paragraph. When the earthquake struck, a minor clerk led the rescue efforts 'with courage and quick thought, and with the efficiency of a general'. The clerk was an ethnic Samili with a sketchy history. Naturally, this clerk interested me. Alas." Kirral leant back into the divan, and the corners of his mouth twitched as if something amused him. "Govan's opinion changed. Now he rants about your lack of manners, your insolence, the ideas you have above your station, how he wants to kick you out of office and send you to count goat-droppings in the Samil." Kirral's voice lowered to a confidential whisper. "Tell me, young man: Are you courting your employer's daughter?"

Dahoud's face fired. Esha's white dimpled cheeks and soft voice had captured him. Whenever they met at work, she granted him a friendly word, and twice he had escorted her to a fantasia show. For the first time in his life, a woman seemed to like him.

"A Ladysdaughter has dynastic obligations," Kirral said softly. "Her offspring will only be Ladysdaughters if fathered by a satrap. If the girl has sense, she will not waste herself on a mere clerk." He popped another nut into his mouth.

"Of course." Esha would marry a satrap, or at least, a chief councillor with promotion prospects.

The moustache blades quivered with every chewing motion. "Two days ago, more news came from Koskara. This is not public knowledge yet. Satrap Zetan is dead, apparently poisoned by rebels. His councillors barricaded themselves into the residency. What do you think of their decision?"

"They're brave." They were foolish. Dahoud remembered the residency: a greenstone palace with pillars and pilasters, fancy and fragile, not designed to withstand a siege. "Are women among them?"

Kirral's lips curved as if the question gave him malicious pleasure. "Would it make a difference to you if there were? If the Black Besieger squashes those rebels, I will make him the new lord-satrap of Koskara."

Dahoud stood very still. Lord-satrap? He checked the Conscrt's posture: leaning forward, hands tented, lips pursed, eyes intent.

"Think about it, Dahoud. No more labouring, no more clerking, no more grovelling before Govan. More power than you ever had as a genera_. Your own satrapy to shape into an oasis of peace where you can keep the womenfolk safe." The Consort's smile spread the ends of his moustache. "And I shall send Esha Ladysdaughter as your bride."

Power, respect, peace, a woman who liked him, all served on a silver platter—if he unsheathed his sword again, if he devastated Koskara once more, if he besieged the rebels' strongholds. During a siege, anger and lust built a pyre on which the noblest resolutions burnt to ashes. He might again become the monster he had fought so hard to leave behind.

"What if I decline?"

Krral beamed as if Dahoud's reaction had lit pleasure lanterns behind his eyes. "Then you will stay here at the palace. I will give you a job suiting your particular talents and interests: torturer in charge of females. You will enjoy that. The choice is yours."

Dahoud's blood chilled. "I'll go to Koskara."

"Good choice, Dahoud. The high general Paniour awaits you."

On his way out, Dahoud sent silent a prayer to the Great Mare, the horse-headed woman who protected Koskara.

CHAPTER 2

The High General

Paniour raised his arms as if to embrace a long-lost son. "My dear Dahoud. Welcome back from the dead."

"Sir." Dahoud snapped a salute with the right palm on his chest. "Kirral commands me to end the uprising in Koskara. Which stronghold do the rebels use?"

"Oubar. This time, you'll conquer it." Paniour's voice exuded confidence. He glanced at the wooden sculpture on the low table: the war god Ikbour held his shield and short thrusting sword raised, poised for attack. "However inaccessible the location, however strong the walls, however vast the granaries and the water supply – no fortress can withstand the Black Besieger. Not even an ancient citadel like Oubar. It's good to have you back in the legions, Dahoud. You belong here." He placed a hand on Dahoud's shoulder. It smelled of soapberries and mint. "Sit, and we'l talk about old times." He gestured at one of the armless chairs facing the table.

Dahoud remained standing. Once Paniour had been Dahoud's commanding officer, his mentor, the closest to a father he had ever had. In leaving the legions, Dahoud had sacrificed the friendship, and he needed to stay detached now. "Tell me about the enemy troops, sir."

"Much the same as last time: Mostly light cavalry in unknown numbers, skilled archers, javelins, throwing knives. Hit and run tactics, violence and destruction, civilian targets. No match for troops led by General Dahoud."

Dahoud could devastate the land again, this time so brutally that the natives would not be able to rise for generations. But he had to shield women from war's violence and from the evil inside him.

There was only way to protect Koskara from the worst: take out their leader. Without him, the followers might lose their fighting spirit, cutting the war short. "This sudden uprising suggested a charismatic leader Who is it?"

"A man named Mansour. He wrestles like a leopard, rides like a desert storm, fights like a god of war."

The usual legends surrounding a Samili hero. Dahoud had met no Mansour during the conquest, but even without solid intelligence, he could piece a picture together. The conquerors had killed all native nobles, so Mansour was a commoner. Samilis revered age, so he was old. Financing a rebellion took wealth, so he was rich. "I need a list of the wealthiest native families, with ages."

"The Koskarans don't make lists. They can't write."

"Satrapy tax records?"

"The late Lord Zetan collected taxes, but—" Paniour gave Dahoud a significant look. "He didn't care to document the money that flowed through his hands."

Dahoud would find out about this Mansour in other ways. Storytellers, rumour-mongers, braggarts and renegades could be made to talk.

"Why did you leave?" Accusation swung in Paniour's voice. "Duty wasn't enough to keep you. Loyalty wasn't. Honour wasn't."

"How many troops are in Koskara these days? Who commands them?"

"Nine hundred, not the Queendom's finest. The best troops are needed for the active fronts. Their commander is Gavinos. Let's say he's no Dahoud."

"Our main garrison is less than half a day's ride from Koskara Town where the residency is under siege. How did that happen?"

"When the rebels attacked the residency, Gavinos withdrew his troops into the garrison, and sent a messenger requesting relief." Paniour laughed. "He feared that the rebels might attack him next. With you in charge, these troops will soon learn to fight. Unless you've gone soft in your cosy civilian life."

He placed a sand-filled tray on the low table between them, and with the manicured tip of his finger traced lines in the sand. "The Yellow

Mountains in the east form the natural boundary against Darria. All this is desert. Grasslands here, here, and here. Oases." He stuck green leaves into the tray and added wooden blocks, clay cubes and charcoal crumbles. "Native towns. Our garrisons. Sites of recent attacks. Will you free the residency first?"

"The residency isn't built for a siege, and its cistern is small," Dahoud said.

"By now they're drinking their own piss," Paniour agreed. "I bet those clueless civilians are regretting their heroics now they've had a taste of the reality of war. When you free them, they'll kiss your toes."

"If they're still alive." Faced with defiant civilians, the Black Besieger would have set fire to the house and ordered the people killed as they came running out. He expected Mansour to do the same.

He jabbed his thumb on the wooden cube in the south-east. "Once I win Oubar, the rest of Koskara will follow." Oubar, ancient and impenetrable, a hundred times besieged, never taken. His passion for conquest stirred. This time, he knew what to expect, would be prepared, would batter its walls and starve the rebels into submission. He would execute Mansour, weakening their structure and their will. Then he would...the opportunities...

Won't that be the Koskarans' fault? If they don't want war, why do they rebel? When we take possession, shall we pick a proud one who'll resist and fight? Shall we teach her to give you the attention you deserve?

"You can do it, Dahoud. Even if the citadel doesn't fall to you at once, the rebel nest will be shut off from the rest of the population. In the meantime, I'll lead a legion and sweep the satrapy clean of insurgents. Once we're done, only obedient tax-paying citizens will be left. Unless..." The corners of Paniour's mouth turned down. "Unless the soft new satrap chooses a more merciful solution."

The djinn would not allow Dahoud to be merciful, not after a siege, not to the women.

What difference does one more time make? What if we take just one rebel who resists us with all her strength?

Indulging the pleasure again, just this once, would take the edge off his need, would still his craving and give him peace. Then it would be so much easier to be a merciful satrap, a loving husband, a man in control of his lusts.

Just once, just Oubar, to punish the fortress for resisting him last time, to prove that he would not be defied.

Yet if he broke his abstinence, the control he had fought so hard to gain might vanish, and the djinn would again be his master.

Peniour rose, smoothing the fine folds of his embroidered tunic. "Enough of this. I have this jug of old Zigazian wine for us to sample. Tell me what you've really been up to these past three years."

Dahoud slammed the palm on his chest for the military salute. "Thank you for the briefing, Sir. I will see you tomorrow when I present my strategy. Good day, sir." He closed his heart to the flicker of pain in his old mentor's eyes.

To win Koskara, Dahoud would not think like a conquering general. He would not think like an aspiring lord-satrap. He would think like a Koskaran rebel.

CHAPTER 3

The Magician

At the sight of the royal palace, Merida's skin prickled with excitement. After three dusty moons travelling in a cramped carriage, the most thrilling time of her life was about to begin.

On the palace façade, banners and glazed tiles showed the bull emblem of the Queendom, and a dozen men guarded the bronze-studded entrance, standing as stiff as their spears. Yet the city clustering around smelled like a village of overripe fruit and animals. Donkeys brayed, chickens cackled, and wheels screeched. Natives in bright clothes balanced straw baskets on their shoulders.

The dust-silvered leaves on the trees curled limply, parched after prolonged drought. Merida would give the people of Quislak rain to revive their land, and the knowledge of the Virtues to nourish their souls. Here, in this primitive country, she could make a difference and gain gratitude for her generosity and skill.

She climbed out of the carriage, stretched her travel-stiff legs, and told her servants to wait. Two guards checked her pass and waved her into a cool atrium, where a further watchman demanded to see the documents again.

"Merida Karr of Hohenhegen," the white-whiskered guard read aloud. "Personal Value 248. Female. Widowed. Age: 24 summers. Occupation: Magician. Status: Diplomat." He squinted at the document as if he suspected it to be a fake. "I've never seen a magician travelling with a diplomat's pass."

"You have now." She unrolled the invitation, a parchment with a huge "K" and a seal with a purple ribbon.

He muttered about magicians and diplomats and about things not being as they used to be, copied her information with a reed brush, and told her to queue at another desk.

The Queendom seemed to have more of those green-clad officials than a hive had bees. Merida yearned to wash the travel grime from her stiff limbs, and to rest in the privacy of a cool apartment, but disciplined herself to be patient. Naturally, the administration in a primitive country would be less efficient than in Riverland.

Many voices had doubted either Merida's ability, or warned her that nothing good would come of the mission. Mother had denounced the plan instantly. "Second Daughter! Mingling with primitives is not fitting for a member of the Karr family."

"It's an honourable goodwill assignment on behalf of the government," Merida assured her. "The poor people of Quislak have been plagued by droughts. They suffer terrible thirst, and their crops are dying. We can't let them perish. They've begged the Virtuous Republic for help, and since I'm an expert in weather magic..."

"Have you no shame, Second Daughter? Cease this boasting at once, and obey the Virtue of Modesty." The matriarch stabbed rapidly at her embroidery. "The whole idea is short-sighted, unconsidered, foolish, immature. Instead of dispatching victuals to nourish the primitives, the government sends another development aid worker. What good will it do? The previous aid workers built wells, sowed vegetables, taught school, preached the Four Virtues. The primitives laughed at the Virtues, ignored the schools, grazed their animals on the crops, and used the wells to water the animals. Flocks increased and the overgrazing became worse. And now —a rain-dancing magician. Ha."

"This is an opportunity to enlighten primitives and spread the wisdom of the Four Virtues." It would also be a chance to see appreciative smiles instead of censorious frowns.

"A Karr has no need to deal with primitives. Can't you give a thought to your family, and what this will do to our value ranking? You may not care that your own will drop from 95 to 64, but you are dragging us down with you." Her voice was as chilled as when Merida had fled from her violent husband and sought refuge with family.

"64 is not too bad." Merida gazed at the mosaic pattern on the square table between them. "It's still more than twice what the average citizen has, and it's only for a year."

"The year of the elections, when every point counts." Mother's nostrils flared. "Stop staring in my face, Second Daughter! How often do I have to remind you that my personal value is 547?"

Obediently, Merida lowered her gaze to her mother's waist, but that did not prevent a tirade. "No longer having a husband does not give you the right to do what you like. A development aid worker abroad is worth no more than a middle-ranker, a tradeswoman, a schoolteacher, a commoner. Having one in the immediate family lowers everyone's points. Just when I have enough points at last to get nominated as Virtuous Vice President, you want to spoil it all. You are unbelievably selfish."

"I'll still have my qualification points from the School of Magic," Merida soothed. "And a foreign magic mission need not mean I'll be a development aid worker. When scholar magician Helva Hein—the Virtues bless her memory—undertook international assignments for the government, she did it with the status of special ambassador."

Mother's eyes lit up. "Special ambassador! This will raise your value to 248, and mine to 551. The whole family will benefit." She dropped her embroidery to rub her hands. "I shall set levers in motion to ensure you are appointed special ambassador. Our nation's greatest weather magician deserves nothing less."

Dizzying excitement swamped Merida's heart. Never would she have dared to dream of such a high value, outranking her siblings, breaking into the top one per cent of society. Everyone would respect her; even Mother's biting contempt would cease. Although the high value applied only to the eight moons needed to travel to the Queendom, do the job and return, she might hold on to the rank, the way Helva Hein had. If Merida completed her mission with spectacular success, she could hope for more assignments and a permanent title. The government might even award honour points in recognition of her services to the Virtues.

"Next!" The official's bellow jerked her back into her the present. "Ah, Merida Karr of Hohenhegen. At last. You've been on the list for ages." He pushed a finger under his moss-coloured turban to scratch his head. "Wait here until a servant can show you to the dormitory."

"Dormitory?" Merida chewed on the foreign word. "You mean, bedroom?"

"The room with the beds, yes."

"Beds? I'm not sharing my room."

His finger slid along a list. "The ground floor dormitory. It's very comfortable, with only a dozen women in the room, and you have your own bed."

"This is a misunderstanding I will not sleep in a dormitory." Merida pronounced the Quislak language carefully so that there could be no misunderstanding. "Especially not on the ground floor. I'm the special ambassador of the Virtuous Republic. My staff may sleep in dormitories, but I will not."

He rifled through a pile of parchments on desk. "Staff? We don't house servants in the palace. And I can tell you, they won't find a stable or roof in town. Everything's full, with Fool's Plea Day coming up. If they're lucky and not too fat, maybe they can squeeze on a roof in the suburbs."

"My contract promises a two-room apartment in a quiet part of the palace, seventh storey or higher, well-lit, fully furnished with private washing facilities, and separate accommodation for my staff." She drew the document from her shoulder bag and unrolled it for him.

He flicked away a fly. "A private apartment in the palace? During the Fool's Plea celebrations? You foreigners have strange ideas."

Merida counted silently to eight. Did this situation call for tolerance about foreign cultures, or for assertiveness? She decided on the latter. "Take me to the Queen."

The man laughed. "Her Luminous Exultancy doesn't receive petitioners."

"The Consort, then. He signed the contract."

"Wait until he invites you for an audience."

"When will that be?"

"Who can tell? In four days, perhaps, or in ten." He made a gargling noise in his throat, and spat.

Merida raised her voice. "Take me to the Consort! Now!"

People spilled out of doors and corridors as if they had been waiting for entertainment, chattering like excited chickens. Their cheap jewellery clinked, and they devoured her with curious gazes.

A bronze-faced man pointed at her. "A new wife?"

Merida perused the crowd with a superior stare. "I'm the special ambassador of the Virtuous Republic of Riverland."

They snickered until a tall woman strode down the corridor. At once, heads dropped into guilty bows.

"What's going on?" Sharpness swung in her voice.

Since this woman seemed to hold authority, Merida explained her credentials and purpose, and waited for a return introduction.

Instead, the woman turned to the guard. "Is your duty too challenging for you?"

He pulled his head into hunching shoulders. "I crave your forgiveness, my Lady, I told her she can't—"

She silenced him with a wave of her hand. Copper bangles clinked. "Let her see the Consort."

"But—" the guard objected.

"You heard me. Let her. Kirral will be amused." To Merida, the woman said, "The Consort's study is at the end of the corridor, the one with the red door." Before Merida could thank her, she slinked away with the fluidity of a snake.

The crowd parted, letting Merida pass. She felt their tense gazes in her back as she strode down the unlit corridor. The clacking of her boots sent tiny lizards darting for cover.

Her knock on the red door yielded no reply. When she pushed, the door whined inwards on its hinges. The temperature dropped. The cool air was thick with incense.

A man reposed cross-legged on a divan. On his head squatted a pumpkin-coloured turban like a fat hen on an egg, revealing little of his face beyond a knife-shaped moustache. Pale legs stuck out of a short tunic and ended in pink pointy slippers with big pompoms. Bent over a Siege gaming board, he did not acknowledge her arrival.

Quietly, she let the door click into its frame and spoke her rehearsed introduction in fluent Quislaki. "I am Merida, second daughter of the First Family of Karr of Hohenhegen, personal value of 248, eleventh-degree magician, special ambassador for the Virtuous Republic of Riverland."

She waited for him to confirm his identity, but he did not glance up. After counting sixteen heartbeats, she assembled the words for her complaint. "I must inform you of a communication difficulty. Members of your staff seem to assume that I'll sleep in a dormitory."

Still not looking up, he twisted a yellow gaming stone and clacked it into a new position.

For a further thirty-two heartbeats, Merida took in the flower-patterned chipped tiles on the walls, the mural of the map of the Queendom, the shelves untidily crammed with scrolls, the lavishly embroidered but badly stained upholstery of the divans. Then she had enough. She pushed her fists into her waist. "Am I addressing His Highness Lord Kirral, Consort to the High Queen of Quislak?"

He tilted his head at her, balancing a green gaming stone on the tip of his pinkie. "Do you play Siege?"

Could this buffoon be the Consort who ruled the nation on behalf of the Queen? Perhaps she had mistaken the door, or the woman in the corridor had played a practical joke on her. Yet an underling would not dare to play Siege against himself during work hours.

"I possess some trifling skill," she replied stiffly. "But I'm not here to play games. If you want rain for your country, you must honour the terms of the agreement. I cannot and will not work magic unless the conditions are right, including privacy for the preparations. This contract promises a private apartment." She waved the parchment at him.

"I am a busy man." His voice had the low-humming hiss of a wasp hovering over rotting fruit. "I do not have time to keep promises."

He clacked the green token down and pushed the other stones rapidly across the gaming board. His aura pulsed with blue hues of intellectual power so strong it made her skin prickle. He appeared to have forgotten her presence.

Merida stepped forward. "Are you, or aren't you, the Consort Kirral?" she demanded. "Do you, or don't you, want rain for your land?"

At last, he raised his face. His eyes flashed at her, green as polished peridots with jewel-hard brightness. His mouth spread into a smile so wide that the moustache quivered. Merida's skin crawled as if slugs were slithering up her spine.

"Yes, I am the Consort." His voice softened to the texture of rubber. "I look forward to playing with you."

A chill crept across her skin, but the furnace of her anger blasted it away. She would have yelled, were such display of unbridled emotion not un-Riverian. Now that she had a personal value of 248, she would always act with dignity. She dipped a curt bow and marched out, letting the door snap shut behind her.

Back in the blinding sun, she assessed what had happened. Clearly, the Consort did not mean to honour the terms of the contract. Perhaps she should return home at once, leaving the Consort to his games, and the people to drought and starvation. It meant admitting her mission had failed, and everyone would remind her they had told her so. She could already see the disdain on Mother's face, and hear her censorious voice stating that her Second Daughter would never amount to much.

To prove her worth, Merida had to stay and bring more rain than anyone could dream.

When she returned to her coach and told her servants that they would have to sleep on a roof, their stricken faces shook her resolve.

"On a roof? Under the open sky?" Her maid's voice broke into quivers. "Squeezed close to strangers?"

"That's what I'm told. For the first couple of nights, anyway." She tried to sound confident. "Maybe things get better once this festival is over. There'll be more space then, even if it's still on a roof."

The second woman joined the sobbing. The man buried his face in his palms.

Merida took pity. "You three go home. You need not suffer indignities for my sake."

Hope shone from the maid's tear-veiled eyes. "Really? We may go?"

"Of course." Merida mustered a smile. "I may even stay for a while in this country and research primitive magic."

The coach driver said, "I don't like leaving you alone in this land." But he was already adjusting the reins.

"I'll be fine," Merida said with more confidence than she felt. "The Virtues will protect me."

⚮

The dormitory smelled of oranges and unwashed feet. A dozen voices shrilled at once about who was wearing what for the forthcoming festival. Tension knotted the muscles across Merida's shoulders so tightly that they hurt. How could she find the refreshing sleep her mind craved tonight, and the privacy to prepare her great act of magic scheduled two moons from now?

Nothing had prepared her for the realities of this assignment. The government had sent her on courses to brush up her already fluent language skills and to learn about etiquette. She had sat through endless lessons about her own nation's history, about the diplomatic immunity of a special ambassador, and the need to set a shining example of a Virtuous lifestyle. To get a better understanding of her host country, Merida had questioned traders and travelling tumblers who had worked in Quislak, but Mother and the government soon prevented contact with such low-value people. Instead, they granted her an appointment with the government's chief ethnologist.

Merida remembered how the old man had received her in his third-floor study, at a square table with his personal value of 260 carved into the surface.

"Merida Karr, eleventh degree magician, personal value 95." Noting that his value exceeded hers by more than a hundred points, she bowed her head to chest level before taking the proffered chair. A servant shuffled in on bowed legs to pour tea. Merida sipped gratefully.

The ethnologist stared at her forehead as he steepled his fingers under his pointed chin. "My child, you must be prepared to witness the most horrendous customs, and brace yourself against succumbing to any of them. Sins and superstitions lurk everywhere in Quislak. I hate to frighten you, but..." His eyes gleamed. "These people cook animal corpses for food. Moreover, they set aside milk to go rancid, and when it's curdled solid they squeeze it into blocks and devour that." He shuddered delicately. The chin quivered.

Merida kept her gaze lowered as befitted someone talking to a person whose value exceeded hers significantly. "What does the solid milk taste like?"

He drew up in affront. "My child, I did not eat their food! But I have seen it with my own eyes, this pale, sour-smelling substance they call *cheese*." He reached across the table to pour himself another mug of purifying sage tea, and swirled the brew in his mouth as if to wash away the memory of the sinful flavour. "That's not all! You will see people wearing apparel in pink, in yellow, even in red. No law prohibits sinful colours, and no spiritual refinement to curb the excess. And imagine..."

Leaning forward, he lowered his voice to a conspiratorial whisper. "They wear only a single outer garment, a knee-length tunic. No trousers underneath. One can see their lower legs." His tongue flicked across his lips and withdrew hastily. "Of course I always kept my eyes averted."

Merida placed her hands modestly in her lap. "I will not let the sight of legs lure me from the path of Virtues, but will model my behaviour on your example."

"They even show toes!" He threw his hands up in disgust. Tea spilled, raining green droplets on the immaculate desk. "They wear shoes especially designed to display these sinful appendages, all ten of them. Nothing but soles and a few thin straps across the instep and ankle. You must not be persuaded into such sinful fashions."

Merida promised earnestly that she would always uphold the standards required of a special ambassador of the Virtuous Republic of Riverland, neither baring her toes nor engaging in any of the other foolish native customs. But she admitted to her deepest self that she looked forward to seeing those sins.

"There's more." His voice drooped with sadness, as if he was breaking news of a tragic death. "The country is primitive to the extreme. No hospitals, no postal system, no sewers. In the southernmost part, the Samil, people still roam without fixed abode. They live in tents, not even square ones, but round."

"Round!" Merida gasped, nearly forgetting to keep her gaze low. That was primitive indeed. "They haven't even reached the threshold of civilisation?"

"In the northern part they have real houses, stone-built and rectangular. But in the south—the so-called Samil—development has not reached the civilisation stage." He admitted he had neither been to the Samil nor seen round tents, but he had heard about them. He warned her that the country was patriarchal. "Although among the lower classes, women and men are equal, you will meet few women in active leadership roles."

It's a Queendom," Merida pointed out. "Surely there's a Queen at the top."

"The Queen's position passes from mother to daughter, but all power lies with her husband. The country's noblemen select her

Consort. I regret having to shock you, but...." Leaning forward, he whispered, "The Consort keeps a harem of concubines."

Merida clapped a hand over her mouth.

"Quislakis are idolaters who worship as many gods as the night has stars, and they don't believe in the Four Virtues." His voice shook. "They are so un-Virtuous that djinns flourish there."

Merida felt the blood drain from her face. "Djinns? Virtues protect us." She had heard of those malevolent spirits which invaded humans, dulling their consciences, stirring their desires, driving them to evil deeds. She had assumed these creatures belonged to the realm of myth. Parents used them to frighten young children into submission: 'Be quiet, or the djinns will get you.' That djinns existed in reality was a chilling thought.

"How can one tell if someone is possessed?"

"As a representative of the Virtuous Republic, you will associate only with people of the highest moral standards. You will not meet djinn hosts." He rose. "Now, if that is all?"

Merida thanked him with the phrases appropriate to his personal value.

At the School of Magic, she commissioned a scribe to copy Scroll 414 from the collected works of the Most Virtuous Scholar Magician, Helva Hein, the section that contained a treatise on *Malevolent Parasitic Entities and their Threats to the Ignorant Human*. When the copy arrived, she packed it into her travel trunks, together with scrolls about *Visual Symmetry and its Role in the Attainment of Civilisation, The Virtue of Modesty and its Rewards,* and *High-Value Persons and their Moral Obligations towards Inferiors.*

❧

Now Merida sat on her bedstead, tried to shut the persistent chattering and human odours from her mind, and wished she had brought a treatise on *Incompetent Royal Consorts and their Meaningless Promises*.

When she pulled her legs into the correct position to meditate upon the Virtues, women in gaudy garments flocked around her, invading her privacy with their high-pitched giggles and perfume reek. They pelted her with questions: where was she from, what was she doing here, what was her father's occupation? They pulled at her four plaits to test if her bronze hair was real or made from spun metal, and stared directly into her eyes as if unaware that this was discourteous and dangerous and therefore taboo.

Resigned, Merida slid from her bed and assumed the opening stance of the ritual exercise routine from the Disciplined Path. Surely they would respect that.

"Why are you standing funny?" a rotund woman demanded.

Three others tilted her top trunk, spilling the contents on the rug. With excited squeals, they fell over the boxes and garment bags.

"You have weird clothes," the plump girl squeaked. She had her arms inserted into the legs of Merida's best trousers, and waved them about. "What's in the cute blue box?"

Merida threw herself across her trunk before they could touch her private garments. "Please leave my things alone!"

Too late. Two women were arguing over possession of a pair of dark grey trousers, each pulling so fiercely at a leg that the crotch seam broke with a *rrratch* sound. Others had discovered her boots and hurled them across the room in a throw-and-catch game.

Disciplining herself into calm dignity, she picked her night suit off the ground. "Where's the bathroom, please?"

The rotund girl pointed to a water barrel in the corner. Merida hesitated to take off her clothes in front of others. Seeing the soapy scum on the surface, she reminded herself of the water shortage, and dipped her hand into the barrel. It came out covered in a greasy-grey film. Better stay unwashed. Using the toilet, however, was an ordeal she could not avoid. Her cheeks heated like fire as she sat on the shared multi-holed bench.

When she crawled under her blanket to change into her night suit, her fingers found brittle stains on the bedding. "This is not clean."

A woman who wore earrings so long that they dangled to her breasts examined the stain. "Don't worry. It's only food, and not even fresh food. Nobody's slept in this bed for over a moon."

Merida tossed the bedding on the ground, then recoiled at the reek of decomposing straw. Only Riverian discipline stopped her from crying. With gritted teeth, she layered clothes from her trunks over the smelly straw sack. Huddled under her cloak, she said a silent prayer to the Virtues of Loyalty, Honesty, Modesty, and especially Discipline.

One day, when she was a celebrated scholar magician, she would lecture about her Quislak assignment, and reveal to her audience how she had slept in a room with other people. First, she had to make her mission a spectacular success. On the day when the Planet of Discipline and the Planet of Honesty formed a symmetrical harmony with the moon, she would summon rain.

CHAPTER 4

Dahoud's Plan

Teruma sat at Kirral's desk, doing the work the Consort was supposed to do, dealing with demanding diplomats, corrupt satraps and rebelling natives. At the same time, she kept an eye on the Consort himself. This morning, he had waxed his moustache into zigzags, always a sign that he was planning something devious.

He and Paniour were engrossed in a board game, and while they were pushing coloured tokens and compliments across the cedarwood table, the air simmered with suspicion and dangerous desires.

Thirty-five years ago, they had been three young people with a hunger for power and a shared passion for strategy—a dancing boy, a studious aristocrat, a Ladysdaughter—who schemed to rule the land.

Paniour climbed up through the legions to command the Queendom's armed forces. His new lifestyle afforded him the dignity he craved, and nobody dared to mention his low past to his face. Kirral married the High Queen, and as her Consort became the official ruler of the land. He had endless opportunities to put pressure on prisoners and politicians. His harem, stocked with a variety of specimens, was his playground for mind games. As his head-wife, Teruma was in charge of palace management as well as the harem. In practice, she governed the country, freeing Kirral for his games and for increasingly bizarre human experiments.

"Your daughter has grown into such a lovely girl, Paniour." Kirral rubbed a yellow gaming stone between his fingers. "How old is she now? Twelve?"

Paniour's hand, with its glassy-white scars and immaculately shaped nails, wavered slightly before he placed his green token. "Thirteen."

"I noticed the new ripeness about her. I like Kadiffe. I really do."

"Your well-stone," Paniour said, his tone even, controlled. "Four moves."

"I'll marry her. Then you'll be my father, won't that be something?" Kirral clacked one of his tokens on the board and brushed away one of Paniour's. "Four moves? I don't think so."

"Keep your hands off my child."

Worry stirred in Teruma's stomach. Kirral would view sex with an under-age girl as an interesting experiment, and when his curiosity hooked into a new subject, he seldom let go. Paniour, who loved his daughter with protective passion, was no feeble adversary. The situation bristled with danger. If the two became enemies, the Queendom's peace would be shattered, and her own position shaken.

Veiling her worry, she grabbed the tea jug to refill their beakers. "There's no need for hasty decisions. The legal marriage age is fifteen - fourteen with a parent's consent. Paniour, if you agree to a betrothal now, and Kirral, if you agree to delay the actual marriage for a few moons, this will satisfy everyone."

With luck, Kirral's interest would wane before the girl reached fourteen.

Paniour's hands balled into white-knuckled fists. "I won't give my consent. Not now, not later."

"I won't wait," Kirral said. "Remember, my friend, I'm the Consort. Without my favour, you're nothing."

The muscles in Paniour's battle-scarred arms bulged, and his fists clenched so tightly around his token that the white scars stood out. "I won't let you defile my daughter."

The morning sun lanced through the window, throwing a pool of light on the crimson carpet at Kirral's feet. He stretched his legs on either side of the table and spread his arms in a wide gesture. "My dear friend, consider the options. Either you deliver Kadiffe to the comfort of the harem tomorrow—or she will perish in a dungeon. The dungeon inmates will be glad to get a female, and they will not fuss about her age."

26

Chills trickled down Teruma's spine. Kirral's moral boundaries were slipping fast.

The mask of dignity slid back over Paniour's face. "What better could I wish for my only daughter than to wed her to my oldest friend?" His voice was butter-smooth as he lifted his palms in supplication, but under the table, his legs remained bent as if coiled to attack. He gestured at the board. "Your well-stone. Three moves."

They resumed their game as if they still were best of friends, but tension seethed, laced with cruel pleasure, fear and fury. Although Paniour's self-control was admirable, it solved nothing. Over recent moons, Kirral's cruelties had escalated. Today, he had turned against Paniour; how long before he turned against Teruma? Of the three, Kirral might do the least work, but held the greatest power. Even if Paniour and Teruma joined forces, they had little chance against him. She would have to make plans.

In the meantime, she would pretend all was well. Returning to the desk, she erased most folk dances from the festival programme and substituted more pleas. Cruel judgements would keep Kirral occupied for a while.

A greenbelt announced arrival of Dahoud, the man who would end the insurgence in Koskara. According to the dossier, he was an ethnic Samili, capable and ruthless, yet apparently handicapped by his conscience. To get out of the legions, he had gone as far as faking his own death with Paniour's reluctant support. This man could be useful.

He stood straight as a spear, snapping a soldier's salute.

"What is your strategy, young man?" Kirral asked without taking his attention from the game. "I trust it is not going to need too many cohorts. We are hard pressed for men on the Zigazian border. As you know."

"I'll go alone and persuade the Koskarans to accept me as satrap. Peacefully."

"Entertaining." Kirral pursed his lips as if judging a dance show. "You think they will listen to your persuasions? The Black Besieger is the man they most love to hate."

"They won't recognise me," Dahoud said. "I had a beard, and I intimidated enemies with a black face mask. Of the people who saw me close up, few stayed alive, and if they remember anything about my appearance, it's the mask. Besides..." For a moment, his lips pressed into a tight line. "Everyone knows the Black Besieger is dead."

"If even one person recognises you, you will be dead," Kirral said. "Your fate will become a favourite with storytellers for years after your demise. The natives will spit-roast you like a goat, or whatever they do with rulers who displease them."

"The Samili custom for an unworthy ruler," Dahoud said calmly, "is to slit his throat."

Kirral's forefinger traced the zigzag moustache. "What a waste. Why not simply frighten them into submission? The news that Black Besieger has risen from the dead should make them tremble."

"If I am to be lord-satrap of Koskara I need their respect, not their fear."

"How will you get there, Dahoud?" Paniour asked. "Without getting killed? Without being taken hostage?"

"Disguised as a trader. Carrying the kind of goods the rebels want: weapons."

Kirral slammed his palms on the divan. "You want to arm the rebels?"

"Samples only, Highness. Once in the citadel, I'll negotiate with their leader. Mansour."

"You need not travel alone." Kirral waved his hand in a generous gesture. "Take ten or twelve soldiers with you. Take twenty. Disguise them as a merchant caravan or a troupe of dancing boys."

At the mention of dancing boys, Paniour flinched.

"They would slow me," Dahoud said.

Paniour pursed his lips and nodded. He was looking at Dahoud with the proud, possessive expression of a horse owner watching an animal he had trained. It struck Teruma how much the two men had in common. The lowly background, the daring strategies, the confidence. Dahoud might become an important ally if she handled him right.

"The plan is brilliant," she said. "I can see that you two have briefed him well." That should soothe the older men's pride. "However, a convincing trader travels slowly, buying and selling along the way. Either you spend half a year on the journey, or you won't be believed. Besides, your presence in the palace has been noted by many people, and your departure will be observed and talked about. Rumour travels fast. If the Koskarans learn about the appointment, they won't fall for your disguise."

"They cannot guess who I used to be," Dahoud said.

"It's enough if they guess who you intend to be. They must not suspect you are the new satrap until you've wormed yourself into their trust."

"I'll ride fast to Djildit Town and change into a trader there. That city teems with traders, so one more won't stand out. I can travel the final stretch at a trader's pace, and still reach Koskara in just over a moon."

"Do you want me to send an agent ahead to Djildit Town to buy your outfit and trade goods? He won't know what they're for."

"Thank you, my Lady." Gratitude shone in his eyes. Good.

"One more request, Highness," Dahoud said. "May I appoint my own councillors? People who are right for Koskara?"

"Of course, dear Dahoud. I rarely interfere with my satraps' staff choices. Just send me regular reports about how your councillors perform. Personal dossiers are so educational. And one more thing." Kirral leant forward. "Like all provinces of the former Samil, Koskara is a cherished part of the Queendom. I cannot stress that enough."

"Quite, Highness." Dahoud's conviction sounded thin.

"What about the palace spies?" Paniour asked. "Even if we keep Dahoud's appointment secret, speculations about his presence at court will seep out, and if the rebels get to hear of it, they may not fall for the trader disguise."

Kirral cast him a hostile look. "My palace does not harbour spies."

"It's riddled with them. There are more spies than rats in this place."

That was true: most of them worked for Teruma. She made her voice sound unconcerned. "If you're concerned about gossip, we'll give an official reason for Dahoud's presence: policing the Fool's Plea celebrations. Dahoud, we summoned you to deal with racial unrest, vandalism and drunken brawls. We'll borrow staff from other sources as well, so you'll be one of many, especially when you wear the official green uniform. The morning after, you vanish among the crowds pouring out of the city gates."

Kirral looked smug, as if he had personally thought of the plan. "Are this year's displays sensational enough to capture everyone's attention?"

"Your judgements will keep everyone excited."

"Excellent, excellent." Kirral stretched his legs forward and dug his slippered feet into the deep rug. "I have a special entertainment to add to the programme. Have you met the magician who has arrived from Riverland? A female, and an interesting one. She claims she can call rain by dancing."

"A dancing magician? Female, and a Riverian of all people?" Paniour's brows lifted. "I thought their religion forbade them to dance in public. Doesn't it offend their Virtue of Modesty?"

Kirral beamed. "Precisely. We will watch her entertain an audience of five thousand."

"What if she needs privacy to call rain?" Dahoud asked.

"Rain? I believe that when it falls on my head. We have had dozens of wizards who claimed to bring rain." Kirral squeezed the ends of his moustache. "Incompetent bunglers and charlatans, and fools hoping for a lucky strike and a reward."

"What happened to them?" Paniour asked. "Are they in the dungeons?"

"Not all of them." Kirral's pointed slipper traced the curving pattern of the carpet. "I gave them choices."

"Even the women?" Dahoud asked.

Silence spread. Incense wafted from a burner.

Kirral picked up a yellow carved stone and twirled it between his fingers. "When Oubar falls, dear Dahoud, I will send your bride."

"If she's willing. I must ask her first."

"That you may not do," Kirral said. "It would endanger your secret. The girl must not yet learn of either your appointment or her betrothal. Win Oubar, and we shall dispatch her. We have ways to make her willing."

"Don't hurt her!"

"Esha Ladysdaughter will wed you willingly when offered the right choices."

Teruma almost dropped her stylus. Esha Ladysdaughter as Lady of Koskara? This was a complication she had not expected, but she kept her counsel.

"I am satisfied about Dahoud's suitability. The decision is the Queen's." Kirral clapped his hands as if summoning a servant. "Teruma, take him to the Queen."

Seething behind her mask of compliance, Teruma rose. "Follow me, Dahoud."

On the way out, she heard Kirral say, "Dear Paniour, you will deliver Kadiffe to me tonight. And pay attention to the game. Your general is dead. Four Moves."

Teruma needed to make new plans fast. Plans which would include Koskara, and Dahoud.

⤨

Dahoud's pulse was beating quickly. Meeting the Queen was an honour most people dreamt about She rarely granted audiences and never appeared in public. What would she look like? What if she examined him about some obscure facet of history or Queendom law? What if she interrogated him about private matters? She must know his true background, and had probably heard about his conduct with captives. Should he deny all?

He followed Teruma into the audience hall. The place was empty.

Dahoud stood very still, mentally revising the subjects about which she might question him. In which year were the Samil provinces integrated into the Queendom? What was the correct etiquette when offering wine to another satrap? Which law scroll dealt with the sanctity of Ladysdaughters? All that came into his mind were the penalties for rape. Not helpful.

The door creaked open. Four greenbelts carried the royal litter into the hall and deposited it on the brocade-draped podium. Dahoud sank to his knees before the textile-shrouded box and touched his head to the woolly carpet.

He heard Teruma's voice. "I have the honour of presenting satrap candidate Dahoud for your approval."

Fabrics rustled as the servants drew the litter's curtains to the side. Dahoud did not raise his eyes. His heart thumped. The green and yellow pattern of the carpet stared at him like snakes.

"You are the new satrap of Koskara?" The female voice was high and flat.

"I hope to be." Dahoud's own voice croaked. What was the correct title for addressing the Queen the first time? Luminous Exultancy or

World-Enfolding Brightness? He offered the address used by those privileged enough to claim longer acquaintance. "Ma'am."

"That is nice. You will defeat the rebels?"

"Yes, Ma'am."

"Good. Rebels are not nice. Now say your oath."

Was that all? Dahoud nearly made the mistake of sitting up in surprise.

"To worship, always and forever... to guard the Queendom with my every limb of my body, with every drop of my blood..." Sweating, Dahoud managed to recite the oath without halting.

"Approach."

Keeping his gaze on the carpet, Dahoud crawled towards the litter for the anointment. He received a quick greasy dash down his forehead.

"Hold up your arms."

He stretched them up for the Queen to tie the purple-fringed bands below his elbows.

A moment later, he heard her clap, and the servants carried the litter away.

Rising, Dahoud marvelled at the bands, purple braid with softly falling silk fringe. He pulled them off and wound them into a tight roll. He would not wear them openly until he had conquered Koskara.

Now he was a satrap. It felt as unreal as riding a storm cloud. Soon he might be a husband as well. But Esha must not feel coerced into this marriage.

He followed the head-wife into the corridor. "Lady Teruma. I have a favour to ask."

She studied him with the gaze of a horse-dealer assessing a bargain. "Come into the rose garden."

As soon as they stepped outdoors, heat scorched like a breath from a potter's kiln. The noon sun slammed short shadows on the dried-up flowerbeds. Where water had once danced in the fountains, empty basins gaped. In these years of drought, even the royals had stopped wasting water on such frivolities. Koskara would be drier still.

Teruma steered him to the dappled shade of a rose arbour where blooms smothered the wooden structure like an army overrunning the land.

He sought to make courtly conversation. "The roses don't seem to suffer in the drought."

"The Consort waters them personally every night." A bracelet of silver scales slithered around her wrist as she sat gracefully on the bench. Fine age lines framed her dark eyes, and a wealth of dark, silver-streaked ringlets tumbled over her shoulders. She had the beauty and bearing of a goddess. "What can I do for you?"

"Will you propose marriage to Esha on my behalf? Tell her I hold her in high esteem. Tell her she'll have time to get to know me before we marry."

Her eyes narrowed. "Are you sure you want to wed her?"

"If she'll have me."

"You must get married soon, and it must be a Ladysdaughter. Does it have to be Esha?"

"Esha is perfect," Dahoud assured her. "She studied statecraft, and worked for her father's government. She'll know everything that I don't."

Unseen grasshoppers ticked in the flowerbeds.

"The choice of unmarried Ladysdaughters is limited," Teruma said. "And competition for their hands is fierce. But they all want to be Ladies, and ready-made lord-satrap is a catch. You can take your pick."

"I met some of them, and they sniffed as if I belonged in a latrine ditch. Today, my title makes me smell like a rose. Esha is different."

Teruma twisted the cluster of beads in her ear. "Esha was raised in an atmosphere of refinement and wealth."

"I'll ensure she has everything she needs."

"Yes. You'll have to do that." Teruma's citron perfume mingled with the fragrance of Kirral's over-heated roses. "The Samil is a tough place for a delicate flower. The heat. The poverty. The violence."

"I can protect my wife."

She picked a blossom and plucked its petals. "This rose variety is almost drought resistant. It's commercially grown in Koskara for its oil. None of the ordinary roses would survive long."

"In her own way, Esha is strong."

"That she is. If your heart is set on her, I'll present your suit. Now let's talk about Koskara." She flicked the nude flower away. "Once upon a time, the Samil was a great civilisation, ruled by an Empress, famed for its architecture, poetry and songs, wealthy from incense trees and caravan trade. Now it's split like a carcass, its limbs owned by different nations who gnaw the flesh from its bones. Koskara is one of the bones, and it has little flesh left."

"I know."

"Your last campaign has bled almost all life out of it. The past four years of Quislaki occupation have sucked the land dry of resources, and with seven years of drought, the land has suffered enough. Will you respect your land and protect your people?"

"I intend to."

"You know that I grew up in the Samil, don't you? My late father was lord-satrap of Tajlit. But that's not my only link with the Samil." She twisted the silver bracelet around her wrist, looked around nervously, and lowered her voice. "I'm descended from a Samili Lady through the female line."

That would make her a claimant to ruling part of the Samil. Impossible. "I thought the native dynasties were killed after the conquest?"

"They were." She leant towards him and held her gaze with his. "My great-grandmother was a Samili Ladysdaughter who married a Quislaki Lord, long before the conquest. My family viewed Samili blood as shameful and kept it quiet." She slid a thin object from the folds of her sash. "I have a gift for you: a seal for the new satrap of Koskara."

The carved stone seal was set into a dagger hilt. The weapon lay smooth in his hand. With its leather-wrapped wooden hilt and plain cowhide sheath, it was the kind of knife a trader might carry, but the bronze blade was of unusual quality, its sharp edge making it a cutting tool, its point designed to pierce.

"My Lady, you honour me."

"I want you to have it now, not on Fools Plea Day with people watching. It's my pledge to help you—as long as you help Koskara. Good day."

Her sandals clicked down the garden path.

Dahoud rubbed his thumb over the seal. Cut from limestone, its emblem was a gatehouse: a fitting symbol for barriers to breach and for boundaries to protect.

CHAPTER 5

Foreign Worlds

When the first morning rays seeped through latticed windows, Merida sought out the regular ambassador of the Virtuous Republic.

She introduced herself with a formal bow. "Merida Karr, personal value 248, special ambassador."

The grey-templed man returned her bow with polite correctness. When he stated his personal value as 251, she basked in the warm pleasure of being almost his equal. Seated on the opposite side of his desk, she levelled her gaze at his thin, long-tipped nose.

After an exchange of correct courtesies, she gave him the bundled messages from the Riverian government. He shoved them to the side, apparently in no hurry to read what had to be the first communications in several moons.

While she told him about the dormitory, he listened in silence with his arms against the edge of the desk, rotating his thumbs around each other. "Considering the delicate state of our diplomatic relations, I had hoped your presence would ease the tension rather than add to it."

"What tension?" Nobody had mentioned any conflict during her briefing. Everyone had emphasised—possibly over-emphasised—the Virtuous Republic's generosity and the Queendom's gratitude.

"Given your status, I had assumed you to be prepared for the political situation." His head shook in pointed disapproval. "The Consort requested to add the Most Virtuous President's daughter to his harem."

"A Riverian as a concubine? Impossible."

Sweat beads formed between the old man's eyebrows. "He took the rejection as a personal slight. You will refrain from further rousing his disfavour."

"You have no idea what the dormitory is like," Merida insisted. "After two moons of this, my nerves will be too frazzled for magic."

His thumbs rotated very slowly. The man had all the vigour of a tower slug. "I urge you to submit your accommodation requirements to the Virtues of Modesty and Discipline. Perhaps I may be of some other assistance?"

"Yes. Who is the person I met yesterday? Tall, female, about forty-five, dark-haired, decked in jewellery. She seemed important but didn't introduce herself."

"Lady Teruma, the Consort's head-wife. Quislaki etiquette forbids introductions, of course."

"Head-wife? She acted as if she had authority."

"She's the most powerful woman in the Queendom." He peered at his rotating thumbs as if the motion was worth studying. "Anything else?"

"Is it true there are djinns in Quislak?"

His face darkened as if she had dropped a shutter. "Never let such prejudiced ideas cross your lips, Special Ambassador! To suggest the presence of malevolent spirits in the Queendom is to insult our hosts with superstition."

"I want to expand my knowledge."

His brows drew together. "The study of djinns is prohibited in this country. Even talking about them is a punishable offence."

"Prohibited by whom? By the Queen? Or by her Consort, the clown?"

His face reddened. "I will inform the Virtuous Government of your inadequacy and ask for you to be recalled. While you're still here, discipline yourself into keeping your mouth shut."

Merida's mind whirled like turbulent water. If the old man complained, she would be stripped of the extra points on return, defeating her dreams of a high-value future. She could only hope that he was too lethargic to push himself into action. From now on, she would guard her tongue. Why was the study of djinns outlawed, and their mention prohibited? Governments restricted the flow of information only if they had something to hide.

She promised to discipline herself into uncritical silence.

On her return, the dormitory was empty and Merida savoured the blissful quietude. She helped herself to an orange from a tray of delicacies, and found it the most delicious fruit she had ever tasted: scented, juicy, honey-sweet, and full of exotic promise.

To make the most of the restful moment of solitude, Merida decided to lie down and read. But when she opened her box of scrolls, the treatise on djinns was missing.

"Special Ambassador!" a hard-faced woman in a green uniform called from the curtained door. "You're summoned to the Queen. At once."

Tension tightened in Merida's stomach. Would she be accused of bringing subversive literature into the palace? She grabbed her accreditation papers and her government's official gift. The necklace of tastefully square-cut garnets would surely make an impression in a country where people delighted in gaudy glass beads.

The guard opened the door to a fume-crowded chamber. Half a dozen braziers each churned out different-smelling clouds. Amidst the fog languished purple divans, tables with blue coral inlays, and cats on cushions of silver brocade. Hanging lamps furnished the light that the shuttered windows refused. Thick carpets swallowed every footstep.

The Queen sat so still, she might have been part of the divan, differing only in colour. Her tunic glittered in red and silver, drenched in jewels. She was the biggest person Merida had ever seen, with a faint silver aura of spirituality. The guard who had accompanied her bowed to the floor and withdrew.

"Your Luminous Resplendency," Merida recited. "It is my privilege to represent, as special ambassador the Virtuous Republic of Riverland..."

The Queen yawned.

Merida hurried through the rest of the rehearsed speech. She had expected a beautiful female to reign in her consort's harem, but this pasty face spoke of poor diet, lack of exercise, and decaying health.

The Queen's splendid stiff dress hid the body, but the pudgy hands and the fleshy folds of her huge neck allowed a guess at the fat softness underneath. The gems embroidered on her gown were real. More than a dozen pendants dangled from her silver crown, white shimmering mother-of-pearl disks, each garnished in the centre with a slice of yellow amber which reminded Merida of fried eggs. She saw the foolishness of the gift. The Queen owned more jewellery than all the ladies of River-land did together, and the necklace would never fit her neck.

"Here are my accreditation documents," Merida said.

"That's nice. Put them on that table. Will you dance for rain?"

"Yes, your Luminous Resplendency. It's my privilege to..."

"That's nice. We need water." The Queen nodded, making the fried eggs wobble. She held the necklace up against the sparse light of an oil lamp. "Nice." She bared a doughy calf. "You may fasten it around my ankle. I look forward to the rain."

Merida did as requested, and the Queen clapped her hands. A brown-liveried maid shuffled in, bearing a basket. After perusing its contents, the monarch selected an embroidered handkerchief. Merida thanked her, wondering what other gifts that basket contained. She suspected that the handkerchief was the one of the lowest value.

The Queen clapped her hands twice, and the hard-faced female guard reappeared to escort Merida away. She was dismissed from the royal presence.

⤝

Dizzy with bewilderment, Merida sought the fresh air of the palace gardens, and found a profusion of lush rose bushes, obviously well watered, though planted without apparent consideration of symmetry and style. Masses of pale pink blooms smothered sagging pergolas with their weight.

Tinkling jewellery heralded the arrival of the chief concubine who the day before had put the guard in his place. The yellow aura buzzing around her like a thousand bees showed an agile intellect. She smelled strongly of mint and citron oils. Merida had been raised to avoid encounters with low-value persons, but curiosity won.

Without greeting or formality, Teruma said, "I can't give you a guest apartment because the palace has none. Once the Fool's Plea celebra-tions are over, you may have a room. Shall we go for a walk? This path here is shady, and we can smell the roses."

The soles of her sandals clacked on the slabs. She was really showing ankles and toes, just like the ethnologist had described. Calves even. Merida averted her gaze towards the flowers.

"We don't have value points here in Quislak, but I believe 248 is quite high. Amazing even," Teruma said. "How did you earn them?"

A glow of satisfaction warmed Merida's heart. At last, someone appreciated her personal value and respected her for it. She explained willingly which factors contributed to an individual's value, such as parentage, family connections, marital status, virtuous living, occupations. "The values are not permanent. It's possible to lose points, and having low-value persons in the family brings deductions."

"What are low-value persons?"

"Prisoners, lunatics, concu..." Merida checked herself. "Prisoners and lunatics. Some families go to great lengths to prevent that happening. They may even kill a relative condemned to prison, rather than take a drop in points. Divorce costs points, too. People go to great lengths to prevent a divorce in the family."

When Merida had run to her parents' tower to shelter from her husband's violence, Mother secretly notified the man and invited him for the night. Then she sent her daughter under a pretext into the guest room, locked the door behind her, and ignored her night-long screams of terror and pain—an unforgettable lesson about how family loyalty mattered more than the individual. Fortunately, the next morning he had fallen from the tower roof in his drunken stupor.

None of these matters would ever be spoken outside the family, especially not to a person of low value, and Merida gave only general information. "Schools teach basic value reckoning, and high-ranking families regularly consult professional reckoners for complex calculations."

"Remarkable." Teruma rubbed an earring. "Your rain dance has been brought forward to tomorrow afternoon. Will this be a problem?"

Merida stopped walking. "That's out of the question. Our astrologers calculated that half moon fifty-five days from now is best, and Kirral confirmed the date."

"He changed it to coincide with Fool's Plea Festival. Five thousand spectators from all over the Queendom are gathering in the arena."

"An audience?" Merida cried, horrified. "Magic needs privacy! The agreement specifies there'll be no one present except the sixty-four musicians, four spiritual leaders, and four representatives of the Queen."

"So you can't cope?"

Merida's head spun. She should have known that laypeople in a primitive society neither understood the importance of astrology nor appreciated the enormous energy a magician had to raise. They assumed that magic was easy, a matter of reciting a spell or two, of snapping the fingers, and rain falling on command.

"By the way, the palace orchestra won't play," Teruma added as casually as if discussing an entertainment programme. "Nor will the legion marching band."

"Won't play? The Consort promised!"

"They worry that the foreign magic could harm them."

"Then he must order them."

"It's not good policy to force people in matters of religion or magic. We respect their fears and give them absolute freedom."

"Then why the prohibition about djinns?" The forbidden word slipped out before Merida remembered to hold her tongue.

For a moment, Teruma went rigid, her face tightening into white hardness. Then her posture relaxed into snake-like suppleness again. "Let's walk some more. The point is we don't force people to do something that goes against their beliefs. How would you respond if Kirral commanded you to dance around that spell tree over there, or to slit a goat's throat in honour of the Mighty Ones?"

"That's different," Merida said. "Riverian magic is safe."

"They don't think so."

"I can't work magic without music. Sixty-four court musicians were to have rehearsed the music I sent them." Panic rose, but she was resolved to cope. "Maybe I can do without the flutes, but I need drummers for the rhythm. Sixteen at least."

"I'll find someone who can drum."

Amateurs, with only one day to rehearse! Things were getting worse. She needed a word with the ruler.

Teruma seemed to read her mind. "Don't argue with Kirral. Keep out of his way as best you can during your stay."

Merida frowned. "As a special ambassador of Riverland, I deserve to be treated with respect."

"Sometimes it's wiser to use caution than to insist on rights."

"Then I'll be diplomatic. I'm a politician's daughter, and I've attended statecraft school." Merida did not mention that she had majored in languages, not politics, and Mother often complained that in three years of statecraft training, Merida had failed to acquire diplomacy. "I'll even play Siege with Kirral if that pleases him."

Teruma coiled a lock of dark hair around her middle finger. "It may not be wise to attract the Consort's attention."

"I'm not afraid!"

Teruma laughed softly. "I've delivered the warning. What you do with it is up to you. Good day, Merida."

Consort Kirral beamed when she strode into his study. Today, his moustache cascaded in ringlets. "Ah, our special ambassador. Have you come to play Siege?"

"Highness. I'm giving a year of my life to bring rain to the people of Quislak. Don't I deserve the courtesy to be consulted about a schedule change?"

Kirral dug in his drawstring pouch for saltnuts. He chewed and spat them on the low table before Merida. "You have invited yourself for half a year at our expense and think you are giving us something?"

Merida was stunned. "But... the government..."

"Your government. Your most Virtuous government," he intoned, spitting as he pronounced the word 'virtuous', "did not ask if we wanted you. They decreed that we should have you."

"Didn't you request help because of the drought?"

He pushed his feet into his slippers and shuffled to the shelf-shrine in the corner. He blew dust from the heads of wooden idols, replenished the incense and rearranged the roses. With his back to Merida, he said, "I asked your Virtuous President to aid the starving people in my country. I asked for water engineers. I asked for grain. He promised to send both, but in the meantime would we please give hospitality to a magician who wanted to try out new spells in dry conditions."

Sinking into the divan again, he let the slippers drop on the carpet and crossed his legs. "I agreed, because at that time I was engaged to your

41

President's daughter. Your Virtuous President broke the betrothal and gave the girl to the Darrian Emperor instead." He snorted like a carthorse. "The marriage was off, the engineers and food supplies cancelled, but the magician was on her way and I was expected to house and feed her."

To learn that she was nothing but an unwanted burden came as a shock. Something had gone terribly wrong, but even if the Riverian government was responsible for at least half of it, loyalty to her country would not let her speak that thought.

"I'll honour my part of the arrangement by bringing rain to your country."

"Nonsense." He pushed the slippers on his feet once more and stalked up and down the room, a curved dagger dangling obscenely between his legs. "We have had foreign conjurers queue at the bronze door promising to bring rain. They begged to be allowed to try." He raised his voice. "None of them had the impudence to demand six moon's lodging at the palace." He raised his voice even more. "In a private apartment! Plus a room for their servants! Plus assistance while they were nosing around. Ha!"

Merida wanted to throw a sharp retort at him. She was not a conjurer, but a member of the First Riverian School of Magic, with skills acknowledged even by her peers at home. She wanted appreciation, welcome, gratitude. "Highness, I can only imagine there must have been a misunderstanding."

"A misunderstanding? What an understatement." He lifted a goddess figurine and clanked it back on the shelf. "Put on a good show. Entertain. That is all I want." His eyes narrowed. "If your magic yields rain, you will find me very appreciative."

※

In a secluded corner of the garden, Merida clenched her fists into tight balls. With insults and indignities hurled at her, she owed it to her nation to leave at once with her head raised high. But preserving her pride here would mean crawling back to Riverland, admitting failure.

Balanced on one foot, she performed The Stork routine which enhanced concentration, followed by The Thundercloud, a particularly empowering martial arts sequence she had only mastered two moons ago.

The great Helva Hein would not have allowed circumstances to defeat her. Therefore, Merida Karr would not either. Indeed, the challenges permitted Merida to prove herself. She had to make this rain dance work, had to make her mission a success. When she returned to Riverland, reporting the obstacles she had overcome, the government practically had to award her honour points for her services to the Republic.

Straightening her shoulders, she assessed the new situation. The energy values of the moon, the planets and the drums had changed, and she had to compensate for the lack.

She had four options—all bad. She could ask other magicians to link their power with hers, but the native shamans would not only be useless but throw her own magic off balance. A second choice was to draw energy from an audience, which was highly unethical. The third option was to increase the amount of fire used to call the element of water. Fire scared her nearly as much as sharp-toothed rodents. Sick fear swamped her even as she thought about being surrounded by large flames.

This left one option: to enter a higher level of trance. Third-level trances were sufficient for large-scale magic under favourable conditions. To rise to fourth level was dangerous, and only ever practised in the safe presence of other qualified magicians. She would be vulnerable during the act, and weakened for a long time afterwards. Merida resolved to risk it.

CHAPTER 6

Dancing for Rain

Even in the early morning hour, the day promised to be another scorcher. Already, the air soaked up heat, and the pale sky stretched taut like the skin of a clay-drum. Vine-ranked banner poles painted sharp shadows on the arena's stone steps. Spectators in straw-hats streamed through a dozen entrances, carrying food baskets and parasols, eager to secure seats from where they could see every flicker of hope and despair on the fools' faces.

Clad in a stiff green tunic and turban, Dahoud greeted the arrivals in his aisle, confiscated their weapons, searched their baskets for hidden knives. Most of the officials performing the same duty in the other aisles were regular greenbelts, but others were borrowed from Lord Govan's staff.

Tarkan strode over as if to compare the instructions on their waxed tablets. "Why are we here?" he asked in a low voice. "This secondment smells like a cover-up. What do you think is really going on?"

Down on the patchy lawn, musicians were trying their instruments. Drums rumbled and leather bagpipes screeched.

"Extra security, because of the uprising in Koskara," Dahoud suggested.

"The Consort has his greenbelts to guard the royal canopy, and if he expected real trouble, he'd call in the army, not a handful of councillors and clerks." Tarkan ran a finger along his smooth jaw. "The herald sought you out in the tavern, a day before the rest of us were summoned. Why?"

"In case of racial unrest." Dahoud tried to keep his voice casual. "A Samili among the security staff can calm things down."

"Why do you have a private room in the palace while the rest of us sleep in dormitories?"

"Look, Teruma is signalling us. Let's see what she wants."

"Tarkan, Dahoud, might I have a word?" Teruma was striding towards them in a jangle of jewellery, a stylus and a waxed tablets in her hands. "Can you play drums?"

"In the Samil, every child learns to drum," Tarkan said, as if his own upbringing had not been that of a privileged aristocrat. He waved at the rehearsing musicians. "Do their skills displease you, my Lady?"

"I need men with courage and sense who can drum and aren't afraid of foreign magic."

Foreign magic? Dahoud looked up, startled. Had a problem with the rain dancer thrown his plan into jeopardy?

Tarkan beamed as if her request gave him pleasure. Perhaps it did. "How may we be of service?"

"A surprise act. A magician from Riverland needs drum energy for her show."

"We're not burdened by superstition, my Lady." Tarkan's eyes crinkled at the corners. "Dahoud and I used to drum together when we were small, and it will be our pleasure to do it again."

During their brief childhood friendship, they had played the goatskin drums for hours, their patterns interweaving with such vigour that a magician could have bundled that power and moved a mountain.

"Good." Teruma ticked the item off on her tablet. "I'll get drums and will call you nearer the time." She strode off, calling instructions to a greenbelt about the schedule for the parade.

While Dahoud searched picnic baskets for concealed weapons, he shut out his friends' probing gaze.

He wondered what the rain dancer would be like, and if her performance would indeed stir much excitement so that his departure tomorrow would go unnoticed. Riverians were famed for their prudery, so the dance would probably consist of a series of stilted strides. Perhaps, if she was a young beauty, she would capture everyone's attention anyway.

Better still would be an old woman: everyone worshipped a crone. The very best would be if she really seduced the sky into giving water.

⨝

On the stone steps around the arena, people sat so tightly together, their hips touched like peas in a pod. Merida was glad that the royal grandstand was spacious and its cushions spaced. When a procession of green-uniformed men carried life-sized idols around the arena, and when priests burned incense and chanted to the Mighty Ones, she took care not to show her disdain.

Listening to native music and watching dances, however, gave her pleasure. On the patchy turf, women hopped and swirled brightly coloured skirts in sinuous, passionate, playful movements while their men clapped out the strange rhythm. She counted the beats. Could it really be a pattern of nine? She had heard mentions of three-count music, forbidden in Riverland, but surely a nine-count rhythm was impossible. Perhaps she should not risk her Virtue listening to those sounds.

She shifted on her cushion. "Teruma, I ought to rehearse with the drummers."

"They're both busy." Teruma selected a cluster of dark grapes from a roving vendor's vine-ranked basket. "Have some grapes."

Hot anger mixed with cold dread in Merida's stomach. "You know I must keep to my special diet for the magic. I told you, sixteen drummers is the minimum, and they must practice with me, so that they can support my magic by nightfall."

Teruma licked at the grapes. "Two drummers is what you'll have. Now pay attention."

The master of ceremonies banged his beribboned staff on the ground. "Here comes the first fool of today: a wheelwright from Quislabat."

Ten thousand feet trampled an excited welcome for the brawny man and his good-speaker.

The master of ceremonies placed the red-glittering fool's turban on his head. "Kneel and speak, Fool. What is your plea?"

The man described how he had carelessly committed a dishonest action, which had gotten him embroiled in further crimes and made him an extortionist's target. "He regrets his deeds deeply," the wheelwright's goodspeaker said, "and wishes to end this cycle of evil."

Waving scarves, the audience shouted for mercy, Merida with them. The Consort, who had looked stern at first, allowed himself to be swayed by the crowds and pardoned the man. The audience cheered and munched grapes.

A young girl wished to marry a poor peasant. Her parents, who favoured a wealthy man she had reason to dislike, threatened to disown her. The girl begged the Consort to intervene. At the sight of thousands of waving scarves, the Consort not only allowed the girl to choose her own partner, but gave the couple a hide of land to settle. The crowd ululated in shrill delight.

"What benevolent rulers the Queen and her Consort are," Merida said. "Even in this totalitarian monarchy they allow the people to decide. Can anyone just turn up to plead their case?"

"We receive more than eight hundred applications every year. From those I chose thirteen. The next case will be interesting."

One green-uniformed official wanted a pardon for raping his virgin niece. This time, no textiles fluttered. The chorus of booing voices drowned out the criminal's and his good-speaker's whiny appeals. Kirral sentenced him to daily public whipping for a moon, starting immediately, followed by eight years of quarry labour.

Merida joined the cheering. Rapists were evil scum who deserved the harshest penalties. But when the whip hit the man's flesh, when he sagged in his bonds and his screams turned to groans, she bit her knuckles. Her guts contracted at every sizzling lash.

"He thought he'd get off lighter here than by confessing to a regular court," Teruma said casually. "But people don't forgive peacetime rape."

"If you knew he had no chance, why did you choose him?"

Teruma just laughed.

Merida insisted. "You should have told him not to apply."

The head-wife plucked a fat grape. "I warn all candidates that they may lose as well as win. I even offer to arrange their safe journey home should they choose not to take the risk. You really should taste these grapes, Merida."

The next fool begged forgiveness for poisoning his neighbour's well.

"Cut off his arm," Kirral said. "Now."

"No! Please, have mercy!" The man tried to run, but two greenbelts restrained him.

Kirral sent the master of the ceremonies back into the arena to announce:

"The Consort offers you mercy. He lets you choose: either one arm, or both hands."

A moment later, the well poisoner's scream shuddered through the arena. Merida tried not to look at his crumpled body on the grass, or the arm on the bloodied block, or executioner holding his dripping sword high as in triumph.

The man with the staff announced: "We will be taking a short break for refreshments now. After the break, we have more performances for you, more fools, more pleas, more executions! For the finale, we have a special act. A dancer has come all the way from Riverland to entertain us."

Merida thought she must have misheard, but he went on: "This kind of dance is used in her home country to bring or stop rain. You may expect a spectacular display, for she will dance on a platform inside a ring of fire. Yes, people of Quislak, a ring of fire."

Merida marched through the massed applause and waving scarves to the Consort's divan. "Highness, I protest! You promised sixty-four professional musicians rehearsing the supplied music in advance, a venue where a river meets a lake, under a watertight canopy, with no more than four observers. At dusk." She flicked her hand at the massed humanity in the arena. "You can't expect me to work magic in these circumstances. Magic requires a special date, a special place, preparation, privacy."

He touched his moustache which today ended in forks like snakes' tongues. "Then we shall announce that the Riverian is not able to perform a rain dance after all. That she has raised the people's hopes with empty promises."

Merida wanted to scream her fury into his face, and to shake his shoulders until that feathered turban fell off. "I'm a qualified magician of the eleventh degree, not a public entertainer!"

He stroked his chin in a slow downwards move. "Be a good girl. Entertain us with a pretty dance."

Wild anger fuelled her resolve. She would prove the worth of her magic by calling more rain than they had ever seen. With none of the specifications met, the challenge was enormous, but she would succeed.

She would draw power from every available source within and outside herself, regardless of custom, sense and propriety.

"Please get the height of the fire square doubled," she told the head-wife. "No, make it triple. Quadruple! Or is there no firewood either?"

"Do you want to meet your musicians while I arrange the wood?" Teruma asked pleasantly.

"No! It's too late. They should have started learning the music and rehearsing moons ago. Just tell them to drum like this: *doum-tek doumtek.* Do you think they can cope with this? Or is a simple four-count rhythm beyond Quislaki intelligence? Or maybe their fingers will be hacked off?"

"They'll manage," Teruma said, unruffled by Merida's fury. "Now listen carefully, Merida. If you want to leave the Queendom, I'll arrange a carriage to take you away right after your show."

"It's not a show!" Merida snapped. "It's an act of magic. Since I'm bringing rain—lots of rain—the roads won't be passable for a carriage for several hours. The very least this country owes me is hospitality." Instincts screamed at her to flee this horrible land, but she would not let undisciplined fear dictate her actions, and she wanted to observe the effects of her magic. "No, you're not going to get rid of me so easily."

Teruma's eyes darkened. "Think about it while you have the chance."

"I have other things to think about. Such as this 'show'."

She would bring so much rain that the people would bathe her in gratitude, the Consort would beg her forgiveness, and the Virtuous Government would award her at least 100 honour points. She would even write her own treatise, *Weather Magic and its Application under Adverse Circumstances,* and her name would be honoured side by side with that of the great Helva Hein.

～

The sun stood three finger-breaths above the horizon, painting the arena in soft gold.

When five green-clad courtiers escorted Merida into the arena, the spectators rose from their seats to cheer as if she were a favourite enter-tainer. The stone idols of the Mighty Ones seemed to watch as she skirted around the dark patches of dried blood. Her white trousers shimmered against yellowed grass, but the ground under her feet contained no earth magic. Not the faintest tingling reached her bare soles.

Wood was stacked for four equal walls of flames higher than any Merida had worked with, but even this would not suffice to draw much rain, not with the moon in the wrong phase, the planets in a pointless place, and the earth's pulse lacking.

Doum-tek doumtek doum-tek doumtek. Merida cast a quick glance at the two green-uniformed men squatting under a striped awning, drums in their laps. At least they had mastered the rhythm, and what they lacked in refinement, they made up in fervency. The acoustics were strong, and the sound carried. But two drums were not enough.

She needed another source. All around her, voices cheered, hands clapped, feet stomped. People. Human energy. Forbidden fuel. Merida had never broken the magicians' code of ethics, never fed on people power. But if she could not draw rain, Kirral would smirk, and she would have to return to Riverland with her head bowed.

She glanced at the rows of excited spectators, sensed plenty of power waiting to be tapped, and wished she could assess its quantity. To make sure, she had better go even higher into trance, not just to fourth level but to fifth.

She climbed the platform in the centre of the firewood square, and spoke the required homage to the four Virtues, as expected from an accredited member of a school of magic. She performed a quick but intense sequence from the Disciplined Path, stroking her own aura and kicking an imaginary foe, and chanted to focus her magic.

The vibrations from the applause caressed her bare arms, her cheeks, tingled through her body's fibres. Resolutely, Merida opened herself up. She allowed the forbidden fuel to flow into her abdomen like liquid into a bowl. She felt her flesh heat and her strength grow. Already her own silver aura buzzed around her skin.

Greenbelts set their torches to the wood. Flames shot up. Now it was too late to back away. She was trapped by the dancing tongues. Smoke scratched her nostrils, and heat bathed her skin.

All she could do was to pull her fear of fire inside her, stir it into positive energy, and focus on her task. She raised her arms to the sky to call for rain. She tossed her head, her shoulders, her body, releasing magic.

Doum-tek doumtek, doum-tek doumtek.

Five thousand people in the audience clapped the rhythm. The liquid strength of the crowd's support surged through her. They wanted the rain, and were willing her to succeed. She drank their appreciation and turned it to power. Her heartflame heated and fuelled her dance.

She surrendered all control to the pulsing of the drums. *Doum-tek doumtek, doum-tek doumtek.* Her arms rose high on one side, then collapsed in the front. The momentum carried her arms up to the other side, her chest and head followed. Sparks of magic crackled in her hair.

She rose easily through the two ordinary levels of trance into the third at which she normally worked major large magic. Then she climbed to the fourth, the dangerous fifth. Power soared through her, sent her blood singing. Weight drained from her body, consciousness seeped away. Almost without effort, she rose to the sixth level, the one no magician had achieved since Helva Hein.

Her mind was lightness, riding inside a cloud-powered bliss. She stirred her inner cauldron, drew the magic through her heart into her head, and contacted the element of rain.

A long time passed before her hands quivered in response. Water had heard her call; now she had to attract it. She pulled the rain clouds she could not yet see. So much power pumped through her blood, she knew she had enough to bring rain, but she wanted more, more, more. Enough water to sate the earth, enough to wipe the smirk off the Consort's face.

Excited cheers greeted the first purple cloud on the horizon.

Then the first raindrops fell on her naked arms, big drops, warm and soft. Shouts of joy and hissing flames nearly drowned out the drumbeats, but she kept going.

The rain poured harder, drowning the flames.

She danced, and danced, and danced. She climbed into further levels of trance, raising yet more energy, calling yet more rain. Her white tunic had lost all substance, a thin textile film glued to her skin.

Violent water crashed on empty white stone steps, ran in streams and cascaded down the corridors into the grass arena.

The cheering spectators cowered under parasols, and eventually left for better shelter in the town. Only the drummers stayed under their feeble awning. Merida dropped to a lower trance to observe them. The descent made her ears ring so loud they almost burst. When drum skins dampened and the sounds dulled, they kept the rhythm going by clapping their hands. Their stamina matched hers.

Doum-tek, doumtek. Doum-tek, doumtek.

Greyness descended, then night-black. Time to stop. She had won. Now was the time to celebrate the joys of victory. After signalling the drummers to slow, she braced herself. As she plummeted into the lower levels, a dizzy void replaced her spent strength, and she collapsed in happy exhaustion.

❧

Servants bustled her into a litter. Once at the palace, tiredness ripped Merida's mind to shreds. In her rush to ready herself, she had not prepared proper aftercare. No honey-water waited to restore energy, no hot brick warmed her bed.

When greenbelts supported her arms on both sides, she was too shattered to resent the touch. They guided her not to the dormitory, but to the palace's audience hall. She needed rest, dry clothes, nourishment, but was too weak to protest. Disoriented and shivering with cold, she dropped into the chair. At least the armrests were wood. Wood energy, though weak, was easy to absorb.

Teruma draped a wool cloak over her.

She could barely hear the Consort's speech of thanks, let alone enjoy her triumph, or compose a formal reply. With effort, she turned the corners of her mouth upwards.

The Queen, fat and stately beside her Consort, spoke. "You will stay in the Queendom, our guest forever."

Merida's mind jerked awake. "No… honoured… some days, then Riverland. Home."

The Consort slapped his thigh. "You will stay in Quislak. If not as a guest, then as part of my harem."

What a bizarre Quislaki custom to express formal gratitude by proposing marriage. Searching for the appropriate phrase, she struggled for strength to speak. "…honoured… regret… return to Riverland."

Sleep. She needed sleep.

"You misunderstood." Teruma said on her left. "You'll be a wife whether you want to or not."

"No," Merida croaked.

Reality and nightmares swam together in her head. She heard Kirral's voice from a distance. "We shall dispense with the traditional rites for the occasion."

Virtues help me, help me, Merida pleaded, but she was too feeble to focus. The room spun. Clutching the armrests, she sought to rally what energy she could muster. Her belly cauldron was a hollow vessel, her heartflame a faint spark. Summoning droplets of strength, she pulled herself up and dropped at the Queen's feet.

"I beg you, Ma'am. Help me."

"I do not involve myself in my husband's harem affairs." The Queen yawned and clapped twice. Greenbelts dragged Merida back to her seat.

"I demand…" She tried to shout, but it came out as a croak. "…speak regular ambassador."

"Quislak no longer has a Riverian ambassador. Diplomatic relations are severed." The Consort held Merida's pass and accreditation over the incense burner.

Her power spent, she could not stop him. Slow-licking flames devoured the precious parchments.

"I … no more magic… never… for you."

"We have ways to make you." Kirral smirked. "Besides, I have other uses for you."

CHAPTER 7

Missed Chance

The crowded tavern smelled of fried mutton, damp wool, and the sweat of festival-goers seeking shelter from the downpour. In the whirring tangle of voices, Tarkan caught snatches of conversation.

"That's four tanni for you," a man wheezed. "I never thought she'd make it. Not after the wizard with the painted pigeons failed."

"Do you remember the hermit?" another voice piped up. "The one who set his hair on fire."

"Well, they didn't bring rain, and the girl did. A Riverian, of all people! - Hey, look at those guys."

Heads swivelled to Tarkan and Dahoud.

"Greenbelts." The wheezy man spat. "They'll have to stand like everyone else."

"These are the ones who did the drumming!"

Several bodies squeezed closer together to make space on their bench. Tarkan called out an order to the harried server for mutton kebabs and wine.

The rotund trader on his right wrung out the hem of his tunic, adding another puddle to the floor. "I hear they were all sent to torture, those mages who couldn't bring rain."

An equally plump woman, whose blue eye-paint had smeared trails over her cheeks, said, "My sister's neighbour has a friend whose brother is a palace guard, and he says they never left the palace alive. I shouldn't really be talking about this…" She leant forward and whispered loud enough for everyone to hear, "but between you and me, the royal palace has dungeons. A whole network of them. The whole of Quislabat is tunnelled underneath, that's where the mages are imprisoned." The trader elbowed her, nudging his chin at Dahoud and Tarkan. She clapped her hand over her mouth. "I didn't say anything, I didn't."

Tarkan smiled to put her at her ease, and sipped his wine.

A girl with over-sized earrings and blotchy skin said, "You'd think these sorcerers would peek into the future before they take a risk."

The young man by her side placed his hand on hers. "You're so right, my dragonfly. What makes them do it?"

"The reward, surely!" The fat woman's voice rose above the tavern din. "This is between you and me, of course, and I shouldn't be saying anything, but I have it from an inside source that she's getting one thousand dinar."

"One thousand dinar!" The boy and the girl gasped in unison, as if unable to understand such a big sum.

"Let's hope it's true," Dahoud said. "She deserves it."

"The Mighty Ones bless her!" The fat woman emptied her beaker in one gulp, and held it out for Tarkan to refill. Her bangles jingled. "Bless her!" she repeated, drank again, and held her beaker out once more.

"I'm glad my wine finds your favour, madam," Tarkan said, "and honoured you choose to drink it in appreciation of the magician to whom we're much indebted. I hope this magician has indeed negotiated a huge fee and the Lord Consort doesn't back out of his agreement."

Dahoud frowned. "Would Kirral break a promise?"

Tarkan refrained from comment. More moisture trickled from his turban tail down his spine, gathered at the hem of his tunic and dripped puddles on the floor.

At the far end of the table, the young couple had lost interest in their surroundings. They gazed into each other's eyes and, from time to time, the man murmured something into his lover's ear. She blushed and giggled. Dahoud was looking away as if tormented by their bliss.

Tarkan tapped him on the shoulder. In a low voice, he asked, "Why did you resign your job?"

"The service here is slow. Where are our kebabs?"

"I traded connections and called in favours to get you the job. Why did you throw it away?"

Dahoud flicked the basil stalk across the table. "Clerking is dull, the pay is lousy, and Govan is a pompous ass. Reasons enough for you?"

Tarkan wished he, too, could leave Govan's service, but the danger would follow him elsewhere. "Has the Consort offered you a more rewarding line of work? Is that why you're here?"

"Why would the Consort give a lowly Samili a good job? Why would anyone?" Dahoud did not meet Tarkan's eyes. "I'm helping out with festival security for a couple of days. Just like you. Just like two dozen other men."

"Our assignments seem similar. Yet, we're on short-term secondment, whereas you left Govan's employ for good. You received an individual letter, delivered by royal messenger, a day before the rest of us were summoned in a curt note." Tarkan ran a thumb along the splintered edge of the tavern table. "The city overflows with visitors and the rest of us sleep on dormitory mats, but you have a private room in the palace. What is going on?"

Dahoud rubbed a hand down the front of his neck. Then he waved to the server. "Hey, hurry up with our order!"

Tarkan knew he ought to let the matter rest. If Dahoud did not want to talk, he would not. Even as a child, orphaned, neglected and hungry, always grateful for meal invitations, Dahoud had never talked about his past. One day, he had simply vanished. When they met again after thirteen years, Dahoud was dragging brick-baskets on a building site like a sweating donkey. Despite picking up the threads of their friendship, and despite Tarkan's prodding, he had never revealed what he had done in the intervening years. But they were grown men now, and friends.

"Dahoud, if you're in trouble, can I help? Perhaps my father..."

Suddenly, conversations around them stopped and giggles ceased. The tavern grew so silent, he could hear the sharply held breaths.

Lord-Satrap Govan stood by the entrance, raising his arm so that droplets sprayed from the purple fringe. "What a fortunate coincidence to find a member of my staff in this place." He shooed the young couple off the bench and sat, combing his fingers through the fringed armbands.

"A real satrap at my table!" the plump woman yelped. "I must tell my husband's aunt."

The time to relax was over, and he had to be on his guard again. Tarkan rose and bowed. Dahoud merely dipped a curt nod.

Conversations picked up.

Tarkan felt a tap on his shoulder and saw a young server.

"Excuse me." The boy's face was shining with excitement. He had an athlete's body with slender hips, and smelled of cinnamon. Their eyes caught. Tarkan willed his gaze away, directing it to the drunken woman's swaying flesh.

The boy tapped his shoulder again. Tarkan turned, and pretended not to notice the blush in the boy's cheeks. With Govan sitting across the table, even a brief glance could be too much. "What is it?" he said gruffly, as if he resented having his attention pulled from the female.

"The boss sent me. He's wondering, er, are you the ones who drummed, because then, er, your food's on the house."

"We're obliged for this gracious invitation," Govan said. "I'll partake of a beef stew."

"But..." the boy said, then caught sight of the purple armbands. "Yes, yes, my Lord."

Tarkan felt the boy's gaze on him, tentative and warm like a caress, and pretended not to notice. Casually, he said, "I didn't know you were in town, my Lord."

"It's my habit to attend this festival annually, although my office cannot spare me for long." Govan combed his fingers through the fringe again. "The vice eradication campaign is in full flow. Yesterday, we drowned a further thirty men-lovers."

Tarkan composed his features into an expression of impersonal interest. "That makes over four hundred. Who would have thought that there could be so many of them?"

"They're clever, those perverts, hiding in ever quarter, in every trade. I'll flush the rats from their holes. Before the year is out, there won't be a single men-lover left in Idjlara. Idjlara will be the first vice-free satrapy in the Queendom."

"A remarkable achievement, my Lord," Tarkan said. "What do you think of the rain dancer?"

Govan licked his lips. "She possesses a nice bosom, not a great quantity of it, but pleasant to view, especially once her tunic was thoroughly wet."

"An enjoyable sight." Tarkan injected a note of male appreciation into his voice.

"I hear she's a special ambassador for her nation. I prefer her to River-land's regular ambassador." Govan scratched the back of his hand. "We should accept only young female ambassadors at court, and oblige them to wear wet garments which cling. You saw her close-up. Did her tits bounce?"

"She was definitely worth watching. How far beyond Quislabat does the rain extend, do you think? Will it reach the parts of the country where rain is needed most? Perhaps she ought to travel to the Samil and dance there."

At the mention of the word 'Samil' Dahoud's eyes widened and his mouth opened as if someone had opened a treasure trunk with gleaming gold, but he said nothing.

With pursed lips, Govan shook his head. "A Riverian in the Samil? That would never work. I have met some. They whine when they see an uncivilised rat or an unauthorised mosquito." He gargled and spat into a puddle on the floor. "They have a strange religion, the Riverians, with rules for everything. Did you know that in their country you can't sneeze, spit or piss without offending some Virtue or other?"

Suddenly Dahoud clasped the table. "I must go," he murmured. "Do me a favour and distract Govan. When my kebab comes, eat it."

A frown formed between Govan's alert eyes when Dahoud rose.

Whatever the reason for Dahoud's request, Tarkan had to act fast. He turned to the drunken woman. "Madam, all the stars of the universe sway in your hips. Will you grant a humble admirer a boon and dance?"

She giggled, loosened her hair and tossed it in an imitation of the rain dance. "The stars of the universe. I'll show you the moon, and the sun, too." Her ample bottom gyrated.

"Incomparable," Tarkan said. "Would you care to mount this table for your performance, and permit me to provide the music?" He drummed his fingers on the table while she climbed up, drawing everyone's attention until Dahoud had disappeared into the rain.

⤞

By the time Dahoud reached the palace, his legs and tunic were splattered in brown mud, water streaming down his back and dripping onto the tiled floor. His mind buzzed with the new-formed plan. Drought-stricken Koskara would welcome a magician who brought rain, and barely notice her drumming assistant.

"I must speak to his Highness the Lord Consort," he told the pair of guards in the dimly-lit antechamber.

One of them yawned, the other sized him up with narrow eyes. "Oh yeah? And who would you be that his Royal Highness would see you?"

"I'm Dahoud. No other name." He was still wearing the green uniform, and unlike the guards', his lacked the fancy shoulder bows denoting rank in the greenbelt hierarchy. "Kirral will want to see me. It's urgent."

The guard had obviously concluded that Dahoud was below him in the pecking order. He unwound his green turban cloth, spat on his fingers, smoothed his sparse hair and put the turban back on, taking time to adjust its position as if it was the only matter of importance to him. "The Consort is in a meeting and does not wish to be disturbed. No exceptions. Not even for Dahoud-No-Other-Name."

If they knew he was a satrap, they would be kissing his feet with courtesy. But the appointment must not get out. "The Lady Teruma will see me."

"She's in the meeting, too. And there are to be no disturbances, by whosoever."

At that moment, the door creaked outwards. Kirral shuffled out, accompanied by a greenbelt who bolted the door behind him.

Dahoud pushed into his way. "Highness. May I meet the rain dancer – The special ambassador?"

"No." Kirral shuffled on.

"It's in connection with what we talked about yesterday."

Kirral stopped. "Ah, yes, but alas, she has left. Her nation has severed diplomatic relations with the Queendom, which upset her so much that she departed at once. She would not even stay to receive gratitude and glory, would not even wait until the rain ceased and the roads became more passable again." He raised his palm. "They are strange, these Riverians."

Dahoud bowed briskly and left. Since the rain dancer was not available, he would follow his earlier strategy: don trader disguise to get into Oubar.

CHAPTER 8

Captive in the Harem

Merida awoke to a clawing thirst, her limbs as lifeless as wilted flowers. High-pitched giggles squealed like a hundred caged birds. Memory slammed into her guts: she was a captive in the Consort's harem.

"You're awake, at last! Do you want cakes?" The owner of the chirping voice was plump, clad in scarlet, with a dozen amulets bouncing on her big bosom.

"Might I have some water, please?"

The concubine plopped on Merida's bed, spreading a smell of overripe pears, and handed her a perfumed concoction. "This is made with fifteen different flowers. I'm Haurvatat, and my father is a Darrian prince. What's yours?"

"I'm Merida." She gulped the drink and shifted away from the woman's smell. "My father's a trader. My mother's a politician, a member of the Riverian parliament as well as a regional administrator. How did you come to be enslaved?"

The woman blinked. "I'm a royal wife."

"Oh. And she?" Merida nodded at the child sucking a honey cake on the adjoining bed, probably a concubine's daughter whose childhood was confined to the harem.

"I'm Kadiffe." The girl rose to plant herself before Merida and pulled her gauzy dress tight, revealing the first buds of womanhood.

"My father's the Queendom's high general, and I'm Kirral's favourite wife."

A thin woman stretched languidly on a divan. "Are you really from Riverland? Is that far away?"

"The Virtuous Republic of Riverland lies to the north-east, two and a half moons by coach."

"Riverland can't be far away," Haurvatat trilled. "Far away is where Darria is."

Two armed female guards clanked into the dormitory. "Which of you is Merida? Follow us. The Consort wants you."

Merida rose at once, ready to give Kirral a piece of her mind.

"Take this." Haurvatat slipped a carved figurine into Merida's hands. "This is great Darrian magic. It will make him want you."

Merida dropped the idol and wiped her hand. "We Riverians don't-"

Haurvatat's eyes widened. "You have strong Riverian magic? You must tell me everything when you come back."

"Remember that I'm the favourite!" Kadiffe shouted. "I, and no one else."

≈

Kirral's apartment was steeped in dark silence and stale, incense-laden air. Wicks glimmered in ceiling lamps, the only light in the window-less room, revealing heaped cushions, dark trunks, carved idols, and murals of hunters netting wild beasts.

Kirral sat on a divan, purple-clad and pearl-trimmed, with the big dagger curving across his thigh. Today, his moustache fanned out like cat's whiskers.

"Welcome, my dear wife." Jewel-green eyes raked over her body. "Be seated."

"I'm not your wife!" Merida disciplined herself into speaking reasonably. "Holding me against my will is unethical and will damage political relations." Lowering herself into the broad carved chair, she mimicked Mother's diplomatic smile. "Arrange my journey home, and we'll forget this ever happened."

He turned a yellow gaming stone between his fingers. "Interesting, interesting. I will get much pleasure from your company."

"I'll never submit to your carnal demands!"

"Carnal demands? My dear Merida, what a crude suggestion." His voice softened to that of a caring father. "I want finer things from you. Shall we play Siege?" He tilted a big beaker, letting tokens clatter into a heap on the gaming board. "Choose: do you wish to attack or to defend?"

"I defend." She built her fortress in a corner of the board. Inside it, she placed the tokens representing civilians, archers, Lady, satrap and the target of the game, the precious well.

Kirral arranged his yellow legionnaires, officers, general and battering rams. When he launched an attack with an officer, Merida responded with an archer. The initial moves brought no contact, no fight, but then he snatched three stones from her fortress wall. At the same time, she killed four of his legionnaires and an officer, while keeping her own figures alive. She placed her Lady by the postern, ready to shoot out and capture his well within three turns.

"I observe the human mind's varied workings, with samples from all ethnicities and professions." Kirral toyed with the officer in his hand, exchanged it for a legionnaire, put that one down as well and finally moved his general forward. "You are my first high-value Riverian study object as well as the first moral magician. It will be educational."

At least she was in no danger of getting raped. Merida prepared the sortie to capture the well, but changed her strategy towards snatching the general.

"Excellent move, my dear Merida." He pinched his chin between his thumb and first finger. "You are amazing: intelligent, courageous, moral. How does it feel to be appreciated for what you are, instead of for the number of your degrees, for your mother's importance, or for the points your family has amassed?"

Haughty silence seemed to be the best answer, so she placed her archer stone, the last but one move before she could kill. "I want to return to Riverland."

"What you want, my dear wife, is of no relevance."

"Will you let me go if I defeat you at Siege?"

He laughed loudly, for a long time. Then he slid a tribune through a breach in the wall and killed her Lady. Merida stared at the chequered board. A moment ago she had been so certain of her strategy, but Kirral had outmanoeuvred her, and the game was lost.

"This was most enjoyable, dear Merida. Now, will you grant me your advice on how to redecorate this apartment?"

A reasonable request. She scanned the blood-red divans, the silk-glistening cushions, the carved idols grinning from shelves. "More light and fewer accessories would brighten the place. The frieze, running on only three sides of the room, lacks symmetry. Consider adding a fourth."

He pursed his lips and stroked a fingernail across the tip of his chin. "The three sections develop a motif. How do you suggest building on it for the fourth?"

She rose to inspect the narrow band of blue figures on white ground, female unclad figures with hands between their thighs. On the second frieze, two bodies cavorted in a series of poses, doing everything a female and a male could possibly do, and several things that were surely not possible. At the sight of the third, shock slapped her in the face and made her step back. She would not soil her eyes by looking at group copulations.

"Have them over-painted with something tasteful. Geometrical patterns, flowers, animals."

"Animals, what a delightful suggestion!" Kirral stroked the dagger on his thighs. "I shall invite the Queendom's greatest mural painter to submit sketches. Will you give me your opinion on them?"

"It will be my pleasure to advise you on aesthetics. However." She put firmness into her voice. "I need a private apartment during my stay, and I insist you arrange my return to Riverland."

"You are too valuable to let go."

"You can't make me stay."

He guffawed so much his waxed moustache vibrated. "You will find that I can. The guards have instructions."

"My mother is a member of the Virtuous Government, a powerful regional administrator, probably the next Vice President of Riverland. She won't tolerate having her daughter abused."

"Interesting." He squeezed one side of his moustache. "I look forward to our next round of games."

With her chin raised, Merida marched out of the room. Green-uniformed guards closed around her and escorted her back to the dormitory. She had to get away from the mad Consort, but how?

Haurvatat's arms snaked around Merida's waist. "Did the Riverian magic work? What did you do?"

"I'll tell you later." Merida disentangled herself. "I'm tired."

She needed solitude and silence to make plans, and the harem quarters yielded neither, with sandals clacking in the tiled corridors, wheels screeching from the street below, and donkey drivers cursing. All day long, concubines giggled, squabbled and squeaked, Haurvatat and Kadiffe competed to see who could clink her finger cymbals loudest, and even the brown-clad maids prattled while emptying wash-barrels and slop-buckets.

When the din of the day finally subsided into wheezy snores, Merida assessed her options. The palace buzzed like a wasp's nest with armed guards who would not let her leave. Even if she managed to sneak out, she lacked the money, maps, transport and knowledge to get home. Magic would be of no help because only in storyteller's yarns could magicians chant a spell to travel bodily to another place.

Mother had the power to help. Since Merida's degradation to minus thirteen devastated the whole family's points, Mother would be desperate to redeem her. Merida would have to grovel in gratitude for the rest of her life, but this price was worth paying. How could she inform Mother of her plight? The country had no postal system, Kirral would refuse the services of a royal messenger, and she had neither funds nor opportunity to hire a private courier. She fell asleep, still wondering how to smuggle a letter out of the palace.

≈

At dawn, the legion band thumped in the square and ripped her out of sleep. Trumpets blared, drums roiled, and an officer yelled orders.

Haurvatat sat under her personal shrine, a shelf where wooden idols stood like trees in a dense forest, while rubbing her feet with a grease. "Take off your boots. I'll massage your feet with this. It's jasmine and caterpillar cream."

"I'd rather not." Merida scraped powder from her inkstick and stirred it into a smooth black liquid. She tried her usual morning exercise of composing a poem in iambic tetrameter, but a dozen chattering females crowded in on her and fingered the parchment on her thigh.

"Oh, you can write!" Haurvatat sat next to her, leaning over the sheet, and cooed. "You're so clever."

Kadiffe dipped her fingers into the ink and licked. "Disgusting. Tastes of sorcery." She shoved the pot. Black ink spilled and spattered.

Merida stowed the precious parchments away and fled to the only place where she knew she would find a pocket of peace.

In the steamy white silence of the bath, she grabbed the hardest bristle-brush and scrubbed the sticky grime of anger and humiliation from her flesh. Only when her skin was almost raw, she wrapped herself in a towel and stretched out on the heated platform to find serenity through meditation. No chatter, no cymbals, no bickering, only the soft drip-drip-drip of water from the domed ceiling. Bliss.

Wooden buckets clanked. "Miracle massage? Nifty nettles? Charm shampoo?" a female voice hollered.

Merida waved the intruder away. "I just want to relax on my own, please."

The woman plunked her buckets down, water spilling over the rims. "Come on! Give an honest masseuse some business."

Merida pulled the linen towel closer around her torso. "No, thank you. It's not done in Riverland for a woman to touch another."

"So you're the new arrival." The masseuse stared. "I've been wondering what you're like."

The woman was clad in nothing but the room's white haze of steam. Merida averted her eyes. Then she realised with a jolt that the woman had spoken Riverian. "You speak my language?"

The masseuse straightened. "Come on, give me some business. Riverians must help one another."

A Riverian? Then why was she doing this job?

"You really touch women's bodies?" Merida's skin pimpled at the thought, even in the steamy heat.

"Men's bodies, too. The palace bookings pay well."

Merida's mind snapped into action. This woman could smuggle a letter out of the palace. "I'm sure a massage would be nice. A shampoo too, and any other service you provide, though I'll have to owe you the fee."

"Don't worry about it." The masseuse filled a sack of white felt with hot soapy water and squeezed it on Merida's belly, spreading soft foam.

"You just choose what you want, and Teruma's greenbelts settle the bill. Believe me, the annual allowance for each wife is so generous, you couldn't spend it all, unless you order gemstone jewellery. So be a darling, divert some palace funds to me."

"I'll be back tomorrow," Merida promised.

"I'm working here only every other day. The wives aren't exactly queuing up for my services. I have high hopes for my new treatment, though. I'm going to whip the wives with nettles, saying it's an ancient Riverian aphrodisiac."

"Nettles?" Merida laughed. "Mother uses nettles for her rheumatism. I've heard that old men use it to stimulate their... blood flow. Why should the harem women want it?"

"Because I'll tell them that nettles make them attractive to Kirral."

The masseuse finished kneading Merida's shoulders, and spread a hot fragrant paste on her thighs. "Beeswax, honey, citron juice. Excellent for removing body hair."

"Remove body hair? You can't do that!"

"Your skin must be smooth if you want to become a favourite."

"I don't want to be a favourite!" Merida cried. "I came to this country as a special ambassador for the Virtuous Republic, with a personal value of 248. Ambassadors are supposed to be inviolate. But I was imprisoned and degraded into becoming a concubine. I have to get away."

"Many women dream of getting into the luxury of the royal harem. You want to get out. So what will you do?"

Merida flushed with hope. "If I give you a letter, will you pay a courier to take it to Riverland? My mother will refund the cost and reward you."

"If I get caught with your letter, I'll not only lose my best customer, but may land in prison." The masseuse ripped a strip of hardened paste off Merida's leg. It stung like fire, and dotted Merida's skin pink like freshly plucked chicken. "Here's the deal. I take the letter, and you promote the nettle treatment. Tell everyone it's an ancient Riverian secret, which bestows erotic powers."

"That's ridiculous!" Merida sat up straight. "I won't soil my tongue with dirty talk, and I won't spread lies."

"Then keep your letter." Unperturbed, the woman tore off more hair with the paste.

Frustrated and sore, Merida returned to the dormitory. She would find someone else to post her message, someone who did not make immoral demands.

⸎

Merida probed the boundaries of her captivity. The harem's courtyard, where pergolas sagged under a smothering mass of pink roses and pebbles baked under a merciless sun, had no exit to the outside world. None of the wives ever left the confines of the harem. The only visitors were a bellydance teacher and traders of silk and cosmetics, and the transactions took place under the watchful eyes of Teruma.

The only means of leaving the harem for even a short time was to visit the devious Consort. Although Merida never achieved victory in Siege, she soon managed to delay her defeat for so long that the match stretched over several days.

Each time Merida returned from their games, the concubines stared at her with more hostility.

"You've bewitched him!" Kadiffe accused. "It's because of your sorcery that he summons you instead of me."

Merida laughed. "You're welcome to him. I don't want him."

"Of course you want him. You're stealing him away from me with your magic. He used to invite me every day until you came. I'm his favourite, don't you forget that."

That poor girl really wanted Kirral. "We're only playing Siege," Merida assured her.

"Liar!" Kadiffe spat. "You stinking slime-bag of a sorceress!"

"Merida is my friend." Haurvatat clung like a burr, stroking Merida's hand. "Her magic potion will make all of us irresistible. Won't it, Merida?"

"I'm sorry I can't help you." Merida pulled herself free from the clinging touch. "Love spells are unethical."

Haurvatat burst into tears.

"We've seen you mixing the potion." Kadiffe claimed. "In that jar." Other women bobbed their heads in agreement and spread their fingers to avert sorcery.

"It's hair shampoo!" Merida dipped a finger into the jar and held up a green glob. "Soapberries, rosemary and fenugreek, pounded into a paste, with a spoon of vinegar."

Kadiffe planted herself before Merida's bed, fists on her waist. "You've robbed the Consort from us with your magic. You're too mean to share your secret!"

"There is no secret. I told you before, it would be unethical to—"

"Sorceress! Sorceress! Sorceress!" a dozen women chorused.

Merida's patience snapped. "It's a Riverian secret. I get myself whipped with nettles by the Riverian masseuse. No man can resist me, and Kirral melts like wax between my fingers."

The lie hooked like a heavy anchor into Merida's soul, but the concubines rushed to book treatments.

Merida used the moment of peace to write her letter, careful to create the correct margins and equal spacing between the lines.

"Mother: Your Second Daughter has the misfortune to inform you of unintended developments. Following the successful completion of my assignment, I was deprived of my diplomatic status and made into what is known as a Consort's Wife, which is a concubine. Please notify the Virtuous President and the High Magician of the School of Magic of this outrage, and assist your Second Daughter in regaining her Value, to the benefit of members of our Family.

Merida Karr, Personal Value..."

She chewed her quill, unwilling to write down the figure. As a concubine, her value had dropped below zero, dragging all the family members down. Her chin broke out in sweat and sticky shame. But the outrage would spur Mother into action to rescue Merida in order to restore everyone else's points.

Merida took a deep breath, summoned her discipline and wrote:

"minus thirteen."

The next day, she joined the queues for the masseuse's services, and gave her the letter.

Now she would have to wait until Mother received it and organised a rescue. Mother, or the Riverian government, would probably spring a surprise on Kirral. To help them, Merida resolved to keep the letter secret. Kirral must not suspect that she had summoned help, so she would pretend to enjoy harem life, would even fake pleasure in the Consort's company.

CHAPTER 9

In the Rebel Stronghold

Oubar loomed above Dahoud's path, yellow walls rising from steep rocks, with archer slits painted scarlet like spatters of blood. Buttressed and towered, this fortress had defied armies, earthquakes and droughts. Saddlebags chafed against the flanking stone walls as he coaxed his horses up the steep, zigzagging track. The corridor was so tight that besiegers could not bring battering rams through it. At every curve, stacked boulders waited in readiness to be released, roll, and gather speed to smash advancing attackers. Four years ago, Oubar had defied the Black Besieger, had repelled his army and his siege machines. Now he would conquer Oubar armed with his courage and his wits.

The gatehouse, part brick-built, part hewn into the rock face, offered a grim greeting. Garlands dripped with scarlet woollen tassels and white human skulls. A dozen spears barred Dahoud's entrance as the guardsmen, leather-clad and hung with daggers, snapped their questions at him. "Who are you? What do you want?"

"The sky's blessings to you. I'm Dahoud of the Desert," he said, giving his almost-forgotten childhood name. "Travelling from Djildit Town and beyond."

"On what business?"

"I bring goods which may find favour in this town." His coned, fabric-wrapped straw hat proclaimed him a trader. The two horses were

Quislaki breeds, with bulging Djildit weave-ware saddlebags and harnesses from Copperland. With a striped Zigazian tunic, an embroidered Darrian waistcoat, and a thick sash from faraway Riverland, Dahoud looked like a man who had seen many places. His costume and gear were serviceable and of the highest quality, but threadbare in places, a convincing disguise put together by Teruma's agent.

One of the guards squinted, deepening a scarred gash on his cheek. "Few traders travel without the protection of a caravan."

"Few caravans travel to Oubar these days. May I step into the shade?"

"A trader with a single pack animal?"

"If my samples find favour, I'll bring more."

"Search him!"

Rough hands pulled his arms back, knocked his straw hat off, patted him down, probed under his tunic. Their commander gestured commands with a hand from which three fingers were missing, the stumps still scarred purple.

More men rummaged through his luggage. Tossing aside his personal clothes, they pulled out silk ribbons, fringe bundles, and pouches filled with beads.

"Fripperies," one of them snorted. Then he whistled. "Look what I've found."

Cloth-wrapped heads peered into the drawstring bag. Hands dipped, metal rattled, bronze arrowheads gleamed.

"Let me see." The scarred commander lifted a piece on his forefinger to hold it up against the light. "Three-lobed. Socketed. Sharp. Darrian-made." He spun around to Dahoud. "Darrian weapons exports are blocked. Where did you get those, friend?"

Dahoud smiled mysteriously, the way an arms smuggler would. "Tell me where I find your leaders."

The guard commander squinted again. "Yes, they'll want to know about these samples. The elders meet at dawn. Up there, just above the gate. Wait outside in the morning. They'll call you in."

Dahoud needed to meet the real leaders of the rebellion, not just the town elders, unless they were the same people.

He pointed to the garland with the dangling skulls. "Are those from ancient battles?"

"Recent." The commander's remaining finger flicked away a fly. "Quislakis. Now listen, friend. If you behave well, you'll get out of here alive, do you understand?"

From inside the town, a chicken squeaked pitifully, as if plucked alive.

"I understand," Dahoud said. "It would be too bad if you valiant warriors had to kill me, and lost your chance to get Darrian bronze weapons."

"Friend, you're not stupid." The guard bellowed to his men to bring the gatehouse tablets, and scratched a mark on the wax-coated wood. Most likely, none of them could read, and recorded only visitor numbers, not identities. "The hostelries are full up. No private rooms to rent either. Lots of people come to Oubar these days. Because of the summer drought and because things are happening here, you understand?"

"I've brought a yurt."

"Put it up on the plateau outside the walls, like the nomads do. Use as much water as you like. Our underground lake never runs dry." He bellowed at one of the guards who brought a yellow pottery bowl. "Drink this. Mares' milk, traditional Koskaran welcome, you understand?"

The milk smelled rancid, but Dahoud swallowed it in a single gulp.

Smells of charcoal and fried onions wafted between dozens of round black-felted yurts. Few vacant spaces remained on the site, none of them offering the slightest shade. After seeing to his horses, Dahoud picked the least rocky one, next to the latrine, and checked it for snakes before setting up his own collapsible dome.

Feeling a curious gaze on him, he straightened. An old woman was watching from the entrance of her own yurt. Yellow scarves swathed her head, baring a single cheek marked with tribal tattoos, skin mottled with age, and eyes as keen as a falcon's, alive with curiosity and caution. She scrutinised his garments as if reading his life history in them.

He bowed to her. "Honoured Mother, will you please keep an eye on my things while I get my bearings?"

She agreed so eagerly that he wondered if she planned to snoop through his belongings. He did not mind. His real secret was safe.

The citadel's high walls enveloped him in their cool shade. In place of the sick stink and deadly silence of a newly conquered town, life pulsed in the narrow alleys, the wooden market stalls, the workshops with reed awnings where hammers clanked on copper and knives scraped on whetstone. Children squealed on rooftops, a woman scolded her husband, hens cackled and a dog whined. Although a few heads turned to stare at Dahoud with open curiosity, nobody cowered at his sight.

Crowds of clucking women with buckets and goatskins clustered around the wellhead in the centre of the town jostling for position as the windlass squealed under the weight. Oubar had enough water—but it could not be pulled fast enough. The narrow wellshaft allowed one bucket at a time to be drawn, sufficient for peacetime demands when around three hundred people might live in the citadel. Since the fortress had become the centre of the rebellion, the number would have doubled, and during the high summer season, there were two hundred or more nomads camping on the plateau.

At the other end of the central square, builders were labouring to rectify this, putting the finishing touches to what appeared to be a well-house. A second, bigger well-shaft would allow the drawing of more water, faster.

He surveyed the bulwarks, the pattern of buttresses, the archer slits. The wall was built from baked brick and pitch mortar in a cellular structure on a socle of limestones. He thirsted to climb up a guard tower, to stand on the curtain wall, to taste the position of a defender. Since he was supposed to be a trader, with no interest in warfare beyond selling his bronze arrowheads, he curbed the urge. Ambling down narrow shaded alleys, he gazed at piled fleeces, peered into sacks of lentils, rubbed felt sheets between his fingers, pursed his lips and nodded knowledgeably. But the yearning to be a commander again tingled in his sword arm and ripped through his chest.

⌁

As the sun was sinking fast, taking the afternoon heat with it, the crone Sirria sat outside her yurt and watched the citadel's walls drop into gloomy shadow.

In the summer months, when the heat sucked life from the soil, and the wandering flocks had devoured even the driest grass stalks, she had no choice but to settle in a water-rich town. The drinking water here tasted sweeter than elsewhere, the underground lake irrigated the pasture slopes, and the town's young shepherd guarded visiting flocks. She wished she could pitch her yurt among them, but the elders of Oubar insisted everyone must stay either inside the town or within a bowshot of its walls. Unlike other towns, Oubar offered a yurt site outside the citadel with open views across the plains below, so at least she did not have to live between enclosing walls.

The young trader returned from his exploration with a cheerful smile, thanking her for guarding his packs.

"Are you from Zigazia, trader?" She pined for news from the land she had fled many years ago.

"I've been to Zigazia several times." His gaze fastened on the sack of charcoal beside her cooking fire. "I forgot to bring charcoal with me. Can I buy some of yours?"

Sirria blinked. If he needed charcoal, he would have bought it in town, which meant he was seeking a pretext for a chat. "I'll trade you some, though not for money rings. Here in the Samil, we don't care for those tokens of evil. Show me what you've brought to trade." Fingering his fabrics would be fun, pleasant memories of the townswoman's lifestyle she had given up long ago. "I'll brew up some tea. How do you like yours, with cardamom, cinnamon or honey?"

When he chose cardamom, the preference of wealthy Zigazians, she nodded to herself. This trader had moved among the upper classes. Something about him was familiar, perhaps the angular shape of his jaw, the slightly crooked nose, the straight-backed way in which he moved, or the curious blend of shyness and aggression in his deep voice. She cast her mind back to when she had been a matron in Zigazia, and later, in Darrian captivity. She had encountered so many traders that memories blurred.

"I'm Dahoud of the Desert," he said.

'Dahoud' was common enough, but 'of the Desert' was unusual, not a name she had met before.

When he spilled out his bolts of silk and spice pouches, the bright colours dazzled Sirria's eyes. Her gaze fell on a bundle of tightly rolled silk fringe, containing lengths in many different colours – sunshine yellow, oasis green, peacock blue, and even the rare snail purple -, but when she reached for the bundle, he snatched it away. "That's, eh..." Mumbling something she could not understand, he showed her a handful of glass beads instead. Even in the dimming daylight, they glistened blue like a river.

Sirria would have loved to own one of those, but to afford it, she would have to trade one of her goats.

He must have noticed the desire in her eyes, because he said, "You like them? How many for half a sack of charcoal?"

Sirria nearly yelped out her surprise. Instead, she said blandly, "Twelve."

He did not laugh at her outrage. He merely offered six, and they settled at nine. The cool beads slid into her palm.

Then he asked questions: how many people lived in Oubar? Who were the wealthy families? How influential were the crones? How many nomads were here for the summer months, and how long did they usually stay? Sirria kept her answers cheerful and vague.

Later, when he had gone, she gazed at the beads, beautifully crafted, shaped like water drops, glistening in the light of her oil-lamp. Not since she was a matron in Zigazia had she owned such precious adornment, and she had never met a trader who did not know the value of his wares. She was certain now: Dahoud of the Desert was no trader. She would keep an eye on him.

⊰

Dahoud lay in his yurt, tense, chasing the sleep that evaded him. His heart still banged like a drum in his ears. Outside, sheep bleated, dogs barked, a stream trickled and gushed.

He was inside the rebel stronghold, still alive. Nobody guessed his identity or purpose. He almost missed the furtiveness and fear in people's eyes, the resentful respect shown to the conquering commander. If he had come to this town as a victorious general, the women at the well would have prostrated themselves begging for mercy. They would not have dared ignore him while they giggled over their water haul.

A trickle of warmth sneaked into his limbs, boldened, grew to heat.

We can still have that. Stay in your disguise, settle, make friends, insinuate yourself into everyone's trust, then call Paniour's legions and open the gate to them. Enjoy the victory, assert yourself, and those women will notice you. Oh, and they will fight. As rebels, they will offer delicious resistance.

Dahoud jerked upright, grabbed the stones he used for strength training, and worked his arms until they screamed with the effort. Exercising his body was the best distraction to drown the djinn's voice. Since the seer's advice two moons ago, he had doubled his efforts, and his arm muscles bulged like hard fruit under his skin.

Shall they not pay for defying you last time? Isn't this fortress the blot on your record of victory? Don't they deserve to be punished for this humiliation?

Dahoud tossed the stones aside to practice push-ups. One hundred... one hundred ten...

When the right woman comes, will you be strong enough to subdue her?

One hundred fifty... His arms trembled but he kept on, squeezing the djinn's treacherous suggestions out of his mind.

He thought back to that last siege, that final rape, when the djinn had driven him to a deed far beyond what could be justified by custom or necessity.

Four years ago, General Dahoud had accepted the surrender of a Darrian garrison he had besieged for two moons, a routine handover. The Darrians would leave unharmed with nothing but the clothes on their backs. There were no treasures to loot, no hostages to ransom, no women to rape.

The officers, all Darrian noblemen with oiled beards and jewelled collars over silken gowns, looked gaunt and hollow-eyed with hunger. Despite the resentment written in their pale faces, they acted with professional discipline, but when Dahoud took possession of the headquarters, he sensed they were hiding something from him. Were they trying to smuggle treasure out? He needed to know. Dahoud the Black Besieger would not be tricked.

Through the eye slits of his black mask, he scanned the room, the light falling through the high windows, the cushions on the floor, the inlaid tables, the statues of the peacock gods. Then he spotted a small clay jar, caught in the fringe of a patterned rug. He pried the lid open. The red paste smelled of olive oil, beeswax and roses. He dipped his finger into the soft substance and smiled. Darrian officers perfumed their bodies and rimmed their eyes with charcoal. But they did not paint their lips.

"Where is she?"

The officers stood stiff, pretending not to know. Their denial meant she was special, neither servant nor whore, but a noblewoman. Yet they had not mentioned her in the surrender negotiations.

"Bring her."

The commanding officer, a black-bearded noble named Baryush, spoke. "I won't permit you to defile my sister."

Behind Dahoud, a centurion chuckled. "Your reputation precedes you, Sir."

Dahoud knew what he meant: The reputation of a man who broke the resistance of every town he besieged, and who took pleasure in raping the captive women afterwards.

"Bring her. Or my men will get her." He let the implied threat hang in the air.

"If you lay a finger on my sister," Baryush snarled. "I'll flay you alive."

Dahoud laughed. "You're hardly in a position to threaten me." To the centurion, he said, "Imprison the officers until I'm satisfied." The fright would serve them a salutary lesson. The Black Besieger was not to be trifled with.

He looked forward to showing his magnitude. Although her menfolk had failed to negotiate her safety, he would treat her with honour. He would take off his mask, assure her of his protection, offer her the use of his quarters while he slept in the barracks.

The young woman who arrived had the bearing of a queen, and coal-black eyes which flamed with enough hatred to torch a town.

"Please be seated," he said in her language, "and allow me to introduce my officers."

She spat in his face. "I'll never willingly submit to your vile advances."

Instantly, the djinn whipped up desire. *She's asking for it.*

Dahoud's temper strained like a horse on its reins, and his loins heated.

"Leave us," he told his officers.

One of them spoke up. "Sir. Rape is not included in the formal conditions."

Dahoud laughed. Protection was not included either. "Get out."

76

He was in charge, and would let nobody meddle with his control. If the Darrians did not want the woman raped, they should have mentioned her, and made her immunity part of the agreement. If she didn't want to be raped, she should have showed him respect.

If she begged for mercy now, he would still let her go. She raised her small white hand and slapped it across his face.

She was asking for it. He caught her wrist, turned it on her arm, and forced her down on the carpet. Darrian females were not trained to fight, and her teeth and nails could not stop him. Her spirited resistance fuelled the djinn-kindled fire. His blade ripped her tunic open. Her breasts spilled free, pink-tipped and white. He felt her struggle and thrash as he subdued her sweet resisting flesh. When he was done, she spat at him again. He raped her once more.

It should have eased his hunger and sated his lust, but his anger was still roaring, and the djinn demanded more. He needed to show her he was in charge, to humble her haughtiness, to punish her for everything women had done to him. He smeared the red paint across her breasts in bold, angry strokes, then called his officers and told them to use her.

When they had done with her, the flame of hatred in her eyes was still not smothered, but burned brighter than before.

"May the gods punish you, you slime-faced bag of dog shit!" she yelled. "May they turn out your ancestor's graves, and peel your skin with a thousand knives."

Hundreds of women had heaped similar curses on Dahoud's head. He doubted that the gods listened.

He called a centurion. "Give her to the men." Being raped by four hundred soldiers would quench her spirit. He poured himself a beaker of confiscated wine. "Make her brother watch. When they're all done, bring her back here."

Sundown stained the horizon when two soldiers tossed her body at his feet. It looked small and horribly still. The face was slack like a sleeper's with parted lips, but her bruised limbs lay broken in bizarre poses. Her eyes, now devoid of life, still stared.

With the cold clarity of shame, he saw that the djinn had made him a monster.

Until that day, he had justified his deeds with the customs of war. All soldiers raped if they conquered a town after a prolonged siege. The act made the victory real. Dahoud had tasted rape when he was four-teen, and liked its flavour. The djinn had showed him how to subdue females and savour the act. So many sieges, so many women, so many opportunities to rape. Every time, the djinn grew in strength and in hunger, and demanded more. Today, the djinn had pushed across the last boundary of honour.

Dahoud was dancing in a storm of destruction. With every future rape, his integrity would shrink, until he became absolute slave to the evil within. Even a host's death could not end a demon's power. Immortal, it would invade another man, and each time a host killed himself, a djinn spawned a hundred more of its kind. Dahoud had to stay alive, and starve the djinn into weakness by resisting its fiercest demands. Whatever happened, he must not rape again. Could he commit to this fight while he still possessed a shred of honour?

He would have to get away from sieges, from warfare, from temptations. Could he summon the courage to leave the legions?

He had no other life, no family or home to return to. A member of the Samili race, he would be viewed with disdain, offered only the dirtiest work. The commander of legions, hailed as hero and glorified for his victories, would become like an ant: at best ignored, at worst crushed underfoot. Every waking moment, he would battle against the torment of the djinn's demands. The future stretched like an unrelenting nightmare.

He ordered the body to be wrapped in linen with spices and perfume, and given to her brother.

Then he sent a messenger to the high general Paniour, resigning his command. Dahoud the Black Besieger, the abuser of women, had to die, so that Dahoud the protector of women could be born.

∾

When the first fingers of dawn touched the sky, Dahoud said his morning prayers and donned a plain tunic in Koskara's national colour, scarlet. Around his waist, he slung a maroon sash and his dagger belt. A maroon headscarf fastened with scarlet cord completed the outfit, so every finger's breadth of him looked like a local nomad and nothing hinted at the black-clad Besieger.

Building work at the new well-house had finished. Women stood on ladders to paint friezes around its pillars, mostly leopards and horses in glistening red.

Vines snaked up on the inside of the gatehouse. Instead of grapes, human heads hung among the parching leaves, tied by their hair, their blood-smeared flesh almost intact. Crimson headbands proclaimed them to be Quislaki legionnaires. Dahoud would have honoured their deaths with a salute, if such a gesture had not drawn suspicion.

Squawking flutters swooped from the sky. A flock of black-winged crows settled on the trellis, jockeyed for position, squabbled over the juicy flesh.

A child's yell scarcely disturbed the scavengers' feast. Then a pounding hail of slingshot forced them to flee. A boy no older than six stuffed his sling into his belt, next to a dagger.

"That was good shooting," Dahoud said to the youngster. "Where do the heads come from?"

"Mansour brought them last night."

Screeching, a woman pulled the boy away. "Don't talk with strangers!"

The rebel chief was in Oubar. Dahoud would convert him to his cause, or kill him.

He peered closely at one of the heads to assess its history. Empty eye sockets gazed down at him because the birds had pecked the most succulent parts first. The man had died two or three days ago, maybe more, so if Mansour had brought it last night, it had been stored somewhere where no birds could peck, most likely in a saddlebag. This meant a recent battle, about three days' ride from Oubar, either in Koskara Town or one of the small garrisons south of it. The crows were swooping again with noisy flutters.

"Dahoud of the Desert. Follow me." A silver-haired man beckoned him up the stone steps into the council chamber.

Light fell through narrow slits in the brick wall. The other side of the room cut into the mountain's yellow limestone, with a scarlet banner of a rearing horse stretched along the curving wall. Two dozen men squatted in a circle on bright-patterned rugs: too many men for a council of town elders, and most of them too young. Some had to be the leaders of the rebellion. Not a single man sat on a throne or even a cushion to raise him above the others, so who was in charge?

Dahoud scanned their scarred arms and faces, their plaited hair, their nomad tunics and knife-studded belts. Since Samilis held age in honour, the silver-haired man with the deep-furrowed forehead and alert eyes seemed the obvious candidate, but this man had come down the steps to call him, and top commanders did not act as messengers. Next to him, a tall man with long plaits and a barely-healed sword gash across his lower cheek sat very straight, exuding confidence, but leaders seldom chose to sit near a corner.

The natural position for a person wielding power was opposite the door below the banner. The man sitting there was a brawny type, not much older than Dahoud, with bare muscle-packed arms, tattooed cheeks, a leopard teeth necklace and a collection of knives strapped to his chest. Town elders would not grant that place to someone so young unless he outranked them, yet he was garbed like a nomad herder, without insignia of rank.

The old man jabbed a claypipe at Dahoud. "Where are the arrow-heads, trader?"

Dahoud had prepared what he was going to say, and spoke confidently in his native Samili dialect. "I'm no trader. I wore the garb to get into Oubar. My name is Dahoud. I'm the lord-satrap of Koskara."

Hands shot to daggers. Heads swung towards the herdsman under the banner.

He locked his hands behind his head, elbows spread wide, and eyed Dahoud up and down as if assessing a horse and finding it inferior. "Quislaki standards have slipped."

"Indeed," the long-plaited man said. "We expected another quill-twiddling bureaucrat. Instead, they've sent a clown."

Ignoring the insult, Dahoud addressed the nomad instead. "Are you the leader?"

The man rose in a slow, fluid motion. "I'm Mansour, Lord of Koskara. My ancestors have grazed flocks on Koskaran lands for thirty generations."

Dahoud took in the bronzed arms, the cheeks streaked with slashes and black tattoos, the rows of nodes above the eyebrows where he had pierced his skin and rubbed ash into his wounds, the knives strapped to the waist, the easy confidence of the pose. Mansour exuded an air of lethal competence, as if he could kill without even raising a sweat.

When Mansour stepped so close to Dahoud their garments almost touched, Dahoud refused to step back. "Will you join my council, Mansour?"

Mansour let out a bellowing laugh.

"I want you as my second-in-command," Dahoud explained. "Support me, and we can bring peace to Koskara. Otherwise, we'll tear the land apart like two leopards fighting over a gazelle carcass."

"The puppy has ideals," the man with the plaits sniggered.

"Will you join my council, Dahoud?" Mansour asked.

"The Queen..." Dahoud started to explain.

"The Quislaki Queen." The plaited man's voice dripped with contempt.

Dahoud held his letter of appointment out.

Mansour did not even glance at it. "What makes you think you'll get out of here alive?"

Several men stood silently, sliding blades of sharp obsidian and shining bronze from their sheaths.

"I bring something you need." Dahoud spoke without taking his eyes from the rebel leader's. "Peace."

Mansour laughed. "Who wants peace?"

"Who wants war?"

Mansour's eyebrows rose a fraction. "Explain, Dahoud."

"Quislak has exploited Koskara, has exploited the whole Samil, for decades. You're fighting to put an end to that. You've fought bravely. You've fought well." Dahoud took a step back from Mansour to brush the warriors in the room with an appreciative glance. "If you keep fighting, you'll keep inflicting losses on Quislak. Yet in the end, your courage is no match for the might of the Quislaki legions. Quislak will win, and with the warriors dead, there will be nobody to protect the land. The abuse will be worse, and Koskara lies defenceless and bleeding."

"Go on."

"If I lead Koskara, I'll stop the abuse. No Koskaran blood will be shed. Instead of exhausting themselves in war, people will put their strength to rebuilding and prosper."

Mansour sat down, leaning against the wall with his hands behind his back, his legs stretched and crossed comfortably before him. "You think you can lead Koskara?"

"Yes."

The plaited man rolled his eyes. "Puppy, go home while you're still alive."

Dahoud kept his gaze on Mansour. "I'm ready to prove myself. I want to address the people of Koskara, as many of them as possible, to explain my plan. Will you call an assembly tomorrow?"

"An assembly?" Mansour ran a finger across the tattooed lines on his chin. "Why wait until tomorrow? Today is perfect."

Deep laughter mocked from many throats. Knives sheathed.

Dahoud wondered what was so funny. He stared into the carved face. "This afternoon. I'm ready."

Mansour's grin bared big teeth. "We look forward to it."

CHAPTER 10

Challenges

Drums rattled and flutes chirped in celebration of the new well. Five of the men from the meeting stood in casual closeness around Dahoud. A priest chanted blessings, and a storyteller sang thanks to Mansour, the sponsor of this water source. The crowd sang his name, seemingly sincere in their appreciation, as if they believed the sun rose and set on Mansour's shoulders.

Dahoud understood: In a land parched by drought, access to water was the most precious gift a leader could make. When the ancient natural well-shaft no longer met the needs of the growing population, the rebel leader had commissioned a new, broader opening into the underground lake, allowing the use of bigger buckets. The well-house crowning the new access was his contribution too, its gleaming new bricks glistening with fresh-painted friezes, with rose garlands snaked around its pillars. As Lord of Koskara, Dahoud would have to grant an even better gift, something much bigger and more welcome than Mansour's wellshaft.

More music followed, chanting and ululations, while weapon offerings were dropped into the wet depth. The priest slit a cockerel's throat, spraying red dots on the golden walls and the already wilting white roses.

The pulley creaked, the ropes squealed, and water splashed. As ladles passed around, everyone claimed that the water from the new wellshaft was sweeter than that from the old.

Then they all walked through the rising noon heat out of the southern gate, past the yurt camp, to the festival site. The arena nestled in the mountains, an oval of grass flecked with sheep droppings, surrounded with spectator seating hewn from the rock. Red and yellow tassels dangled from ropes and bright banners blazed in the noon glare.

Mansour directed Dahoud to sit beside him in the front row, answered some of Dahoud's questions and ignored others. Drums throbbed and bagpipes squeaked. Girls danced, their arms linked, their bare toes beating the hard-baked ground. Swords clashed in mock duels, and performers offered more music, more songs, more praise for Mansour.

Dahoud rehearsed in his mind what he was going to say, how he was going to paint a vision of a peaceful, flourishing land. The day was auspicious. Even if their goodwill focused on Mansour, their exuberant mood would make them listen favourably to Dahoud's proposals.

When Mansour strode to the grassy centre, ululations shrilled so loudly they seemed to make the mountain tremble. With a wave of his arm, he silenced them.

"Koskarans!" Mansour's voice carried throughout the arena. "To celebrate this special day, I give you a special entertainment. A clown has come all the way from Quislabat for your amusement."

Sweat ran down Dahoud's neck and glued his clothes to his skin.

"He has a letter from the Quislaki Consort which says that he is the Lord of Koskara. Please welcome Dahoud of the Desert." Laughter roared along the seated rows.

With his head raised and his back straight, Dahoud strode into the arena. He needed to impress the natives on their own terms. Fortunately, he understood Samili custom, and knew a skill or two which would work.

"Normally we honour acrobats and clowns with their nation's banners." Mansour said. "Alas, we have not a single banner of Quislak in Oubar." More laughter.

"People of Oubar!" Dahoud called. "I thank you for honouring me with the horse banner. I'm proud to represent Koskara."

A splinter of silence, then crashing howls.

"We don't want to hear the fine speeches you've prepared, Dahoud of the Desert." Mansour's voice dripped with sarcasm. "We want to see what you can do. Since you want to be Lord of Koskara, surely you're good at all our local sports. In this fantasia, you'll compete against the best of Oubar."

"I look forward to it," Dahoud said with all the confidence he could muster. At least Mansour had said 'fantasia'. A contest of sporting skills was better than a clown show.

He was about to strip off his garments, when he remembered that Samilis practised sports clothed.

At a wave of Mansour's hand, the tall plait-headed man from the morning's meeting led in two horses, silver Koskarans with yellow tassels in their manes, carrying padded rugs and leather girths with strap grips.

Dahoud held back the urge to yell in triumph. Unknowingly, they were presenting him with a chance to shine.

"Can you do trickriding?"

"I hope so." Dahoud pretended uncertainty, even as his heart thudded with the thrill.

"You'll compete against me." The man's voice dripped with patronising pity. "I'm Idrahad, and these are my horses. We copy each other's routines. This is how it works…"

Dahoud could have told him that he was familiar with trickriding rules, but thought of a better strategy. "Aren't the horses on a lunge-line?"

From the front row, a child shouted "Booh!"

Idrahad guffawed. "Frightened already, are you? We don't use lunge-lines in Koskara. I've picked a docile horse for you, the pretty mare here."

With a show of hesitation, Dahoud placed his hand on her warm, muscled rump. "She looks big."

This drew snorts of derision.

While drums rumbled a saidi rhythm, Dahoud quickly stretched his arms and legs to prepare them for the strain. Restless, the horse tossed her head. Dahoud rubbed her withers, then ran alongside her and jumped up. Her pace was steady, and she responded fast to commands. With her ears pricked forward and her neck proudly arched, she seemed to delight in showing off. Dahoud swivelled with straight legs, the way he had been taught many years ago, knelt on the saddle blanket, and stood on the horse's back, arms outstretched.

Idrahad aped the straight legs and pointed toes, mocking the riding school style. Then launched into handstands and one-footed poses in rapid succession. "Copy this!" he shouted.

Dahoud did it with ease, faking effort. Then he dropped the pretence of being a novice, leaped into the routine that had once made him legion s trickriding champion, layering somersaults, back flips, a dive under the horse's belly, hanging on her side. He let his caution flutter away, hung head-down with his legs locked around her head. Two handspans below, hooves thudded and the ground raced past. Blood throbbed in his head, air rushed against his cheeks, and joy coursed like wine in his veins.

He landed with a precise somersault, his heart pounding in triumph. The crowd roared with admiration of his skill. The mare danced and tossed her head, basking in the spectators' awe.

Idrahad insisted on copying what he could, before he waved to acknowledge defeat. When Mansour raised Dahoud's arm to proclaim him winner, Idrahad said, "You fooled me, Dahoud. I took you for a novice."

"I ve competed in fantasias before." Dahoud did not mention the legions.

While the audience ululated, the two men clasped elbows.

"Well done, Dahoud. This was a fantastic performance. I'm proud to have been beaten by you." Idrahad's words said admiration, but the brief crinkling of his nose said otherwise, and the voice swung with resentment.

"Let's have a rematch one day," Dahoud suggested.

"Yes, sure." Idrahad was walking away.

Sweat streamed from Dahoud's forehead, and dripped into his eyes. He had impressed the natives. Surely now they would allow him speak, to argue the Quislaki cause. First, he needed a rest. He scanned the surroundings for the nearest shady spot.

Mansour brought him a jug of water. "Next match. Can you wrestle?"

"Of course." Dahoud had been one of the best wrestlers in the legions, and had recently practised with Tarkan. Although he was unused to Samili style, which featured different rules, leather loincloths and oiled bodies instead of bare dry skin, he would manage. "Who's my opponent?"

Grinning, Mansour took off his tunic. His broad, bronzed chest bulged with muscles.

While putting on a stiff oxhide loincloth and slathering himself in oil, Dahoud assessed his opponent who was flexing muscles under glistening skin, bursting with balled confidence. No doubt he possessed great skill as well as unusual strength, but the limbs of most heavily muscled men did not bend far. Dahoud would pitch his own agility against his opponent's muscle mass. He stretched his ride-tired legs and back before they could settle into stiffness.

Head to head like angry bulls, they locked arms. They dropped to their knees, then their oil- and sweat-slick bodies slipped, rolled, gathered grass and dirt. Mansour's mass, heavy as a mountain, threatened to crush Dahoud to pulp. Dahoud managed to hold him off and twist out of his grips. At last, he pinned Mansour belly-up, and strained to hold him while the referee counted. "Five... six... seven... eight..."

Almost won. Dahoud squeezed all his strength into the hold to keep it one moment longer. Suddenly, Mansour's arms clamped around his chest and squeezed the air from his lungs. A wave of muscle crashed against him. The mountain weight leant on him, bending him so heavily that he thought his spine would crack. Breath leached from his body. Lights danced across his vision. Desperately, he stabbed his thumb at a tender spot between his opponent's fingers, which brought a moment's release and a lungful of air. But in an instant, he found himself flipped belly-down, with Mansour squatting over his back in a camel clutch. However much he struggled, he could not free his arms, let alone his neck. The seer's advice throbbed in his head: *get stronger arms... stronger arms... stronger arms...* She had known this fight would happen. He should have listened better. He should have worked to strengthen the full length of his arms, not just the upper part. Pain soared through his shoulders. He had no chance.

"You win," he said. With his jaw squeezed, it came out as "Ywfffn."

Mansour bent closely over his face. "You sure?"

"Shfffff."

"...eight, nine."

Released from the grip, Dahoud rose, gasping for air. The match was over. They clasped elbows.

While Dahoud gulped down more water and rubbed a towel over

his dirt-sticky skin, Mansour stepped into the centre of the arena. "A short break, then dagger fighting." Mansour's voice was loud and effortless, as if he had not exerted himself physically at all.

Dahoud massaged his burning neck, rallying the stamina for another contest in the blistering heat, knowing that this time he had to win.

Joining Mansour in the centre of the arena, he forced confidence into his voice. "I look forward to it. Who'll be my opponent?"

"The best dagger fighter of all Koskara." Mansour's face gleamed with malice.

Hands clapped. Feet stomped. Voices squealed with delighted anticipation. Koskara's dagger champion was obviously a fighter of renown. Dahoud prepared to see a vicious man of huge build and merciless violence.

At a flick of Mansour's hand, a slender figure darted from the audience.

"Meet Yora." Mansour's teeth flashed. "She'll enjoy defeating you."

Dahoud did not want to raise a weapon against a woman, but refusal would brand him a coward. Silently thanking the Mighty Ones for the Samil custom of clothed contests, he accepted the armguards and tunic of thick leather, and the yellow tabard worn over it.

"One long and one short dagger each." Mansour said. "Obsidian blades. Slash the tunics only, not the flesh. Afterwards, we count the cuts."

Dahoud tried to focus on the knives which lay smooth and heavy in his hands, but his eyes refused to obey. His opponent's breasts were tiny mounds under the duelling tunics. She was young. A child almost, although the small crosses tattooed on her brown face proclaimed that she had reached womanhood. Her hair was braided in a mass of plaits. Wherever she moved, the glass beads at their ends clanked together. Her eyes sparkled with glee.

They circled each other in a fierce dance, their hands weaving in gestures and feints. Their eyes locked, caught every shift, every tension, anticipated every move. Yora's attacks came fast, tight, and ruthless. Breaths laboured, blades clanked, feet swished on grass.

He could not slash with full force at a woman. Obsidian was so sharp, the mere touch on skin would slice deep into flesh. Despite the leather undertunic, she might get hurt. She shot into attack. Dahoud deflected. Knives flashed. Fabric ripped.

Dahoud sweated under the leather. The djinn painted a vision of the Yora without clothes, naked with small brown breasts. He blinked the image away, but the moment's distraction cost him two slashes.

He switched to straight lunges and stabs as in real combat, twice catching her tunic before she could pull away. Blade rang on blade, forearm to forearm. He deflected her lunges, tried to slow the match to a safer pace. She refused to be slowed. Her body shot forward and back, knives slashed from the side.

When Mansour ended the contest, Dahoud's yellow tunic hung in tatters, while Yora's showed only a handful of cuts.

She waved the black knives, beaming. "This was fun."

"You fight well." Another contest lost. Against a woman.

"Enough fighting for today," Mansour announced. "Tomorrow there'll be spear throwing, foot racing, stone slinging, archery. Now, we have food. Wine. Dancing."

Although Dahoud's tortured muscles screamed for a rest, he sat in a relaxed pose during the celebration meal, lightly answering unimportant questions from Sirria and devouring as much roast camel with fried onions as anyone. Two out of three matches lost. He would have to do better tomorrow, much better, but the next day's trial did not favour his strengths. He was skilled at archery, mediocre at javelin-throwing, and inexperienced in stone-slinging. Yet he had to prove his valour to get accepted and avert war.

He declined to have his beaker filled with date spirit, and sipped only as much of the dark wine as courtesy required, since he needed to wake up with a clear head.

At last, people poured back into the citadel and into their yurts, including Mansour, who had apparently chosen to live on the yurt-site, reminding everyone that he was a nomad.

Dahoud stretched out his battered body to review the contests. The trickriding performance had probably been his best ever, but in the wrestling, he had made a big mistake. Next time he held an opponent pinned, he would keep his guard focused until the referee had counted to nine and the match was truly won.

The dagger duel had been a disaster. Shocked to have a female opponent, he had allowed inhibitions to slow him. Next time he fought against her, he would discard his scruples, would throw himself into the fight, would show her what he could do.

She has spirit. She'll resist. Won't she be fun to fight? Shall we show her how strong we really are?

Dahoud's loins heated.

From the citadel came the sounds of celebration, the throbbing of drums, the nine-count rhythm of languid passion.

When sleep washed over his burning body and aching limbs, he dreamt of wrestling. His favourite fantasy took flesh, meeting the longing that reality refused to fulfil. A woman desired him so much that she fought to force herself on him. Cat-agile and naked from the waist up, she knelt over him with parted thighs, pinning his arms behind his head. Yellow eyes locked with his. He pushed his pelvis up towards hers, but she evaded the contact. Her laughter made everything vibrate, his body, the air, the ground.

Dahoud woke and grappled with reality. This was no dream, nor was it the wine dancing in his head. The ground was truly shaking. He grabbed his clothes and bolted out of the yurt.

CHAPTER 11

Death of a Citadel

The mountain roared. Before Dahoud's eyes, the fortress cracked. Three towers tumbled. A fourth arched, held its place for a heartbeat, then collapsed. Water splashed. Beasts and people squealed. A mass of rock broke and plunged the rest of the citadel into the gurgling abyss.

Less than a bowshot from Dahoud, a void stared where the town had been. He pulled his tunic on while he ran to the disaster site.

The large moon, round like a battered shield, shone its pale light on the scene. A huge hole gaped like a scurvied mouth, with ruined remnants sticking out like rotten teeth from bleeding gums. Yellow dust filled the black air, swirled and settled over a brown sludge below. Unseen survivors screamed. The mountain above stared in black anger at the wound in its flesh.

Dahoud crawled to the edge to asses the site. Sixteen man-heights below, houses had shattered into dense heaps of rubble and were sliding into the water where the bricks melted into thick mud. He could guess the cause of the disaster: Mansour's new well-shaft had fractured the ceiling of the underground lake.

This was like the earthquake he had witnessed last year. But in Idjlara, stone-built walls had created gaps that could shelter survivors. Here, mud-bricks turned to rubble and dust. In Idjlara, the broken structures had crashed onto firm ground. Here, the remnants were drowning. In Idjlara, disaster had struck during the day, and the town's uninjured quarters had supplied everything they needed. Here, he had to act in dust-shrouded darkness, with no resources but what nomads kept in their tents.

The town was beyond saving, but if they acted fast, they could get out some of the survivors. Rescuers would have to contend with darkness, unstable surfaces, sinking debris, choking dust, lack of gear, the risk of drowning, and the threat of more of the mountain crashing down.

He needed ropes, spades, torches, and he needed them fast.

From the yurt site, where the earth had not cracked, people came stumbling. Their low whispers shrieked of despair. "My nieces! My nieces are in there."—"Punishment from the gods."—"Where's my mother's house? I can't see my mother's house."

Dahoud took charge, directing their panic into action. "You, you, and you. Get ropes. You two, torches. You over there, blankets and tools. Shovels, cleavers, spades. Hurry." Some rushed to do as told, others stared with hostility. To them, he was the enemy, the usurper sent by Quislak. He scanned the growing crowd for competent lieutenants whom the Koskarans would trust. The town's elders and crones would be drowned or trapped. He spotted the nomad woman who had traded him charcoal. People would obey a crone. "Sirria. You're in charge of evacuations. Dismantle the yurts, drive the flocks down, summon the healers. Then report back to me."

She gave him the kind of look most people reserved for particularly stupid persons. "What healers?"

Hostile mumblings reminded him that Quislak forbade the study and practice of healing arts among conquered natives.

"Away from the edge, everyone," Mansour's voice bellowed in the darkness.

Here was the perfect lieutenant to whom the Koskarans would listen. "Mansour, I need you to organise supplies. Tell these people to bring ropes, torches, tools."

The rebel leader stood with his elbows spread. "Get out of the way."

"I know what I'm doing," Dahoud assured him.

"Out of the way!"

The sinkhole gurgled and slurped.

"Mother of Mares!" Dahoud shouted. "We don't have time for this.

People are trapped, the ruins are sinking, the mountain is about to collapse. Why can't you just do as I tell you?"

Mansour shone a torch over the abyss. "I'm Lord of Koskara. We Koskarans take care of our own."

With the voice which had made legions obey, Dahoud barked: "Get the supplies! Get helpers! Get everyone else away from here!"

The mountain rumbled, and another section of rock crashed into the void. Screams ripped the silence.

Rather than wasting precious moments arguing over leadership, Dahoud gave in. "What do you want me to do?"

"We'll climb down in stages. First, we'll land on that wall. The top is broad enough to hold us all. Then we'll tie the rope around a merlon and abseil from there."

"Don't!" Dahoud said. That segment of the curtain wall was dangerous. To the untrained eye, it might look solid, barely tilting and broad enough at the top to hold a dozen men, but Dahoud had seen walls of this type tumble. Had made them tumble. On both sides of the intact segment, chunks of wall had already fallen, and the stumps were at identical heights. He could draw a mental line from the top of one broken part to the other, a crack-line which ran straight through the seemingly intact masonry. All it took to make this wall collapse was to attach a rope to its top and pull. Which was exactly what Mansour proposed to do.

"Mansour, that wall will collapse," he said quietly. "It will hold while you're standing on it, but the moment the first person climbs down its side, it will fall."

Idrahad stepped forward. "I'll toss this puppy down the hole. That'll stop the yapping."

Mansour silenced him with a wave of his hand and eyed Dahoud up and down. "Know a lot about walls, do you?"

"I've worked on building sites, and in demolition."

For two heartbeats, Mansour stood with thumbs hooked in his belt, considering. "If you know so much, show me a better spot." Aloud, he announced, "We'll have two teams. I will lead one, and our guest from Quislak the other."

Dahoud pointed at a slab of rock directly below them. "This should hold. How many people were staying inside the citadel?"

"Can't tell without the gatehouse book. Right, we'll go down here.

Each of us takes half." Mansour stabbed a thumb at the section where wrecked walls had not yet slid into the sludge. "That part is your responsibility."

A hundred volunteers clamoured to join Mansour's team. Mansour chose twenty to come with him as well as several strong men to hold the rope, told the rest to follow Dahoud's orders, and vanished into the void.

Dahoud scanned moon-pale faces of the remaining volunteers, all of them eager, all of them unknown. Did any have what it took? Time pressed.

One face only was familiar: Yora. His instinct screamed to keep women out of danger, but the girl was agile, fast and brave, and she knew everyone. "Yora, you come with me. Pick twelve good climbers with strong ears and eyes to come with us."

Dahoud instructed the rest to create makeshift stretchers from tentpoles and blankets, as well as knot more tethers into ropes.

With a torch between his teeth, he rappelled down the almost vertical limestone into the abyss, demonstrating the quickest way to get into the sinkhole. When his last helper's feet touched the rock slab, he grouped them in pairs. "Whatever happens, stay close enough to your partner to touch hands, so when one gets trapped or sinks, the other can help at once. We're taking risks, but not foolish ones. Too many people have died already. You're more useful alive than dead."

He allocated a section to each pair, selecting spots with stone walls and timber where air pockets offered a chance of survival. They could not save everyone. The aim was to rescue as many as possible before time ran out. "Keep shouting, so they know help is on its way. Listen for responses. When you've covered your section, report back to me."

Everyone submitted to his command. In the middle of disaster, he was in control again, and it felt good. A rat scurried from the light of his torch. Spiders squatted on bricks and darted into crevices.

The debris shifted under their steps. Smells of wood smoke and dust warred in the air. Torches prattled and chickens screeched.

Hands and heads stuck out from the mud, limp and still warm. Rescuers sobbed when they found friends and familiar faces: the gatehouse guard with the finger stumps, the silver-haired elder, the priest who had slaughtered the cockerel, their skulls crushed, their torsos mashed.

Dahoud allowed his helpers no time to dig out the dead or to grieve while they had living people to save. It was like walking across a limb-strewn battlefield, counting corpses and finding comrades. Crying did not bring anyone back to life. 'Don't waste strength on pity while there's work to do,' Paniour used to say.

Coughing and spitting dust, they climbed, they fell, they listened, they dug. They responded to every noise that might have been a tapping or a groan. On bare feet, with naked fingers, they shifted mud-bricks, shards and half-crushed timber, hoping they were not piling debris on an unseen survivor.

One torch after the other burnt out until the fingers of darkness clutched the scene. Water trickled, sludge gurgled, rodent feet scurried. They dragged, burrowed and scraped, clutching at uncertain supports to stop their feet from sliding down-slope into the soup.

Sweat glued Dahoud's shirt to his chest even while the cold night air bit his cheeks. His fingers, cut and bleeding, groped through slippery stones, through cold mud and mangled flesh.

The broth gurgled and swallowed the section where they had dug a moment ago. Any moment, the sinkhole would devour what was left. He would have to send everyone back to safety.

A whimper led to a woman curled in conscious agony beside the single pillar that remained of the well-house. Fluids seeped from her wounds, drenching her garments, soaking the white-rose garlands and the mud. Her cheek was torn, her side ripped open, her intestines spilling forth. Dahoud had known enough battle deaths to be certain she was dying, in torment but too weakened to scream. Her contorted mouth moaned, bubbled blood and syllables. He leant close, brought his ear to her lips.

"Baby. Baby. Baby."

He glanced at the mangled remains of children nearby. Aloud, he said, "I'm sure your baby is fine."

"New baby."

Now he understood. He ripped his knife through the woman's sodden fabrics, reached into the soggy mess between her legs to pull the newborn out. It looked blueish, covered in blood and white-cheesy slime. A white fleshy rope dangled from its belly. Dahoud knew how to deal with battle-broken bones or sliced limbs, but about midwifery he had no clue. Was he supposed to cut the cord? He drew a dagger.

"Let me. My knife is cleaner." Deftly, Yora held up the tiny creature by the ankles, fiddled with it, and placed it on the mother's chest.

The woman twitched, trying to hold her child, then screamed. The full pain had finally hit.

Her shriek sliced Dahoud's insides.

"Yora, take the child!" he commanded. "Now. It needs… It needs all sorts of things. Ask the crones. Quick." He did not want her to see what he had to do.

When Yora was out of sight, he stroked the woman's good cheek. "Your child is safe. All is well now." He positioned his knife below the ribs and drove it straight into her heart. The screaming stopped.

He climbed down the tilting ground where several survivors were trapped between chunks of stone wall. He worked rapidly to free them before this section of ground sank and they drowned. Around him, debris bubbled and folded like the skin of boiled milk. Wall remnants tilted, slid and sank.

"Get out, team!" he yelled. "Climb up now! Fast."

Back on the plateau, he checked the casualties they had lifted, many injured first from the collapse, then from getting bumped against the rock on their way up. His team had rescued four time as many as Mansour's. Good. He did not allow himself to think of the ones they had not saved.

He and Mansour were clasping elbows like two competitors in an arena when a terrified scream shot through the air. It echoed in the emptiness, died down.

Moonlight shone through thin, corpse-pale clouds. Narrowing his eyes, Dahoud searched where the scream had come from. He could just make out the remains of a house clinging to the steep rock-face like a fly to a wall. If someone was in there, they were trapped between the abyss below and a sheer rock-face above.

The scream lashed again. A woman.

The only chance was from above, twenty man-heights of sheer cliff where no climber could find a hold. He could not send anyone down that rock face on a makeshift rope.

He looked at Mansour. Their eyes held for a heartbeat. Then Mansour gave a small nod.

⨏

During the descent, the rope sang with tension, and Dahoud prayed that the knots would hold. As soon as his feet touched the ruined roof, he unstrapped the improvised harness and sent it back up. Kneeling, he groped for a way in and found a jagged hole where the ceiling had fallen. It would be safer to wait for Mansour, but the wreck could collapse any moment. He squeezed through the hole, lowered himself into the black void, sought for a foothold. His soles slipped on sliding stones. The debris rolled under his feet, scraped against the floor, and moments later, splashed in the distant depth. Dahoud's skin crawled. This was no enclosed chamber, but a ruin whose walls had fallen away, open to the clouds that whispered across the low moon disk.

While his eyes adjusted to the darkness, his nostrils noted the smell of human fear mingled with that of spilled olive oil. A woman cowered on her knees in the corner closest to the rock, hands clutched to her face, clothes soaked with panic piss.

"Come up on the roof. There's a rope that'll lift you to safety."

Fear-rooted, the woman ignored his outstretched arm.

The ruin around them cracked and groaned. Bricks crumbled from the ceiling, scraped across the floor, vanished with a hiss.

Kneeling before her, he lowered his tone as if talking to a skittish horse. "I'm here to help you. Your friends are already waiting."

A crack jolted through the floor, then another. The ruin shuddered. A section broke away and fell outwards. Many moments later, a splashing thud came from far below. Only a few feet of space remained to stand on. Unless the woman cooperated, they would both die.

"We have to get out fast now. Really fast. You understand that, don't you?"

She did not budge. When he tried to wrap his arms around her, she pushed him away and screamed.

More brick crumbs hailed down from the ceiling, and Mansour landed beside them.

"Out of the way, Dahoud." Mansour punched the woman's temple with a fast hook. She sagged to the floor. "Problem solved."

Mansour pulled himself up through the ceiling gap and then reached down. Dahoud lifted the woman's limp body so Mansour could pull her to safety. Under their weight, debris crumbled and rained down on him.

A crack like the lash of giant whip jolted, tilting everything. Dahoud pressed himself against the back wall which was sheer rock. Bricks pelted crashed at his feet. The ground beneath his soles heaved, thundered and fell. He was standing on a ledge of no more than a foot wide, all that remained of the floor. The air chilled.

With his eyes squeezed shut, he sought a handhold, found none. He bent his knees to grip that sliver of ground on which he stood. The slightest tilt forward, and he would fall. He must not look down.

Squinting upwards, he saw that most of the ceiling had gone, too.

"Mansour?" he called.

From above came nothing but silence. Had the rebel used this mission to rid himself of a rival? Cold sweat ran down his sides. Below, gurgles sucked.

At last, debris rained down.

"Reach," Mansour told him from above. An arm appeared, then a face, shoulders. "The roof is cracking. You have to come up here." The rescuing hands dangled before him above the void.

Could Mansour, hanging upside down, hold Dahoud's weight?

Dahoud pushed himself into a standing position, wiped his fear-slick palms on his tunic, grabbed Mansour's wrists and stepped forward into the empty space. With nothing under his feet, he clung to his rescuer's wrists. As the void pulled him downwards, his muscles seemed to tear.

Memory of the seer's words bounced in his head. *Get stronger arms... stronger arms... stronger arms...*

Arms hooked under his, dragged him forward. Rope knotted around him in a harness. Mansour yelled a command. The rope bit into Dahoud's flesh. His body scraped against limestone, his skull bumped against rock. At last, people pulled him onto the top of the cliff. Never had solid earth felt so good. An eternity later, Mansour emerged, his face bloody and bruised.

Again, they clasped elbows.

"The real test still comes," Mansour said and walked away.

CHAPTER 12

The Rebel Leader

At the first pink streaks of dawn, the camp stirred to life. Camel feet shuffled in the sand. Goats bleated, kicked up dust, and slurped up the last of the water.

Sirria gazed up the mountain where the citadel had stood, glad she had insisted on living on the yurt site. Staying inside town walls brought death and disaster, suffering and sorrow, and she had had enough of those. Where should she go next? During the sun-blasted months, her flocks would not find enough fodder on the savannah. This left the towns, either Koskara Town in the north or the nearer oasis of Ain-Elnour. Most people were already loading their pack animals for the trek across the desert to the oasis of Ain-Elnour, joking loudly as if no tragedy had happened. Sirria knew the mood only too well. People who had seen death needed laughter. It proved they were still alive.

Dahoud, the puzzling stranger, had turned out to be the enemy, yet helped with the rescues. He was working hard, carrying baskets and strapping yurt-poles on donkey backs, chatting with everyone, his clothes caked with mud and blood. This was no quill-twiddling bureaucrat, but a man who belonged to this kind of life.

She congratulated herself that she had known he was no trader. Since he turned out to be the satrap, the mystery was solved. Or was it? The unease of a buried memory still niggled in her stomach.

Kind and courageous, harmless and helpful, he was a man she wanted to like, but could not trust. If his trader image had been a pretence, he might carry other secrets under his skin. He was like a leopard pretending to be a domesticated cat.

He greeted her with warm praise. "You did a great job with the evacuation and setting up this camp, Sirria. It can't have been easy in the dark."

"Not as difficult as what you did last night. I've heard of your deeds." She helped him fasten a donkey's straps. "Tell me something, Dahoud. Most Samilis wear their mother's or father's trade as a belongname. Why don't you?"

"My father was not known. My mother's trade would shame a child." Before she had the chance to say something sympathetic, he added. "The clan's crones named me Dahoud of the Desert."

It sounded plausible, but explained nothing. "Since you're no trader, what really is your line of work?"

"I'm the Lord of Koskara."

Sirria laughed. "And before you came here?"

"Government clerk. Bricklayer. Day labourer. For a while, I worked with horses." He groped inside the saddlebags. "Sirria, what happened to the trade goods I brought with me?"

"Looking for something?" Mansour asked behind him.

"Some of my belongings have vanished."

"I took them. Take your yurt and horses, to travel back to Quislabat. We keep the rest."

"You're welcome to most, though some small items are important to me."

Mansour opened his balled fist, revealing the purple fringe. "You mean this?" With a quick flick, he tossed it into a fly-buzzing puddle of cow shit. "Are you able to find the way to Quislabat, or must I give you an escort?"

"I'm the Lord of Koskara," Dahoud said. "I'm staying."

The two men stared at each other with flaming hostility, neither of them backing down. Last night, they had worked as a team, but now, it seemed, they were enemies again. Sirria still did not know where she had seen Dahoud before.

As herd after herd departed, the earth rumbled faintly under hundreds of clopping hooves.

Suddenly Mansour bared his teeth in a smile. "I have matters to see to in Koskara Town. You'll be useful, Dahoud. Will you come?"

"It happens that I have matters to see to in Koskara Town. You'll be useful, Mansour. Let's ride there together."

"Hurry up, then. Idrahad and I are riding at once."

Despite the agreement, the air between the two men simmered with tension.

"I'm coming to Koskara Town," Yora chirped. Her many plaits danced, the glass beads sparkling in the sun. "I want to be with you."

"Go to Ain-Elnour," Mansour told her. "The crones there will find a family to take you in."

She tossed her head back, sending a dozen beaded plaits flying. "I don't need a family. I have my own yurt, and I'm not a child."

"I won't have time to look after you."

"I can look after myself." She tapped the dagger hilts on her waist. "I want to be with you, and with with you, too, Dahoud. We'll be very best friends."

Danger warnings stirred in Sirria's stomach, and she made up her mind fast. "With your permission, Lord Mansour, I'll come to Koskara Town. I'll leave my flocks in a friend's charge to ride with you. I have no family here." The flicker of pain in Mansour's eyes made her look to the ground. "I want to say how very sorry I am about your wife and daughters."

Mansour jerked his chin up. "Let's move before the noon heat hits. We'll need three days to get to Koskara Town. We'll make a short detour. I want to show you something, Dahoud of the Desert. If you have the stomach for it."

Dahoud wrapped his scarves to guard his eyes from the glaring sun, and his nostrils from the sand that drifted like wafts of smoke. "Whatever you want to show me, I'm ready."

✑

In the noon heat of the third day, Mansour steered the riders towards a ruin which Dahoud recognised as the remnants of a legion post. The horses raised their heads, rolled their eyes and worked their nostrils, sidestepping as if trying to get away from the blackened buildings and stink of scorched wood.

Four years ago, this had been a garrison, functional, fortified, defended by a hundred highly trained men, expected to withstand attacks from all but the best-equipped armies. Now, only the outer walls stood intact, casting short shadows, and remnants of burnt roofs sagged over broken houses, the result not of battering rams but of post-conquest demolition. The attackers had defeated the fortress without siege machinery, and Mansour's smug smile revealed who had led the assault.

Dozens of carcasses piled in a single heap taller than a man where crows flapped and squawked, fighting for the best bits of what remained of the human flesh. At Dahoud's side, Sirria made a gagging noise. Luckily, Yora was at the back of the group, shielded from the gruesome sight.

Dahoud handed his reins to Sirria, and strode to the carcasses. The crows fluttered, took off, circled above.

Animal scavengers had plundered the uppermost bodies, leaving shreds of red fabric and pale bones. He shifted the dry remains. Further down, the corpses had the rotten stink of soft moist flesh, and crawled with maggots and desert ants.

The carnage was recent, six or seven days ago at the most. Most men wore crimson uniform. Some might once have fought under his command.

"Feel free to puke," Mansour said from high on his mount.

Dahoud straightened. "Immediate assault or siege?"

"Siege. We stopped their supply caravan and waited. Those who didn't like starving opened the gate."

Dahoud nodded. Starvation and treachery had brought an end to many sieges. "Did you reward the traitors?"

"Generously. We made them watch the others die, from sunrise to nightfall. Then we got a woman who could write to tattoo their brows with the word 'traitor'. After that, we gave them horses and let them go."

Dahoud pointed at the corpses. "How did these die?"

Yora rode forward, her face shining with excitement. "Knife-throwing. We tied them to posts, to use them as targets. First the fingers and feet, then arms, legs. Hearts and necks at the very end. We made it last all night."

Dahoud had witnessed executions, had ordered them, had carried them out, but the sight of this child-woman's joy churned his stomach.

"Mighty Ones, Mansour! Can't you get grown men to do the killing?" When he walked around carcass pile, his sandals sank into the blood-caked ashes. "Not all of the corpses wear uniform. Did you kill the civilians the same way?"

"Only the men. The children we killed fast."

Dahoud did not need to ask what they had done to the women.

"So you know the uniforms, do you?" Mansour asked.

"Who doesn't?"

When he returned to his horse, Sirria was clutching the bead strings at her throat. Her mouth was open as if she was about to be sick, and she stared in wide-eyed horror – not at the corpses, but at him.

"Sorry you had to see this." He took the reins from her hand.

She leant away from him as if he carried an evil disease.

As they forged northwards through the broiling heat, Yora attached herself to him, her eyes shining. "Your fight with Mansour yesterday was so exciting! You must teach me to wrestle like that. I want to become a champion. We'll practice every day."

At the thought of wrestling this girl, he went deathly still. She would let him pin her lithe body. Better still, she might pin him, use him, force her attentions on him. He wanted to measure his own strength against a female's.

The djinn cheered, leaking poisonous desires into his limbs. *Do you see how she lusts for the contest? Will we win?*

The breasts under her tunic were small and high.

"Say yes, Dahoud." She tilted her head and fluttered her lashes at him.

She had not only a woman's body, but a woman's instincts.

"Yora, if you want to learn wrestling, you must practice with other women."

"The women wrestlers aren't good. Not like you or Mansour." Her dark pink lips pulled into a pout. "Mansour won't wrestle me either. Why not? It's unfair if you don't want to practice with me just because I'm a woman."

The djinn sent pictures of Yora's slender body pinned naked under him. *Is she asking for it?*

"It's not because you're a woman," Dahoud explained. "It's because we're men."

"You're as boring as Mansour. I thought you were exciting, but you're really just afraid of me."

He wanted to throw her to the ground and teach her a lesson, but she was almost a child, without a woman's understanding of what she was suggesting, and he was the satrap of Koskara. He would protect the women of this land, even from himself.

He stared straight ahead into the sun-glaring desert. "Let's do something else together." Anything that did not involve touching her in combat. "I've always wanted to learn dagger throwing. Will you teach me?"

She clapped her hands. "I'm the best dagger-thrower in Koskara. Next time we have an execution, you and I will do it. Mansour says he's going to round up men-lovers to kill. They'll be naked and tied to posts and we throw to pierce their eggs first." Her eyes sparkled.

"Drowning men-lovers is quicker."

"Mansour says that would be a waste of good water. Anyway, knife-throwing is much more fun."

"We'll see." He would kill the vermin to stop the man-loving vice spreading in Koskara, but he would not let Mansour dictate the method.

He considered Yora's threadbare clothes and the fortune's worth of knives in her belt. "These are fine daggers. Some obsidian, some bronze, right? Where did you get them?"

Beaming, Yora pulled out one weapon after another. "My father brought me this flint blade from Quislak when I was a child, and this bronze one from Zigazia. This here is from a Quislaki soldier and this from an official. When I kill an enemy, Mansour lets me keep their knives."

"Do your parents travel a lot?"

"My mother died at my birth. My father was a trader and every year, he visited me and brought me presents."

Dahoud got the picture: a half-orphan whose father had fled the responsibility. "Did anyone look after you, Yora?"

"Oh yes. Lots of aunts and uncles. I've lived in many places all over Koskara. I was born during a storm, the worst storm there ever was in the Samil. My father said there were animals and tents flying everywhere."

'I remember that storm," Dahoud said. "My clan was crossing from Djilcit into Zigazia, and we sheltered in mountain caves. I was eleven."

During that storm, he had fallen victim to the djinn. Better not dwell on that. "Have you fought with Mansour often?"

Where Sirria had been reticent, Yora chattered happily: Mansour came from a poor nomad family with more children than animals, had multiplied his flocks through skill and hard work, and was now one of the richest men in Koskara. About his leadership style, she had little to say beyond that he supported whatever she wanted. "Everything, except wrestling."

$\gtrsim$

The sun stained the horizon scarlet when they neared Koskara Town. Long before the dark wall of the southernmost date palms came into sight, the smell of animal sweat and manure reached Dahoud's nostrils. Shadufs creaked, lifting water from the river, and irrigation channels gurgled in the shadow of the olive and date plantations. The wall circling the town was barely man-high and in bad repair, a crumbling structure useless for defence.

A fat stone bridge squatted above the river, leading to an even bigger stone-gate, both too monumental for the yellow brick town, both erected by Zetan to celebrate his rulership of Koskara. Rebels had vented their anger on these structures. Marble statues, toppled from the bridge railing, lay face-down in the reeds and drowned on the river ground, and the fine picture reliefs of the gate were smashed, its walls smeared with anti-Quislak caricatures and curse triangles. The giant statues of the Queen and her Consort stood beheaded; someone had stuck goats' heads on their stony necks.

Word of Mansour's arrival brought people spilling from their houses, ululating and chanting his name. Women rushed to offer him mares' milk and to kiss his tunic.

A mother with a baby on her hip begged him to take refreshment in her abode. The room was crowded with half a dozen children and another woman who was trying to get the young ones to sleep.

Mansour naturally took the position of power opposite the entrance and Idrahad claimed the spot on the reed mat next to him, leaving Dahoud to sit on Mansour's left. Sirria and Yora, not jostling for status, sat by the door.

After pouring water for her guests, the woman tried to get her younger children to sleep.

"Lie still," she warned them. "Or the Black Besieger will get you."

Dahoud's breath stalled, but he kept his face impassive.

"I m not frightened," a youngster piped up. "The Black Besieger is dead."

"He will come back from the dead if you don't obey."

This prospect seemed to frighten the child into obedient silence.

When their hostess offered them a basket with the first summer figs and chunks of salty cheese, they ate under the attentive stares of her six older snot-nosed children who seemed fascinated by every movement the guests made. Dahoud savoured the sweet juice of his tenth fig when he noticed that Mansour still held the first fruit in his hand, bringing it to his mouth many times and biting without taking flesh. Puzzled, he raised his eyebrows. With a minute flicker of the eyes, Mansour pointed at the children.

Dahoud understood: those figs were the family's only food, and what he had read as curiosity in the children's eyes was sheer hunger. He declined another helping, assuring his hostess he was too sated to eat more.

"Time to look at the residency," Mansour said. "I hear three men tried to get out and were shot."

"Yes!" one of the boys piped up. "We shot them. Quislaki soldiers."

Dahoud laughed. "Soldiers? You're joking." To his knowledge, the residency held only sixteen foolish civilian patriots.

"I've seen them myself," the boy insisted, even as his mother squeezed his arm to hush him. "I even touched one of them when I took his belt."

Silence spread.

"Forgive us, Lord Mansour!" the woman whispered, touching her forehead to the ground. "He's only a child, he didn't know what he was doing, and we didn't mean to keep the belt. I'll bring it at once, but I beg you, have mercy."

"Let him keep it," Mansour said. "When he grows up, he'll be a fine warrior."

"Show us the belt, please," Dahoud requested.

When the boy brought the item, Dahoud fingered the crimson-embossed leather with the scabbard loops. Legion issue. He smiled at the boy. "A bit big for you still, but you'll grow into it. What do you think, Mansour? Is this the kind of belt Quislaki soldiers wear?"

"Without doubt," Mansour said. "We'll find out why. The men in the residency are fools. I offered them free passage to the border, days ago. They said they'd rather drink their own piss."

"I hope they like the taste." Dahoud grinned. The men in the residency were fools, but they had the guts to defy his rival. "They'll stay or leave as I tell them, because I'm their rightful satrap."

"I look forward to it." Mansour rose. "Let's go."

The sparse stars of the Great Horse and the Mighty Warrior lit the blackening sky. Crowds with prattling torches followed them to the residency, the two-storey status building the previous satrap had erected outside the city walls, upriver, at a hygienic distance from the natives. Glazed tiles, painted pilasters and arched windows imitated the royal palace, a feeble structure only a fool would try to defend.

"You can come out now, councillors," Dahoud called. "I'm Dahoud, the new satrap of Koskara."

Bolts creaked, and he was able to thrust the dark wooden door open. Unasked, Mansour pushed in after him.

In the entrance hall, sixteen pairs of dull eyes stared from pale faces, hostile in their dejection. Above the expected stink of piss lingered a sweetish smell, showing they had smoked joy-flowers to alleviate their hunger and fear. Dahoud made himself look past the anger and despair in their faces at the competent councillors he knew them to be, every one of them a veteran of statecraft, a seasoned politician and skilled administrator, an expert who would help him rule Koskara.

"Who's been acting as the regent?"

A heavy man with sagging cheeks and sluggish movements identified himself with a hoarse voice as Esmat, chief councillor and, since Lord Zetan's death, regent of Koskara. He studied Dahoud's appointment letter with unfocused eyes, mopping his brow. "This, ahem, the Consort, the seal..." His hoarse voice tipped into aggression. "How did you get this letter, you filthy nomad?"

Dahoud glanced down his tunic, still smeared with blood and mud from Oubar. Wishing he was wearing the purple-fringed armbands, he braced his legs and hooked a hand into his belt. "I'm Lord Dahoud, satrap of Koskara. Tell me, Esmat, why you didn't leave when offered free pass."

"If you're the satrap, you shouldn't need to ask. We risked our lives to hold this residency, to maintain the Quislaki presence in this latrine of a province, even when the centurion wanted us to give up."

"You ignored an officer's advice?"

"Those military men are all cowards. You owe it to us that you still have a residency." Esmat looked around for support and harvested nods.

Dahoud's patience snapped. "You brother of a braindead bat! You were sitting here like hens in a coop. The rebels could have wiped you out with a single attack. The only reason they didn't was because you were convenient hostages. Had I arrived with a legion marching against Koskara, they would have used you to press us into leaving." A glance at Mansour showed a grin and a nod. "When your cistern ran dry, the soldiers— the ones you call cowards—gave their lives trying to get you water. Where did they come from, anyway?"

"From a garrison the rebels had attacked. The three of them were the only survivors of an atrocious carnage. Severely wounded, and sought refuge with us."

"What kind of wounds?"

"Their heads, mostly."

Events locked together into a coherent story of how the garrison's traitors had redeemed themselves by their heroic if useless deaths, whereas the councillors had shown nothing but stupidity.

Esmat said, "The first thing for you to do is change out of these filthy rags so you don't look like a Samili."

"I am Samili, and proud of it."

"You sheep-witted camel turd dare call yourself a satrap?"

Dahoud squared his shoulders and fixed Esmat with a hard stare. "Watch the Words that Burn Your Tongue." He pronounced the traditional formula of warning in a calm deep tone, making every word hum with danger like an arrow in flight.

Several of the councillors drew breath. The Quislak formula was a warning that someone had committed a verbal offence against one of the sacred institutions of the Queendom: the Queen herself, the satraps and the Ladies. If an offender did not retract the insult at once, he could be condemned to lifelong forced labour or beheading.

Esmat hooked one hand across his other arm and raised his chin in defiance. "So you want me to grovel? You expect me to respect you as a satrap if you do not behave like one?"

Dahoud stepped forward, so close that only two finger-breadths of space remained between them. Esmat took a step back.

Dahoud stood still, waiting.

At last, Esmat raised his hands in submission. "I beg you to return my words to me. After so many days of captivity, my mind is not working as it should."

"Accepted," Dahoud said coldly. Even if he made allowances for many days of suffering, sickness and joy-flowers, Esmat was unsuitable as his second-in-command. He had met men who had endured worse during longer sieges, yet still acted with sense and courtesy. If the chief councillor was an incompetent ass, the others were probably worse. Yet they had the training and experience he sorely needed, and would be difficult to replace. Without them, he would struggle like a camel in a river pretending to be a fish.

It was better to fight unarmed than to carry useless weapons, Paniour used to say.

"All of you are relieved of your posts. You will be given food and will leave Koskara immediately."

"You can't dismiss us." Esmat flung his arms back. "We've defended the residency!"

Dahoud drilled hard stare into him. "You will leave." A satrap could let a council go if he put a new one in place, and Kirral had granted him the right to choose his own councillors. "Mansour, will you be my chief councillor?"

Mansour, in the relaxed pose of an observer, said, "No."

"If you agree, I can send them to Quislabat."

"It's quicker to kill them. I no longer need them as hostages, now that I've got you."

"Please let them go," Dahoud said. "We don't need bloodshed."

"All right." Mansour leaned lazily against the painted wall. "They can go. Appoint who you like for your Council. Pick people from the street."

Even for a temporary council, Dahoud did not want street pickings. He needed advisers with local knowledge. The Black Besieger, after beheading the leaders of conquered citadel, used to place the local crones in positions of power. They knew everything, commanded everyone's respect, and were skilled at managing local affairs.

"The crones of Koskara Town will be my temporary Council."

"The crones?" Mansour laughed. "I look forward to it."

Esmat guffawed. "You want to run a Queendom province with a bunch of old women? That will never work."

"I trust your stay in the residency has been memorable."

⨘

Outside the residency, Mansour said, "You're not a hostage, Dahoud."

"I'm glad to hear it."

"Have you heard of the Feast of the Stallion?"

The Feast of the Stallion was a traditional Samili festival. A long time ago, the Lady chose a new consort every year who killed his predecessor. If she desired to keep her man for another year, a stallion was killed in his stead. Eventually, it changed to the ritual slaughter of a horse and a public feasting on its flesh.

"I attended as a child in Djildit," Dahoud said. "Is it celebrated in Koskara?"

"Enjoy the last forty-three days of your life, Dahoud."

Mansour had manoeuvred him into a situation where there could be no backup plan. Dahoud had to withdraw or risk all. If this was a test, Dahoud could pass by staying. If it was not, he would find out when he stood in the arena with a thousand people wanting his death.

Mansour raised his brows, waiting.

"I know how the Feast of the Stallion works," Dahoud said. "I'll be around."

CHAPTER 13

Koskara Town

Early next morning, Dahoud explored the residency. Four years ago, he had paid a courtesy call on Lord Zetan here. Now the cool greenstone building was devoid of life but for lizards that darted about the walls, tongues flicking. Naked male statues stood forlorn around the courtyard cistern. Among the sumptuous silk draperies, the stink of siege still lingered, that sour-sweet odour of sweat, piss and fear.

He sat in the carved chair in the study, claiming command of the residency. He would undo the harm his predecessor had done, and wipe the tray clean.

Floor-to-ceiling stacks of scrolls mocked his aspirations. When taking charge of conquered towns he had only managed their immediate needs: executing leaders, sending statues to the Consort, burning corpses, whitewashing bloodstained walls. It had not prepared him for governing a satrapy which rejected his rule.

A massive mural of the Queen stared at him with eyes like bulging raisins in a lump of pale dough. He would have it replaced with a portrait that gave the monarch the beauty she deserved.

He spat on the ink palette, stirred in a pinch of powder, and started work.

"Dahoud, Lord-Satrap of Koskara, greets The High Lord Kirral, Consort to the Queen of Quislak. Oubar destroyed. Six hundred dead, rest

cooperating. Request amnesty. Residency freed. Outgoing council provided with subsistence and escort. Request Esha Ladysdaughter in marriage."

He signed with a capital D.

His next letter was to Esha.

"Dahoud, Lord-Satrap of Koskara, greets Esha Ladysdaughter, in the satrapy of Idjlara: Will you be my Lady, please? D."

A least a moon would pass before she received his message and another or more before he could expect her reply. If she accepted him, he would make up to her for all the harm he had done to women in the past. He would wrap her in his love, worship her and bathe her in his gratitude.

The third letter was to high general Paniour who needed to know how a garrison had fallen by treachery and how the traitors had ended. This was easy to compose in the terse language of the legions.

The next letter was difficult. Squeezing the quill, Dahoud sought the right phrases to explain to Tarkan why he could not make him chief councillor. At last, he simply invited him to visit Koskara for a hunting holiday. He did not expect Tarkan to accept.

He stabbed the dagger hilt into clumps clay, sealing the letters with the gatehouse emblem. Now he needed a courier. A general could dispatch soldiers, the Consort used heralds, Govan had mounted messengers on his staff. But Dahoud had no messenger at his disposal. He had to wait for a travelling trader willing to take letters as far as Djildt Town from where Lord-Satrap Adil would send them on.

A fifth message would go only as far as the legion garrison less than half a day's ride away. Dahoud was commander-in-chief of the armed forces in Koskara. Centurion Gavinos would assume this a nominal rank, which suited Dahoud. He penned a polite note of little content.

He left the residency, pleased to have completed his first tasks. Outside, the sun was already beating down on Koskara Town, ripening the smells of musk and manure. A seething stream of donkeys, carts and people jostled along the road.

"Dahoud! Dahoud!" Yora waved wildly.

He waved back. "Yora! Good to see you. How have you fared?"

Scarf-wrapped heads turned, noting the friendship between the Quislaki satrap and the local girl. Yora, shunted from relative to relative, had lived three years in Koskara Town, knew everyone, and was the best guide he could want. At the same time, he could protect her from the dangers of her naïve enthusiasms—as long as he also shielded her from his djinn.

"Uncle Wurran has given me a job. Today we've been gelding yearlings. It's fun."

"Wurran?" Dahoud remembered a man of that name, a horse breeder who had steadfastly refused to sell animals to the Quislaki legions.

"He breeds the best horses in Koskara. The best horses in the world!" She agreed to help him find a riding messenger who would carry his letters. Then she said, "Mansour says he'll kill you at the Feast of the Stallion. Are you disappointed?"

"Very." Especially with himself for not anticipating Mansour's move. He had misjudged the rebel leader, expecting public challenges and open aggression. Instead, Mansour had set about eliminating the problem quietly, giving Dahoud forty-three days to get frightened and flee. Dahoud would stay, and use every day to prove himself worthy and unafraid.

"The old way of cutting the throat is very quick. I'm sorry." Her voice brightened. "But there'll be lots of people watching, and music and feasting."

Dahoud put on a pleased face. "I'm sure it will be exciting."

"You and I going to have fun together until then," Yora chirped. "Dagger-fighting, knife-throwing and shopping. Mansour says you must spend all your money. You'll buy clothes from my aunt, and goats from my other aunt, and a horse from Uncle Wurran."

Dahoud did not point out that he had two horses already, nor mention that he knew the man. He had tried to persuade Wurran to sell him horses, met with refusal, and confiscated the needed mounts. If anyone in Koskara could recognise the Black Besieger, it was the horse trader. But their encounters had been brief, and Dahoud had worn the black mask.

"Let's look at his horses," he agreed.

The breeder's stables sprawled outside the northern wall, their brickwork gleaming in the sun, with no sign of vandal damage. Dahoud's nostrils welcomed the familiar acrid smell of straw dust, dung, leather and sweat. Horses snorted into their hay, cribbed their teeth on wood. A thin cat shot past and vanished behind bales of straw.

Even from behind, Dahoud knew the man shovelling straw with a pitchfork. His back was twice as broad as any other man's. He put the fork aside and peered at the arrivals. His bushy white beard was shaved off in the centre to reveal a triple chin. "Good day, young Yora. I wasn't expecting you until noon. I see you've brought the pretender with you. What does he want? He can buy a horse while he's here, a fine animal to take with him when he departs."

"I won't depart," Dahoud said.

Yora added, "Mansour will kill him at the Feast of the Stallion."

"A snake that comes out of the cave during the day can't expect to live long." Wurran dug his fork into the soiled straw and tossed a load over his shoulder. "I hope he can afford a horse. Does the Consort pay pretenders well?"

"Well enough." A satrap's salary, while too narrow to uphold the kind of lifestyle most Lords indulged in, was many times what he had earned as a clerk. "And the name is Dahoud. Lord Dahoud of Koskara."

The Black Besieger's name had also been Dahoud, but that was a common name. Still, it might trigger recognition. Dahoud waited.

Flies buzzed. Two settled on his arm, tasting his sweat.

The skin folds under Wurran's jaw wobbled. "What kind of horse does he want?"

Dahoud glanced over rows of grey rumps. "Your best. I can afford it." The prospect of silver should buy some courtesy. He wondered if Wurran would try to foist an inferior animal on him.

Wurran tilted his jaw at one of the rumps, sending his chins into another wobble. "This five-year-old mare here, name of Peace. Sleek enough to pull the sun's chariot across the sky, if he ignores the unfortunate matter of her tail."

From the front, the mare looked divine: tall, glossy, white-maned, with the dark grey coat of youth not yet turned silver, bursting with health. The tail's colour was that of damp wool soaked in piss.

"She has good wind, never refuses an order." Wurran watched as Dahoud checked her eyes, teeth and nostrils. "She'll do anything he wants her to, with a packsaddle, a riding saddle or a legion saddle without stirrups. She carries anything, she does trickriding, and she does a good pace. Mind, she's is no racer, and she gets a little spooked by mountain terrain." He helped saddle her and led her out of the stables. "Of course, horse prices have gone up recently."

Dahoud mounted. "I'm glad your trade is flourishing. I would have thought with the war and the drought, few people can afford them."

"The Lord Mansour keeps me in business."

"How many horses has Mansour bought?"

Wurran picked up his fork to toss a load of straw. "Young Yora, tell the pretender to take Peace for a trot."

The horse's canter was smooth. She sidestepped carts and obeyed verbal commands promptly. Without thinking, he used legion signals, and was startled that she responded to them eagerly.

Since Wurran had not recognised him, he could be almost certain that nobody else would.

Back at the stable, he asked Yora what she thought, as if he needed her views before choosing a horse.

"The price is right," she said. "Horses with yellow tails don't live long, but you'll need her only for forty-two days."

≈

Yora's great-aunt, a crone swathed in melon pink from whom he bought a ceramic cooking pot, was the first vendor to acknowledge he was in Koskara for more than a visit. "The Lord Mansour says we are to be your temporary council. We meet tomorrow at dawn."

"Come to the assembly hall in the residency."

She sniffed as if he had served her a dish of rancid meat. "We meet in the arena."

Dahoud felt a sharp tug at his tunic.

"Are you the new satrap?" The speaker was male, small, wiry. "Will you re-open the copper mines?"

"Is there a reason why I should?"

"My family worked in the same mine for sixteen generations. My great-great-grandmother unearthed this." He lifted a gnarled copper nugget from his chest. "I mined copper from the day I was old enough to crawl. I was a miner, a foreman, a tunnel engineer. These days, I work shadufs and dye wool, but there's nothing I don't know about that copper mine."

Dahoud understood: The man hankered after the status and income he had lost twenty years ago. "Thanks for telling me. If I ever want to reopen the mine, I'll be sure to ask you. What's your name?"

"Criton. They claim there's no more copper in those mountains, but they've never made a proper search. The shafts and tunnels still exist. That mountain has more holes than a piece of old wormed wood, and we can extend the network until we find a new vein."

"I ll bear it in mind, Criton."

"People kept dying when the tunnels flooded, but believe me, the mine is safe to work!" Criton had a beggar's whiny voice and a sergeant's persistence. "It's just the water pockets in the limestone karst which kept flooding the tunnels, but I know where those are and can avoid them when we prospect for a new vein."

"Water?" Koskara needed water, and if Criton was right, ready-made tunnels existed to lead it to the surface—a mad idea, worth pursuing. "At another time, I look forward to talking with you about those mines."

～

Soon after the first rays of dawn kissed the earth, Dahoud sat in the arena, his native tunic now washed and mended, his legs crossed the nomad way. He needed to absorb local habits, every nuance of them, and make them his own.

Brightly coloured dresses swished, bangles and anklets chinked as the town's oldest women filed in. They laughed, they chattered, and cast him curious glances.

The gathering of crones was a remnant from the Samil's past when women were in charge of almost everything. Although today, the crones' authority was restricted to female concerns and sometimes advising the town elders, they still yielded immense power. If he impressed them favourably with his leadership, he would be accepted by the townspeople, and eventually all of Koskara.

With their knowledge of local matters, they were the perfect people to help him rule until he appointed a council.

As the sun rose over the distant mountains, the altar and statue cast long shadows into the arena. In this spot, forty-one days from now, his fate would be decided.

When all nine had taken their places in the circle, the senior crone, a slight woman with pointed chin, turned to the altar and spoke a prayer to the Great Mare.

"Honoured Mothers, thank you for joining me. Together, we will make Koskara peaceful, prosperous, and safe. We will-"

"Quiet." The senior crone stabbed the stem of her claypipe at him. "We have business to attend."

Startled, Dahoud glanced at their wrinkled faces, some grave, some smirking. He had been tricked. Loyal to Mansour, the crones had let him believe they would serve as his council, and sidelined him into attending one of their regular meetings where men had no say.

"I'm on your side," he assured them. "We can work together. Please"

"Quiet!" Nine voices choroused.

Yora's pink great-aunt added in the sing-song voice women used when talking to a child, "You may stay, but you must not disturb. Why don't you brew us a nice pot of tea?"

Anger churned in Dahoud's stomach, speeding into a spiral of fury. Women were shutting him out again. If they knew who he was, and what he could do, they would not dare treat him so. Slowly, the djinn's poisonous tendrils reached into his mind. He had the power to unleash a storm of terror, to bring these women to their knees.

No. He was no longer the Black Besieger; he was the Lord of Koskara. Alienating the crones would gain him nothing. Nominally, the crones were his council; formalities were met. Did it matter that they refused to work with him? His real rule would not begin until the Feast of the Stallion, when he would appoint his real council.

For now, the crones were a source of information, the kind of information few men and no outsider would ever hear. Information was the gatehouse to power. He unclenched his fists and switched strategies. He would learn from the crones what he could, absorbing every droplet of local knowledge.

He bowed. "I'm honoured to witness your wisdom."

For an hour, he stoked the brazier and replenished beakers with mint tea, while they discussed the need for a women-only day at the bathhouse, the lack of midwives and healers, how many women had died in childbed last year. A woman named Naima drew the crones' admiration and their scorn, because she campaigned to improve health but had impractical ideas how to achieve it.

"Naima is mad." The speaker waved her arm, rattling bangles. "She wants to move the animal pens away from the river! What does this have to do with childbirth?"

With a sideways glance at Dahoud, the senior crone raised a warning finger to her lips. While Dahoud pretended not to notice, he guessed what secret they were guarding. Perhaps this Naima was an illegal healer.

He sat in respectful silence – until he heard about a mother rejecting her child. "It doesn't matter if she doesn't want the child," the oldest crone declared. "She gave birth, so it's her duty to care for it."

Damp chills ran down Dahoud's back. His own mother had exposed him to the murderous desert sun. When he was discovered just in time to survive, well-meaning crones had restored him to his mother, insisting she bring him up. His mother had fed and clothed Dahoud, but had never grown to love him, and showed him nothing but contempt.

Not once had she willingly touched her child, nor spoken a single word to him. As the clan's whore, she received only the men who were prepared to support her with gifts. She had cradled their heads between her breasts and bathed them in her caresses, while her small son looked on with the pain of longing. Whenever he tried to attract her attention, she hit him, the only kind of touch he could gain. Once he reached his eighth year, she made him wait outside the yurt until each customer had left. The crones, having done their duty to the newborn, did not care.

Now another child was about to face a similar fate.

"Some women act strangely after giving birth," another crone said without taking the pipe out of her mouth. "They feel low and lack affection. The phase will pass, and she'll learn to love her child."

Contradicting the crones would be a mistake, but Dahoud had to act or another child would become a ready victim for a djinn.

"Honoured Mothers."

Their heads spun, faces painted with disapproval and surprise.

"I'm honoured to learn from your experience. How will you assess the success of your scheme?"

"We will... we will..." The senior crone pulled at the bead hanging in her ear. Her frown showed the grinding mill of her thoughts. "We will check on the child once a moon for the first year, and once a year after that."

"Thank you, honoured mother." Regular visits would flag up the worst kinds of abuse. Dahoud settled back into the role of respectful listener.

At the end of the meeting, he extinguished the brazier. He had not established himself as the leader, but had not alienated the crones either; he did not have a council, but had a source of insider information other satraps would never access.

CHAPTER 14

The Consort's Games

Masses of jewellery jingled on wrists and ankles. Hips swayed, shoulders quivered, and henna-stained soles stirred up dust as they shuffled across the crumb-strewn carpet. The air reeked of over-sweet perfumes and sweaty armpits.

Merida decided to feign pleasure in harem life, so Teruma and Kirral would think she had surrendered to her captivity, and not suspect that rescue was under way. Joining the bellydance practice was the perfect opportunity to fool everyone.

"Now bend your knees, and shimmy." The visiting teacher, an overweight greying woman of boundless energy, shook her hips. "Faster, faster. Pelvis forward, knees soft, relax."

With Riverian discipline, Merida copied the contortions. Shoulders circled back, hips rotated to the right, and at the same time, hands were supposed to weave while the feet slid forward and the abdomen fluttered. The layering of movements challenged the mind as much as the body, and it felt good to work muscles which had been idle for most of her life. The sweat of her efforts trickled down her thighs, soaking her trousers and slicking her felt boots.

The hip movements grew obscene: twists, drops, swivels, spirals, even forward thrusts. Worst of all, the women seemed to have fun. They tittered and squealed.

Something in Merida's body threatened to feel good. Energy

flushed her thighs, hips and abdomen, like a cramped captive suddenly freed. Merida longed to let the pleasure of the release carry her like a river carried a boat, but she guarded against this sin. Bodily pleasure of any kind had to be kept under strict control.

The teacher bounced her plump body. "When I entertain in a tavern, the tables come up to my waist. So the patrons, they cannot see what I do below. I must use my upper body, roll my shoulders, like this. Try it. Look over that shoulder, smiiile. The men, they looove this."

None of the harem inmates would ever get to leave the palace, let alone dance in a tavern. Only Merida had a life waiting outside, and she would never lower herself to bellydancing for an audience.

"The costume I wear for tavern dancing has tassels here and here, and they swing—bing-bong, bing-bong—from just rolling the shoulders. Now, finger cymbals. If you don't have your own, borrow a set from my basket."

Merida tied copper disks to her thumbs and middle fingers. Soon a cacophony of chinks and rings filled the room. Merida focused on repeating the teacher's patterns, all based on four counts: *Click-clack, click-clack, click-clack, click-clack and Clink, clink, clicketeclick.*

"Your sense of rhythm is fantastic," the teacher praised.

Merida tried to stay Modest by ignoring the compliment, but the praise flowed like wine in her veins.

"Now let's try some other patterns," the teacher said. "Six counts, a popular rhythm in Darria, perfect for entertaining. Step-ball-change to the left, step-ball-change to the right, and with the cymbals you play *ding-ding-dak, ding-ding-dak.*"

All virtuous rhythms had four counts. Two and eight counts might be tolerated, but six counts were forbidden. What now? If she refused to play this on the grounds of Riverian virtue, it would reveal she still planned to return home. Playing a six-count rhythm could not be a severe sin since it was based on four plus two. Back in Riverland, she would atone for the transgression. The rhythm was cheerful, airy, uplifting, and Merida's forced smile soon turned into a real one.

"Listen to Haurvatat," the teacher said, "She's a master at the six-count. It's clear she's grown up with Darrian music."

Hauravatat's whole body radiated joy at being the focus of everyone's attention, and her aura beamed with pleasure.

Kadiffe snorted. "Foreigners. It's easy for them."

"I'm not a foreigner!" Haurvatat cried, her pleasure crumpled like a collapsing house. "I'm Darrian!"

"Darrian is foreign," Kadiffe insisted. "Enemy, even. My father says the Queendom will crush Darria."

"Next, the nine-count," the teacher said. "This one is tricky, so pay attention."

Kadiffe chucked her cymbals into the basket. "I don't like the foreign stuff."

"It's a traditional rhythm from the Samil, and the Samil is part of the Queendom. Perhaps, as a patriot, you want to give it a try?" the teacher suggested, but Kadiffe sat in a corner and sulked with her knees drawn up and her chin on her hands.

"In Riverland, we use four-count rhythms," Merida contributed. "They're more natural, because they relate to the left-right walking pattern. They don't rouse the blood, and they clear the mind. You should try them."

"Riverland, Riverland, Riverland. I give a donkey's spit about Riverland!" Kadiffe snapped.

"You would benefit. Riverian researchers are the best in the world, and they've found—"

"The Samili nine-count," the teacher announced loudly. "One-two-three ratata. One-two-three ratata."

Merida wanted to point out that *one-two-three ratata* added up to six, not nine, but the instructor's glare made her keep quiet. Apparently, the *one-two-thee* part was slower than the *ratata,* thus counting double.

The teacher sang, a wailing tune of aggression, longing, and sensuality, and clinked her cymbals. "Stop thinking. Just feel it, let it flow into your hips, just move on the first count. Stomp like you're squashing a cockroach, and at the same time clap your hand like you're catching a mosquito. Gracefully. Stomp forward, three small steps back, and on the last step lift your other knee."

Nine counts were definitely sinful, but Merida had to keep up her act. What did a small transgression matter if it helped her get away from greater sins? With the assertive stomping, a glimmer of fun sneaked into Merida's mind. Languid, passionate, and utterly sinful, the rhythm pulsed through her body, with a sensual power that stirred the blood and heated the senses.

This was wrong, wrong, wrong. She slipped the cymbals from her fingers before the music could seduce her into bodily pleasure and sweep away her self-discipline.

"All right, enough cymbals for now," the teacher said. "Take them off, and we'll practice floorwork. Lie down, and I'll show you some really sexy moves..."

Merida fled.

For once, she was alone in the dormitory. With a damp cloth, she wiped the sweat off her limbs, and changed into a freshly laundered suit.

The air here stank worse than in the social room: stale sweat instead of fresh, and mixed with incense and the sour reek of slop buckets. The latticed shutters were nailed closed, keeping the women out of the world's sight, and the world out of the women's, and preserving the harem stench. With the bronze tongs from the incense burner, Merida pried the nails of one of the shutters open and inhaled deeply. Even the heat-boiled street smell of dust, manure and rotten fruit was an improvement over the foetid harem air.

Under a sky so pale it was almost white, endless yellow buildings sprawled, stacked without overall design or thought to symmetry. Laundry bleached on the roofs. Merida gazed towards the far north-east. Somewhere out there was Copperland, and beyond that, the Mountain States, and still further, the Virtuous Republic of Riverland. Her home. Her freedom. The place where she would again breathe virtuous air, untainted by sin and sensuality. How long before help arrived? Two moons and thirteen days had passed. With luck, Mother had already received the letter, but it would take at least the same time again before an answer came.

The precious moment of privacy did not last long. Haurvatat rushed through the rattling door curtain to wrap her arms around Merida. "Don't be sad! I'll show you how to dance lying down." She still smelled of pear perfume. "Come, lie on my bed, let your body go soft, and I'll hold your hips and move them."

As gently as she could, Merida shifted away from the squeeze of the girl's perfumed body. "Will you teach me to play the six-count? You do it wonderfully well. How do you make yours ring so brightly?"

Haurvatat beamed. "It's easy. I'll show you." *Ding ding ding.* Each sound vibrated for many heartbeats before it ceased. "Now you do it. To get a good sound, open your fingers fast and wide."

When Merida hit the disks of her right hand together, she got a dull *clack clack clack.*

"Faster. Wider. Don't think about closing your fingers. Think about opening them."

Merida tried. *Clack clack clack.*

"I'll teach how to make a really bright sound." She held the fingers of her right hand so the disks were parallel but a distance apart. The disks of her left were also parallel, but almost touching. "Now you put the left cymbals between the right cymbals, and then you move them to and fro very quickly, so the inner ones hit the outer ones, like a vibration." *Rrrriiiiiiiiiiiiiiiiiiiiiiiing.* "This is perfect for performing a hip shimmy. I can do it for a long time."

She jumped to her feet and quivered her hips at the same time as her cymbals. The sound shrilled on and on in Merida's skull.

"How did you learn to play so well?" Merida shouted over the din.

"My mother taught me."

"Do you miss your mother? Does she write to you often?"

"Write?" Haurvatat brow creased in puzzlement. "My mother is a woman. All mothers are. The trick is to click them very fast, and open them at once. Like this." *Ding.* The metallic ring filled the air.

Merida's heart filled with pity. To be illiterate was worse than having to wait a long time for a letter. Like her, the girl was a stranger in this land, probably as confused about customs and values as she was. "Is your home country very different from Quislak?"

"Oh yes, very different. It has its own moon and everything. Now practice. You can try mine if you like. One hit on the left, opening them really fast. One hit on the right, opening not quite so much." *Ding tak ding tak ding tak ding tak.* "Now, neck slides, and shoulder rolls, backwards in big circles." Hot hands pressed on Merida's shoulders to coax movement out of them. "Feel the pleasure ooze."

To free herself from the touch, Merida leant away, examining the cymbals in the shine of the oil lamp. "The engraved palm trees are so pretty. Three slender trunks entwined. They look almost like they're dancing."

"My mother used to play them until she was sold."

Merida dropped her hands into her lap. "Sold?"

"When she got too old to please my father." Haurvatat held one of the polished metal disks before her face and watched her face in its reflection. "Since he sold her as a mine slave, she had no more use for the cymbals. The palm trees are my father's family emblem, which is on everything he owns, on cups, on concubines, on cattle." She beamed. "My father owns many many things."

"What happened to your mother after she was..." Merida struggled to get the word out of her throat. "Did you hear from her? Did you miss her?"

"It's not like my mother was my father. Not family. She was just a slave, a dancer he'd captured in the war, and she was really getting old. She had wrinkles." Haurvatat spat on each of the disks and polished them with the hem of her skirt.

"I'm so sorry, Haurvatat. So these finger cymbals are all you have to remember your mother by. Did you ever try to free her?"

"Free her? How? Why?" Haurvatat frowned as if struggling to understand Merida's horror. "My brother, who is an officer and also owns many things, he went to the mine to buy her back, but she was already dead or sold on or crippled or something. Now try again, *ding-ding-ding ding-ding-ding*."

Aghast at a society that devalued the bond between mother and daughter, Merida clinked the cymbals. They seemed to shriek with a slave woman's anguish.

"Wonderful!" Haurvatat clapped her hands. "You're playing like a Darrian! Now I'm your best friend, aren't I?" She pressed Merida's hands between her pudgy fingers. "Say that I'm your best friend."

Startled by the demand, Merida sought for an answer. She had no friends in the harem and wanted none. Haurvatat was kind, but also stupid, and her clinging neediness was a trial. Merida wished neither to cause hurt nor to tell a lie. She hesitated too long.

Haurvatat burst into tears. "You don't like me! Nobody likes me!"

"It's not you," Merida soothed. "I'm just a bit of a loner. I don't have friends here."

"But you have me!" The girl's arms clasped around her. "Why don't you want me?"

Merida was almost glad when the other women swarmed back into the room.

Kadiffe yelped. "That window's broken."

"I'm letting air in," Merida said.

"Air?" Kadiffe shrieked. "The foreigners want to kill us all! Merida has vandalised the place. Guards! Guards!"

"Fresh air is healthy. You should read the treatise, *Air Quality and the Reduction of Sickness*. In Riverland, we open the windows every morning, and we spend much of each day outdoors."

"I piss on Riverland!" Kadiffe marched off in search of a greenbelt.

Merida turned towards the window, bathing her face in the light and air before it could be nailed shut again. She would have to suppress her anger and to pretend she was adapting for a little longer. Rescue would arrive in two moons, four at the most. Soon, she would be back in civilised Riverland.

Until then, she would have to put up with the noise, the dirt, the stupidity, and pretend to like it. Hopefully, the Consort would summon her again soon, pulling her for a short time out of the morass of boredom. Playing Siege with him, she could measure her mind against a worthy opponent.

That evening, Teruma, stylus and wax tablet in hand, took her aside. "I wonder if you could explain something to me about the Riverian language. I've been studying the basics, but the word 'modesty' stumps me. I believe it's an important concept in your culture, but it doesn't translate well. What does it mean?"

Merida was glad to help. "Modesty is one of the four Virtues," she explained. "It's an attitude as well as a behavioural code, and is mostly about what not to do: for example, not drawing attention to oneself with bright colours or adornment, and not rousing lust in others through movement or baring flesh."

"Ah." Teruma made a note on her tablet. "It's as I thought, then: a translation problem. In Quislaki, we don't have a word for just that. Our word 'modesty' is less specialised. It encompasses many other things, such as not boasting of one's achievements and status, or of the superiority of one's family or nation."

"Riverian modesty includes all that too," Merida hastened to add. "Modesty means refraining from all forms of boasting and arrogance."

"Really?" Teruma's brows rose two finger-breaths and stayed there. "You surprise me, Merida. You surprise me very much."

While preparing for bed, Merida puzzled over the head-wife's comment. Did it imply that Merida was boasting, that she lacked Modesty? True, she had let everyone know her value points, but that was only courteous. True, she had emphasised Riverian superiority in certain things, but that was only because she wanted to be helpful. Without Riverian example, how could the harem women aspire to better minds, lifestyles and morals?

As she snuggled into her blanket, her fingers found a lump in the hem. She examined it: half the body of a cockroach, wrapped in silver thread and tingling with faint magic. Whatever the purpose, it was an amateur's attempt. Merida guessed it was Kadiffe trying to harm her with a primitive spell. Quietly, she disabled it and went to sleep as if she had not seen it, letting the perpetrator believe the malice was working.

≈

Kirral inspected his moustache in the mirror of polished bronze. Stiff and sharp, the shape still lacked originality. He applied another layer of beeswax and experimented with angles.

All day, he had written letters, signed agreements, seen to dull tasks, and the evening offered little entertainment. Just the usual harem women, or Siege with a greenbelt.

Shall we invite the Riverian? How will she react to the little entertainments?

Yes. He had a couple of things to show her. Studying Merida's reactions was always educational, especially when denied something she thought was her right. He would take something away from her. Maybe her trouser suits, or the boots she insisted on wearing.

Why don't we give her something she wants? Something she yearns for deep down, such as appreciation?

Kirral tweaked one side of his moustache up, the other down, and contemplated the effect: an interesting symmetry, but not the kind Riverians liked. He rubbed another blob of beeswax between his fingers and massaged it into the moustache to stiffen the shape. Yes, luring Merida with appreciation would be interesting, especially once she realised she had been fooled.

When Merida breezed into the room, she wore a cheerful smile. "Life in the harem is such fun I'm learning all sorts of things I'd never thought I'd do. Painting my face, playing finger cymbals, bellydancing."

Kirral raised his arms in greeting. "Your visits are a breath of fresh air. Such a welcome stimulation. Not many people possess your intellect."

She stopped, a hint of suspicion in her face, her shoulders tense, her head tilted, and her eyes thin. Then she straightened and inclined her head in acknowledgement.

Kirral pushed on. "You obviously possess a cultured taste. I want to consult you about the interior decorations again. What kind of lamps do you suggest?"

"Square." Her shoulders relaxed, and her face grew animated. "These round bowls and wreath shapes are pretty and no doubt appealing to undeveloped tastes, but for the cultured mind, the aesthetically most pleasing design is a perfect square."

"I remember you recommended four-part symmetry for the new friezes."

"You can get further harmony by putting them in the centre of each wall."

"I was told two thirds were the most aesthetically pleasing arrangement."

"For the uncultured mind only. But the refined intellect values perfect balance. In Riverland we aim for absolute symmetry in everything."

Shall we spring our surprise now or enjoy the suspense a little longer?

"Thank you for enlightening me." Kirral rubbed his hands. She had taken the bait. "Should I have it repainted at all? Or are murals unsophisticated?"

"Painting is one of the highest art forms," she told him. "Almost as permanent as architecture and sculpture, and therefore nearly as valuable."

"Are there high and low art forms then? What are the lowest?"

"Music and dance. They are impermanent, existing only in the moment in which they are performed."

Kirral stored that information for future use. "The artist has already submitted her sketches for the new friezes. I would cherish your opinion on them."

Merida followed him eagerly through the curtain-hung doorway into the adjoining chamber where four narrow bands of pale linen lay stretched on the carpet. "I'm not at all certain if they are realistic."

She bent a knee to study the repeated motif of the first charcoal sketch. Kirral saw her jerk when she realised the man was copulating with the goat. Instantly, her features composed, and she picked up the second piece, a nude reclining woman being pleasured by a monkey.

Merida dropped the sketch in disgust and stood, glowering. But obviously her curiosity won, and she glanced at the other images: three dogs licking a woman's breasts and genitals, and a woman hanging under a donkey's rump for copulation.

Blood coloured her cheeks.

"Do you not approve, dear Merida?"

She crossed her arms over her chest and raised her chin. "The whole series is tasteless." Her voice barely trembled. "One might expect an adolescent boy to appreciate this kind of thing."

"Tasteless, yes, I feared so." Kirral rolled up the sketches. "It is astonishing what artists believe my taste to be. I shall have to give more precise instructions."

She blinked.

Are we letting her leave now, or shall we show her the other exhibit?

"Do you favour fish, Merida?"

"Paintings of fish would be delightful."

"I have purchased a display of living fish. Come, enjoy them."

He led the way into his third chamber, and lit the wicks of a lamp bowl, illuminating the six narrow, vertical glass vases on the table. "The traders who still come to Quislabat charge incredible prices, but the expense is worth it. These vases are Darrian glass. No glass-blower from Quislak could make glass so fine that it is almost invisible."

"A Riverian glass-blower could." Then her hand flew too her mouth. Each narrow upright container held a single red-shimmering fish, their tails down and their heads just under the surface, with almost no room to move. "Fish need space to swim. Put them into one big bowl."

"Oh no. These are fighting fish. If they get together, they kill one another. Do you see how they change colour? That is because they feel anger with one another. Sit over there and watch."

Kirral relaxed into a divan. The shimmer changed from blue to purple while tails flapped against glass and mouths gasped up for air. Even more interesting were the changes in Merida's face, the working of the muscles around her mouth, the teeth gnawing at her lip. "Purple means they're angered by the presence of another male, and when their fury grows unbearable, they go red, even yellow. That is the painful stage, and they stay in this state until they have killed another fish or exhausted their energy. Then they return to blue. Fascinating, is it not?"

She squeezed her balled fist together. "Why do you have to hurt them so much?"

Kirral folded his hands behind his neck and stretched out his legs. "They are hurting themselves, which is more entertaining. They choose to work themselves into a state of pain."

"Please release them."

She wants it. Shall we test how much?

"My dear Merida, If I offered you the choice between letting you go, and freeing those fish—what would you choose?"

"Will you?"

"Educational as it would be to watch your dilemma, I will forgo that pleasure. You and the fish are both too entertaining to let you go. Observing fish tells me a lot about the nature of human beings; these fish serve an educational and therefore worthy purpose, do you not think?"

She took the bait. "If you want to learn about human nature, observe humans."

"I will, dear Merida, I will. I learn so much from observing human responses." He snapped the trap shut. "You shall watch. Have dinner with us tomorrow night."

⁓

Kirral surveyed the guests he had invited to dinner, so many that the chairs at either side of the table had to be replaced with benches. It was going to be very educational.

Teruma's nose crinkled. These days, she disapproved of most of his experiments, but she had the sense not to interfere when they were underway. Haurvatat, the plump Darrian, had painted her face for the occasion and wore a low-cut silk dress in attention-screaming red. She kept leaning forward into Kirral's field of vision, rolling her shoulders to make her cleavage heave. Prim Merida had enclosed herself in a stiff trouser suit and piled up hair into four towers of strictest symmetry.

The Queen looked more than ever like an oversized flour sack, but the eight commoners were clearly overawed to be in her presence. Without exception, they had dressed beyond their station, probably in borrowed garb. They clutched their wine beakers as if terrified of spilling a drop. Kirral hoped they were not too intimidated for conversation. Having found eight natural stutterers, he looked forward to hearing them talk.

As servants piled the table with platters, the men's eyes widened: roast lamb and crispy chicken, fried sparrows and pickled mice, lentils and chickpeas, slices of okra and aubergine, and a nutty soup where carrots bobbed amidst specks of pepper and curls of onion.

The Queen clapped her hands. The door curtain lifted once more, and in came the peacocks, a procession of stately birds dragging long tails behind them.

All the guests managed to hide their confusion by focusing on the food. Only Merida's nostrils twitched. A year ago, when the Queen kept leopards as pets, guests had been more disconcerted when she had the leashed animals brought for feeding in the dining room.

The men, shy in the presence of royals, dared not speak. Every clearing of a throat, every splash of pouring wine, every squeaking of a spoon drawn across the bottom of a bowl sounded loud.

The Queen paid no attention to her subjects, but stuffed herself with food, pausing only to toss bread to her tailed companions.

Shall we start livening things up?

"Have some lamb, my dear Merida," Kirral invited. "It is so young, it has tasted neither grass nor its mother's milk."

The corners of her mouth turned. "Riverians don't eat dead animals. Eating flesh soils the body and weakens the mind."

"Eeeeee!" Haurvatat clasped her throat, staring white-faced at the bowl of glazed figs before her. She had discovered the large spider topping the dish, dead with its legs curled inwards.

"You do not fancy the figs?" Kirral asked pleasantly. "I had them prepared especially for you. Aren't they your favourite?"

Haurvatat retched.

Teruma pressed a cup of water into her shivering hand.

"Spiders," Haurvatat croaked. "Spiders are terrible!"

"A phobia," Merida said authoritatively. "Many people have them. Mine is rodents. Drink the water. Then we'll go into the garden for some fresh air. That will make you feel better." She rose.

"Poor Haurvatat has my permission to leave, of course." Kirral put a concerned father's kindness into his voice. "You, dear Merida, will stay."

While Haurvatat headed to the door, Merida demanded, "How did a dead spider get into the food? Don't the cooks check the dishes before serving? In Riverland..."

Teruma cut the lecture short. "I know, in Riverland you eat only living spiders."

A flash of anger blazed from Merida's eyes, but she quickly contained it behind lowered lids.

As if the spider incident was proof that the royal table was part of the normal world, the strangers relaxed. The tension vanished from their shoulders, and they piled their plates.

Soon they would talk, and then the fun would start.

"Wi-will you pass me the ch-chi-chickpeas please?" the heavy-muscled wheelwright asked.

The other pushed the bowl at him. "Help yours-s-self."

Kirral rubbed his hands under the table.

"How d-d-dare you mock me!" Both their faces reddened as brightly as the bellies of the fighting fish, but after a quick glance at the Queen, they fell silent.

For a long time, resentment simmered as the diners fought to suppress their fury in the royal presence, their lips pressed tightly together, their nostrils flaring. Kirral waited, and watched.

The Queen kept on eating, and feeding her peacocks.

"Have you tried the aubergines?" Merida said to the man on her left.

"De-de-de-licious," he replied.

"B-b-bastard!" The wheelwright shook a meaty fist in the air. A flush of angry blood coloured his face.

The strangers glared at each other across the table. Moments later, they had jumped up, embarrassment and anger making them forget their manners. The first arm shot out, a punch landed. Red blood streamed, and eyes blackened.

Wine spilled. Sauce splattered. Merida held her food bowl out of the way of the flying fists.

Kirral sat back comfortably, with his outstretched legs crossed at the ankles, and traced the zigzags of his moustache. It had taken time to find natural stutterers with a short temper, but it was worth it.

As fists hammered and stuttered insults flew, the Queen said, "This is not nice. I don't like these men." She dipped a piece of bread into the sauce. "Punish them."

"At once." At Kirral's shouted order, the greenbelts waiting outside dragged the prisoners away. "My dear Merida, choose the punishment. Shall we cut off their fists or tear out their tongues?"

Merida pressed a hand across her mouth as if she was about to vomit. "I refuse, Highness."

"Then each man shall decide for himself." Kirral smacked is lips. "These sparrows are the best I have ever sampled."

Dinner had been a great success, and Merida's presence had added interest to the research.

Shall we have some real fun with Merida next time?

Kirral licked his lips. Yes.

∝

Back in her apartment, Teruma sat on her hardest divan. Worry tugged at her stomach. Kirral's obsession with cruel games was escalating as if he were possessed by a djinn. Of course, those creatures existed only in myths, but... A shutter fell aside in Teruma's mind. All those years ago, Kirral's first act on becoming Royal Consort was to outlaw the study of djinns—precisely what a djinn host would do to keep his secret.

For two decades, he had played with the minds of harem inmates and condemned criminals. Recently, he had started tormenting both bystanders and friends. Did djinns stir their hosts to greater evil as the years passed? Teruma had to find out. But since the study of djinns was forbidden, few people possessed information, and fewer would admit to it.

Teruma took the scroll she had confiscated on Merida's arrival from the trunk. *Malevolent Parasitic Entities and their Threats to the Ignorant Human.* She tapped it on her desk. Her knowledge of the Riverian language was too limited to read the work. She sent for Merida.

∝

The Riverian arrived with her arms crossed over her chest and her chin struck rebelliously forward. "What do you want?"

Teruma treated her to a disarming smile. "Thank you for helping Haurvatat. You did well." When Merida's posture relaxed, Teruma poured mint tea for them both. "Have you settled into your new life?"

"Very well, thank you," Merida said stiffly. "Everything is lovely, the food, the bellydance lessons."

Teruma sipped, studying Merida's prim garments and stiff stance. "It must be pleasant not to have anything to do."

"There's no virtue in idleness."

"I m sure we can find work for you. You said you'd not work magic, so perhaps you will empty and scour the slop buckets."

An angry flush coloured Merida's cheeks. "That's low-value work."

"Aren't you a low-value person now?" Teruma asked softly. "Perhaps even below zero. Criminals, prisoners, concubines... If you don't like the slop buckets, there's no useful work for you here. Unless you're able to do translations."

Merida swallowed the bait. "I speak and write six languages."

Teruma tossed the treatise into her lap.

"You!" Merida gasped. "You stole it."

"Took charge of it," Teruma corrected. "For your protection. You might have been imprisoned for bringing subversive literature into this country."

"Aren't I a prisoner anyway?" Merida snapped, revealing her true attitude. The act of being happily settled was a sham.

"Can you translate it into Quislaki, or would that be too difficult?" Teruma asked pleasantly.

"I can translate anything, but isn't the study of djinns forbidden?"

"Are you sure this isn't too difficult?"

Merida pondered, then lifted her chin. "I'll need a quiet private apartment, so I can concentrate on the task."

Teruma laughed. "As a qualified magician of the eleventh degree, you are not able to close your mind to distractions?"

"Someone will see me writing about a subversive subject."

"Don't worry. You're the only concubine who can read."

When Merida had left, Teruma reviewed the report of the silver discovered in Tajlit. If her suspicion about Kirral proved correct, she would push on with her plans for a Samil Empire. This meant that nobody must learn about the silver until Teruma was ready to exploit it. She did not want the revenue to flow into the Quislaki treasury. It would be needed to finance the new empire's standing army.

Teruma, Empress of the Samil. The title had a nice ring to it. Much better than 'head-wife'.

She refined the story of her mythical Samili ancestress, improving on what she had invented for Dahoud. To stir native emotion, the girl had to survive a massacre when the heroic mother shielded the child with her dying body. Storytellers would enrich the tale with a kindly shepherd, a barren noblewoman or a she-wolf.

Next, she needed to place more allies in the Samil. Dahoud was the right man in the right place. Who else could she put in a position of power?

She scanned several personal dossiers. Tarkan Ladysson. Educated in law and in statecraft. Descended from an aristocratic family. Raised in the Samil. Diplomatic. Well-mannered. Ambitious. Currently, Lord Govan's councillor of law. Almost certainly a men-lover, though he hid it well. Teruma liked men with secrets which she could threaten to expose. She caressed the scroll.

Then there was Merida. Her greatest use lay in keeping Kirral occupied. While he experimented with her principles, he did not commit atrocities.

Intelligent, with courage and conscience, able to call rain, Merida might become useful, if only she was more perceptive, far-sighted and adaptable. Viewing palace life as primitive, she would never cope with the harsh realities of the Samil. Nor would she willingly go to the Samil.

Teruma placed the Merida dossier with the other Samil scrolls, next to the one about Dahoud. Here was an interesting combination, worth thinking about.

⇌

When Merida returned to the harem, Kadiffe waved her fist, rattling bangles. "He should have invited me to dinner! I'm his favourite! You have no right to his affections."

"Leave me in peace."

"You've bewitched him! You've made me invisible to him!"

"I did no such thing," Merida said. "I wouldn't if I could, and I could not."

"Oh yes, you did. You muttered things in your foreign language, and you burnt my toenail clippings!"

"Because they were unhygienic. You left them on the rug before my bed."

"You're a spy, sent to poison our Queen with your magic."

"The Queen is in fine health. Now let me sleep."

Merida climbed into her bed, ready to wrap herself into serene mediation. Her toes touched a lump. Hairy, cold, stiff.

She tossed the blanket off and checked the object in the shine of an oil-lamp: A rodent corpse with slick brown fur, naked tail, and glassy eyes, the mouth gaping with yellow teeth.

Merida's stomach heaved. She slid into fighting stance number 18, The Angry Bear, with spread legs, bent knees, and both hands fisted before her. "Who did this?"

Giggles ran around along the bed-benches. Only Haurvatat was quiet, looking almost as sick as when she had discovered the spider, and reached for her idol shelf.

Kadiffe clapped. "Rats like sorcery. They always bed down with a sorceress."

"Sorcery! Sorcery!" a dozen voices chorused. Several women slid out of bed to advance on Merida. Their rhythmical hisses came closer. "Sorcery! Sorcery! Sorcery!"

Merida's fury pulsed as a painful purple cone in her chest, and the thin thread of disciplined patience snapped. "You want sorcery? I'll give you sorcery!"

She banged a copper tray on the floor, and placed a lit oil-lamp in its centre. With much head-tossing, she danced around it, chanting ominously, "Go to sleepland and beyond, the moon shines on the duckling pond," followed by another lullaby, "One, two three, sister catch a bee. Two, three, four, brother catch a boar."

Jaws dropped. Eyes widened. Bodies backed away.

Merida flicked her fingers at the flames. In a sinister voice, she recited the multiplication tables in her mother tongue, and drew the Riverian sign for 'public latrines' mysteriously in the air. When she howled four times like a wolf, the women's auras tinged green with fear.

Haurvatat trembled. "Please call off your magic! You can borrow my gods and sleep in my bed."

"No, thanks. I'll sleep next door. The one who put the rat into my bed will suffer, and so will the one who tried to harm me with the cockroach spell."

She grabbed her writing supplies and strode to the social room which was empty at this hour.

Who had done this to her? It had to be someone who knew about her rodent phobia. Teruma was devious, but sticking dead rats into bedding was hardly her style. Kirral would do it only if he could be around to see the response. Haurvatat was too kind to play nasty tricks, but she might have traded Merida's secret to Kadiffe. Merida could trust no one.

The parchment supplied by Teruma was unevenly cut and dirty, with previous writing scraped off by an unskilled hand. Merida dipped her quill into the slimy ink, wishing she had thought to bring her inkstick with her. She placed the title on the first sheet, as symmetrically as the flawed shape allowed. The ink splotched on the uneven surface.

Treatise on Malevolent Parasitic Entities and their Threats to the Ignorant Human, from Scroll 414 of the collected works of the Most Virtuous Scholar Magician, Helva Hein, Magician of the 14th Degree, Personal Value 288; translated by Merida Karr, Magician of the 11th Degree, Personal Value....

There was the problem again. Her personal value was minus 13. But once Mother had rescued her, she would resume her career and her status as magician. *Personal Value 95.*

She started putting the great Helva Hein's words into Quislaki. Djinns gained nourishment by compelling their humans to do evil. The more evil acts a host committed, the more the djinn grew, and the more evil it demanded in the future. Possessions were most common among men, and always began in adolescence. The great scholar magician speculated that djinns selected boys who had potential for greatness. They promised to fulfil a desperate need, and the boys agreed without understanding what was involved. At first, the djinns satisfied the boys' desires, then they added variations which over the years grew into horrific evil. By the time the hosts were grown men and understood the situation, it was too late.

Each djinn apparently had a speciality. Some made their hosts rape, others made them strangle strangers or mutilate children. Djinns could be neither killed nor exorcised, and a host's suicide multiplied their number. At best, a host could hope to starve them into weakness, but djinns retaliated with painful withdrawal symptoms, and manipulated their hosts by perverting their good intentions into evil deeds. Helva Hein also noted that some djinns suddenly changed their techniques, taking their hosts by surprise. Most hosts did not even try to resist anyway, but simply enjoyed the pleasures of evil.

Merida wondered why Teruma sought to read the treatise. Did she know someone possessed by the djinn? Or was it a case of royals doing what they forbade their subjects?

She worked on the translation until her eyes tired in the sparse light, and exhaustion clawed at her mind. She brushed pastry crumbs from a sagging divan and stretched out on it, covering herself with the scraps of fabric that were the women's embroidery projects.

Just as sleep finally washed over her, a series of screams from next door shrilled her awake.

Merida hurried into the dormitory. Kadiffe thrashed. "My baby, I'm losing my unborn child!"

Concubines were kneeling by her bed and holding her hands.

Merida knew better. Pregnancy created a pale blue aura; Kadiffe's aura was unaffected. The concubine was pretending.

"Shut up and let us sleep," Merida said, but nobody listened to her explanation about auras.

They just cooed over Kadiffe.

Faked moans and panicked chatter lasted the night. In the morning, Kadiffe called servants to carry her to the royal healer, and returned with a face full of triumphant pain. "I have lost my baby!" She pointed a long finger at Merida. "It's her fault!"

"You never carried a child," Merida said. "Nobody here is pregnant. That's obvious."

They all looked at her with horror and hatred in their eyes. "Sorceress!" they chorused, as if their barren state was her fault. "Sorceress!"

A woman in greenbelt uniform pushed the entrance curtain aside, interrupting Kadiffe's hysterics, and dipped her lance. "Pray for her Luminous Majesty. The Great Queen has been taken ill. She retches all the time. Her sight is blurred, her belly burns, her whole body is bathed in fever. The healer suspects sorcery."

All stares pointed at Merida.

CHAPTER 15

The Bride Arrives

Dahoud pushed the residency door open to shoulder his duties as the new satrap. His nose picked up an odour that had not been there before. Charred wood and wool.

In the study, the shelves lay toppled, the imposing chair thrashed to splinters amidst a stink of piss. The mural of the Queen had the eyes scratched out. The roof surrounding the courtyard sagged above broken pillars. The statues lay tossed in a pile, their noses and genitals smashed. Of Koskara's records only a heap of ash remained, with orange sparks glowing at fragment edges.

Dahoud's stomach felt as if someone had filled it with pebbles. While he was convening with the crones, Mansour's men had ransacked the place. He refused to let this intimidate him.

From the groves across the river came the rhythmic *thwack-thwack-thwack* of sticks hitting against branches. With a show of calm, Dahoud walked across the broken bridge into the olive grove.

The place smelled of parched grass and distant cooking fires. A faint wind took the edge off the heat but sucked the last moisture from the plants. Dogs yelped, children squealed, and shadufs creaked under the weight of precious river water. Nearly a hundred Koskarans were at work, mostly nomads who had come to town while the land was too dry to nourish their flocks.

He picked up a harvest staff.

Mansour, with a bulky basket on his back, eyed him up and down. "This work is too hard for a Quislaki quill-twiddler."

"I've picked olives in Djildit." His clan had worked as hired harvesters for the dry season when Dahoud was ten. He slammed the stick into the nearest tree to bring the fruit raining down on blankets.

Hour after hour, day after day, he whacked his staff against the branches, even during the hottest hours when the hired nomads napped in the shade. His face burnt and blistered, his sweat streamed, and his shoulders ached under the cumbersome sacks he lugged to the oil mill.

After eight days of labour, his efforts were acknowledged with curt nods, and after ten, people forgot he was the enemy long enough to pass him a waterskin.

The fruit and the oil pressed from might hold off the worst poverty from Koskara. Yet, he would have to send it as tribute to Quislak. He did not say it. The staff-armed harvesters would rather beat a satrap to death than pay their oppressors a single jar.

On the first day of olive moon, the arrival of a small caravan caused a stir. Many workers dropped their staffs, running to see who had arrived.

Dahoud kept working. Only twelve days remained until the Feast of the Stallion when he would be judged. He hoped he had read Mansour right and the period was a test. If Mansour planned a simple execution, scheduled on a public feast day to entertain the masses, Dahoud would not find out until it was too late. But he would stick to his decision and stay. At least, there were no lives at risk but his own.

Yora returned, panting with excitement, "Dahoud, Dahoud! It's a Quislaki lady who claims she's your bride."

Could it be Esha? While his heart yearned to have his marriage proposal accepted, his head saw a gazelle wandering into leopards' hunting grounds.

Curious children swarmed around the camels kneeling by the residency. The palest animal bore a large, fringe-trimmed litter. Its curtain was lifted, and the pretty woman inside waved regally. Esha.

He hurried to welcome her.

"The Consort informed me that you were seeking my hand in marriage." Esha's voice sang like a bird at dawn.

"I'm honoured that you've come." Having sent the written proposal a moon ago, he had not expected to hear from her for three moons at least, let alone to see her in person, before his own position was secure. "I'll take you to the caravansary."

"Not to our residency?"

"The guest rooms are being refurbished."

"The caravansary will be absolutely adequate for now." Her dazzling smile did not waver even as she glanced over his olive-stained tunic and his dusty bare feet. Taking his hand, she descended gracefully. The polished copper disks on her pink dress threw red sun-glints.

When she linked her arm through his, he caught a whiff of her flowery scent. Clean and fresh as a cooling breeze, she strode at his side, her silks rustling and her anklets clinking with every step. He guided her quickly past the vandalised workshops, speeding his steps so she would not have time to be offended by the anti-Quislak graffiti.

Esha's dainty feet stepped over piles of horse apples, and skirted around fresh cakes of cow dung. She never ceased smiling. From windows and workshops, curious faces gawked. Dahoud wondered how many of them were already scheming her death. She raised a hand and tilted her head to the side in the graceful gesture of a noblewoman greeting her subjects. Her retinue and the flock of curious children followed. A herd of cattle rumbled past, throwing up clouds of dust.

At the caravansary, the landlord gaped and bowed. Dahoud glanced at Esha's retinue. He had never made arrangements for servants before. For how long should he book the room? The sooner Esha ended her visit, the safer, but she might need more than one night's rest.

Esha took over. "I'll have your best, finest, coolest room," she instructed in her clear voice. "Another room for my companion." She nodded at a small, leather-clad woman. "For several days. My retinue will sleep on the roof and depart at dawn. I borrowed them from the satrap of Djildit and he will be anxious to have them back. Make a comfortable bed in my chamber for my dog. Cloud is most sensitive, and exhausted from the journey." She turned to Dahoud. "Wait for me in the dining room."

"There's no dining room," Dahoud said. "A tavern down the road serves food at dusk."

"I'm hungry now."

The landlord bowed many times in rapid succession. "I can serve light refreshments in the courtyard. Figs, or yoghurt if you prefer."

"We'll have figs," Dahoud said at once, just when Esha said, "Yoghurt."

"Yoghurt," he hastened to agree.

"Figs," Esha said at the same time.

Their laughter met and mingled. Her smile warmed his chest, but he dared not let it reach his heart, because he was not worthy of her.

While she retired to freshen up, he checked the courtyard and found it a dump where chickens sheltered under broken furniture from the sun. He carried the two least-splintered benches and an almost intact table to a corner where a faded awning made the heat less broiling.

He thought about marriage, its dangers and its gifts. Some women did not resent coupling with men. He had heard that some even sought the embrace, not for gain, but for pleasure, enjoying the act as much as men did. Perhaps that was true, although in twenty-five years, he had never felt a woman's willing touch.

When a figure emerged from the door, it was not Esha, but her leather-clad companion. "A word please, Lord Dahoud."

She was the first person to address him with his title. "Please, sit." he said. "Is Esha coming?"

"Esha always needs time to change." She chose the part of the bench with the least chicken droppings and swivelled her legs to sit. "Have you appointed your councillors yet?"

"I'm sorry if you've come all the way in the hope of a job. My council will be Koskarans only."

"I am Koskaran, Lord Dahoud." She raised her chin. "I'm also statecraft-qualified."

If this was true, she was the answer to his problems. He studied her: a young face, but lined with worries and pinched around the mouth. Age unguessable, probably a few years older than he. Her hawk-alert eyes and straight posture, with both hands open on the table, exuded openness and confidence. Small, so slender to be almost thin, but filled with wiry energy. No breasts to speak of.

"Tell me about yourself. Do you have family?"

"All Koskaran. Mother: potter, dead. Father: trader, dead. Five siblings: dead." Her voice was as dry as a stalk of straighthorn grass.

"Married?"

"That is hardly relevant." Her glare told him she thought his question impertinent. "I'm Keera Pottersdaughter. The first Samili to attend statecraft school. One of the few women to qualify. The best student of my year."

He filled the second beaker and pushed it at her. "How did you get to study statecraft?"

"I grew up here Koskara Town, picked up skills from visiting traders, taught myself to write, then worked as a scribe for local businesses. Then I took a job in Quislabat which led to work for the royal family, and finally to statecraft school. I graduated as the top student, hailed as success. Alas." She shrugged one shoulder. "Satraps don't give senior positions to Samilis. While my peers landed councillor jobs, I was lucky to get any work at all."

Dahoud nodded. He knew a Samili's prospects in the Quislaki bureaucracy, and for a woman it was even tougher.

She lifted the beaker, took a sip. "Half a year as a palace clerk, until Teruma made me her assistant."

"Does Teruma know you're here?"

A smile curled the corners of her lips. "She suggested it."

Dahoud needed competent councillors with the skills he lacked, and Teruma was a shrewd judge of character.

"I'm familiar with etiquette, I know the laws like a lawyer, and I'll do almost anything for a councillor position," she offered. "Give me a chance, and I'll find a solution to any problem. I'm sure you have plenty of problems, Lord Dahoud."

"What new satrap doesn't?" He was not going to reveal his half-formed strategies to a stranger. He wanted to welcome Keera, but the position of councillor in his government was as safe as a job shepherding leopards. "I'm not making appointments yet."

She studied him. "Because of the Feast of the Stallion? I can wait twelve days. In the meantime, you face a challenge greater than any satrap before you: you need to be accepted as one of Koskara's own." She stroked a hand down her chin. "Until you prove otherwise, people will assume you're like Zetan, extorting taxes and killing priests. You know what he did to the boys at the school, don't you?"

"I've heard the rumours."

If even a fraction of them were true, it was surprising someone had not killed Zetan sooner. Dahoud had met Zetan once. A courtesy call: the general visiting the local satrap. A pale-faced man, overweight and flabby from lack of exercise, Zetan had been jovial and generous. Nothing about him had suggested child abuse. On the other hand, Zetan's arrogance towards the natives had been evident, and his errors of judgement had fuelled the rebellion.

As a rule, Quislak left locals to worship whom and how they pleased. The Koskarans had abused this religious freedom and rallied around the priesthood. The high priest preached resistance; his priests spread the rallying cry, the temples became centres of rebellion. Zetan's patience snapped. He had the high priest arrested to force his submission, but the old man had died under torture without giving in.

Zetan declared the high priest had been an imposter whom he had executed to protect Koskaran spirituality. He found – allegedly with divine guidance—the true high priest, a compliant pro-Quislak candidate. All other priests above the age of fourteen were killed.

The priests' martyrdom fanned the rebellion into a fire that only the Black Besieger's brutality could quench.

As far as Dahoud knew, the Quislak-approved high priest kept to his mountain monastery where he trained a new generation of suitably meek priests, and ventured into Koskara Town only twice a year to officiate at major festivals.

Dahoud would have to tread very carefully in matters of religion. In matters of children, too, it seemed. In all matters. Any step he took might place his foot into a cow pad or a trap.

"I'll prove I'm not like Zetan."

"If I may make a suggestion." Keera stroked the rim of her beaker. "The residency stands for everything the Koskarans hated about Zetan."

Dahoud nodded. "It's been trashed by vandals and needs complete refurbishment before we can move in. It will be difficult to get locals to do the work."

Her leathery lips pursed. "The law requires a satrap to have a residency. It doesn't say he has to live there. You can use it to store council records and live in a townhouse."

He liked the idea at once. "Or in a yurt?"

"Or in a yurt," she confirmed. "It will take the edge off their anger."

"This is a good thought. Thanks." He considered her face again, the pointed chin, the leathery skin, the pinched lips. "I'm sure you were a useful asset for Teruma. Why are you giving up that job and coming back here?"

"To be councillor," she said. "That's what I want to be, and of course I want to help Koskara. I want that more than anything else in the world, and I will do what it takes. You can count on me."

"I think we may be able to help each other. If you're not afraid." Dahoud smiled. He liked Keera's direct manner, competent thinking and undisguised ambition. "About the priests: I understand that Zetan -"

Then Esha drifted into the courtyard in a cloud of blue silk.

Dahoud rose at once and bowed. "Sit here, so you don't have the sun in your eyes."

The landlord carried a bowl of yoghurt, a platter of figs, spoons, beakers, and a jug of citron water with mint sprigs floating. He hung around to water the wilting pot plants, sneaking glances at Esha.

"Leave us," Dahoud told him.

Keera jumped up. "Is the olive harvest on? Then I'll make myself useful. It's been a long time since I thwacked a stick."

Alone with his bride, Dahoud squinted at the chattering chickens that waited to pick crumbs from the ground. He had to advise her to leave Koskara for her safety, and to admit he was djinn-possessed.

"Is your room comfortable?" he asked. "Do you have everything you need?"

"Quite comfortable, thank you." She tilted her head and played with her hair.

He cleared his throat. "Esha, you can't stay here."

Her eyes widened with alarm. "Don't you want me?"

He could smell her perfume, her hair, her skin. Her locks danced around the white skin of her neck, down over her tunic, over the swell of her breasts. "I'm glad you've accepted my proposal. Only... I didn't expect you so soon."

"I departed as soon as Kirral informed me of your proposal. I managed to arrive here so fast because we didn't travel by camel all the way. Camels are unbearably slow. Instead, we took a river barge all the way to Djildit Town. And I didn't endanger your secret either." She beamed a grey-eyed smile. "I know all about your secret, how you infiltrated innermost rebel stronghold with your cunning disguise, so I didn't tell anyone I was on my way to marrying you. Teruma worked out this clever plan and I pretended to visit Lord Adil in Djildit Town. Because he's widowed, the gossips naturally thought I was going to marry him. Then I pretended to hear for the first time that the Lord of Tajlit was sick, and I visited him as an excuse to travel still further south and get very close to Koskara."

"Good strategy," Dahoud approved. Teruma had thought of everything. Her brilliant plan had not only maintained his cover, but had ensured the rebels did not snatch the pretender's bride to press him into leaving.

Esha smiled as if he had complimented her. "The camels and servants we borrowed from Lord Adil. He's a most amazingly generous man."

"He is." Dahoud remembered Tarkan's father from many years ago. "Perhaps you would like to stay with him for a while. I'm sure he'll enjoy your company."

"I've come to get married."

"Esha, there are a few things you need to be aware of," he said carefully. "Koskara is very hot at this time of the year, and there are some local problems with rebels."

"Teruma says a big wedding will help pacify the locals. She grew up in the Samil, and knows everything about the native people and their quaint traditions. They adore weddings, so we'll have the biggest celebration they've seen for ages, four days long, with lots of food and entertainment. I'll do absolutely anything that's necessary."

A traditional wedding might indeed make them popular. "Anything? Would you be willing, for example, to live in a yurt?"

"A yurt? You mean living a tent?" For a moment, her face stiffened as if she had seen a poisonous spider on her spoon. Then it relaxed, and her eyes narrowed like those of an officer assessing battle plans. "That's a fabulous strategy for getting popular with the natives, and I'm not in the least afraid of discomfort."

She ate little, lifting her spoon daintily with small white hands. She talked about how peacock fans were fashionable at court this season, how tiring the journey had been in the summer heat, and how annoying she found the presence of poultry.

Dahoud drank her beauty as thirstily as a camel sucking up water. Her skin was creamy-white like a lamb's fleece, her hips curved like a succulent fig, and her breasts plump like a pair of cushions to sink his head into.

He had to tell her the truth about himself, but the words stuck in his throat.

"Are you sure you want to wed me?" he managed at last.

"Absolutely, and I'm ever so grateful you asked for me. It was simply the only way for me to escape my horrid betrothal."

"Betrothal?" he repeated.

"To my father's former chief councillor. He seemed destined to become a Lord, but grew addicted to smoking joy-flowers until his mind was utterly befuddled. It was disgusting. When my father sacked him, this failure of a man couldn't find work elsewhere. Now he's a greenbelt at the palace, doing utterly useless things such as carrying standards in processions. If I had to marry that revolting wreck, my daughters would be commoners. I kept petitioning the Consort most fervently to release me from this abominable betrothal. Finally, he let me choose between that appalling feeblehead and a ready-made Lord, which is the most wonderful opportunity. The Mighty Ones have poured the most magnificent gifts into my lap, because my very first daughter will be born a Ladysdaughter... and also because I like you, Dahoud." Her cheeks tinged with a becoming blush. "I can speak freely of it now, can't I? I really think I'm amazingly fond of you."

His heart was aflutter like a bird, ready to soar. A woman liked him. But she did not know the truth yet.

"We need not marry at once. We can delay until you're used to me, and to Koskara."

"Dahoud, I'm fully aware that Koskara is a dreadfully backward province. I've travelled here to marry you and beget a Ladysdaughter. I want to start without delay." Her lash-veiled grey gaze sent hot blushes into his cheeks.

"There's something you need to know. Nobody else in Koskara does." Cold sweat ran down his temples. "I was a soldier once."

"Oh." For a moment, her mouth drooped, but her face quickly recovered its radiance. "It doesn't matter. You're a lord-satrap now. I won't hold your lowly origins against you, or disclose them to anyone."

"Sieges sometimes went on for moons. Soldiers missed female companionship, and -" He broke off, unable to say it.

Esha's lips thinned. She put down her spoon. "Are you a men-lover?"

"What I mean is, when a town was conquered... the captive women... the final act of subduing the enemy... the rights of the victor..."

She blanched. "You raped a lot of women?"

A hen cackled.

"Yes."

She rubbed fingertips across her palm, and her face turned whiter still. "You caught a disease from those women? One of those horrible diseases that mean you can't father a child?"

"I'm healthy."

"Then you're the man I want for a husband, Dahoud. I've researched the great dynasties. Those whose matriarchs choose men from other races always grow healthy, numerous and powerful. I will infuse a Samili strain into my bloodline. How soon can we marry and have our first daughter?"

"It may be a boy," he cautioned.

"I consulted a brilliant soothsayer who said that if I marry you, my first child will definitely be female." She added, "Later, we'll have boys. They can marry into other dynasties to strengthen our connections. I want at least a dozen children."

Dahoud's heart warmed. Unlike his mother, Esha would never abandon a child to die in the desert. If necessary, she would fight fiercely to protect them.

Marriage to a Ladysdaughter would validate Dahoud's position as satrap. Esha, too, would get her most fervent desire from this union, breeding the children she wanted. Most importantly, Dahoud and Esha were fonder of each other than other couples betrothed for political reasons. In time, their affection would ripen into solid love. By bestowing this precious gift, the Mighty Ones had filled his bowl with happiness.

Perhaps he did not need mention the djinn after all. A sweet girl like Esha would never trigger dark desires. Marriage would soothe those angry _usts, and with Esha welcoming him into her arms, surely the days of the djinn's power were past. There was no need to expose this lovely woman to worry, to make her carry his dark burden. No, he would protect her from the tormenting knowledge, and from ever finding out.

CHAPTER 16

The Wedding Night

Koskaran nuptials had more rituals than the royal legions had rules. For the four days of the celebration, the daylight hours were filled with special meals, auspicious garments, soothsayers, whiteseers, bellydancers, priestly blessings, the cutting of hair and the henna-ing of feet. The festivities swept hostility away, and the town oozed goodwill towards the new satrap and his bride.

On the final wedding day, dawn painted dramatic cloud patterns against a cool orange sky. Depilation at the bathhouse was Dahoud's first duty. On the way there, the crone Sirria joined him. Ever since their arrival in Koskara Town, she had kept her distance, but now she walked by his side, her bright scarves fluttering.

"Plucking time? Is Naima doing it?" Her voice oozed mock sympathy. "Did you know that she trained in Riverland and in Darria?"

"Trained in what?"

"Healing and torture." Sirria chuckled.

He recalled the crones talking about a woman passionate about improving healthcare. "Is Naima a healer?"

"Tsk, tsk. If she was a healer, do you think she would want you to know? She manages the bathhouse. Steambaths, scrubbing, depilation, all perfectly legal."

"Of course." If Naima was an illegal healer, it made sense that she had avoided meeting him.

"And personal torture for those who like it. That's what she learnt in Darria, what she's best at. The Darrians let a woman be breeder or a tormentor, a healer or a whore." Her voice dripped with pained cynicism. 'Or a concubine to be discarded when her youth petals fade, when they send her to labour in the mines so they can squeeze some final usefulness out of her. All Darrians are dogs. You know all about Darrians, don't you?"

More than he wanted to remember. "Not really."

She hooked her arm around his. "Now, Dahoud, do you need a little pre-wedding chat with a crone?"

"Do you mean to tell me about the stallion and the mare? Not necessary." He freed himself from her grasp and strode faster.

"Where are your manners?" she called. "When a crone speaks, you stay and listen."

He turned and bowed.

"And you answer her questions." Sirria stabbed a henna-stained finger at him. "Does your bride know what kind of man she's about to wed? Does she know you were in the legions?"

He looked down the road, at the wooden balconies, at the honeysuckle smothering the mudbrick walls. "What makes you think I was in the legions?"

"What makes you think I was always a nomad?" Sirria leant against the wall. "Imagine me eight years younger, in the gown of a Zigazian matron, instead of this." She pulled at the side of her tunic. "Eight years ago, Dahoud. Eight years. Do you remember Ain Ziggur?"

Ain Ziggur. A city he had besieged under Paniour's command, before he had become a general, before he had campaigned in Koskara, before he had started wearing the intimidating mask. He had not expected anyone from those days to cross his path here.

At Ain Ziggur, the djinn had been in charge. Recall squeezed a fist around his throat. The siege. The women. His orders.

While the conquerors beheaded the surviving men, women barricaded themselves into the main temple and refused to come out. Centurion Dahoud had broken the door, and the women's resistance. He had ordered every woman raped.

He would have eaten the dust at Sirria's bare feet if he could undo the past. Nobody must know what kind of man he had been.

The rising sun glared on the town. Already, the air started to cook. The dry air burnt the back of Dahoud's throat.

"Because I remember, Dahoud." Sirria's voice was as sharp and unforgiving as an executioner's sword. "I remember every day the Quislaki legion besieged us, starved us, abused us. I remember our chief tormentor standing in the charred ruins of my home, with the bodies of my husband and my son at his feet. A man named Dahoud."

"Dahoud is a common name. Why do you think there's a connection?"

"Do you think the women of Zigazia would forget that name? Do you think we would forget what you ordered, and what you did? Do you think we would forget your face? You did not wear your famous mask then."

"I'm sorry, Sirria. More sorry than I can say." The words sounded inadequate even to his own ears. "I've changed. I'm not the man I was eight years ago. Can you believe me?"

A string of camels padded softly through the lane, laden with bales.

Sirria waited until they had passed. "I survived, fled to Koskara, became a herder. Then war came to Koskara, too, and with it came evil in the shape of a Quislaki commander, a man without scruples or conscience. A man so ruthless that some said he was possessed by a djinn. A man whose whispered name was enough to make women cower in fear. The Black Besieger." Her eyes pierced him like dagger points. "Did you know that when the Black Besieger died, the women in Koskara lit lamps of joy at every altar?"

It was bad enough if the Koskarans found out about his legion past. If anyone connected him with the Black Besieger, he would have no chance. Far from accepting his rule, they would roast him alive, and if he died, there would be more slaughter in Koskara, more war, more suffering.

He tried a different evasion. "You're happy now as a nomad, aren't you, Sirria?"

Her eyes darkened like thunderclouds. "Does the Black Besieger live? Was his funeral pyre faked?"

Below the tribal tattoo, her left cheek was mutilated, as if someone had slashed it with an angry knife.

"How did you come to Koskara, Sirria?" His palms sweated.

She adjusted her crimson shawl, covering the scar, without taking her eyes off him. "How did you come to Koskara again, Dahoud? How did you dare to?"

Dahoud's stomach knotted so tightly he could feel the pain. He dropped the useless shield of denial and faced his attacker. "I'm sorry for Ain Ziggur, and I'm sorry for every other citadel. I'm sorry for every death and every suffering, but it was in the past, Sirria. I've changed as much as you."

"Doesn't your bride have the right to know she's wedding a beast? Doesn't every woman in Koskara need to know that a monster rules the land?" She stepped so close to him that he could feel her searing breath on his throat. "Why shouldn't I scream the truth from the roof? Why shouldn't I tell Mansour? Why shouldn't I expose you as the impostor you are?"

Dahoud's mouth was drier than desert sand. "What's the price for your silence?"

"When the time comes, I'll let you know." She laughed softly and pointed at a curtain of clay-bead strings. "Here's the bathhouse. Enjoy the experience. Have a water-filled day, my Lord, and a pleasant wedding night."

She floated away in a swish of coloured shawls.

~

"Strip off and stretch out there." The cinnamon-skinned beauty pointed to the heated brick platform and tossed him a towel to drape across his loins. "I like your body hair. I'll start at your chest." Licking her lips, she waved what looked like a Darrian torture instrument in shiny bronze.

Standing at the platform's head-end, she bent so low that her linen-swathed breasts brushed his cheeks. They promised to be high and firm, the perfect size for cupping in a man's hands. Her jasmine perfume teased. Then the bronze pincers pulled one hair after another, inflicting tiny pricks of pain.

"I like seeing strong men helpless before me." Naima's lips curled from one tattooed cheek to another. "I enjoy seeing them struggle for self control."

If only she knew who he was, she would not dare treat him this way. He knew how to make her tremble. He could grab her and pin those arms to the hot platform, and make her flap and struggle and plead for his mercy. She was fortunate he had renounced that part of himself, that she would never meet Dahoud the Black Besieger. He was Dahoud of Koskara now, the protector of women, patient and kind.

"There's so much pleasure to be had from a hairy male body." Her palm slid over his now smooth torso and thighs.

"I hear you trained in Darria. Is it true? Have you been to other places?"

"Darria, Zigazia, Riverland. Now the real fun begins." She whipped the towel off.

His hands shot down to keep her fingers away. "You're not going to pluck down there."

"You must be smooth for your bride tonight. Be a man and let me get on with it."

"Shave it."

"Shaving is no fun at all. Now lie still," she instructed. "Or I'll do it the Darrian way. That's singeing the hair off with glowing nutshells. Burning the hair without scorching the flesh is an art I have not mastered yet. Do you want me to practice between your legs?"

"Keep plucking," Dahoud said through gritted teeth. "How does Koskara compare to Darria and Riverland?"

She ignored his question. As stabs of pain lanced his privates, he sank into the soothing fantasies of what he could do if he still was the Black Besieger. He would grab those wrists and wrestle this female into submission. He would pin her to the platform, rip her tunic with his knife, bare those perky breasts. He would feel her buck and rear beneath him, fighting to free herself. Every moment of her imagined resistance was soothing, sweet, delicious. If only he could experience the pleasure for real, just once more...

Pain jerked him into reality.

"Oh, sorry," Naima said. "Have my pincers pinched your eggs? Does it hurt?"

Her gloating smile did not look as if she was the least bit sorry.

✑

The evening sky flared up in hues of crimson and purple. Esha took her place at the head of the bridal procession around the arena, comfortable in the knowledge that Dahoud was wrong. The Koskarans loved them. At least, they loved her. She could see it in their cheerful waves, their happy faces, their trilling ululations. Her heart rode on the wave of sincere blessings and adoring applause, and her blood sang with excitement. This was her big night, the beginning of her life's purpose. Every astrologer had agreed that the best date of the year for conceiving a female child was the twenty-third night of the olive moon, and a wonderful soothsayer had even guaranteed that she would succeed.

If only she could start begetting a Ladysdaughter at once. But the procession returned to the carved chairs by the altar, and she had to take her place at Dahoud's side while snot-nosed children showered them with wilted rose-petals. She stifled a rising yawn as the fourteenth bellydancer in four days swirled into the arena. The dancer was a vast woman with breasts which nearly reached her navel. She lathered her dance with suggestive gestures, thrusting her hips and rubbing her fingers, making the women spectators roar with approval. Dahoud was leaning forward, seemingly mesmerised by every flick of the scarves and every quiver of the hips, and his fingers drummed the rhythm on the armrests.

Then a priest, dressed in a flame-coloured kilt and a cape of leopard skin, pranced around like a dancing pony. He leaped high, lunged low, shook a rattle, sprinkled milk, chanted in deep tones to bless the couple's fertility. Esha appreciated the purpose of the performance, but wished he would hurry up.

With a smile fixed on her face, she visualised improvements to the arena. The stone steps would be clad in painted wood, and there would be a shaded gallery offering comfort to her family and her guests. A large stone entrance building would welcome the people with life-sized carved reliefs of the Great Queen and her Consort. On top of it, overlooking the arena, a statue of Esha herself, tall in pink marble, the matriarch of her dynasty. Maybe a statue of Dahoud, too. The arena, the whole town, indeed all the province would be transformed into places of beauty and artistry, worthy of the Queendom, and worthy of the new dynasty that was about to be born.

At last, darkness sank like a soft blanket. Dancers with wooden clappers and tambourines led a noisy path to the couple's yurt.

On the way there, Esha glanced at Dahoud. Even in the garish local garments, his body shone with health. When he did not return her gaze, she squeezed his arm to get his attention.

"You need not be frightened," he soothed.

Esha was not afraid. Some women loved marital couplings, others hated them, but either way, fear was a waste of energy. Only conception mattered.

On reaching the yurt, the natives crowded around the couple, kissing their hands and touching them for luck. Esha dipped into the darkness of her new home, and waited for Dahoud to follow. The space was cramped and smelled of wool, with mere cushions and fleeces instead of comfortable beds and divans.

Outside, the drums banged on. People kept dancing around the yurt to wish the couple luck. Their noise and presence intruded into what should be a private time. Esha wished they would leave. At least the yurt shut out curious stares. One of the ancient Quislaki rituals, still extant though seldom enacted these days, demanded public consummation for a Lady and her Lord. This often ended in disaster, because some men could not perform with an audience watching.

Dahoud snuffed the oil lamps and kissed her lightly on the cheek. "Good night, Esha."

The air filled with oily smoke.

"Dahoud, please!"

"Don't be frightened. I won't touch you, I promise."

"You're supposed to. This is our wedding night."

"We can take a long time to get to know each other first," he said softly. "A moon or a whole year or even longer, and nobody needs to know."

Was he planning to back out of his duty? Or had he lied? Was he unable to fulfil his part of their contract? Was he a men-lover after all?

"I want to get pregnant," Esha said firmly. "Now."

"Are you're sure?" He sounded reluctant. "It will probably hurt the first time."

Esha sighed with impatience. Of course the first time hurt. That was one of the facts of life. Childbirth would bring even worse, longer-lasting pain, and she planned to go through that many times. What was a quick stab, if it opened the way to a dynasty?

"I'm not afraid of pain." She slid off her stifling woollen garments.

"Please hurry, Dahoud."

At last, he lay down in her embrace, burying his face in her bosom and sucking like a starving child at its mother's breast. His lips felt hard, hot and hungry. With her arms wrapped around his head, Esha noted that the sensation was surprisingly pleasant. However, creating a child required more than mere fondling. She opened her legs, grabbed his buttocks, pulled him where she knew he needed to be and clenched her teeth. The pain was sharp but ceded soon.

Dahoud was thrusting in time with the drums that still banged outside. His hot breath wafted in her face. Then he started fondling her breasts once more, and groaned as if in pain. To comfort him, she ran a hand through his hair, as if he was a small child in need of comfort.

"I love you," he cried. With a final grunt, he rolled off her.

Esha understood that her husband had delivered his seed. She lay still so that none of it would get spilled. The coupling had not been too bad. She would do it again, as often as was necessary. Since tonight was the most auspicious date of the year, she would get Dahoud to repeat the act at least once. Men needed rest between performances, so she would let him sleep a little before working him again.

≈

Dahoud woke to a hand blazing a trail down over his chest, kindling a thousand fires. He kept his eyes closed in the darkness, pretending to be still asleep, savouring the caressing strokes. Thrills of pleasure pulsed through him. After a lifetime of rejection, a woman wanted him. It was like finding an oasis after a long thirsty walk in the desert.

Esha's fingers slid further down his front, sending his blood racing. "Come on, Dahoud," she whispered.

He drank in her closeness, her smell of milk and roses. If he feigned reluctance, would she increase her efforts? How would it taste to be seduced? "Another time," he muttered.

She pulled his shoulder. "Do your duty!"

Her forceful touch fuelled the flames of desire. She was taking charge, launching an attack. Here was a chance to measure his strength against a female who wanted him. For once, he would submit rather than subdue. His heart pounded louder than a kettledrum.

"Make me." His voice croaked with excitement. "Wrestle me." He imagined her astride him, her thighs straddling him, his arms pinned behind his back, her soft breasts brushing his face. He wanted to feast on those breasts. They were the perfect size to overfill his mouth.

Her hand stopped. "Wrestle?" she asked, as if tasting a slug in her mouth.

"Yes. Fight me." The words came rapidly as he imaged her mounting him. "If you win, I'll serve you in any way you wish. You'll love it."

She withdrew her hand. "I will certainly do no such thing."

"Yes, Esha. Yes." He spoke with the urgency of his pulsing need. "It's a game, we're just playing. It will be such fun. I won't hurt you. I'll even let you win."

"Keep your perverted tastes to yourself," she told him. "I'm not a siege captive. I'm a lady and deserve respect."

"I promise I'll let you win." His loins burnt with the heat of a town on fire. "Pin me, mount me, make me helpless, take what you like."

"Mount you?" She shifted further away. "Don't you know that it's extremely rare to conceive that way?"

"Then pull me on top of you. I'll submit." A woman forcing him to do her will would rub out much of his old guilt. "Please."

"Dahoud! I absolutely refuse to wrestle you. Perverted couplings lead to deformed children. I've researched it."

"Let's just play, we don't have to make children." He tried to press a lid on his passionate craving, but his body burned for her touch. He had to make her understand. "Come, Esha, please!" He ran a finger over her breast.

She slapped it away. "You disgust me!"

Her disdain struck him like the lash of a whip.

Anger and hurt churned in his stomach, and in its scalding spiral, another kind of lust rose. The djinn leapt to life, feeding on Dahoud's frustration and fury. The woman was resisting him, showing him contempt, like all the others. It was time to subdue her, to let her feel who was in charge.

From an arm's length away, Esha said, "There will be no more fondling in future. It only gives you ideas. Only straightforward matings, and only until I'm pregnant."

He could pin her, feel her writhe beneath him. She was practically asking for it. Oh yes, she would wrestle then. She would fight him off with her limited strength, and he would prolong the period of her struggle, then part her legs, and penetrate her, slowly, savouring every moment...

The djinn was gaining the power. This was a battle for Dahoud's integrity, and with every fibre of his body on fire, he was about to lose.

Isn't she asking for it? Won't you take her?

Clenching his teeth so hard it hurt, Dahoud rallied his self-control. No woman was ever asking to be raped. He had learnt to resist the djinn's words, but the urgent fire in his loins was a different matter. Hurriedly, he dressed and went out into the night-cold silence. He would not rape his wife. He would not! Would not. Would not...

CHAPTER 17

The Feast of the Stallion

On the thirteenth day of Olive Moon, Dahoud laboured long after most of the workers had left. Esha had slipped away at noon to beautify herself for the festival. Dahoud stayed to show his willing usefulness, thwacking the stick with violent fervour. Only when the large bright disk of the sun hung low above the horizon, surrounded by a lilac-orange haze, and the last of the olives were stowed in baskets, did he stop.

In the yurt, Esha was oiling her cream-white body. She had laid out his official green tunic, together with the green turban and the purple-fringed armbands.

"Not this one." He searched through the clothes trunk. "Where's the striped tunic I wore to the wedding?"

"I've given it away. The garish nomad colours were ghastly." She pushed the uniform at him. "We must look our best."

If he dressed as a Quislaki greenbelt tonight, the mob would tear him to pieces. That left his patched scarlet tunic, sweat-soaked and oil-smeared from the olive harvest. It was not festive, but it was Samili, and the stains came from honest work. He retied the maroon sash.

"Dahoud, you can't wear those dirty rags tonight. They're an insult to the purple fringe."

"I won't wear the fringe, and you'll look beautiful for both of us." He kissed her cool, rose-scented cheek. "Esha, if anything should happen, if I'm unable to protect you..."

"What should happen? Why would I need protection?"

"This used to be the day when people killed the Lords who displeased them."

"That was when the Koskarans were still wild, before they had four years of civilising Quislaki influence." She laughed a little. "They won't dare to kill you. You're a satrap."

"Just in case, if things get out of hand..." He spoke calmly as if his heartbeat wasn't thumping in his throat. "Tell Mansour you want to leave Koskara. He'll probably let you go unharmed."

"You expect real danger?" She put down her oil jar. "Then, by the Mighty Ones, wear the green tunic and the fringe! They'll respect authority."

"They won't. Hurry. We mustn't let them wait."

"Wrong. We'll arrive when everyone else is assembled, to impress them with our entrance." She dipped her finger into the paint pot and stained her lips crimson. "I'm the Lady, and I represent Quislak. I won't be hurried."

"I'll meet you there." He pecked her on the cheek. "Just be careful."

In his rush, he stumbled across a lump of something outside his tent. A big lump. A human body.

Although he had never seen the man, he knew who it was: only the high priest wore a kilt of leopard skin. This was the hierophant appointed by Zetan. His shaven head had been brutally bashed. Grey and pink matter spilled from the skull, mixed with clots of blood and splinters of bone, and black flies buzzed around the wound. No blood had soaked the soil. Dahoud knelt and probed the dead flesh. The muscles had already stiffened, but the skin colour was still even. He turned the body to check the face. A cloudy film covered the eyes.

The man had been murdered early this day, and his killers had dropped him here, as a message for Dahoud.

Quickly, Dahoud rolled the body away from the tent so Esha would not have to see it, and strode to the festival site. Koskara Town shimmered in the crimson wash of the setting sun.

By the time Dahoud reached the arena, only a glimmering thread of daylight remained. Children chased one another across the patchy grass, squealing. Adults milled around in clusters, murmuring and surging like a swarm of wasps. The town's year-round residents were joined by the harvest workers and hundreds of nomads who had come either to partake of the stallion's flesh or to watch the pretender Lord die.

The chattering stilled as he walked in. Adults nudged one another. Heads turned, gazes followed him. Dahoud took hope from the glow of cooking pits besides the altar. They might signify that people expected the stallion to be killed.

The hard earth still felt hot under his naked soles, but the temperature dropped rapidly, and chills brushed his skin.

Everything depended on whether he had read Mansour right. He only knew that Mansour put Koskara above everything, even his own ambitions. And he had said 'The testing isn't over.' Dahoud hoped the death threat was a test, and that by showing fearlessness he was passing it. If his assessment was wrong, he would die.

The rebel leader met him, dressed in a black tunic with a brown sash, obviously new. "We're waiting, Dahoud of the Desert. I thought you'd run away."

Idrahad, the arrogant trickrider with the plaited hair, was waving the storyteller's staff. "Three men from different countries decide to rape a girl. The well-mannered Darrian bows, saying, 'Allow me to help you to divest yourself of your lower garments. The sudden rising of a certain member forces me to make use of your delectable body.' The Riverian is next. He invokes the virtues of Loyalty, Honesty, Modesty, and Discipline, and says..."

Drums roiled at the entrance, announcing that the stallion had arrived. Idrahad ceased mid-joke. Before the sacrificial animal, strode the Lady Esha, who had timed her entrance so everyone was looking at her, as if the drums and the ululations were all for her. The disks and beads on her white dress glittered in the light of torches. Her silver-blond hair shone. She looked like a goddess. She acknowledged the applause with a regal wave of her hand before walking into the arena. The stallion and its handlers followed behind.

"Pretty," Mansour said.

"Don't harm her."

Mansour laughed. "Why should I?" He joined in the ululations with a deep-throated cry. "You can both leave. Pack up your yurt, your purple fringe and your bride, and ride away. I'll kill the stallion, and we all forget you ever came to Koskara."

"I'm the Lord of Koskara, and your only chance for peace."

"Then it's time for the killing," Mansour said. "Come to the altar, my Lord."

As they walked to the altar, the chattering ceased, and silence sank over the arena. The moon's thin curving blade stood in the sky, offering scant light. The cooking fires had dimmed to a low glow.

"Meet our new high priest. The previous one had an accident."

Above the stark stone altar, stood the magnificent statue of the Great Mare, with a mature woman's body, the wise face of a crone, and a horse's legs and tail. Next to it, waited a man in a thick collar and leopard kilt who raised a serrated knife in greeting.

His muscled chest gleamed with oil like a wrestler's. The face above the dark collar was too young to belong to a true high priest, but too old to have survived Zetan's slaughter. Had Mansour sidestepped the genuine priesthood and planted one of his own men?

The priest raised his arms in a theatrical gesture, and his deep-voiced incantations carried across the arena. The thick collar shifted, widened, uncoiled. A forked tongue tasted the air.

Not a real priest then, and not a warrior either, but a showman, a snake charmer, an entertainer hired for the day.

"The goddess has chosen Zun to be her new high priest," Mansour said. "He has returned to Koskara in this time of need. Are you ready, Dahoud, or will you change your mind and leave?"

"I'm Lord of Koskara. Will you change your mind and be my chief councillor?"

Their eyes locked, and the moment stretched like a taut bowstring.

Mansour raised his arm. To the throbs of drums, two men led the stallion to the altar. Hemp-drugged and docile, its head lowered, its torso garlanded with yellow and red tassels, the animal staggered between them. Its eyes rolled.

Dahoud's heart wanted to fly with relief. Yet something in Mansour's grin warned him to stay on his guard.

Then Esha strode up, a goddess of victory, and took the dagger from the priest's hand. The flint blade glinted in the torchlight. She stroked the curve of the horse's neck from the head down, as if he was a favoured pet. Without breaking her smile, she slit his jugular.

The stallion gargled and sank forward. Its blood spurted, spattering

Esha's dress with dark splotches. The crowd yelled approval.

With the dramatic grace of a trained performer, Zun sank to his knees to catch the blood in a vessel of painted clay which he presented to Dahoud.

The blood tasted salty.

Mansour pulled the blood-dripping tassel garland off the carcass and draped it around Dahoud's neck. "Welcome to Koskara, my Lord."

While stallion chunks roasted on spits above charcoal fires, the crone Sirria waved him close and bowed in mock deference. "Everyone is calling you Lord Dahoud now, instead of an older name. I wonder if they'll regret accepting you." She stabbed the stem of her pipe at the blood-sodden tassels on Dahoud's chest. "Wash the tunic soon or the stains won't come out. Will you name your councillors tonight?"

In the light of the torches, the scars on her cheek stood out: a violent wound, inflicted by a person who hated with passion.

Dahoud decided quickly. Appointing Sirria was a small price for keeping his secret. "I'll be honoured if you join my Council."

Sirria laughed. "Thanks for offering, but I don't like life behind town walls. Tomorrow, I'm off with my flocks."

"Then what do you want?"

"When the time comes, you'll know. For now, give Koskara peace— if you can."

"I promise. Sirria, the scar on your cheek..." Violence, hatred, infection. Had it happened under his command?

Sirria's lips curved, and she pulled the scarf further back to expose the grotesquely knotted skin. "I did it myself." She laid a hand on his arm. "Everyone talks about the Quislakis – what the Quislakis have done to us, what the Quislakis will do to us, how we can guard against Quislakis or take vengeance on them. All the time, the Darrians are waiting just behind the Yellow Mountains." She jerked her chin towards the east. "They've always been there, so Koskarans don't see them as a problem. But the Black Besieger won't close his eyes to the threat."

Dahoud nodded. From a Darrian perspective, Koskara was not worth the bother of a conquest: sparse population, poor soil, no industry and no mineral resources. However, Koskara was now part of the Quislak, and Darria was at war with Quislak. An unguarded Koskara would be a temptation.

"I'll protect Koskara," he promised.

"That's all I want for now. Farewell, Lord Dahoud, until we meet again."

The time had come to select eight more councillors, people who would help him rule Koskara. People who brought skills which complemented his own, people whom he could trust.

Keera, with her statecraft training and troubleshooting skills was an obvious choice for Councillor of Law. The healer Naima was assertive and unflappable, knew life outside of Koskara, and had a passionate vision. She would be in charge of health.

Dahoud considered Mansour's trusted lieutenant, but so far, Idrahad had offered nothing beyond insolence and hostility, and seemed to want only Mansour's approval. Dahoud rejected the idea.

Wurran, the horse breeder, was hostile as well, but he had principles and a passionate loyalty to Koskara. In addition, he would bring his business acumen and local knowledge. Dahoud was almost certain now that Wurran would never recognise the Black Besieger.

However, when Dahoud invited him, his mouth curled in distaste. "Whoever walks with unworthy people becomes unworthy. Why would I join a Quislaki Council?"

"Mansour is the chief councillor."

"Is that so?" Wurran pursed his lips. "It's better to get walking than to curse the road. I'll follow Mansour."

The other councillors also hesitated until they learnt that Mansour had joined.

Garlic scented the air. Burning bay leaves crackled and dripping fat hissed. Dahoud's stomach opened in anticipation, but he did not join the crowds jostling around the spitroasts yet. Others needed the food more than he.

He remembered what it was like to be a hungry nomad. The children had only dates and milk, and never enough to feel full. Meat was a rare treat. Keen to please the natives, the satrap had enacted a semi-authentic stallion sacrifice festival. Dahoud's clan travelled there for the food. The place smelled of rich roasted beef and mutton. They had never seen so much food, and waited many hungry hours while it was being prepared. Dahoud had never before tasted beef. A thousand or more people waited. The satrap's family ate first. Then the council. The elders. The merchants, the craftspeople, the military, the visiting greenbelts, all the people who were used to having meat every day. The nomads were told to give them precedence. They took so much that nothing remained for the nomads.

With an angry hollow growling in his stomach, the ten-year-old Dahoud had marched to the awning where he'd earlier seen Lady and Lord. He was going to confront them, but found that the Lady and her husband had already left the feast. Only their children stayed behind, playing.

One of the boys, a little older than Dahoud, seemed keen to befriend the ragged nomad child. "My parents make me eat mutton every day. I think the stallion meat was great. What did you think of it?"

Dahoud, startled by the concept of daily meat, told him why he had not had any.

The other boy was outraged by the injustice. "This is bad. If I'd known, I'd have shared mine. Are you still hungry? I'm Tarkan and I live at the residency. My parents allow me to take guests home; come with me."

Dahoud had only a vague idea what a residency was, but a house where people ate mutton every day had to be a good thing.

Tarkan's parents had delighted in feeding the small nomad's big appetite. The Lady gave him more attention than he had ever had from a woman, and the Lord promised to have more animals killed the following day, so everyone could eat their fill.

Dahoud's clan, their pride insulted, refused to stay, but the friendship between Dahoud and Tarkan had begun.

He hoped that today was the start of another friendship—but he doubted it. Mansour had handed over the leadership of Koskara far too easily to be trusted.

~

Dawn scratched orange streaks into the purple sky. The trampled arena ground was dotted with sheep dung and defiant tufts of grass, and the air still smelled of charcoal from last night's cooking fires.

While Dahoud spread incense on the burner to invite the blessing of the gods, he studied his new councillors, twelve people whose support he needed to win. They sat cross-legged in a semi-circle on the desiccated turf, lips pinched, faces tight with distrust. Only Esha, kneeling on a silk cushion, with a stylus poised over the wax tablet on her thigh, exuded happy confidence.

He opened the meeting with a prayer to the Mighty Anour, god of judgement and wise counsel, and another to the Mare Mother, patroness of the Samil, under whose stone statue the council was gathered. He needed the divines' help.

As soon as he invited the councillors to swear loyalty, arms crossed over chests.

"We're Koskarans," Wurran said. "We won't pledge obedience to the Quislaki Queen and her Consort."

Dahoud had expected the refusal. "Will you-"

"But you absolutely must!" Esha hit her stylus on the tablet. "You can't be a member of our council until you do."

"I'll take the oath, Dahoud," Keera said. "You can count on me."

"Some folks will swear any oath." Wurran's nose crinkled as if at a bad smell. "Some folks are so ambitious, they serve abusers. Some folks desert in a crisis to throw their lot in with the enemy."

Keera remained unflustered, not a single muscle twitched in her face. "In war, brave people take up arms and fight. Clever people infiltrate the enemy. Cowards do nothing and just wait until it's over."

The reddening of Wurran's cheeks revealed that the arrow had hit. "It takes a thousand years for a lizard to grow into a snake," he hissed. "And only one year for a disloyal person to grow into a traitor."

Wurran's sole known act of courage had been the refusal to trade with the Black Besieger. Did he carry the shame of cowardice? But Dahoud would not encourage rancour in his council. He sent Keera a warning glance, which she answered with a shrug.

"I don't want your oaths to Quislak," Dahoud said. "What counts is your loyalty to Koskara. Are you prepared to swear that oath?"

They remained silent. Then their heads turned to Mansour, waiting for his command.

"We will," Mansour said. "Will you?"

Pairs of eyes drilled into Dahoud, as if assessing his conflict, as if expecting him to back out.

There was no conflict: a satrap served the Queendom by protecting his satrapy. "Of course."

Standing before the statue of the Mare Mother, he recited the ancient oath. "My body shall be the soil from which Koskara's greatness grows, my blood the water that sustains Koskara's life..."

He understood the severity of the pledge, and meant every word of it: he would protect his satrapy with the last drop of his blood.

He sat and folded his legs under him, looking at them calmly. "Back in the days when the sun shone red," he said, using the traditional opening of Samili storytellers, "two gazelles saw that a leopard had come into their territory. 'I'm not afraid of the leopard,' the first gazelle said. 'I'll show him how brave I am.' Fearlessly, she walked straight up to the leopard and told him to leave. When he didn't respond, she hit him with her hoof. The leopard killed her and ate the meat. The second gazelle was clever as well as brave. Fearlessly, she walked straight up to the leopard and bowed. 'Master of the land,' she said, 'I wish to swear fealty and pay homage to your might.' Flattered, the leopard accepted, and when other animals threatened the gazelle, he drove them away. He protected her from the lion, from the cheetah and the wolf. The gazelle's life was long prosperous."

Postures relaxed, but eyes remained wary.

"Paying tribute we can't afford—do you call this friendship?" Wurran asked.

"The tribute to Quislak is counted in jars of oil," Dahoud said. "The tribute to war is paid in blood. What do we value more—olive oil or Koskaran lives?"

The councillors glanced at one another, at Mansour, at the ground.

"What costs more—taxes, or waging war?" Dahoud pressed. "Have you weighed the costs of armour, of time away from fields and flocks, of rebuilding and replanting? If we pay Quislak, they'll not only keep out of Koskara. They'll do our fighting for us, keep the Darrians away—like the leopard that guards the gazelle—and we can put our resources to making Koskara prosper."

"What resources?" Wurran demanded. "Quislak has already taken most of our flocks, our copper, our harvests, our lives."

"Koskara's greatest resource is the people's spirit. Nobody can take away Koskaran courage," Dahoud said. He waited for a response but none came.

Heads swivelled, this time not to Mansour, but to the man striding towards them with measured, muscular steps. It was Zun, wearing a leopard kilt around his loins, a snake around his left arm, and a lot of oil on his chest. He stopped before the assembly, flung his arms open in greeting, and lowered himself in a spot opposite Dahoud.

Dahoud could almost hear the accompanying drum roll. He nodded a brief greeting. While he welcomed the high priest's presence in the council, he would not encourage theatrics.

"How can we make life better for the people of Koskara?" he asked. "If there was a single action which could bring a drastic improvement, what would it be?"

He smiled encouragingly at Naima to let her know that he was open to her 'mad' plans.

"Move the cattle pens away from the river," she replied at once. "We'll all be healthier if we don't drink animal-soiled water. We'll see a difference in under a moon, especially with the very young."

Dahoud nodded. This was what he needed: a project which brought quick victory with measurable results. "What stands in the way?"

"Tradition. Lethargy. Ignorance." She rolled her eyes. "The pens have been by the river since the days when the sun shone red, and if the animals aren't near water, people will have to carry water to the animals. I've been talking about it for years, but they won't listen. Most don't believe there's a connection between sickness and animal faeces in drinking water."

Although Dahoud did not see the connection either, it was worth trying. At any rate, the water would taste better. "We'll do it. As councillor of health, you're in charge. Get the pens moved immediately."

Her eyes flashed with enthusiasm, but she glanced at Mansour until he waved his consent.

Dahoud wanted to do more to improve healthcare. From the gathering of crones, he knew that most girls married on onset of puberty, and many died giving birth not much later. Quislak law forbade marriage until the age of fifteen, by which time the young bodies were better prepared for the strain. But the Koskarans would be hostile if he tried to enforce Quislak law. This was a change to introduce gradually, a goal for the future.

For now, they needed a goal they could all embrace enthusiastically. "What does Koskara need most?"

"Rain," a dozen voices replied at once.

Rain. If only he could give the drought-stricken land the water it craved. If only he could have brought the Riverian rain dancer to Koskara. But it was no good staring after an arrow which had left the bow.

Zun raised his arm. A scaled head lifted and licked the air. "I'll tell you what Koskara needs: A school of healing."

Esha clapped her hands. "Yes! That's just the sort of civic monument Dahoud and I want to sponsor. A greenstone façade with relief carvings of the gods of health and longevity, and columns of finest pink marble: The Lady Esha School of Healing."

"Healing schools are illegal," Keera pointed out. "There's a prohibition on the healing arts in Koskara, by order of the Consort." She scratched her chin. "We can get around this by calling it a school of sheep breeding, and quietly offer classes on human as well as animal health."

"Sheep?" Esha crinkled her nose. "You're asking us to sponsor a Lady Esha School of Sheep?"

"There's no rule against teaching torture either." Keera's voice sounded dry like a desert breeze.

Naima's face lit. "My torture teacher in Darria was awesome. If we get a Darrian expert, I'll sign up for refresher lessons."

"The Lady Esha School of Torture." Esha rolled the words around in the mouth as if tasting their flavour.

"We'll call it a school of literacy," Dahoud said. "There's no law against teaching people to write."

Naima's eyes sparkled. "Such a useful skill, writing. Especially for tattooing traitors."

"We'll employ the best architect in the Queendom, import the highest quality greenstone for the school, and commission fabulous sculptures," Esha said. "I'll write to the Consort for recommendations."

Building a school would be a strong signal that Dahoud had Koskara's well-being at heart, but the project had not fired his councillors' enthusiasm. He needed to give them a goal they could wholeheartedly embrace.

The sun was rising rapidly, brushing the place with colour and heat. Spectators milled on the stone steps, poking stares at the council until Mansour waved them away.

"We need another town, to replace Oubar," Wurran said. "The loss of Oubar has dealt a blow to the economy. There are only two towns left in Koskara, none at all in the south."

Eyes shone, and heads nodded in eager agreement.

Dahoud thought quickly: a town would be a spectacular gift to Koskara, practical and valuable, far outdoing Mansour's ill-fated well-shaft.

"We'll build a new town," he declared. "Oubar will live again. The mountains in the south are limestone karst which contains water pockets. We'll find a place where we can safely drill for underground water."

His real plan was more daring. Criton had mentioned ancient copper mines which were closed because of flooding. They had the potential to channel water from deep inside the mountains.

Wurran nodded appreciatively, his layered chins quivering. "The new town needs to be further north than Oubar was, closer to Ain-Elnour. If it's within a day's ride for a camel caravan, it can become a trading centre, especially once the Darrian border opens again. As for the building cost, local materials—limestone, bricks made from Koskaran mud—won't cost us much. For the manpower, we can recruit nomads whose flocks have starved. Villagers whose waterholes were overrun by dunes. Farmers who lost their living when the Black Besieger salted their land."

Dahoud agreed. Paying those people to work on the new town would not cost much more than giving them free food, and they would feel better if they supported themselves by their own labour.

"But it will still be expensive," Wurran said. "Far more expensive than Koskara can possibly afford."

"My father, Lord Govan the satrap, will contribute to Lady Esha Town," Esha offered happily.

"We'll get the Queendom to pay for New Oubar," Dahoud said.

"You're joking." Wurran shook his head, frowning. "They never give us anything. They take, take, take."

Dahoud notched his best arrow. "They will give—because I'll ask on Koskara's behalf."

Wurran rubbed his eyes. "A promise is but a cloud in the sky. Fulfilment is rain."

"I'll get the funds from the Queendom. That's what a satrap is for." Surely Kirral would agree. Teruma had already offered to sponsor a public building in Koskara, and the High General Paniour would part-finance the fortifications from the Queendom's military budget.

"New Oubar will be better than the old citadel," Dahoud promised. Based on his experience in laying siege, he knew how to make a fortress invincible. "It'll be located near water, inaccessible to attackers. It'll have two curtain walls, a triple gatehouse, battlemented parapets. There'll be a forum, a temple, a caravansary below in the plain, a yurt site, and yes, a school of healing..."

"Building a citadel like that takes five hundred years," Wurran said.

"We'll build it in five."

Mansour glanced up from his spindle. "I look forward to it."

While he had everyone's enthusiasm, Dahoud pressed forward. "New Oubar will be our fortress which keeps us safe. Free from the pressures of war, the herders will tend to their flocks, the artisans will practice their crafts, the traders will sell their wares far afield. Koskara will prosper, and each of us will play a part. Mansour, your help will set things straight. And for this I thank you."

The former rebel nodded like an aristocrat accepting thanks for a cup of tea.

"Naima. Wurran...." Dahoud looked into every person's eyes as he spoke. "So, where do you stand? Will you help to make Koskara great?"

The councillors exchanged glances. Then Mansour tapped his hand on his thigh. Once, twice, and he continued. One after the other, the councillors imitated him.

It was important to end the meeting on a high note. "We've made real progress. Thank you for supporting Koskara."

Mansour waited until the other councillors had left. "Nicely done, Lord Dahoud." He stashed his wool into a leather pouch and stretched lazily under the pulsing sun. "In future, get my approval for your plans beforehand."

Dahoud's stomach soured. "I'm not your puppet ruler."

"Aren't you? You preside, Esha prances, and I rule. You keep the Consort happy with reports, and once a year you go to Quislabat to wipe his arse."

Dahoud rose. "No."

Mansour stood as well, and hooked his thumbs into his belt. "Remember our wrestling match? I cheated."

"You won fairly."

"I didn't cheat to win. I cheated to almost lose."

"What do you mean?" Dahoud had barely finished the question when he found himself on his back, his arms pinned.

"...seven, eight, nine," Mansour said. "Try again?"

As soon as Dahoud scrambled up, he fell and was pinned again.

". .eight, nine. Do you get it?"

Dahoud rose and knocked the grass off his tunic. "Why didn't you fight like this at the contest?"

"To make you look strong. For the good of Koskara, even the puppet ruler ought to look good."

"I'm the Lord of Koskara. You're my number two. I'll do the work of a Lord, and you will treat me as the Lord."

"Even better." Mansour's smile bared teeth. "In times of crisis, a stallion is not enough. One day, we may need a Lord to die. Welcome to Koskara, Lord Dahoud."

CHAPTER 18

Betrayed

Kirral did not request Merida's company for a long time, and without his games, the days of her captivity crawled.

At the beginning of Almond Blossom Moon, two guards pulled Merida by the arms. "The Consort wants you."

Was she going to be formally accused of sickening the Queen by sorcery? She held her head high and mentally rehearsed her defence, as she strode between the guards down the corridor to Kirral's apartment.

When the door squealed open, she thought she had stepped into the wrong room. Gone were the murals, the knick-knacks, the rugs. Grey cloths draped the walls.

Kirral sat on the sole divan, with his elbows on his knees, his head bare, his tunic plain. Neither jewels nor weaponry glittered. Even his moustache drooped.

"Highness?"

"The light of the Great Queen's life has dimmed, and it is my fault." Self-reproach slurred the edges of his voice. He buried his head in his hands. "I am flawed, not worthy to kiss her toes. Even less worthy to govern the Queendom on her behalf."

She searched the bare room for somewhere to sit. "Highness, if the Queen is ill, it is not your fault."

"Compared with me, you are wise," Kirral said. "You are compassionate. You are blessed with Virtues I do not possess."

"I'm not so Virtuous at all." She traced the tip of a boot along the bare floorboards. "Sometimes I find it difficult to submit to Modesty."

"Is that in itself not a sign of your Modesty? Your compassion shines like a star. Few people would have cared for the well-being of my fish, and fewer still would have had the courage to take me to task about their abuse."

"Did you set them free?"

"Alas, my remorse came too late for them." His voice sounded hoarse and subdued. "For my amusement, they died a cruel death. How could I possibly atone for their fate?"

Merida folded her hands. "In Riverland, the sinner visits temple, confesses to a priest, and carries out a penance. And of course, he submits to the mercy of the Virtues."

"The Virtues," he said, like a starving beggar might say 'bread'. "Loyalty, Honesty, Modesty, Discipline. Which of the virtues would be the wisest for this worm?"

"Any of them would be good, but Discipline offers the strongest self-control." Merida explained the concept.

He sucked up every word like a soul starving for salvation, then sighed. "I want to rise and greet the day as a new man, but sinful habits cling to me like old dirt."

"No sinner reforms in a single day. Only slow changes are lasting changes."

"Your presence is like a lake in the desert, refreshing and clear. Life-giving, even. Your spirit is inspiring, your intellect excites me." He sat straight. "The stimulation transcends the boundaries of my spirit and takes physical manifestation."

Confusion stirred. "What do you mean?"

"My spirit, as yet untrained, cannot contain all the stimulation it receives, and is overflowing with excitement. It spills into my mind, my body. It awakes physical reactions."

Prickling doubts whirled through her mind. "I'm not sure I understand, Highness."

"Your chaste intellect affects my loins."

"I—I find that hard to believe, Highness."

"Look, my dear Merida." He wiggled on the divan, raising the hem of his tunic to his mid-section. "Take a good look."

Fire shot into her cheeks, and she jerked her head away. Should she scold him, or scream? He meant to shock her, so she would deny him the satisfaction of a strong response. "As I said, the Virtue of Discipline lends itself to … "

"Tell me more," he rasped. "I like it."

Reality hit her in a sickening wave. How could she have believed in a reformed Kirral? She mustered what dignity she could. "I beg to be excused."

"Certainly, my dear. It has been educational playing with you."

❦

To punish herself for her stupidity, she pushed her body through the most gruelling sequence of the Disciplined Path, from Number 48 The Ravens in Darkness to Number 47 The Poison Toad's Vengeance, taking each stance to its extreme. With her full weight on one leg, she lowered herself almost to the floor and held the pose until her knee crackled and her thigh screamed. Then she did it again on the other side, waiting for physical discipline to purify her mind, but the shame stayed.

❦

"There must be a letter," Merida pleaded while the masseuse pummelled and scraped. "It's been five moons and twenty-nine days!"

"Count the days as often as you like." The woman squeezed foam from a cloth bag on Merida's face. "I have no letter."

Had a dishonest courier absconded with the advance fee, or an honest one been waylaid? Had she expected too much from a country without an organised postal system?

"I sent your message with my own," the masseuse said. "My family has already answered."

If the masseuse's letters had reached Riverland, so had Merida's. But why had she not received a response?

❦

On her knees, Merida scraped the dormitory rugs with a borrowed brush, directing her anger into loosening the tangles of hair and caked crumbs. Dust clouds thickened the air.

Kadiffe, seated on a bed, sneered down at her. "I see the sorceress now has to do servant work. Serves you right."

Merida did not halt her rhythm. Honest work never demeaned anyone. If these rugs had ever been cleaned, it was years ago.

"Why doesn't the Consort send for you? Are the nettle treatments not working?" Kadiffe clucked with mischievous laughter. "I have a real secret which will make him love me again."

Merida scooped up dirt with her bare hands, thick wads of dust dotted with cake crumbs, squashed raisins, ashes, hairs, toenails and dead beetles, and dumped them into the waste bucket, while calculating. Clearly, her letter had reached Riverland, but Mother's reply had gone astray. No doubt, the Virtuous government was already applying pressure for her release, and the head-wife would know about it.

⚮

Afternoon light filtered through filigree lattices, dipping Teruma's study into pale gold. Merida inhaled the cool mint scent.

Barely looking up from the piles of parchment on her desk, Teruma pointed at a yellow divan by the window. Merida plunged onto it, expecting to sink into its sumptuous depth, but beneath its silken softness, it was hard and ungiving. A sleek cat uncurled from an embroidered cushion and stretched, baring claws. Then it yawned and settled back to sleep. A caged bird twittered and fell silent.

"Have you had a chance to study the treatise on djinns?" Merida asked, and was surprised to see Teruma's face harden. "Are you pleased with my work? Perhaps I can translate something else for you?" She glanced at the scroll-filled shelves. "If you wish to expand your library, I have brought several treatises including *The Virtue of Modesty and its Rewards* which I can translate for you."

"That would be a waste of parchment." Teruma dipped her reed brush into ink and continued writing. "Now go. I have a national crisis to deal with."

Merida sat up straight. "What national crisis?"

"You have to ask?" Teruma put the reedbrush down. "The Queen has been sick for three moons and has no daughters. The economy limps, the currency plummets, and rivals fight about the succession."

Merida understood. In a monarchy, these things would happen. If only the Queen had taken measures to preserve her precious health. A person of her girth needed frequent exercise and a cautious diet.

"When the Queen dies, her successor's husband will be Consort, won't he?" she probed. "What happens to Kirral? As a common citizen, he won't be permitted a harem, will he? Will all the wives be set free and escorted to their homes?"

"Kirral will keep one wife only," Teruma said drily. "The pregnant ones will be spared. The rest will be drowned in the pebble pool."

Sickness churned Merida's guts. Teruma could be calm about this, because as Kirral's head-wife she was the favourite he would keep, while the others lost their lives. Unless Mother sent help soon, Merida, too, was in danger.

"This is barbaric."

"They know the rules when they marry the Consort," Teruma said.

"If the Queen had a daughter, the succession would be clear, wouldn't it? Why then does the Consort waste his time with concubines instead of doing his duty with the Queen?"

"How many children have you seen in the harem?"

"You mean, Kirral carries no living seed?"

"The slop buckets need scrubbing."

Apparently, Teruma had not received communications from River-land. At least she was too preoccupied to suspect a plot to free Merida was under way.

Knowing of the fate awaiting the concubines should the Queen die, Merida felt intensely sorry for them. For the first time, she understood their desperate need to get pregnant.

With her new sympathy, she tried to be kind to everyone, even if their manners grated. She would have been pleasant to Kadiffe, but the girl was receiving a guest in the visitor's room, her father perhaps. At least the child was not wholly cut off from her family. But what kind of father would sell his young daughter into concubinage with an impotent old lecher and at the same time sentence her to an almost certain early death: He was an officer, Merida recalled. Military men were the worst, they killed people for money and had no honour. Maybe he had traded his daughter for a promotion. Poor Kadiffe.

"The sandal-seller has arrived," Haurvatat chirped, linking her arm through Merida's. "Come, Merida, come!"

Merida greeted the basket-laden vendor with courtesy and attempted to interest herself in the leather goods. The concubines tried on pair after pair, squealing with delight.

"These are so cute!" Haurvatat trilled. "I must have them. Those as well, and the green ones, of course, and the red."

"Don't you already have one thirty-five pairs?" Merida said.

"Yes, but none with turquoise ankle-straps. What do you think of those pink ones with the glass beads? If nobody else has them, I'll be the only one. Or these ones here? I love those tassels. Which ones should I buy?"

Merida considered, then pointed to a pair in dark leather with a muted pattern of squares.

"You think they're pretty?" Haurvatat held them up and turned them over as if searching for hidden glitter. "All right, I'll take those, too." She gathered a dozen pairs to her bosom and took them to the greenbelt who was administering the budget. "Which ones are you buying, Merida?"

"Not this time. You've taken all the pretty ones." Until her return to Riverland, she would get by with her old leather boots, although they were splitting at the seams, and with the felt house-boots she had sown. Nothing would make her reveal naked toes in sandals.

⚞

Merida counted the days and calculated. The masseuse's own message, dispatched at the same time as Merida's, had already received a response. Why was Mother's reply delayed?

Captivity was devouring a chunk of Merida's life, time she should devote to her studies and career. To make the most use of her time, Merida practised all sixty-four drills of The Disciplined Path, a water-bowl balanced on her head. On her return, she would prove such proficiency that she could apply for a sparring licence.

Merida would like to be among the chosen ones allowed to spar. She would enjoy measuring her skill against a real opponent.

Every day, she practised the drills, stretched her limbs and lifted buckets to gain strength. She punched and kicked, leaped and rolled, jabbed and stabbed, aiming for fluidity, serenity, power and grace which would yield her the permission to spar. Unfortunately, not only strength and skill were assessed, but a candidate's virtue too. If anyone in Riverland ever found out that her value had dropped below zero, and that she had been nominally a concubine, she would never be considered. But nobody needed to find out. Mother would help hush it all up.

Merida's fluidity improved, but she was not certain the priesthood would be impressed with her serenity. Fury fuelled most of her moves. With every punch of the Woodpecker she thought of smashing Kirral's nose, with every Boar's Tusk she imagined gouging his eyes, and each Leaping Trout delivered a kick at his insulting groin. This was not the desired mental attitude, but it felt good.

⤙

The next time the Consort summoned her, Merida had her strategy ready. If he dared to expose himself, she would laugh loudly at the display. Embarrassment would cool his ardour.

The apartment was back to plush purple, vulgar murals, and splatters of crimson bric-a-brac. Kirral wore a gold turban hung with strings of coral and pearl, and his moustache was waxed into a straight bar.

"Sit down, dear Merida. Guess what I have here?" He balanced a small scroll on his outstretched palm.

She expected another distasteful picture, but then she recognised the expensive creamy vellum her mother favoured, and the moss-green wax of the splintered seal. Hope lapped at her heart like water at a riverbank: Mother had written to the Consort demanding her release, and he was giving in to the pressure. The hand of freedom was reaching out to her at last.

Kirral scraped off his pink pompom slippers, pulled his feet up under his thighs, and rubbed his pudgy fingers. "Read, dear Merida."

Merida leant under the light of a hanging wreath-lamp to read it.

"*Second Daughter: I can think of no explanation for your letter. The Royal Consort's own correspondence indicates that you are highly esteemed as your nation's Special Ambassador. If you mean to create tension between the Virtuous Republic and the Queendom, I will not be so misled. This family benefits from your Personal Value of 248, and you would do well to remember it. I will not write again.*"

The letter was a cold slap in Merida's face. She swallowed the defeat clogging her throat, trying to convince herself that it was a misunderstanding. But the more she looked at it, the clearer it became that Mother had cast her off like a stained garment.

Kirral smirked. "I've been looking forward to this letter, ever since reading your outgoing one. You have a lot to learn about human nature, even your own kin."

She stared at him coldly, clasping at a detail in the hope the big issue would go away. "You told me diplomatic relations between our nations were severed, and the regular ambassador had travelled home. How, then, can anyone believe that the special ambassador remains at Court?"

He steepled his fingers and touched them to his mouth. "My dear Merida, you must have misunderstood. No correspondence was exchanged severing diplomatic relations, and the unfortunate regular ambassador had an accident."

Merida felt the blood drain from her cheeks. Murder. And the Virtuous Government was not even aware their ambassador was dead.

All her hopes had collapsed like a badly-built tower. With her head held high, as if not in the least upset, she rose to march out of the room.

"Wait. I have not finished with you yet, dear Merida."

Merida gritted her teeth to keep her composure rather than allow Kirral to see her hurt.

"There is the delicious matter of punishment. Caning the soles? Whipping?" He stroked his chin. "Are those too crude? Then you shall have your writing materials confiscated. Your notes and scrolls, too. That is appropriate penalty, is it not?"

He had no right to steal her inks, to deprive her of intellectual pursuits. Without the chance to read or write, her mind would dry up and shrink. She tried to protest, but the words came out as a choked sob. Protests would be futile anyway, so she answered with haughty silence.

"On the other hand, I may leave your inks and your scrolls, and punish you with solitary confinement. Ten days without human contact should chasten even you, dear Merida. Which penalty do you choose?"

Ten whole days without chanting, without chatter chatter, without bickering, just restful silence? What bliss!

Pretending to ponder, she delayed her answer. "Confinement."

"Are you sure? You will feel very lonely with no other human in the room. Of course, you can always try to tame the rat and teach it Discipline."

"The rat?" Merida squealed. "There's a rat in the room?"

Kirral rubbed his hands. "I hear it is amenable to human company. It eats from the same bowl, sleeps in the same straw..."

"Take my inks," Merida said.

"What an interesting choice, my dear. Now you have my permission to leave."

Merida hurried down into the pebble yard and clenched her fists so hard that the knuckles stood out white and the nails dug into the palms. Mother's attitude made horrid sense: Loyalty to the family came about loyalty to the individual, and Mother was cutting her off, the way one might amputate an infected limb to protect the whole body. By disbelieving the call for help, she had even preserved the special ambassador points for the family.

But the point loss from Merida's shame would be for a short time only, rectified as soon as she left captivity. Mother was not willing to undergo even a few moons of humiliation for Merida's sake.

Merida cried until her head ached. Then, with a throbbing skull and gritted teeth, she straightened. If Mother refused to send help, she would escape by her own wits.

CHAPTER 19

The Lady Esha

Theo noon sun glared on the pale limestone walls of the legion fortress. Familiarity pulled at Dahoud with longing, as if he was returning to a long lost home.

"Lady Esha and Lord Dahoud, to see Fortress Commander Gavinos," Dahoud said.

"That's all right," one of the Siege-playing guards under the gatehouse arch said placidly. "He's expecting you. Go right through to headquarters."

Dahoud drilled a hard stare into him.

Flushing, the sentry stood and saluted. "Commander Gavinos is expecting you, my Lord."

"Announce us!" Dahoud barked. Then he remembered to act like a civilian. "Would you be so good and show us the way to headquarters?" he asked, as if he did not know the pillared building in the centre of the garrison.

"I'll get someone to escort you, my Lady, my Lord, and to see to your horses." The sentry mumbled an order to his subordinate, who laced up his sandal before scuttling off.

Paniour had been right. The troops left in Koskara were not the Queendom's finest.

Waiting in the shaded arch, Dahoud watched his wife with concern. Despite the broad-brimmed straw hat, she seemed to be wilting in the heat. "What's wrong, Esha?"

"It's awfully hot. I need to sit down." She perched on the edge of the wall niche, next to the life-size limestone statue of the Mighty Ikbour, god of discipline and martial valour. "Ikbour won't mind sharing his space with me, will he?"

"I'm sure he won't." Inside the dusty crook of Ikbour's elbow, a yellow spider was settled in a web. "Do you need anything?"

"Some water, but that can wait until we're inside. I trust Gavinos will show us more respect than these soldiers did."

"Probably." Dahoud lowered his voice. "But he'll resent that I'm in nominal command of the armed forces in Koskara."

"Then we'll establish our authority," Esha said.

"No. Let's assure him we won't meddle in his affairs. That's the best way to stop him from meddling in ours. Act impressed with what you see here and flatter him."

"Why?"

"Can you do it?"

"Absolutely."

Dahoud planned to fool Gavinos into thinking he was clueless about legion life. The dark green tunic of a Quislaki official helped, but he must act the part. When a couple of legionnaires escorted them to the command building, Dahoud pulled his turban cloth deep into his face. He hunched his shoulders, shuffled his sandals across the gravel, and gazed the barracks with curious awe.

Inside the cool command building, dusty light filtered through curtained window. On the desk stood a silvered statue of Mighty Ishara, goddess of love, wisdom and war, clad in nothing but a helmet and girdle.

After bowing to Esha, Gavinos clasped Dahoud's elbows with jovial enthusiasm. "Lord Dahoud, I'm so pleased to welcome you to this humble fortress. I've been waiting ever since I heard you're to be in charge. Sit down, sit down." He gestured at carved, cushioned chairs. "Do you know much about military matters?"

"Little," Dahoud said. "If we might have some water, please? The Consort puts some of us satraps in nominal charge, the Mighty Ones know why. I'm sure you can do without a meddling civilian."

"Haha." Gavinos held his belly as he laughed. "I like your sense of humour. You're right, of course, absolutely right. There's no need to bother yourself with legion matters, apart from annual sacrifices to the martial gods." He stroked a finger down Mighty Ishara's girdled flank. "Inspecting the troops, giving a speech or two, that's all you need to do as the nominal head. Don't worry, I'll teach you to create a good impression. Of course, if we ever have to go to war..."

"I'm sure your soldiers can win any war." Esha fluttered her lashes. "Everything in this camp looks absolutely efficient. Your soldiers seem so well trained, surely they're simply invincible."

Gavinos lapped up her praise. "I made a lot of improvements in my two years here. I wouldn't be so sure about well-trained troops, though. The men they send me are the dregs of the legion barrels, and the officers aren't great either. Koskara is a penalty posting where they send incompetents. I ask you, is that fair on me? How can I do my job if half my officers are failures?"

Esha smiled sympathetically, but she had not regained her colour.

"We would be grateful for water," Dahoud said. He waited until Gavinos had shouted an order into the corridor before asking, "How many men are based in Koskara?"

"Only a fifth of a legion. Is this a joke, or what? Just because this province was integrated into the Queendom four years ago, they think it can be left to itself. I keep asking for more troops, but they turn me down, every time. Of course, it's all about politics and money pouches. If they sent me more men, they'd need to make me a general, and they're too stingy for that."

Dahoud kept his face blank. Standing armies were expensive. It was impossible to keep one in every potential trouble spot.

"What happened, I ask you?" Gavinos went on. "The Koskarans rebelled They burnt fortresses and even besieged the residency. With so few men, there was nothing that could be done."

With nine hundred men, Dahoud could have relieved the residency. "If you could have done anything, you would have done it, I'm sure of it."

Gavinos beamed. "I'm glad you understand. We'll get on well, you and I. It was a terrible time, I tell you. What if the rebels had attacked the garrison? Ah, here's the water, and some wine. I'm afraid it's impossible to get good wine here, but perhaps you don't mind drinking this."

"The water first," Dahoud said.

Esha emptied her water beaker before sipping daintily from the wine. "Absolutely delicious."

"After forty years of service, I deserve at least command of a legion," Gavinos said. "But these days, it's about politics and connections and who you know. A hard-working officer like me has no chance. One of my predecessors, the one they called the Black Besieger, was given a legion and made a general. I'm doing the same job as he, but they deny me the promotion." He refilled his beaker, drained it, and refilled it again. "I should have gone into statecraft, that's where careers happen nowadays. With my brains, I could easily have been a satrap. Still could become one, I suppose."

Dahoud gazed at the lump of incompetence and said nothing.

Esha said, "This wine reminds me of the one I had when I dined with the royal family. The Lady Teruma chose it, I believe, and the Consort said it was his absolute favourite. Of course the Illustrious Queen is very fond of yellow wines."

Gavinos watched her lips as if they were dripping jewels. "If there's anything I can do for you, just ask."

"There is," Dahoud said. "If you have competent engineers, I want to borrow them."

"I have most urgent need of a really good soothsayer," Esha said.

"Sorry, my Lady, we don't have soothsayers in this backwater garrison." Gavinos drained his beaker again. "Engineers, yes. What for?"

"To survey a site for a citadel, and draw up plans for it." Dahoud wanted to give Koskara a new town to replace Oubar and to outdo Mansour's donation of a wellhouse. In his mind, he could already see it rising from the rock: solid brick walls on a socle of golden limestone, so high no ladder could scale them, so thick no ram could batter them, with projecting parapets, curved merlons and archery slits, and every amenity the people could want. "Would the south-east be a good place to build one? Say, a two-day ride from Ain-Elnour? Maybe on the slope of the Yellow Mountains?"

"Ah yes, we need a fortress down there. I keep telling them that the south-east is woefully unprotected against Darrian invasion."

"I'm glad that your judgement confirms my amateurish impression," Dahoud said.

"I can lend you a couple of engineers. You'll need to use your court connections to find the funds, and I don't think the high general will send me the troops to staff it."

"I'm grateful for your expertise and the loan of your engineers." The citadel would be a military marvel. He would give it a double gatehouse, or a triple one even. There would be two curtain walls, a bailey, watchtowers, and an approach so steep and so guarded no attacker could bring up siege machinery. Based on Dahoud's war experience, the town would be invincible. He would keep his people safe. But he needed engineers to survey the site and plan the structure, and he needed someone like Gavinos to be the official designer.

"It will be my pleasure. Time to inspect the troops," Gavinos said. "The men will be lined up. You just walk before them, slowly, pretend you're checking them."

"Who are your officers?"

"I'll introduce them to you, if you like," Gavinos said.

"A list of their names will do."

Gavinos fumbled through several piles of parchments. "In this place, nothing is ever where it should be. I'll have to send it by messenger when it's found."

"I'll be obliged." Dahoud walked onto the gallery to look down where the men assembled for the inspection. Any one of them might have served in Koskara, or in Zigazia. Any one of them might recognise the Black Besieger who had not worn the mask before his own troops.

"Why not wear a uniform?" Gavinos suggested. "Dress up like you're one of the men, that always goes down well. Or put on the general's uniform I keep in my study."

The sight of Dahoud in a crimson and black tunic might waken memories of a man who was supposed to be dead. He laid an arm around his wife. "Esha, how would you like to wear a uniform and take the inspection?"

A few heartbeats later, Esha stood, radiant in general's regalia, her former tiredness forgotten. Her naked legs in the very short tunic looked white, and with the tight-cinched belt, her hips curved like a succulent fig.

"Very pretty," Dahoud approved. "Do you mind the men seeing your legs?"

"My legs are perfectly shaped," she told him.

Gavinos licked his lips. "The men will love her."

Beaming, Esha walked very slowly past the soldiers, giving each of them a smile, swaying her hips. Dahoud kept to the shade, with his shoulders slouched, and waved a most un-military salute.

For Esha's sake, Dahoud agreed to hang around the garrison and drink more of Gavinos' wine until the day's fiercest heat was spent, so they could ride in the cooling hours. However, he declined the invitation to have dinner with the officers, since the risk of recognition was too great. In future, he would send Esha to inspect troops in his stead. She would enjoy it as much as the men did, and Dahoud's secret would stay safe.

⁓

Esha's legs ached, and tiredness gnawed at her mind. She yearned to sit on a divan, toss off her muddied sandals and have a servant wash her feet while she sipped hot tea from a dainty beaker. Instead, she had to crawl into the dark felt tent with its reek of rancid milk and greasy wool. There was no divan, no chair, no decent bed, just her trunks and heaps of fleeces.

"You did well," Dahoud said. "They liked seeing you. You can take future parades."

Cinching the uniform belt had been a mistake. She sank into the bedding. The animal odour sent a wave of nausea from her stomach. "I really need a proper bed."

A voice rang outside. "My Lady, my Lord! I bring messages for you."

Finally. The first messenger in three moons to come to this backwater.

Dahoud fetched the handful of wooden tablets and scrolls. Esha's family sent gossip and the satrap Adil of Djildit a courtesy note, while the Lady Teruma asked how she could help to boost trade.

Dahoud was shaking his head over a parchment. "Tarkan is coming. He's on his way, currently staying with his father in Djildit, looks forward to working with me. What does he mean?"

"Wonderful!" Esha said. "He's a most amiable person. We'll definitely make him chief councillor."

"Mansour is chief councillor."

"Tarkan is qualified, experienced, descended from the best blood-line," she reminded him.

"I'll deal with it later." He dropped the letter on a trunk. "Now you've had time to settle in, we have to get you started on a real job. Have you decided what you want to do?"

Confused, she said, "I'm the Lady."

He bent to kiss her cheek. "How about seasonal labour: Picking olive one month, rose petals the next. Figs, dates, grapes..."

"Isn't it enough that I keep council records like a scribe? Do you expect me to do labour in this ghastly heat?"

"If the heat is too much for you, do indoors work. Why not be a teacher at the school that will be named after you?"

"When the school is built, of course I'll be delighted to teach those sweet little children."

Fortunately, it was not built yet. The mere thought of those stinking brats with their dripping noses, their rashes and their pus-swelled eyes stirred her sickness. She sat up, tore a chunk from the flat bread and chewed. It lacked flavour but quelled the nausea.

"It's also time for you to learn everything a real Koskaran can do, so the people accept you as one of us. I'll show you how to shear a sheep, and milk a camel, and trim a goat's hooves."

"I'm sure those are useful skills," Esha said. "For common people. Perhaps you have forgotten that I'm a Lady? Why do you treat your horses better than me? They get to live in the residency stables while I'm stuck in this tent. I need servants, I need furniture, I need a Lady's lifestyle."

This time he heard. "What are you blabbering on about? Nobody in Koskara has servants."

She had to tell him, although she would have preferred to wait until a good soothsayer confirmed what she knew. She threw the words at him. "I'm pregnant."

He stared as if she had just grown green wings and a purple moustache.

"So you see that all this talk about work is utterly inappropriate, and I must have servants and personal messengers and live in the residency."

"Haven't we agreed to shun the residency?"

"I agreed to live in a yurt for a little while to help your strategy. Now you're established as a satrap, it's time you behaved like one."

"I'm satrap of Koskara, Esha. Not of some elegant place in the north." He looked at her belly again, as if expecting to see it swell. "How many moons?"

"Almost two, and all the signs are strong." The soothsayer who had promised conception during the wedding night had lied, and she would ask her father to have the man punished, but it mattered little. Before the year was out, she would have her first daughter.

"Be very careful about the work you do while you're pregnant. Koskaran women carry water and dig the fields until the day they give birth, but you're not as strong as they. Helping the weaver or the trader won't be so strenuous. You like handling fabrics, don't you?"

"I won't risk the health of the first daughter of my dynasty by doing common work." She held her hands protectively around her belly. "And I really need servants."

"If we employ a woman to help you, we have to be tactful about it, so people won't think you arrogant."

"Don't worry about offending Koskaran sensibilities. I'll get Quislaki maids. Don't worry about affording the cost, either. My father – who, I remind you, is Lord Govan the satrap – will pay for it, just as he'll pay for the refurbishment of the residency."

In silence, Dahoud heated water over the brazier, then gave her a beaker of tea. "I'm sorry, Esha. But moving into the residency would make a statement that undoes everything I've worked for."

"I suppose you're right." When undermining a man's resolution, it was always best to pretend to agree with him.

She suffered his sweat-smelling hug, but when he ran his hand down her flank, she shoved him away. "We will not do that any more. It could harm the child most dreadfully." She folded her hands protectively over her abdomen. "Anyway, now that I'm pregnant, we don't need to do that again."

"Don't need to..." he repeated, as if he doubted what he had heard.

"We'd better not endanger my unborn daughter." She cuddled Cloud to her chest and rubbed her ears, marvelling how docile the little dog was, how devoid of smell compared to the reeking skins of dead sheep and the odour of the living man. Cloud's black eyes shone in adoring gratitude.

The idea came to her in a bright flash. If Dahoud agreed, it would solve all her problems at once. The way to make a man consent to something that went against his principles was to make him believe it was his idea.

"You're absolutely right. The natives wouldn't stand for a satrap living in the residency, and by living in a yurt, you show that you are different from Zetan and the others. Of course, I'll support you, whatever it takes. It's just that sometimes it's difficult—without a bed, the heat in the yurt, the... aaargh." She curled, clutching her belly.

"Esha. Why don't you move into the residency until the child is born, and I stay here?"

"What a wonderful idea! This is the perfect solution." Esha gave him her most adoring gaze. "You're so clever, Dahoud."

⸺

At the end of Almond Blossom Moon, when the earth was supposed to erupt in fresh green, the land remained brown, baked and barren. Dahoud watched the nomads urge their flocks out of town on their annual journey, desperate to claim the sparse sprouts. Most animal pens stood in deserted silence, and where dozens of family tents had squeezed together on the yurt site, only a few solitary domes remained.

The new council yurt was ready, a large round tent which would not provoke hatred the way the residency did, but still shut out eavesdroppers and heat.

The yurt smelled of tea and frankincense. Inside, the councillors sat with their legs crossed, passing the incense burner to hold it beneath their tunics for fragrancing their bodies and killing pests. Only Esha shifted frequently on her cushion of silk, as if demonstrating the discomfort of meeting in a tent instead of a well-furnished residency.

Dahoud invoked Mighty Anour, god of wise counsel and thunderstorms, and the Great Mare who nurtured Koskara.

The main concern was water. With the seasonal torrents were nearly two moons overdue, Koskara faced the seventh year of drought. More crops would fail, and dunes would swallow yet more grazing rounds. Dahoud thought of the succour the Riverian rain dancer might have brought to Koskara.

Failed crops fuelled discontent. Only Mansour's loyalty could prevent another outbreak of rebellions.

Mansour said, "I want your permission to flush out men-lovers and make them targets for knife-throwing."

Dahoud's stomach chilled. Mansour expected him to sanction torture. "Give them quick deaths."

"Knife-throwing," Mansour repeated, adding carded wool to the thread. "A slow public death deters others. Problem solved."

"My father, Lord Govan the satrap, had them all drowned," Esha said. "It has been most effective in eradicating the vice totally."

"Why not castrate them?" Naima's pink tongue flicked across her lip. "They'll never sin again."

"The law demands death," Keera said.

"Knife-throwing, I say." Fire gleamed in Mansour's eyes. "Right into their eggs."

Keeping Mansour happy was the price for peace. To protect the people of Koskara, Dahoud had to sacrifice a few. "Knife-throwing. But I won't have innocents killed. There must be at least one witness to the vice."

Esha wrinkled her nose as if she despised Dahoud for his weakness, but Mansour fingered a hilt as if impatient for the first execution.

Spreading the parchment plan on the rug, Dahoud presented his own project. "This new fortress will protect Koskara. It will be the safest citadel in the world. Impregnable."

"If you'd seen war," Mansour said, "you'd know that no fortress is impregnable."

"We'll make it as close to impregnable as it can be. Gavinos has advised me on the basic design—"

"Gavinos?" Mansour laughed.

"I'll welcome your suggestions for improving it." Dahoud knew the citadel was perfect: he had designed it himself, based on his experience in besieging fortified towns. Situated on a steep rocky outcrop, with its own secret water supply, surrounded by three thick curtain walls, with powerful towers, projecting battlemented parapets, curving merlons and a triple gatehouse, it would be invincible.

Mansour viewed the plan with a furrowed brow, seeking a flaw where none existed. At last he said, "I look forward to it."

⨼

Afternoon heat held the land in a fiery embrace when Esha took possession of the residency.

As she directed people to unload her property from the donkeys, the residency stared, a cold witness in unmoving stone.

Dahoud told himself this was but a brief separation, triggered by the fancies of pregnancy. When the child was born, they would reconcile in renewed harmony.

Mansour, leading a donkey loaded with straighthorn grass for kindling, halted to make way for Esha's train, and watched the unfolding scene with undisguised curiosity.

"Hurry up, woman!" Esha scolded. "I'm not paying you to stand around. Carry that trunk upstairs."

"Yes, my Lady." The woman held her face down and was struggling to lift the box off the donkey's back.

When Dahoud hurried to help her, he saw with horror the way her belly bulged. Surely Esha, so protective of her own unborn child, could not have overlooked this woman's condition?

"I'll carry that trunk," he said.

Esha wrinkled her nose at him. "Why do you indulge those natives so much? You should have seen how she begged me to hire her."

The desperation of these people's poverty shamed him, and Esha's ruthlessness roused his anger. He wanted to grab her by the shoulders to shake sense into her.

Esha adjusted the folds of her silk gown. "They're not at all delicate like we are. As you pointed out, they can easily work up to the day they drop their litter." She snarled at the woman. "Pick up that basket, you lazy camel fart! Careful there, Cloud is extremely sensitive."

Cloud in her basket started yapping on cue, a sharp, high-pitched bark, as if to prove how sensitive she was. Esha hurried to press the bundle of noisy fluff to her chest. She strode into the residency, as tall and straight as the stone pillars at the entrance, leaving the others to cope with the luggage.

Dahoud carried one of the trunks, although he knew the action would make Esha detest him further.

He avoided Mansour's eyes, for fear of what he would see in them - contempt, or worse: pity. The Koskarans would despise him for his lenience towards Esha. Nobody could know how much he needed to atone for what he had done to women in the past.

When he had put the trunk down, he waited for an invitation to sit.

"Go now." Esha flicked a hand as if sending away a servant.

He complied. The door slammed shut. The bolt screeched into place.

Dahoud stared at the wooden door, wanted to break it down, to force entry, to make Esha accept him into her life. His anger roared with the same howling fury as on the night of the storm, fourteen years ago.

The other children had selected their teams for the trickriding contest and left him standing, as usual. They seldom included the whore's whelp, unless they needed to make up numbers. Dahoud marched up the mountain slope to a secluded spot where he practised ferociously: cartwheels across the rock, backflips, somersaults. If he became a spectacular gymnast, his skill might win him their acceptance.

For hours, he jumped, leaped and ran, his knees scraped, his wrists jarred, his legs bruised, his only audience the mountains and the sun. Most tricks required a run for momentum. He could do a handstand from standing still, and planned to perform other tricks without a run.

If he could arch his arms back until the hands touched the rock, and if he could heave himself up to perform a backflip, this would make him stand out. The afternoon heat on the slope of Sentinel Mountain faded, and the length of the shadows suggested it was time for the communal meal.

Dahoud scrambled across the ridge to climb down the other side of the mountain where his clan was camped. The sky had a strange texture, spongy like uncarded wool, and the colour of curdling milk, with a band of purple on the horizon. The air was so dry it sucked the moisture from his breath, yet it smelled as if someone had doused a charcoal fire with water. He squinted at the horizon. Between the grey earth and the purple sky, a yellow band formed. Even as he stared, it grew.

He ran downslope to his clan's tents —but they had gone. The people must have seen the sky's change long before he had, folded up the yurts, and sought shelter. Whatever the threat, it meant the danger was real. Where had they gone?

The wind picked up. The sky grew more purple and more yellow.

He scanned the mountainside. While guarding the goats the day before, he had seen a cave, large enough to shelter a family and their belongings.

The wind grew and whipped desert sand against his naked legs. He scrambled up to the cave mouth but found it blocked with sacks of produce.

"Let me in!" Dahoud called. A weaver peered through a gap between the sacks. Seeing him, she crammed a blanket into the space, shutting him out.

Debris hit him, twigs, grasses, chunks of dead wood. Balls of fire were racing across the plain below. "Please!" Dahoud screamed.

The entrance stayed shut. He huddled against the sacks. Over the storm's howls, he heard another woman's voice, "Is someone out there?" and weaver replying, "Nobody. Just the whore's whelp."

Chunks of rock were breaking loose, thundering down the slope. The wind buffeted him, tore at him, threatened to hurl him from his precarious hold. "Please!" He pounded the sacks and screamed, but the wind carried his voice away. "Where are the others? Let me in! Please!"

The entrance remained blocked.

Pelted by sand, he scrambled for shelter, and found none. No further caves, no crevasses, no stream bed, no gorge.

He curled up behind a boulder, but it offered little protection. Sand scratched his eyes, ground in his nose and throat. Fireballs zinged against the rock face, not ten feet from him. A goat's body whirled, smashed into the rock, spattered him with blood.

See those rocks up there? Behind them you'll be safe.

Where did that voice come from? Soft, almost a whisper, yet audible over the storm's howls. He must be imagining it. But that group of rocks might offer more shelter than this current spot. With shoulders hunched high, he scrambled up the slope. The space between the two rocks was just wide enough for a boy to squeeze through. It was a cave. Cool, wind-still, safe.

Dahoud sat through the night, his arms locked around his knees, listening to the storm's angry howls, thinking about the woman who had refused to shelter him because he was nobody. Anger spiralled inside him, matching the storm's howling fury.

The women have no right to treat you so. You deserve better. The voice again, very close. Low, resonant, smooth, persistent like a musical drum. *How would you like it if women noticed you, treated you with respect, feared you? How would you like to be someone they dare not ignore?*

He would like that a lot. To have no more entrances shut in his face. To be someone women noticed. To be important. To matter. To be able to make others pay attention to his demands. But he was just a nomad boy, the whore's unwanted child, so this could not happen, could it?

Are you willing to do what it takes?

"Who are you, and what do you want from me?"

I'm the part of you that makes you whole. You need to take me in to become someone who matters. I need to be inside you to be strong, and my strength will give you power.

"Power over other children?" He would make them select him for their game teams.

Power over all those who mock you, those who taunt you, those who shut you out.

The storm lashed against the rocks.

"Are you really part of me?"

As soon as you invite me to be.

"And my power will make everyone respect me?"

More than that. The women will fear you. Together, we will be invincible. Would you like that?

"Yes," Dahoud said. "If you really can change how people treat me, and make me powerful, then I will help you grow strong. What must I do?"

At once, a cool, soothing substance swished inside him, settling his burning resentment, infusing him with strength and calm. *Sleep now. Tomorrow, when the storm abides, don't return to your clan. Let them assume you've perished. Go to Djildit Town. It means five days trekking, but you can make it. The Quislaki army is seeking soldiers. With my help, you will become a commander of warriors, a man of power who earns respect.*

Courage poured into his limbs. He felt older, stronger, a grown man. With his new ally showing him what to do, everything would be well.

Now fourteen years had passed. He was an adult, and everything was not all right. Yet again, a woman was shutting him out.

The djinn pulsed like a second heart, pumping fury. *When will we punish her?*

CHAPTER 20

Loyalty

Tarkan stretched his legs under the table, sipped tea and soaked up the sun. Coming to the Samil was like returning to a mother's bosom, far away from Lord Govan's vice-clearance campaign and persecution of men-lovers. The letter from Dahoud had arrived just at the right time. By pretending it contained a job offer, Tarkan had been able to withdraw before the net closed around him. Now he needed an actual job.

"A pleasant caravansary," he said. "Is Esha still whitewashing the guest rooms in the residency?"

"I thought you'd be more comfortable here," Dahoud mumbled. "Near the amenities."

"I've brought some of the things you left in Idjlara. I hope I made the right choices. A saddle, a belt...and this." Tarkan placed the sword on the table between them.

Dahoud's face lit up as he gripped the hilt and stroked the sheath. Then his mouth tightened so briefly that Tarkan nearly missed it. "Yes, thanks. It's good to have these."

A poor clerk might own a sturdy belt and a saddle, but only the wealthiest civilians owned bronze weapons. Even the short swords issued to soldiers remained legion property. Tarkan sensed a secret. "I don't know much about swords. Isn't this long curved blade rather unusual?"

Dahoud shrugged. "Probably Darrian."

A common clerk did not own such a valuable item without knowing its provenance, any more than a common clerk became satrap. The mystery deepened.

Tarkan raised his beaker of hot, fragrant mint tea. "The gods' blessings on this town, on your satrapy, on your marriage. I look forward to working with you. Have you appointed a chief councillor yet?"

Dahoud's face was tight, as if it pained him to speak. "Yes."

"Can we shuffle him diplomatically to an important-sounding post?"

"Mansour is the local leader. Appointing him was the price of peace. It's how I won Koskara."

"Which councillor post is still vacant? Obviously, law is my speciality, but I'll serve in whatever capacity you need me."

"I've created a council of natives."

Tarkan laughed. "Will I also have to let my tunic fray, cover my feet with dust, and sit cross-legged on an animal skin?"

Dahoud watched the cluster of skinny chickens between the tables as if their pecking was of greatest interest to him. "You're not a Samili. Sorry."

Tarkan drank his tea slowly. He had escaped the men-lover hunt with his reputation intact, but with his career stalled. It could be years before he found another councillor job, unless Dahoud changed his mind.

"Far be it from me to criticise your strategy with foolish objections, Dahoud, but have you considered that the council made up of Koskarans is ruling the satrapy on behalf of Quislak? When a conflict of interests arises, do they offer sufficient loyalty? Can you count on them to keep their oath to the Queendom?"

"They've sworn no oath."

Tarkan closed his eyes. With a rebel as chief councillor, and a council that had not sworn loyalty, Dahoud was standing on the edge of an abyss. "I'm familiar with Samil culture and sympathetic to it, and my political skill may help reduce risks."

"We'll have a good time while you're here. The hunting is excellent: gazelles, antelopes, sometimes even leopards. We'll hunt, and wrestle, and ride." Dahoud emptied his beaker and called for a refill. "What's the news? Any exciting developments in Quislabat or Idjlara?"

Far too exciting. Most of Tarkan's friends in Idjlara were dead, drowned by Govan's zeal, and denunciations were spreading like lice. He did not want to think about it. Better talk about Quislabat. "Have you heard about the treason?"

"Treason? No. What happened?"

"The high general tried to murder the Consort."

"Impossible."

"It's not official, mere hearsay, but probably based on fact. Apparently, they were close friends but they fell out when Kirral developed a tenderness for Paniour's daughter. Paniour didn't want his girl to be part of the harem and refused his consent. When Kirral took her anyway, Paniour plotted to kill him." Tarkan sipped. "He almost succeeded, too."

Dahoud's face had gone as white as if he had heard very bad news about a member of his own family. "Will he be hanged?"

"Here comes the most interesting part, if it's indeed true. Rumour has it that in his youth, Paniour used to be a dancing boy in seedy taverns, until Kirral made him an officer. Now Kirral gave him the choice: either Paniour would return to be a dancing boy. Or he would be bricked up alive."

"Paniour would never give up his dignity," Dahoud said. "He chose the slow death."

Interesting: Dahoud had known the high general well – unusual if he had indeed been a common soldier.

The pigeons warbled with excitement as Esha glided into the courtyard in a cloud of white silk, her head held high like a queen's, her arms extended as if permitting the men to rise from their benches in greeting. "I'm ever so glad you've come, Tarkan," she sang. "You'll be our chief councillor, of course."

"I've already told him he won't be," Dahoud said gruffly.

Tarkan bowed in deep deference. He praised the health of her complexion, the shine of her hair and the cut of her gown, and was rewarded with her warmest smile. Govan's daughter was a born manipulator. Through her, he might yet get his appointment.

She chose to sit an arm-length from Dahoud, who barely glanced at her. This was not the behaviour of a newly-wed pair in the thrall of shared passion.

Tarkan placed her family's gifts on the table: a peacock feather fan, a box of inlaid sandalwood, a jewelled collar for her dog. Esha clapped in childlike delight.

Two more people entered the courtyard, a woman and a man. The woman was young, with sun-sparkling glass beads in her many plaits, and Tarkan made a point of appraising her slender figure.

The man had thickly muscled shoulders, tribal tattoos on the cheeks, and hostile eyes burning with fanatical fire. From the way he filled the courtyard with his presence, Tarkan guessed his identity and knew at once that Dahoud had made a grave error in appointing his chief councillor. This was not a man who would meekly assume the role of second-in-command and submit to orders.

The girl sat on the bench beside Tarkan as if they were already acquainted. "Are you married?"

"Alas, no." As if confessing a personal secret, he lowered his tone, but spoke loud enough for everyone else to hear him. "Ambition thwarts my desires. To become a satrap, I may marry nobody but a Ladysdaughter." He caressed the girl with a meaningful gaze. "However strongly another woman attracts me, I must keep myself free for a suitable marriage."

"Will you wrestle with me?"

He digested the girl's proposition. Respectable women did not wrestle men, but a whore would not promote her trade in the presence of the province's dignitaries. To wrestle or not to wrestle, was a familiar dilemma, but normally it was about the danger posed by close physical contact with male bodies, and the suspicions roused if he refused. Most men would grab the chance to roll on the ground with a pretty girl, wouldn't they?

Eight pairs of eyes waited for his reply.

"What a charming idea," he said. "I feel flattered, though on consideration it may not be entirely appropriate."

She sulked. "You're boring, just like Mansour and Dahoud."

"I crave forgiveness for disappointing you, and hope you will grace me with your company for other activities."

"Will you go hunting with me? I like hunting with knives."

"An excellent idea. Now, if you will please excuse me, I want to find the bathhouse to wash off the travel dust. I trust your local bath has a good steam-room?"

Mansour said, "We fire steam on the day of the new moon. Use the river. Or better still, hurry home to Quislak where you belong."

"Thank you for your original suggestions. I'll keep myself clean with olive oil and a strigil."

Esha said, "You're welcome to bathe at the residency. The bathroom is out of order, but there's a courtyard cistern with good clean washing water. Better than that mud-stinking river."

"You live in the residency?" He must have misunderstood Dahoud's mention of a yurt.

"Esha is with child," Dahoud explained. "She's moved to the residency for the moment. The local climate is a strain."

The air was heavy with unspoken words.

"My sincere congratulations on accomplishing pregnancy so soon, my Lady. I accept your offer of clean washing water with gratitude. Once I've settled into my room here, I'll call on you in the residency."

Even if her relationship with Dahoud was as fragile as a cracked clay pot, Lord Govan's daughter was now a person of power, and he would persuade her to use her influence on his behalf.

≈

By the time Tarkan had purchased local garments, the late afternoon sun was dipping the town in a dark golden glow and casting long shadows.

Esha's bracelets clinked as she guided him to the cistern in the residency's courtyard. She had changed into an embroidered court dress, reddened her lips and hung her ears with jewel drops.

"I'm extremely glad you're here," she gushed. "My father, Lord Govan, often said you were one of his best councillors, absolutely indispensable."

"I am gratified by this flattering assessment."

"I know you're absolutely competent. Your experience as a lawyer, your education, your personal talent all mark you out for high office."

"Thank you, my Lady." This was easier than expected. It was as if she was trying to give him a job, without him having to beg.

"Here's the cistern. I've put out a bucket and soapberries and everything else you may need."

"Thank you." He gazed around. Naked male statues lay toppled, their genitals smashed. Someone had loved male sexuality enough to collect its artistic representation; someone else had hated it enough to destroy. The former had to be the late Lord Zetan who had lived here for twenty years. The latter... Tarkan thought of the fanatic fire in Mansour's eyes.

The building was laid out like residencies all over the Queendom, with function rooms and a main entrance in the front, stables and a small exit at the back, bedrooms and service accommodations on the sides, all arranged around a colonnaded courtyard. From the stables came the snorts and soft shuffles of at least half a dozen horses. How typical of Koskarans to vandalise the artwork but to keep the stables in use.

"I know you're intelligent, experienced, utterly dedicated. A real politician." Esha stood closer to him. Her rose perfume smelled sweet and strong in the summer heat. "Why do you allow Dahoud to use you? You got him the job with my father, Lord Govan. Now that he can finally return the favour, he doesn't. I'm ashamed of him."

"The final word on the issue is not spoken." Tarkan hoped she would offer to intercede on his behalf.

Instead, she sat on the edge of the well-head, dabbing her brow with the hem of her stole. "I can't bear this dreadful heat. Goats and sheep are everywhere, and midges and mosquitoes. Even the natives show me scant respect."

"I'm sorry to hear that. What would you have me do?"

She grasped his wrist. "Rescue me and my unborn child. Take us away from Koskara."

"Why do you consider yourself in need of rescuing, my Lady?"

"There's not a single decent soothsayer in Koskara, there's no healer, there's no entertainment. Dahoud wants couplings even though I'm pregnant and he forces disgusting perversions on me and he wants me to shear sheep and to clean the hooves of dirty goats." She broke into a series of sobs.

When he did not respond, she stopped and sat straight. In a voice as clear and hard as crystal, she said, "I know it's difficult for you to deflect certain suspicions, to be on your guard all the time."

"What do you mean, my Lady?"

"If you were married," she said, "any speculations about men-loving would cease."

As always when this subject was raised, he said, "Naturally I wish to marry, but with ambitions to become a satrap, I may only wed a Ladysdaughter, and there are very few of them in the whole Queendom. In the meantime—"

"You don't fool me, Tarkan." Her smile was soft, her gaze hard. "I need to get away from Koskara, and you'll take me."

"Should Dahoud be unable to arrange an escort for your journey, I'll gladly oblige."

"Wedding a Ladysdaughter will numb the nasty rumours, and raise your career prospects. If you get me out of Koskara, I'll marry you."

Thoughts and questions whirled in his head and his heart, but he kept his face and voice steady. "Your offer honours me, my Lady. However, it may not be entirely appropriate, since you are already married."

With a quick wave of her hand, she flicked that argument away. "I'll get the marriage annulled."

As a lawyer, Tarkan knew annulments to be almost impossible."On what grounds?"

"Non-consummation."

He looked at her belly.

She laughed. "We'll say you're the father."

It was plausible. Before her marriage, they had moved in the same circles. If they both claimed the child was his, the ensuing scandal would ensure everyone believed it. No one would watch him narrow-eyed again. He would not even need to mate with a woman. Esha would never expose him, because it was in her interest to maintain the pretence. Being married to a Ladysdaughter would make him a leading candidate when the next satrap position fell vacant.

"Once you're a satrap, my daughter will still be a Ladysdaughter, the start of a great dynasty." She smoothed the purple fringe on her arms. "We'll both get what we deserve – you the career and I the lifestyle – that Dahoud tried to cheat us of."

The churning thoughts in his mind settled. "My Lady, I've often dreamed of allying myself with a suitable spouse, and imagined what she might be like. There is one quality I value above all else. Hearing you brings this precious quality to mind."

"Yes?" she whispered, "What is this quality?" Her eyes were wide open with hunger for praise.

"Loyalty. You, my Lady, don't possess an eggshellful of it." He bowed. "May the Mighty Ones cradle you in peaceful sleep."

Pelted by her curses, he strode to the stable exit.

In the darkness of the stables, Dahoud was standing, a grain sack in one hand, a hoof-pick in the other, his face grey.

Tarkan would give anything to erase the conversation. It was a terrible way for a man to learn of his wife's treacherous nature. "I'm so sorry you had to hear this."

"Pregnant women have odd notions." Dahoud's voice sounded flat and devoid of life. "She didn't mean a single word."

CHAPTER 21

Attacked

At the next meeting, everyone sat cross-legged on animal skins, except Esha, who queened it in a big chair. Dahoud found the council yurt crowded. Zun the high priest could attend whenever he choose, but what was Idrahad doing here?

While Dahoud spoke the invocations and burned incense, the air felt thicker than the wafts of frankincense should. Something was wrong, very wrong.

The entrance felt lifted for another arrival. For a moment, a streak of bright light shone into the yurt, then it was gone.

"I am honoured by the chief councillor's invitation," Tarkan said. "How may I be of service?"

Mansour pointed his spindle at the empty spot between Naima and Idrahad.

Tarkan crossed his legs elegantly and ogled Naima's cleavage. His headcloth was creased in neat folds, and his tunic as crisp as if newly cut from the weaver's loom, without a speck of dust or stain.

When the incense burner passed from hand to hand, Idrahad took it from Tarkan, screwing up his face as if the item stank.

Dahoud went through the first points of the agenda: A leopard stealing sheep, an epidemic of skin rashes, disputes over water rights, Zun demanding a school of healing. Esha wrote everything on waxed wooden tablets with her usual efficiency. A council meeting like any other in the past seven moons – except that people wiped their palms more than normal, and nobody met Dahoud's eyes.

"Idrahad has something say," Mansour said.

Dahoud tensed. Idrahad had resented him from the start, for sneaking into Oubar in disguise, for besting him in trickriding, for not making him councillor, for ousting him from Mansour's regard.

Fabrics rustled and rubbed against leather.

Idrahad cleared his throat. "There are men-lovers in Koskara Town. Hasn't this council sworn to hunt down men-lovers and put them to death?" His eyes gleamed like those of a leopard about to pounce on its prey. "The men-lovers are not only in Koskara Town – they are in this yurt."

A knot tightened in Dahoud's guts at the thought of executing members of his council. "Who do you accuse?"

Idrahad flicked a quick glance to his left. "The Quislaki."

"Tarkan?" Dahoud almost laughed at the ridiculousness of it: Tarkan was a decent, honourable man. "Very well, we'll hear your evidence." He sent an apologetic glance to his friend for having to put him through questioning. At least, this gave him a chance to demonstrate impartiality. "And who else?"

The yurt was silent with heavy expectation. Idrahad straightened like an uncurling snake. "The satrap Dahoud."

The knot in Dahoud's stomach tightened further. "That's absurd. What evidence do you have?"

Mansour held up his hand to examine the new thread. "Since you're accused, you don't get to ask questions. Idrahad, proceed."

"I saw them last night by the river, doing the vile thing." Idrahad spoke with the calm assurance of a storyteller who held his audience bound in a spell.

"Last night? This is a misunderstanding." Dahoud laughed with relief. "We were wrestling in the Quislak style, which is dry-skinned and nude. Only in the Samil style do wrestlers wear leather and oil."

But the air did not clear. Shoulders stayed tense, jaws set.

About the vice of men-loving, these people had neither tolerance nor mercy, and they might not have much sense. The Koskaran penalty for men-lovers was death by dagger-throwing. Dahoud himself had sanctioned it.

"Are you, or are you not, a men-lover?" Mansour demanded.

"I am not," Dahoud said.

Was this how he was going to die: not in battle, not at the hands of an enraged woman, not in atonement for his deeds—but executed for a mere misunderstanding?

"And you?"

"Of course not." Tarkan turned up his palms. "Would I come to Koskara if I were? Your ferocious stance against the vice is famed throughout the Queendom."

"Flies seek out carrion." Wurran's chins quivered. "Tarkan sought out Dahoud."

"Wrestling," Mansour said. "Without spectators. Without clothes."

Several fists balled, and Naima's smooth face crinkled with distaste. A sense of menace swelled. "Disgusting."— "Unnatural."— "Just like Zetan. He did it with children. Locked them into the schoolhouse so he could have his way with them." - "All Quislakis are perverts." - "Castrate them on the spot."

The temperature in the tent rose as if a coppersmith had pumped his bellows into a furnace.

"We don't tolerate men-lovers in Koskara." Mansour's voice was calm, but his eyes flamed. "We execute them by knife-throwing."

Idrahad rose, stroking the daggers in his belt. "Slice them right in the eggs."

"Tarkan doesn't fall under our jurisdiction." Keera's voice was as dry as a stalk of straightthorn grass, with as much emotion. "And a satrap can only be sentenced by a court in Quislabat."

At least one person still had sense. Dahoud blessed her for her calm and her loyalty.

"Who cares about Quislak law?" Mansour laughed. "We do it the Koskaran way. Dahoud himself ratified the method of execution – as long as there is a witness. Let's hear what the witness has to say."

"Idrahad, Idrahad!" the councillors chanted. "Mansour! Knives! Eggs!"

The place no longer smelled of frankincense but of angry sweat. Hatred burned with enough heat to torch the tent.

"They deny the sin, but we will find the truth." Mansour's eyes glowed like angry coals. "If they're guilty, they'll suffer. Keera, you ask the questions and write down the answers."

Keera took up a waxed tablet and pointed a stylus at Idrahad. "Where and when did you witness the act, and what exactly did you see?"

"Yesterday at sundown, the southern river bend. I saw the two of them, writhing naked in vile embrace. Do you want to know what I heard, too?"

"Did penetration take place?"

"The way they were going on..."

"How close did you stand, and long did you stay to watch?" she asked with such detachment, she might be enquiring about the purchase of a clay pot.

"I didn't need to get close," Idrahad said, "because it was obvious what they were doing."

Tarkan sat with a politely attentive face, as if watching a performance that did not concern him personally.

"Is it your normal custom to go the southern river bend at sundown?" Keera asked.

Idrahad straightened. "I went there because the Lady Esha alerted me to what was going on."

Halting his spindle, Mansour looked from Esha to Dahoud, from Esha to Idrahad, and to Esha again.

Esha leant in her chair, her silver-blond hair snaking over its back, her bejewelled fingers calm in her lap. "That is correct."

"Tell them we were wrestling," Dahoud implored. "The way we used to in Idjlara."

A metallic glint flickered in her eyes. "Your vile perversion has finally come out."

Cold comprehension slid down Dahoud's spine. He could no longer shut out the truth: Esha was scheming his death.

Keera took up the next tablet. "Tarkan, your statement, please."

"We were wrestling," Tarkan said pleasantly. "I regret having, in my ignorance of local customs, caused offence."

"We need not listen to this filth," Wurran said.

"Some people's suspicions reflect the scope of their own desires." Tarkan brushed a fleck of dust from the back of his hand. "Councillors are supposed to have loyalty and intelligence."

Esha stabbed a finger in Tarkan's direction. "He's always going to the Old Traders Alley in Idjlara to consort with men prostitutes."

Could there be truth in this accusation? Surely not. Dahoud had known Tarkan most of his life, and known him well. During their long evenings together, or when they wrestled, he would have noticed if anything was amiss.

And yet.... fingers of doubt sneaked into his mind. What did he really know about men-lovers? How much did he really know about his friend? In Djildit, they had been mere children. The adult Tarkan was always spraying females with his charm, but words were as common as desert sand. Whenever Tarkan claimed passionate love, the woman was married and therefore unavailable.

In the three years of their adult friendship, Dahoud had kept the djinn from Tarkan; it stood to reason Tarkan might have kept a secret, too.

Shivers crawled like spiders up his back. Suddenly, it all made horrid sense: Tarkan had come to Koskara looking not just for a job, but for sanctuary from persecution, and Dahoud had failed him.

"What went on in Idjlara doesn't concern us," Mansour said. "Koskara matters."

"But this is evidence," Esha insisted. "And Dahoud had a room near that neighbourhood, so it was easy for him to sneak there every night."

Tarkan smiled. "Aren't you forgetting something, my Lady? Your father, the honourable Lord Govan, has cleansed his satrapy of vice. Male prostitution no longer exists. How could anyone visit boy whores in Old Traders Alley when there are none? Are we to understand that Lord Govan reported untruthfully to the High Queen, an offence punishable by death? It is noble of you to expose your own father."

"This isn't about my father. It's about ridding the world of perverts. If Idrahad is afraid to say they were copulating, I'll say I witnessed it. I'm a Lady, and my word must be believed."

Keera raised the hand with her stylus. "This is an important statement: The Lady Esha says that if Idrahad is afraid to say they were copulating, she will say she has witnessed it as well." Keera emphasised every syllable while she pressed the stylus into the wax. "She is a Lady and her-word-must-be-believed. Have you all heard this?"

Dahoud saw the councillors' frowns and narrowing eyes as the truth seeped into their minds. He could have hugged Keera and kissed her.

"So this is the truth." Mansour put the spindle down. "There are no men-lovers in this yurt, only a snake spewing poison. We've heard enough. The case is closed."

"But..." Esha protested.

Keera placed a hand on her arm. "Perhaps, my Lady, you wish to retire and rest?"

When Esha had left, Mansour said, "Idrahad and I are hunting the sheep-thieving leopard today. Join us, Dahoud." Then, with less warmth, he added, "Your friend is welcome, too."

"I'll join the hunt, if I may." Naima's significant look at Dahoud made it a statement of solidarity, the nearest to an apology he would receive.

Wurran interlaced his fingers and rubbed them up and down. "I'm no coward, but..."

"The fewer people, the better," Mansour said. "A leopard hunt is dangerous."

Zun, with the heavy snake across his shoulders, surveyed everyone in the yurt. He exhaled noisily, as if coming to a decision in a weighty matter, and said nothing.

"I'll be delighted to join your hunt," Tarkan said.

In the cool shelter of the residency, Esha collapsed onto the divan. Sweat streamed down her neck and sides. Everything ached, from her shoulder tips to the small of her back. Her breasts hurt as if the skin was being stretched and could no longer contain them. Waves of nausea alternated with belly cramps, and her guts turned to liquid fire. For the sake of her dynasty, she accepted the suffering, but it would be safer in civilised surroundings, away from the violent sun, from the insolent stares, from the native stink. She hated Dahoud for exposing her to the unsuitable lifestyle, for treating her with insolence, for making perverted demands and for smelling of sweat. She hated him for caring more for the well-being of his horses than for his pregnant wife, and most of all, for defying her scheme.

If she stayed here, she and her child would wither in the hostile heat. She had to escape before her belly swelled further and her sickness increased.

Travel to Quislak or Idjlara would take almost three moons, an unthinkable strain. The nearest safe shelter was the residency in Djildit Town, which she might reach on horseback in under ten days. The kind old satrap, Lord Adil, was sure to offer her hospitality. A thought clicked into place: Lord Adil was widowed. There was potential.

The sickness eased, and her stomach relaxed. She would send a letter first, one that alarmed Lord Adil so much that once she arrived, he would be glad she was still alive and would treat her with every kindness.

"My life is in danger. I have proof of a secret which Dahoud is desperate to hide. For the sake of my unborn child, I will try to escape. By the time you get this letter, I may already be murdered."

After signing off with an 'E' and blowing sand over the moist ink, she felt much better. Taking the parchment and her parasol, she slipped out of the residency to bribe the travelling silk trader. Even in the absence of a messenger service, it was possible to send speedy letters by promising sufficient reward.

She might even pay the trader to escort her out of Koskara, but Dahoud's riders would soon catch up with a mule cart. Perhaps she could use her husband's two-day absence to get away. Better still: she could trick Dahoud into aiding her escape. She hurried back to the residency and packed the items she could not do without: favourite dresses, a few jewels, and of course, darling Cloud.

The shadows were already shortening, and the landscape was fading to pale in the harsh daylight. Esha padded up the dusty road, her heart pounding, not looking at the crowd of natives gathered to see the hunters off. Mansour, Tarkan, Idrahad, the healer Naima, that wild girl Yora and Dahoud sat on their horses, laden with weaponry like mounted warriors, and greeted Esha with hostile scowls.

Everything depended on how well she knew Dahoud after five moons of marriage, and if what she had seen of him was a true picture of his soul. In silence, she walked up to him.

Heat flared in his eyes, so scorching that seemed to singe her skin. "What do you want?"

She dropped to her knees on the packed dirt. "To beg your forgiveness, my Lord." With both arms stretched before her, she lowered her face to the ground and maintained that pose until the discomfort grew too great. "I feel shame too great for words, and I want everyone to know I was wrong. I totally misread a situation when I should have trusted you."

Dahoud shifted in his saddle.

She clasped his sandalled foot. "Please say you'll forgive your foolish wife."

They were the only two people in the world. His eyes held hers with hunger. He needed to believe her the way a thirsting animal needed water. She watched the emotions fight in his face, longing and hope in a battle against resentment.

For a long moment, he gazed into the distance, as if seeing something in the faraway past. Then he looked at her again. "I forgive you, Esha." He bent to pull her up. "We'll talk tomorrow when I come back."

"Don't leave me, Dahoud." She held her hands up imploringly and whispered: "Some of these people are waiting to tear me into pieces as soon as you're gone. Don't leave me unprotected."

"I'll detail a guard for you." He scanned the crowd for people who could take responsibility for his wife.

"They all hate me. I fear they'll arrange an accident for me. You may return to find me dead. I'm so frightened." She widened her eyes and raised her brows in the way that always roused his protective instincts. "Please protect me. Let me ride with you."

She sensed him softening.

"It's a hot brisk ride without rest until afternoon," he warned. "And then we hunt on foot."

"If it's strenuous, it's the punishment I deserve. Thank you Dahoud, thank you!"

Now she had an escort for the first part of her journey north. Once they got to the nomad tents, she would plead tiredness and stay behind to rest while the others went hunting. As soon as they were out of sight, she would hire some of the nomads to travel as her servants, and bribe the others to say she was asleep when the hunters returned at night. Dahoud would not realise her absence until morning, and by that time, she would be out of Koskara. She just hoped she would not get another phase of sickness like she had had earlier. The spots of blood between her legs had been most alarming.

The high priest who had looked so quaint at her wedding was chant.ng in an ancient tongue, apparently to call a blessing on their hunting venture. He danced with low-squatting steps, slowly, ominously. Snakes writhed around his arms, tongues flicking into his face. The deep notes from his throat vibrated her bones and shattered her confidence. She wanted to clasp her hands over her ears and flee, but was trapped like a mouse held by a snake's stare.

℞

To Dahoud's surprise, his wife rode uncomplaining in subdued silence despite the murderous heat. They crossed an endless expanse of parched land, blasted flat and colourless by the sun, recent growth already flattened into submission by drought. A scattering of trees defied the heat, clipped and crippled by hungry mouths. If the drought continued for another year, the last living trees would fade away, despite roots eight men-heights deep in the ground, and even the toughest grasses would vanish, turning the savannah into desert. The heat haze shimmered, and cicadas burred incessantly.

The nomads welcomed the group to the cluster of black tents, two dozen women and men with sun-carved, heat-scorched faces, hungry for gossip and thirsty for news. They boiled up tea and shared their sparse food, a bowl of warm camel milk topped with a head of frothy scum, and dates gritty with sand. When they talked about the goats the leopard had taken, they addressed Mansour, still the rightful leader in their eyes, and treated Dahoud with wary courtesy.

After the meal, while Idrahad and Mansour set up yurts and Naima treated infected eyes, Esha held court under the awnings, allowing the nomad women to fuss over her.

Dahoud took the hunters' skins to refill at the waterhole where the camels and goats were slurping. The level of liquid was so low it would not last another year. A pair of martins circled above the pond, undaunted by the heat. Dahoud bent to draw the scum aside and dipped his cupped hands into the water which was so clear he could see tiny red worms swimming. He filled the skins. In times of drought, water was precious in any form.

Returning to the yurts, he wondered about sleeping arrangements.

If Esha was serious about outward conciliation, they would spend the night in the same tent.

Esha groaned, curled forward. At once, a dozen women flocked to hold her hand and dab her brow with cool water. "The heat," she croaked.

Dahoud's eyes saw a haughty schemer, but his heart saw an exhausted woman he had sworn to protect. He hurried to scoop her up and carry into the shielding shade of his yurt. "I'll stay here with you."

"No, no, you must go on your hunt. I'll be perfectly well soon, and if there's any problem, the women of the camp can look after me better than you could. Just bring my luggage, will you?"

Carrying her baskets, he said, "We'll be back by nightfall."

She yawned. "Don't wake me when you come back."

"Yap-yap-yappyappyapp." There was no mistaking that high-pitched noise from the reed basket. How did the dog come here?

With an agility that belied her claims of sickness, Esha jumped up to silence the yapping dog and cuddled it to her chest with soothing words.

Dahoud's stomach chilled. Esha would not have brought the pet on a short journey from which she expected to return. She had tricked him again. Bitterness bloomed in his chest, burst into anger.

Does this woman still deserve your protection?

He twisted her arm on her back, hard enough to hurt. She yelped.

"Don't touch me!" she yelled. "My father, Lord Govan, will…"

"Your husband, Lord Dahoud, demands an answer. Why did you bring your dog?"

"Yap-yap-yappyappyapp!"

"Your shouting upsets darling Cloud! How dare you!"

The djinn whipped his fury into a blaze. He grabbed the dog's body in one hand, the head in the other, and twisted. The yapping stopped.

Esha screamed.

He tossed the dead dog aside and pinned the woman. Rage surged through him like a hot desert storm. Everything had been a lie. Her pretence of liking him. Her claims about pervert relations. Her fake conciliation. Her pleas for forgiveness. She was probably not even pregnant.

If she screams, will anyone come to her aid? After what she did this morning, will anyone care? We can do with her what we want. Isn't she our wife?

For a long moment, Dahoud savoured the soft flesh beneath him, the female scent, the squealing resistance.

He pulled himself off. "Get up!"

When she did not respond fast enough, he tossed her out of the yurt into the soaring heat. Smiling coldly, he announced, "The Lady Esha will accompany us on the hunt."

~

The afternoon heat seared Dahoud's throat with every breath, but it was the best time to hunt a leopard. Daylight made the spotted predator sluggish. The beast might even be asleep, drooping in the branches of an ancient tree.

While Idrahad and Mansour sought the cat's tracks, often bending to read traces in the scattered stones and the high yellowed-tufted grass, Dahoud kept a wary eye on Esha, still nurturing his anger at her deception. She was not an ally who had erred, but a devious enemy who had never ceased to scheme. He would not let her out of his sight, would not allow her a moment in which to scheme another plot. Now she seemed determined to cause trouble, frequently demanding that Naima act as her maid and carry her parasol. Her complaints were loud enough to wake a sleeping leopard and drive it away.

Mansour led them to a half-dried water-hole. Butterflies glided low over the purple-tinted surface, red like large splotches of blood. On the gravel edge, small, long-tailed birds picked worms from the footprints of larger animals.

"To find the predator, find the prey," Mansour said. "This waterhole is used by gazelles." He bent to study the prints. "Here's our leopard: round prints, no claw-marks. Problem solved. A female, about four feet. When those prints were made, the soil was still damp, just before the water receded to the current level. She was here last night, and she'll come here again." He picked up his spear. "She's nearby, resting, probably in a tree. But be careful, she may not be asleep."

When the first rim of the golden disk touched the horizon and the dusk breeze blew across the plains, they still had not found the beast, and their spears were growing heavy.

"Too late for today," Mansour said. "At night, leopards are invincible. We'll try the same spot again tomorrow."

"You made me walk for hours and hours and it was for nothing?"

Esha wailed. "I won't take one step further! Bring me my litter."

"You know your litter is in Koskara Town," Dahoud said, weary of her complaints, frustrated by their lack of success. "If you want to sleep in a tent tonight, get walking."

Without warning, a leopard broke cover and leapt across their path.

Dahoud threw his spear. The weapon hit, but did not kill. The cat went to the ground, then vanished behind acacias and horsedeath trees.

"A wounded leopard's fury is deadly," Idrahad growled. "Nobody will be safe tonight."

"I'll kill her," Dahoud promised.

Idrahad laughed. "How many leopards have you killed to be so sure? Leopards are stealthy. They don't wait around for a satrap, and pose until he gets his aim right."

"Let's walk back to the camp," Mansour said. "We'll warn the nomads, light fires and post guards."

"You go back, I stay," Dahoud said. By wounding the leopard, he had endangered the people he had set out to protect. "Even if I have to hunt her all night, I'll make the kill."

"We'll hunt her together," Mansour said.

"But it's getting dark," Esha wailed. "Dahoud promised we'd be back by nightfall."

They found the broken-tipped spear, but the trail of blood led into the undergrowth and petered out.

The sun was sinking fast, taking the heat with her. Evening wind brushed the undergrowth, and grasses whispered all around them so they could no longer hope to hear the wounded cat move. They were still a long way from the camp.

"At twilight, leopards get dangerous," Mansour warned. "Be on your guard."

Esha sat down and sulked. "I'm feeling faint. Bring me my litter."

"Get walking, or we'll leave you behind as fodder for the beast." Dahoud threatened.

She responded with a theatrical moan. Only Yora fell for it. Kneeling at Esha's side, she mumbled soothing words, while Dahoud marched on, shutting out Esha's wails.

He had taken half a dozen paces when Yora shouted, "She's bleeding."

He spun. "What?"

Esha lay curled in the grass. Yora cried, "Mother of Mares, she's bleeding between her legs. Naima, what—"

A movement flickered in the darkening undergrowth. Two yellow eyes gleamed.

Dahoud leapt to throw himself before the women.

The beast's weight sent him into a staggering spin. Through ripping pain, he saw the leopard hang from his arm, its claws and teeth in his flesh. By spinning, he could keep the hind legs away from him. If he slowed for an instant, the claws would tear into his guts. A belly wound meant certain death.

Through haze of agony, he saw Esha's curled pink form on the ground. Yora was crawling. The men clutched spears they did not dare to throw.

Stronger arms. Memory of the seer's words pounded in his heart. *Get stronger arms, stronger arms, stronger arms...*

His feet started to slip on the blood-slicked grass. He must not fall.

Yora stood, knees bent, arms stretched in front, a dagger ready to throw. Could she hit the right target in this whirling tangle?

The knife whizzed, grazed the cat's hind flank. The beast recoiled.

Dahoud snatched the moment. His free hand found and yanked out his dagger, stabbed at the cat's head. The blade hit the skull and slid off.

"The heart!" Mansour yelled. "Into the heart!"

As Dahoud tried to get his blade in behind the front flank, his spinning pace slackened. Her hind legs ripped into his thigh with roaring pain.

I can give you the strength to win, the djinn said. *Won't you ask me for it?*

Yes. Yes, yes, yes!

Instant power surged.

She's a female. Strong and devious. She needs subduing.

Yes, yes, yes!

Dahoud's eyes locked with the attacker's yellow-flaming fury. Both wounded, they would stay clasped until one's strength gave out.

He urged his body into renewed speed and drove the dagger into her flesh. As they collapsed in a bloody embrace, he rammed his weapon deeper into her. His guts burned with agony and his veins flowed with fire that singed his flesh. Then the pain faded and the world around him sank into orange, then black.

$\mathcal{L}$

At last, life returned to his limbs and the haze cleared from his brain. He recognised the people in his yurt: Naima, Mansour, Keera, Yora.

"Does your belly hurt?" Yora asked. "It was all open, and I could see your guts, like with a butchered sheep. Naima made the men piss into your belly. Tarkan didn't want to, but Mansour did."

"Drastic measures," Naima said. "Patients with belly wounds seldom survive. Thirteen days, Dahoud. I've never had a patient hover so long in the valley between life and death."

"Thirteen days?" Dahoud sat up as best he could. "Then I must -"

She pushed him back into the fleeces. "You must rest and drink lots of garlic juice."

"Obey Naima and rest," Mansour said. "I'm ruling Koskara."

Dahoud's mind groped back to the day of the hunt, searched for memories, found little. Legal concepts were even more elusive. Yet something was wrong: if the satrap was ill, the Lady took over the government. "Esha is the regent."

Yora squeezed her hand around his.

"The Lady Esha is dead," Mansour said.

Mansour had to be mistaken. But a picture of Esha's curled pink shape on the ground seeped into Dahoud's mind. She had been bleeding.

Guilt gnawed. "I made her come on the hunt."

"It would have happened anyway." Naima's voice was unusually gentle. "Esha was carrying a child outside her womb. Her body expelled the poison fruit too late."

"Don't worry about anything," Keera said. "Mansour is acting regent, and I handle the correspondence, the administration, the formalities. Between us, we're taking care of almost everything."

Dahoud sensed an omission. "What is it you're not taking care of?"

"The Consort summons you to Quislabat."

Once a year, every satrap had to serve the Queen in the palace for three moons, performing pointless tasks such as watering the rose

STORM DANCER by RAYNE HALL

garden or feeding royal pets. This Quislaki tradition allowed rulers to keep an eye on the satraps and prevent uprisings.

"My court service isn't due until Date Moon."

"This isn't about court service." Keera's voice was dry as ever. "It's about a letter Esha sent before she died."

CHAPTER 22

Merida Plots her Escape

Kirral looked forward to breakfast in the rose pavilion. His chosen companions would enhance the entertainment. On his left, was Kadiffe hanging on to his arm, giggling and trilling for his attention. On his right, Merida strode stiffly.

The guard at the pink-pillared entrance bowed to his toes. "Everything is prepared, Highness. Number two, he's been active overnight. Tried biting his wrists."

"Excellent." Kirral rubbed his palms. "Get breakfast ready at the number two hole. Three settings."

Inside, carpets and sumptuous cushions granted comfort, while incense burners neutralised the latrine odour. Only Merida wrinkled her nose.

"Come, my dear wives." He showed them the cushions around the four-foot round hole. "This is where the Queendom keeps its special guests. One in each cell. They are here permanently. The defectors, the rebels, the traitors."

Kadiffe clapped her hands. "My papa is a traitor! May I speak to him?"

"Of course, dear Kadiffe, that is why I brought you here. First, let us enjoy breakfast and the view of this inmate here." He clapped for a servant. "Eggs, almonds, sausages."

"Let me out!" The prisoner from number one wailed. "Pleeeeease!"

Kirral yawned. Number One was still at adjustment stage, and predictable. Number Two was much more interesting. He leant forward to peer down the hole to check on that prisoner's progress. The guard had reported wrist activity. Indeed, the man was lying curled, and the scent of blood came wafting up.

"Prisoners are a precious research resource. Merida, you may share my studies of the human nature." He offered her the tray of sliced fruit.

Although she took a slice of orange, she did not eat it, but pressed her lips together as if trying not to throw up.

Shall we tease her national pride?

Kirral opened his arms, encompassing the room. "These dungeons are four generations old, but their design is remarkable. Each cell enables the prisoner's survival. Every day, the guests get the finest dates and freshest bread dropped into their cells. There's a basin of water, fed from the outside, fresh every day. Slits in the wall allow sunlight in. A hole in the floor takes the body wastes into an underground chamber which gets flushed once a moon. Impressive, is it not?" Kirral sucked a juicy fig. "The engineer who created it was Riverian."

Merida stared straight at the opposite wall, her face a rigid mask.

"Listen, please, please, listen," the prisoner in Number One wailed. "I'll do anything but let me out!"

"The poor man feels the boredom of two moons without company," Kirral said. "Kadiffe, drop him some raisins."

At once, Kadiffe grabbed a handful of raisins and tossed them down the Number One hole. "He's picking them up!"

"Thank you, kind person," the prisoner cried. "Talk to me. Please. Just a word."

"Now, dear Merida, what do you wish Kadiffe to do? Stay silent, or ease his despair with a friendly chat?" He nibbled at a roast rabbit leg. "Before you choose, consider. Everyone who takes up residence here knows he will not leave except as a carcase. In the four generations that this accommodation has been in use, nobody ever left alive. Yet this does not stop them from hoping. It appears the human mind creates hope where none exists. Hope may be a necessary ingredient of sanity. However, my studies show that hope prolongs suffering. So, do you wish Kadiffe to communicate with him, giving him a morsel of hope, which will increase his despair? The choice is yours."

Merida pressed her lips into a tight line and gave a minute shake of her head.

Excellent. She would hear the prisoner's pleas in her sleep, and berate herself for depriving him of the small solace.

"Now consider this specimen here," Kirral said. "He has completed Phase Two, the descent into insanity, which generally occurs at the beginning of the forth moon. I find the pattern consistent. They smear the walls, and themselves, with their faeces. The collapse into ranting madness is always educational to watch."

Merida held a clenched fist to her throat. The muscles in her jaw worked, but she pointedly looked away from the hole.

"I regret if the smell offends," Kirral said. "One would assume that confinement is in itself an unpleasant enough state, yet these people go out of their way to make it even more unpleasant. Some regret it, and try to clean the walls. However, this enlightened moment lasts a mere two to twelve days, then they resume their active sloth, until they lie in a bed of faeces. It fascinates the studious mind."

At last, Merida's composure broke. "You monster."

Shall we grant her a few moment's peace to recover her control, or shall we provoke her until she has no control left?

Provoking Merida was fun. Sometimes she responded with insults, sometimes with lectures, sometimes with silence, and he had not yet worked out the pattern.

"This specimen has completed Phase Two and has reached Phase Three, the suicide attempts, my current research focus. Naturally, we do not facilitate self-harm. The water basins are constructed to prevent prisoners from immersing their faces, the food contains no bones for stabbing, and without clothes, they have no textiles for hanging. As a first step, they try to refuse nourishment, but they cannot keep it up, not with fresh water bubbling and fragrant bread dropping into their cell."

Kirral nibbled a nut-stuffed date. "After that, they get creative. Some hit their heads against the wall, but it is nearly impossible to summon enough force, so they merely get a headache or a fractured skull. Others bite off or swallow their tongue, or rip their throat open, or bite their wrists, which is what this guest has done." Kirral gestured into the hole. "Can yo see the blood, Merida? Naturally, he lacked the willpower to succeed."

Kadiffe snuggled against his chest, demanding a share of his attention. He patted her head.

"Is it not disappointing that he performed his first attempt at night? Would it not have been entertaining to watch it at breakfast?"

Kadiffe tugged at his moustache. "Can we see Papa now, please?"

"Yes, dear. Pick up your cushions, and we shall view the prisoner in Number Five. Merida, you will like him. He has been with us for four months, and is still sane. He does not beg, he does not scream, he does not soil himself. A marvel of discipline, and so clean. It will be interesting to watch when he finally cracks."

Shall we stimulate her mind? How will she respond to a personal taunt?

"Before you view the prisoner, dear Merida, here is a hypothetical question for you. Assume that a person must choose between loyalty to their country, and loyalty to their family, which path should they take?"

Although she held her lips in tight refusal, her eyes worked, showing that she was pondering the question.

Kirral bent over the hole. In the strip of light spearing from the window slit into the cell, Paniour was walking, his naked body as straight as if he was marching on the parade ground. Five steps one way, five steps back, that was all the cell allowed. Squats.

Merida was looking too.

"His discipline is admirable, almost Riverian, is it not?"

She spoke at last. "What has this man done?"

"He made a bad choice." Kirral wrapped his moustache around his forefinger. "He acted on his own values, and assumed that his loyalty would be reciprocated." He bit into a sausage and chewed without taking his eyes off Merida. "He forgot that other people had different values, and they also had choices to make. A member of his own family choose to further her own status over protecting him. Terrible, is it not?"

"Yes," Merida said, her eyes wary like those of animal that sensed the trap but could not see it yet.

"Naturally, such a situation would never arise in Riverland. Or would it? Would a Riverian protect their own status – their value points—by abandoning a family member to their fate?"

Merida's nostril's flared.

Kirral pressed on. "My research shows that humans are very ready to sacrifice others if they can pretend it is for the greater good. Your Mother convinced herself that she acted not out of self-interested, but to serve the rest of the family, or even the Virtuous nation. Dear Kadiffe sacrificed her father who had given everything to protect her. According to her conscience, she was serving the Queendom by revealing a traitor."

Kadiffe, hearing her name, purred.

"Had our guest studied human nature the way I have, he could have anticipated what she would do. Alas, he did not, and he still does not know who betrayed him. It will be so educational to watch his reaction."

He leant forward and called into the hole. "Paniour! My dear Paniour. I've brought visitors."

Five steps. Turn. Five steps. Squat.

He slapped Kadiffe on the rump. "Talk to him."

Kadiffe leaned over the hole and waved. "Papa! Look at me, Papa."

The prisoner stopped pacing. He looked up. He stared. His mouth opened.

"Kadiffe?" His anguished cry tore through the building.

"Would you like sausages, Papa?" Kadiffe upended the bowl, spilling the pieces on his head.

"Kadiffe!!!!!!" Paniour screamed with the anguish of a mortally wounded animal.

"Well done, dear." Kirral patted his thigh, and Kadiffe crawled onto his lap.

"I saved the Queendom, didn't I?"

"You did, dear. Without you, Paniour would have led the legions against us. You're a heroine of the nation."

Kirral looked forward to watch the erosion of Paniour's sanity. Life was becoming more interesting every day.

What shall we do to Merida next?

≈

Teruma shifted through piles of documents, with thoughts chasing in her mind. Kirral's djinn possession and the Queen's fragile health clawed at her position. She needed to act fast, to place more supporters in the Samil, and to channel more funds into developing the region's satrapies, before she made her move and declared the Samil an independent nation.

To avoid rousing Kirral's suspicion, she had to carry out her routine tasks. With every staff member Kirral executed or dismembered, more duties fell to her. Updating the palace expenses records alone would take days. The last thing Teruma wanted was a visitor wasting her time with complaints.

Merida wore her hair in a tight bun, and her lips in a wide smile. "Greetings. I hope I find you in best health."

Her voice carried a lot of confident gaiety for someone whose plans had been foiled and who had recently been betrayed by her own mother. Teruma did not believe the cheer.

"I'm busy." Teruma stood, pointing at the spout of the clock, where fine desert sand ran like water. "State what you want, and be quick about it."

Merida's smile refused to shrink. "I want to work. Not magic of course, and not slop buckets."

Teruma held a finger into the stream of sand running from the clock-spout.

"Why don't you let me keep accounts?" Merida waved an arm towards the stacked scrolls and tablets on the desk.

"Prove that you can."

She watched Merida sort the documents into neat piles, draw parallel lines and columns on parchment, and write.

When Teruma checked at the end of the day, she found the entries meticulous and the calculations correct. The expenditures for the entertainment of diplomats were listed in the same straight script as the costs for repainting Kirral's apartments. Only in the entries for torturer's fees did the handwriting wobble.

Day after day, Merida worked under Teruma's watchful eye, using her skill to sneak into the head-wife's trust, at the same time gaining knowledge about trade, prices, and the outside world. She had been a captive for eight moons, and since that horrible breakfast, she knew that being Kirral's captive meant more than mere humiliation and discomfort. She was in real danger. Since no escape route existed, her only chance to flee was by cunning, and for that, she needed access to information, fast.

In Teruma's study, windows allowed natural light, fresh air circulated, and no noise intruded beyond the occasional twittering caged bird or purring cat.

The Quislaki currency lacked logic. Thirteen coppers made a bronze ring. Twenty-one and a half bronzes made one silver.

Merida sorted, copied and calculated. She attributed the costs of face paints, perfumes, skin-softening clay, nettle massages, dance lessons and servant wages to individuals and to palace overheads. Once the backlog was cleared, she drew up an annual budget. It felt good to hold an inkbrush again.

"Shouldn't I dress as a greenbelt while I'm doing this work?" she asked. A greenbelt's uniform would be the perfect disguise. The palace was riddled with them, and they went in and out all the time. The bulky turban would hide her conspicuous hair.

"No," Teruma said.

Merida considered disguising as a servant, but servants went bareheaded. Perhaps she could disguise herself as one of traders who came to the harem to peddle their fripperies. If she wore a cone-shaped straw hat and carried several baskets, she might be able to get out of the palace unrecognised.

She bought items she did not want from the sandal-seller and the perfume purveyor so she could squeeze them for information about the outside world. She discussed with the tailor whether it was possible to copy her trousers or to patch up the threadbare parts. She even bought a big pot of skin-softening clay, a pair of purple slippers, a sewing kit and a pile of coloured felt pieces. She observed every trader's mannerisms until she was certain she could impersonate them. Next, she had to persuade one of them to leave her distinctive hat and baskets behind, but she could not trust them. Any of them might betray her the way the masseuse had.

The saffron-yellow uniform of a royal herald would be even better. With her hair hidden under the turban, she could ride fast on a horse borrowed from the stables, pretending to be on the Consort's business. Nobody would dare to delay her. Herald's uniforms were washed in the palace laundry.

She went to Teruma. "We keep sending the bed sheets to be washed, but the fruit stains never come out. I could teach the laundresses how stains are treated in Riverland." Red-scrubbed hands were a fair price to pay for access to heralds' uniforms.

"I doubt they would care for your lectures," Teruma said. "No. We're going to be busy. The Queen is well again, thank the Mighty Ones. There'll be thanksgiving celebrations throughout the country, and I have to organise them. You, Merida, will arrange a party for the palace staff."

Nearly five hundred people were to be entertained. Merida checked the archives for previous events of a similar nature, and hired musicians, bellydancers, whiteseers and acrobats, and continued plotting her escape.

On the day of the celebration, flags and bunting fluttered. The garden smelled of perfumes, sausages and frying fat. Pigeons padded along the paths, and squawking sparrows fought for crumbs of cake.

It felt good to be out of doors, for the first time in ten moons in a garden much wider than the harem courtyard, where the air tasted of freedom. But whenever Merida strayed to the exit, stern guards blocked her way.

With a jug of honey-sweetened wine in her hand, she strolled to the musicians, whom she had briefed to play decent four-count music with their flutes and tambourines, and then on to the crowd clustering around the whiteseers.

Instead of forming orderly queues, people jostled for position. Kadiffe had secured the first consultation, probably to ask advice how to monopolise Kirral's affection.

Merida watched the seer who was sniffing at the girl's palms: a skinny woman, with face, hair and arms covered in thick layers of white clay. Her aura was much larger than her slight body, pulsating in intelligent yellow, spiritual silver, and the deep red of serious magic.

Although the seer looked like a charlatan with her white dress, clay-covered hair, and painted arm rings, her power was real. Merida wanted to shout with joy at meeting a colleague, someone who would understand her, at last. She disciplined herself into patience until her turn came. Surrounded by curious onlookers, she could not ask for aid in escaping. Ten black rings painted on the seer's left arm stood for magic degrees attained. If Quislaki magic degrees were similar to Riverian qualifications, the seer was trained in thought transmission. Could they communicate without being heard?

Merida absorbed the rhythm of the music, converting it into magical energy.

Now the seer was speaking, giving the eager Kadiffe the customary single sentence of advice: "Learn to play Siege."

Merida nearly laughed out loud at the appropriateness of this advice, but Kadiffe sulked. "Yes, but what can I do to make him really interested in me?"

"Next," the seer said coldly.

Standing straight, Teruma held out her hands. "How can I achieve my goal?"

Merida thought this was a good way of phrasing a question. Nobody would know what it meant.

The seer scratched, slapped and sniffed. Dropping the hands, she said, "Seize the moment when it comes."

Teruma looked startled. "Yes, but how do I know when the moment is right?"

"Next," the seer said rudely, ignoring Teruma's high rank.

When she took Merida's hands, the touch prickled like nettle stings.

Merida asked a bland question that the bystanders could hear: "How can I be happy?" but silently, she sent the real message, "I'm a magician, imprisoned in the harem. How can I escape?"

The seer performed her scratching and sniffing. In a bored voice she said, "Fulfil your new role."

While Merida waited for a discreet thought transmission, the seer dropped her hands. "Next."

Either the seer had not received the real question, or she did not want to help. Another hope was crushed.

With clinking cymbals and spinning fabrics, a bellydancer whirled into the room. Her hips rolled, her arms swayed like branches in the wind, her shoulders quivered like ash leaves in the autumn. Her hands made scarves dance like flames, and the shivers of her belly could have brought rain. She was a cat, she was a snake, she was a woman. There was beauty in this dance, no vulgarity. Merida watched, mesmerised, glad for the distraction from her pain.

Then drums rolled for the performance Kirral had requested, an escapologist who claimed the ability to free himself from any fetters. People clustered around the wooden cage. On one side of the partition, the actor was roped to the wooden bars, on the other waited a growling leopard. The sand clock spouted a stream of silver sand into the bowl. Once it was spent, a spectator would pull up the partition, freeing the beast to maul the man. The performer succeeded in undoing the knots and fleeing the cage just as the last grains of sand trickled from the spout.

Kirral congratulated him warmly. "An excellent performance, most educational. I wonder if you would care to repeat it." He rubbed his hands. "If you escape a second time, I will treble your fee. Bear in mind, however, that I have observed closely how you undid those knots. This time, I will tie them so you cannot undo them by the same method. Will you take the risk?"

Merida guessed that if the performer survived, Kirral would tempt him with higher rewards into further and further repeats, each with a higher risk of failure.

An angry female voice lashed across the room. "You don't know how good you've got it, what a sheltered life you lead." Heads turned, necks craned. The seer with the ten magic rings was yelling at a couple of concubines. "Always enough to eat, even when the rest of the country goes hungry. What do you have to complain about?" Her voice rose to a screech. "Most of us would change places with you happily. We're anonymous – unknowns who look alike, act alike. Nobody will recognize us if they see us again the next year because even our rings will have gone or been added to. We have no name, no family, no home, nobody to mourn us when we die. We carry no possessions, own nothing but our gift for seeing, often go hungry..."

Teruma linked her arm through the ranting seer's to steer her away from the crowd. "Haven't you been treated well? Tell me about it in my study."

"Oh, we've been treated more than adequately. We've had a bath, a new white robe, as much food as we could eat, thank you very much. An offer for a dormitory bed, even, for those who want it." She fixed Merida with a stare. "You spoiled concubines don't know how lucky you are."

Merida boiled in anger. To be called a spoiled concubine! Ha! She would change places with the whiteseer any time. She would happily trade her captivity for occasional hunger. As for anonymity, by the Four Virtues, she would give anything to be able to move without being noticed.

She stopped in sudden understanding. Shutters fell away: While the harem teemed with seers, all looking alike, a white dress and lots of clay were all Merida needed to fade into obscurity. Her and the seer's glances met. The seer winked.

While most people's attention drew to the escapologist in the leopard cage, Merida ambled back into the harem wing as if answering a call of nature. There was no time to carry out research or perfect her plans. She had to use the chance at once.

In the deserted dormitory, Merida ripped the sleeves from the tunic she had worn for her rain dance, and slapped on white skin-softening clay. Kadiffe's face-paints provided rings around the arms: eleven in black for Merida's magic degrees, and two in blue for the years of celibacy since her husband's death. A white fabric square from the embroidery kit, tied with string, made a pouch of the kind the seer had worn on her waist.

By nightfall, her disappearance would be noticed, but pursuers would be seeking a Riverian in a grey trouser-suit and leather boots. Merida dropped her boots into the latrine shaft. Haurvatat would not miss the plainest of her forty-seven pairs of sandals.

⨯

"Who's that?" the palace guardsman by the bronze doors barked.

Her heart beat so wildly, she could feel the rhythm in her mouth, but she gave him a haughty stare and strode on.

"It's only a white one," his colleague said. "The Lady Teruma hired a dozen of them for the celebration."

Once outside the palace, Merida walked fast, but with a show of absent-minded arrogance, and blended into the afternoon crowds bustling through the city gate. As long as she kept to the north-east direction, she would eventually reach the safety of the Copperland border. To get there, she would have to keep marching for many days, and nobody must suspect she was not a whiteseer.

CHAPTER 23

Dahoud at Court

The painted walls of the Consort's anteroom closed in on Dahoud. He shifted from one buttock to the other, longing for the open grasslands of Koskara.

At last, Teruma glided through the arched doorway stretching her hands out to him. The copper bangles on her arms clinked. "Welcome to the palace, Lord Dahoud."

"What did Esha say in her letter?"

"Later." Linking her arm through his, she steered him down the corridor. "Have a bath first."

"No time for that. I want to get this problem sorted at once."

"Kirral has booked a special treatment for you." Her tone lowered. "The Consort's good will may not last much longer, so enjoy it."

"Lie down," a female voice commanded in the misty white steam, her accent foreign and harsh.

Dahoud lowered himself onto the hot marble. Bone by bone, muscle by muscle, ligament by ligament, she kneaded him into passive pulp. Surprisingly, the djinn stayed silent.

"Now comes the special treatment. It's an ancient Riverian tradition, a secret from the Temples of Discipline. Turn over." Lashes whipped down on him, needles bit into his flesh, covering his thighs, his buttocks, his back in red heat.

"You enjoyed that," she told him, pushing her hands into her waist, emphasising arm muscle. "Remember, this is a Riverian speciality."

"I'll remember." Dahoud resolved to avoid all dealings with Riverian females.

Once he would have been roused by her ruthlessness, and the djinn would have tormented him with desire. Now, only a fleeting fancy had passed his mind. Four years of near-abstinence had strengthened Dahoud and weakened the djinn. He had as good as conquered the demon. From now on, it would be easy to resist.

◆

Dahoud's buttocks still prickled when he stood in Kirral's study.

The Consort sat with a long curved dagger across his thigh. His turban was the colour of freshly butchered meat.

From her chair in the corner, Teruma flashed him a sliver of a smile, and continued shifting parchments.

"I had hoped to congratulate you on your success in Koskara. Instead, I have to execute you for murder." Kirral leant back on his dark red divan and unfolded a parchment. "Lord Adil forwarded this. *My life is in danger. I have proof of a secret which Dahoud is desperate to hide. I will attempt to flee for the sake of my unborn child. By the time you get this letter, I may already be murdered.* Entertaining, is it not?"

"Esha had an accident."

"A noblewoman reaching out from death to accuse her killer is convincing." Kirral stroked the parchment along his moustache. "The people who received copies are eager for your blood, Govan especially. The penalty for killing a Lady is being torn apart by two bulls."

"Five people witnessed the accident. Our healer says—"

"Your healer? Interesting. The penalty for healing in the occupied territories is the cutting off of both hands. Is this healer a woman?" Kirral's lips curled. "I thought so. How will you enjoy watching the amputation?"

The incense-laden air suddenly seemed very thin. "Highness, the other witnesses—"

"Rebels who refused to swear loyalty to the Queendom."

'Tarkan Ladysson is oath-sworn."

"Ah, yes. Tarkan, the former councillor of law, who left Idjlara in a hurry. Will his lifestyle stand up to scrutiny in court? The penalty for men-lovers is drowning." Kirral adjusted a crimson cushion. "Is he a good friend of yours?"

"Highness, we were hunting a leopard, when—"

Kirral raised a hand to silence him. "I know the story from the report your councillor Keera sent. A remarkable woman. Statecraft-trained, oath-sworn. Quick-thinking, too. How unfortunate that she destroyed the evidence by having the body burned instead of embalmed."

"Burning is the local custom."

"Destruction of evidence is a crime. The penalty is a lifetime of chained labour."

"Highness, believe me, Keera had nothing to do with Esha's death. It was an accident."

Kirral's smile was knife-edge thin. "What I believe is irrelevant. What matters is what I choose to do about it. I can execute you and punish your friends. Or I can deflect the accusations and clear your name – if you agree to render me a small favour by starting your annual court service early, with a special assignment."

Dahoud's scalp prickled. "A suicide mission for which nobody has volunteered?"

Teruma rose from her chair, snake bracelets jingling, and studied him as if he was a token in a complicated game. "A task which suits your particular talents. Find a missing woman before she comes to harm."

"One of my dear wives has vanished," Kirral said. "We fear for her safety."

"Vanished by choice, or abduction?" Dahoud asked.

"It appears she left of her own will," Teruma said. "If word were to spread, it would reflect badly on the Consort. We need you to be discreet."

"What's she like?"

"Tall, medium build, long hair—between light brown and reddish blonde—and amber eyes. Her name is Merida Karr, a Riverian national from the upper classes. She has no relatives or contacts in the Queendom."

At the mention of 'Riverian', the memory of nettles prickled across Dahoud's skin. "Any particular skills?"

Kirral and Teruma exchanged a silent glance. Then Teruma said, "Magic. Her speciality is the weather."

Several items in Dahoud's mind clicked together. "The rain dancer!"

"You remember her?" Kirral twirled his moustache. "Good, then you will recognise her."

"I only saw her from the distance. I thought she had returned to Riverland?"

"She changed her mind."

A successful hunter needed to understand the prey. "Highness, as a renowned scholar of the human mind, how do you assess her?"

Kirral laughed. "Prim, prudish, patronising. You'll probably find her lecturing to sheep, wrapped up in fabrics while everyone else is going naked in the sweltering heat. Her Siege-playing is decent, but predictable. She dislikes trying anything new, and I could foretell most of her moves."

"She lacks social adaptability," Teruma added, "and complains that the palace wants Riverian refinements. Surviving without comforts will be a struggle. We expected her to give herself up after one night. Six days have passed, and we fear for her safety."

"What steps have you taken?"

Teruma smoothed her hair back. "The border guards are watching for a woman of her description. I also asked a whiteseer, who told me to get the one man who can bring the woman back: you." She pinned Dahoud with the stare of a desert hawk watching her prey. "Merida may not be willing to return."

"I'll get her."

Teruma's eyes showed the smug satisfaction of an owner whose horse had just won a big race. "You'll start your hunt tomorrow. Tonight, you're dining with us. I want you to meet the Queen."

Dahoud stood straighter. Few subjects were honoured to meet the glorious woman who represented Quislak's power. He had been in her presence once for the anointing. Today he would share her meal and conversation. He needed to make a good impression.

The table was laden with more food than most Koskaran families saw in a moon, with exotic dishes set out on copper trays and in delicate red earthenware bowls, steaming with spices and the smell of fried meat.

The Queen's big body filled an ivory-inlaid chair that would have been broad enough for five ordinary women. She had a face as pale and shapeless as unbaked dough, with tiny eyes like black desert beetles. Her eating sticks clacked rhythmically on her teeth and her bowl.

From time to time, she threw pieces of meat at her peacocks. Five of those long-tailed white creatures strode around the room on scaled, silent feet.

Platter piled upon platter: fluffy couscous topped with melting butter, crisp-fried dormice, glazed garlic, saffron-gilded lentils, generous slices of lamb, and what looked like an insect the size of a bird.

Kirral pulled off a leg and dipped it into salty butter. "Locusts are pests who strip the plants bare, even my rare roses, but they taste good."

The Queen spoke up. "You are the new satrap of Koskara."

'Yes, your Luminous Glory, Ma'am."

Teruma said, "Dahoud has been successful in Koskara. He tamed the rebels there, thus saving the Queendom a lot of trouble."

"That is nice." The Queen said. "He married Govan's girl. I remember her. Studied statecraft. Very suitable."

Silence descended. A peacock tried to turn, but had to change its mind when its long, dragging tail became trapped between the legs of Dahoud's chair. Its cold yellow eye seemed to blame the inconvenience on Dahoud. "Heeah-wou!" The accusing scream shrilled so loud it threatened to shatter the ceramics. "Heeah-wou, heeah-wou, heeah-wou!"

The humans kept eating, apparently used to piercing peacock cries at dinner. Dahoud wondered if Kirral had thought of serving fried peacock.

Teruma spoke calmly. "Unfortunately, the Lady Esha had an accident. Dahoud is widowed."

"Make him marry someone else." The Queen s stuffed her mouth with bread, like a well-fatted ewe intent on grazing.

"We will." Teruma said. "I have already compiled a list of eligible Lacysdaughters. We think Dahoud succeeded with the rebels because he's a Samili himself. The Tajlit province needs a new satrap. They have a rebel problem there too."

236

"Yes, I heard that the Tajlit satrap has died," the Queen said. "It is a bad place, the Samil. People there keep dying."

Dahoud kept his eyes firmly on the food. So this was the Queen he had worshipped from afar, the most powerful person in the country, the one whose decisions could alter the course of history! Perhaps it was just as well she left the day-to-day government to her shrewd Consort.

"Dahoud is Samili," Kirral said. "That is why he is good at putting them to order."

"Appoint another Samili in Tajlit," the Queen ordered. She crumbled bread, fed half to her peacocks, and stuffed the rest into her mouth. "Samilis survive longer and are good with rebels."

"What about an almost-Samili?" Teruma said, as if the idea had just occurred to her. "Tarkan Ladysson grew up in the Samil. Didn't he study law, then statecraft, and even work as a councillor? Son of the satrap and late Lady of Djildit. He might be a good candidate. Dahoud knows him."

The Queen's beetle eyes focused on Dahoud. "Will Tarkan Ladysson be good with rebels?"

"Very good, Ma'am," Dahoud assured her with a straight face. "And he'll live for a long time."

"Appoint Tarkan," the Queen told her Consort, and tossed the peacock at her feet a buttered locust leg.

※

Impatient as Dahoud was to pursue the runaway, he would not ride on a hunt with a strong bow and an empty quiver. He needed clues.

In Teruma's study, sunlight slanted through latticed slots. Under the watchful eyes of the head-wife, he checked the vanished woman's workplace: ink powder, quills, a reedbrush, neat document stacks, meticulous accounts with figures in straight columns like well-drilled foot soldiers. No personal ornaments, no dried fruit snacks, no desk statue of a patron deity.

When servants dropped the fugitive's trunks on the carpet, he knelt to dip into her possessions: boxes within boxes, bundled scrolls, and drab clothes, devoid of scent.

"Merida's garments are all grey." Teruma stroked the kitten in her lap. "She never wears anything but trouser-suits and boots. She should stand out."

Dahoud dropped the trunk's lid shut. "Unless she's in disguise, my Lady."

"Unlikely. She thinks colours are immodest and sandals are sinful. She'll be wrapped up in fabrics to her neck, and she can't open her mouth without delivering a lecture. She's probably headed for Riverland. Bridge guards on the roads north and east have been given her description, of course without information why we want her. I've also sent my most discreet greenbelts to comb the land. Nobody has found a trace."

He rose. "A foreigner who has no resources and doesn't adapt to local customs can easily come to harm."

"I trust you to find her before she has an accident." The glass in Terume's earrings tinkled. "Also, remember the Queen's order to wed. Rumours about you and Tarkan being lovers are spreading faster than locust swarms. I've prepared a list." She lifted the cat off her lap to pick a parchment from a shelf. "Thirteen unwed Ladysdaughters—the total sum of eligibles in the Queendom."

His throat scratched as if he had accidentally swallowed a firefly. "You want me to marry one of those?"

"Before you return to Koskara. You have first pick. Tarkan second." She returned his stare with the attentiveness of a cat for its captured mouse. "If you still grieve for Esha, her sister is a similar type and may fill the gap. If you seek someone loyal and mature, your predecessor's widow is fifty-six and a marvel of loyalty. Wherever she goes, she carries a jewelled casket with her late husband's final faeces."

For a moment, Dahoud wanted to run away with a tavern dancer, but he was a satrap, with duties to the Queendom and to Koskara. He would have to wed whoever made the least disastrous Lady for his land.

First, however, he had to catch that concubine to save his friends.

In a noisy tavern near the palace, Dahoud found a seer whose many painted rings promised competence. Skinny with a triangular face, she might have been the one who had advised him nearly a year ago, but all white ones looked the same under their pasted layers of pale clay.

"I need to find a missing person," he murmured, cautious of curious ears.

After probing his palms, she said, "Go to Djildit Town."

"Djildit Town?" He must have misheard her words over the tavern din of clinking cymbals and raucous laughter. "The person is between here and Copperland. She's not in the Samil."

She dropped his hands with such force they slammed into his thighs. "You heard me. Go to Djildit Town."

She spun so fast that her clay-clotted hair whipped into Dahoud's face, and strode away.

He stared after her. Whiteseers were always right, even if at first their advice made no sense. At the first pink of dawn, he would start the long ride to Djildit Town.

CHAPTER 24

Merida in Disguise

Without looking right or left, Merida marched steadily northeast. It would take twenty days or more before she reached the safety of the Copperland border. She was a strong walker, but sandal straps chafed, and dusty grit rubbed between her toes. The merciless sun tried to squash her spirits, the dry air burnt the back of the throat, and the thefts weighed on her conscience.

Wearing no trousers felt strange, but in this heat, the ventilation between her legs was pleasant. The layer of clay hid her skin as effectively as a garment.

"Hey, seer!" The male voice nearly sent her ducking into the cover of the thorny roadside shrubs. "Where are you headed?"

A donkey cart rattled to a halt. She jabbed a thumb vaguely eastwards.

"Hop on, seer. I'll trade you a ride for a reading."

Grateful to get the weight off her blistered soles, Merida climbed on the cart and sat between sacks of lentils. For the rest of the afternoon, the donkey trotted through the smothering dust.

When they reached his village, he held out his hands. "Tell me, seer. Ought I wed my girl, or wait for a better match?"

She had no choice now but to play the role. Imitating the whiteseers she had observed at the palace party, she sniffed his palms. They smelled of leather and donkey sweat. His aura was that of a common man:

mostly physical, with flickers of spiritual energy. Wanting to reward his kindness with real advice, she willed herself into a mild trance to catch random glimpses into his possible futures. She struck lucky. His sweetheart would shortly inherit some wealth.

"Marry her soon," she said.

He enfolded her in a sweaty embrace. "Come, see my mum. She'll give you a meal for a reading."

❧

Merida ducked into the hovel, willing to give one more reading to fill her stomach and get out of the glaring sun. A dozen neighbours who had heard of a seer's arrival stretched their calloused hands at her, demanding advice.

Modelling her act on the seer in the palace, she said little, serving single-sentence advice of spiritual significance. "Stay faithful to your friends", "Disdain the lie", "Be humble", "Practice self-control." They lapped it up and enveloped her in gratitude. No missionary could have hoped for warmer acceptance of Loyalty, Honesty, Modesty, and Discipline.

The meal of gritty bread and olives shamed her, not because of its sparseness, but because the people were obviously proud to serve up such a feast in her honour. That night, she slept under the stars with no bedding but prickly straw.

❧

For eight days, Merida strode eastwards. She squeezed the juice of tutsan leaves on her blisters and accepted offers of cart-rides and food. Neither bridge guards nor other officials bothered her. They simply waved the whiteseer on.

At last, she reached the river that marked the Queendom's eastern border. Even in the dry heat, it smelled of rich wood and moist grass, like the rivers at home. All she had to do was cross the bridge into Copperland, and claim diplomatic assistance.

The green-uniformed border guards under the striped canopy were tougher than their colleagues at the bridges and village gates. "Your pass, seer!" one demanded.

A knot tightened in her stomach. "I'll trade you a reading if you let me through."

He drew himself up. "I won't be bribed."

"Attempting to bribe a border guard draws fifteen lashes," his colleague added.

"I've lost my pass," she tried.

"More likely, you never had one. Typical seer. No idea how the real world works." He stabbed a stylus at her. "Who's your sponsor? To which temple do you belong?"

Knowing too little about whiteseers to bluff her way through an interrogation, Merida pretended unworldliness. "Blessings, good man. I'll come back another time."

With a show of unconcern, she strode away, but heard a guard say to the other, "There's something not quite right about her. Have you seen her hair?"

She knew her hair's copper glint was shining through the remnants of white clay. Over the past days, she had depleted the white stuff in her jar. This morning, she had spread the final crumbs on her face.

"It's not our problem," the other guard said. "Why bother, as long as she doesn't cross the border."

"It's our duty to follow up suspicious..."

Merida did not stay to listen to the outcome, but ran to the river.

Several barges lay roped to the wobbly wooden quay. One of them was leaving. She jumped in.

"I'll trade you a reading for a ride," she told the astonished bargeman.

"I'm going Djildit Town," he said. "Ten days, maybe twelve. You're coming all the way?"

Djildit Town was in the south, in the wild Samil region which even the Quislakis viewed as primitive, the place where nomads roamed and lived in round tents. She wanted to go north, to safety and civilisation.

But if Kirral set his henchmen to pursue her, they would check the roads north. Nobody would think to look for her in the Samil. The detour was worth it.

"All the way to Djildit Town," she confirmed, settling between bulky jars and coils of rope.

The barge ambled past patches of copper-coloured sorrel spiked with purple loosestrife, reeds and rushes, and crack-willows hanging over the water where dagger-shaped weeds floated. Children slid squealing down the slippery clay banks into the water, tinting it white with milky clouds. Flocks of dirty-brown animals drifted around clusters of black tents. For the first time in months, Merida felt serene and free.

After nine days of silent drifting, the barge moored outside the honey-coloured walls of Djildit Town.

Having thanked her bargeman with profuse blessings, Merida strode along the riverbank until she found a willow-shaded section abundant with abundant white clay. Here she could fill her jar and renew her body paint. The substance slid silky-soft and cool between her fingers. It felt so good that she slapped it on by the handful, and finally burrowed herself in the silky mud. This place was rich in magic energy. For a long time, Merida lay on her back, with her limbs spread and her eyes closed, to absorb the earth's blessing and listen to the river sucking softly at the banks. She drifted into healing, blissful sleep.

A horse's neigh, followed by excited giggles, jolted her awake. A small crowd had gathered on the riverbank to stare at the sleeping seer.

She jumped up, pulled her hair forward over her chest lest any female forms should be visible under the still-damp fabric, and clambered up with as much dignity as she could muster.

"A reading, a reading! Seer, a reading!" a dozen voices clamoured at once. She obliged with recommendations for a virtuous lifestyle, and collected copper rings in her pouch.

Suddenly the air sang with danger. A rider vaulted off his grey horse. The sight of his moss-green tunic and plaited belt hit her guts. This was one of the Consort's henchmen, a thousand miles from the palace. Had he come to arrest her?

She took a step back, poised for flight.

"A reading, please, seer." His voice was deep like a slow-flowing river, smooth on top but dangerous beneath.

She allowed herself to meet his eyes, as if she had nothing to fear from his kind. Although his mouth smiled, his eyes were bitter-dark like olives. An aura of vibrant intelligence was enveloped in intense bitterness, and under his cheerful courtesy, pain radiated from him like heat searing from a fire.

Her instincts screamed at her to pull free from the dangerous power before it could burn her, but a genuine wandering seer would not panic at the sight of a palace official, and bolting would draw his suspicion.

She forced herself to stay in her role. "Your hands," she demanded, careful to hide her accent.

The hands were wrong. Brown, with short dirty nails, calloused, rough and ridged with old scars, they did not belong to a courtier, nor even to a guard.

At the moment of touch, shock surged through her, sending tingles all over her body. Her stomach felt as if a pestle was running along the inside of a stone mortar. Several futures flashed by her vision, too fast to hold, then his past dragged her in. She heard screams of terror and pain, and smelled the stench of burning flesh. This man was burning in the fire of his own soul.

Gasping for breath, she jerked away. "I can't… your past…"

His hands clasped around her wrists. "I'm sorry you had to see that, but please look beyond it if you can."

"I can't advise you on a problem of that magnitude." She tried to pull free from his crushing grip.

"I'm not asking about that. I want advice for a current mission." He lowered his voice to a confidential whisper. "I'm looking for a concubine escaped from the royal harem. A colleague of yours told me I might find her here."

She forced slow breath into her lungs to slow her thudding heart. Shutting out the danger tinglings as best she could, she rubbed the man's palms, traced the lines with her nails, sniffed at the fingers. They smelled of leather and horse.

Caution prodded her to send him on a false path, preferably back to distant Quislabat, but Honesty would not permit her to speak a lie, not even to a despicable greenbelt, not even to protect herself. Instinct warred with honour like two cubs tearing the same piece of flesh. She searched for a sentence that contained the truth he sought, without exposing herself to danger.

Finally, she said, "Don't underestimate that missing person," and dropped his hands.

When his brows tightened in a frown, as if he was about to ask for clarification, she raised her chin haughtily in the whiteseer manner. "Next."

"Thank you, seer." He pressed a copper ring into her palm and mounted his horse.

Merida scanned an old woman's hand, but from the corner of her eye she watched until she was certain the silver horse and green tunic had vanished in the distance.

She finished the fifth reading and placed the grateful client's payment in her pouch when a girl of Kadiffe's age planted herself squarely before her. "Why you be readin' today? It be the solstice."

Scarf-wrapped heads exchanged bewildered glances. Voices, laced with suspicion, muttered about 'solstice' and 'seclusion'.

"The solstice?" she repeated brightly. "Of course. How could I forget the seclusion! I'd better not do any more readings today. Thank you, good people." Cursing her ignorance about seers' customs, she strode off with enforced calm.

Before long, the greenbelt would realise the seer had worked on a forbidden day, concluding she was a fake. If he found her, her freedom was forfeit. She must not stay in seer disguise a moment longer.

Out of sight of her erstwhile clients, she immersed herself in the river. The water carried away the clay, and the dress dried quickly in the searing sun, but she was still wearing a white dress, and her long copper-coloured hair was conspicuous.

She needed a new disguise.

✂

Djildit Town smelled worse than a cattle pen. Crippled beggars wailed their pleas while tavern-keepers accosted passers-by with promises of jugglers, dancers and storytelling acrobats. Crudely painted signs advertised bellydancers, tattooed maidens and women with two heads. Vending stalls with copper pots and earthenware crowded the narrow alleys, and Merida dodged bickering shoppers, donkeys and sheep.

The town's broadest road led to a heavily guarded bridge across the river. Beyond that lay the country of Zigazia, blue in the heat-mist. The uniformed men at this border took their duty seriously, checking passes, interrogating and body-searching everyone leaving the Queendom. Merida still had no pass. What now?

Evening sun slanted from the rooftops. Daytime was running out.

Merida returned to the warren of alleys where she tried to blend into the crowd of shoppers, but among the yellow and orange garments, her white dress stood out. She fingered the coppers in her pouch. Five tanni might buy a decent headscarf, but no dress. No longer a whiteseer, she did not even have the means to earn more.

"Look at my lovely clothes," a rag-seller trilled. "Lovely, lush, luxurious! Anything from this stall for just one tanni."

The thought of wearing someone else's cast-offs was revolting, but it was the only way to change her appearance fast. Merida dipped her hands into the heap of garish fabrics. "Have these been laundered properly?"

"My clothes are very clean," the woman assured her. "I wash them myself. Lovely, lush things they are. Buy two, get the third one free."

Merida knelt on the packed dirt, next to two bony cats sunning themselves in a patch of receding light, and rummaged through the baskets. She found only one tunic, much too short for her, with the underarm seams split and the hem frayed, as red as the sinking sun, the most sinful of colours. But even now, the greenbelt might be scanning the streets, asking questions about a woman in white.

Already, the sun was vanishing behind the houses, the shutters of shops clattered shut, and vendors rolled up the awnings of their stalls. With a pointed glance at her indecisive customer, the rag-seller started to stuff her wares into baskets.

Merida grabbed the tunic and added two garish shawls with unravelling tassels. She tossed two coppers on the table, and changed behind the stall's curtain. The tunic was not only too short, but too low at the front, showing almost a whole finger-breath of Merida's breasts. She draped the yellow scarf to hide the cleavage. Her arms and calves remained bare, and she could not even cover them with clay. She felt very sinful.

A uniformed watchman prodded a beggar with his spear. "No loitering in this town at night."

Merida marched fast, pretending to have a purpose. Darkness fell fast and nothing remained of the day except lingering heat.

The inn near the bridge had a huge canine painted on its façade, next to a sign promising *Darrian Dansers Evry Night. Eksotig and Apsollutly Gennwin*, complete with a drawing of a female torso with unrealistic curves. The clacking steps of spear-armed guards drove Merida into the inn's courtyard where camels slurped from a trough. A smell of jasmine was even stronger than the reek of animal sweat and dung. Torches waved their yellow flames in the descending gloom.

Several people argued in the doorway. "Promising dancers you don't have," an old man grumbled. "I call that cheating. I'll complain to the authorities."

"Please," a black-haired man with drooping cheeks beseeched him. "We be havin' full music tonight, and dancers be back tomorrow."

The woman pulled her husband by the arm. "There are other shows in town. Let's enjoy the rest of the night and see the woman with two heads. Tomorrow we'll complain to the authorities."

Merida waited until the incensed customers had left, and addressed the drooping-cheeked man. "Excuse me. Are you the landlord of this establishment? What are the prices for one night's accommodation?"

He eyed her up and down, and obviously judged her to be of an un-lucrative client class. "Six tanni for a place on the roof."

She had three tanni left and nowhere else to go. "I'm afraid -"

"You be wantin' a place, or not?" he barked through big pointed teeth. His drooping cheeks wobbled. It was easy to see how the Black Dog Inn had gained its name. "The roof be getting' full fast. Pay now, you be squeezin' in."

"Squeezing in?" she repeated feebly. That sounded worse than a dormitory. Maybe there were even men sleeping on that roof.

Another cluster of patrons left, grumbling about the cancelled enter-tainment. The Black Dog wrung his hands, entreating them in vain to stay.

An idea shot into Merida's head. "Are you seeking to hire a per-former for tonight? I'm an accomplished dancer with lots of experience. From Darria." A lie. A shameful, sinful lie. She would have to atone for it later. For now, she trusted he would not guess her foreign accent's real origin. The dancer at the palace had earned thirty tanni. Provincial prices would be lower. "Fifteen tanni."

"You be gettin' no tanni from me." He shimmied his shoulders. "Wobblin' titties, like. Gettin' tips." His gaze travelled down the front of her dress. "Where be your costume?"

She plastered her most charming smile to her face, unwrapped the yellow scarf from her chest and knotted it around her lower torso. "Will this do?"

When he gazed at her cleavage, a hot flush burnt her face. Now she had added gross indecency to her list of sins. Once she got back to Riverland, she would have to do heavy penance to purify her soul.

She flicked four technically refined hip-drops. "I want a meal and accommodation for the night."

"Very fine." His lips pursed in contemplation of the exposed cleavage. "You be getting' food leftovers from the kitchen, and a space on the roof."

"I'll eat leftovers, but I insist on a private room."

His lips widened. "Private room, yes. Very private. First, you be dancin'. Be quick."

A drum started to throb, and a harp's strings silvered the air.

Without light or a mirror, Merida used the stolen black face-paint to draw a hasty rim around her eyes. Recalling everything the teacher had told the concubines about tavern dancing, she hurried to make her entrance. If only she had finger cymbals or a tambourine!

The torch-lit dining room smelled of coriander and roasted flesh. With a confident pose copied from the palace dancer, Merida floated into the river of welcoming applause.

The drum delivered a clear rhythm: *Doum tek, doumdoum tek, doum-tek, doumdoum-tek.*

Four steps forward, eight to the left, eight to the right... Not enough space between the benches. Hipdrops, hiplifts, shimmied circles.

The rhythm switched to the Darrian six-count: *Doum-doum-doum doum-doum doum.* As a supposed Darrian, she had to cope. Three-step shuffle left, three-step shuffle right. When the women at the table clapped, her feet slid into the pattern, and the joy of music and movement seeped into her limbs. This was supposed to be work. Was she permitted to feel pleasure?

When she added the Darrian neck-slides Haurvatat had taught her, women, rather than men, cheered her on, yelping and ululating with pleasure. These were respectable-looking tradeswomen in almost decent clothes, so perhaps bellydancing was not an entirely sinful act. Merida absorbed their response and converted it to magical power. Soon she was rising inside a cloud of a happy trance.

She remembered to keep her hands near her throat to hide her cleavage, but it seemed the custom to drop coppers down her front.

Fortunately, it was only the women who did it. The cool rings slid down between her breasts and jingled below her waist.

One-two-three, one-two-three.... Merida danced happily towards the far end of the room, giving the people at every table a sincere beaming smile. The final corner was almost dark, and she launched into a full-body shimmy before she saw the man's face. The greenbelt.

He was not wearing the turban, and his green tunic looked grey in the dim light, but it was him, and his eyes grazed her with hunger. Did he admire her dance, did he desire her body, or did he suspect who she was? The drum of fear beat in her chest.

Wanting to bolt, Merida forced herself to keep dancing. He stood, holding up a copper ring in one hand and beckoning her close with the other. Before he could drop his tanni down her front, Merida fled to the safety of the friendly tradeswomen.

Shutting out the greenbelt's presence and assuring herself that he could not possibly guess her identity, she danced until the musicians put their instruments down.

In the kitchen, she asked for a jug of water and the promised meal. A gruff female cook pushed a bowl into her hands, the kind of dish dogs in Riverland ate from. Gristly bones stuck out of the grey mush, and a chunk of yam showed bite marks. These were not remnants from the cooking pots, but what the patrons had left on their plates.

"Would you show me to my room, please?"

The cook squinted. "Your room?"

"Black Dog... I mean, the landlord, promised me a private room for tonight."

The woman jerked her head at the staircase. "Up there, corridor to the left, the door at the end."

The tradeswomen, chattering in good spirits, were withdrawing for the night. They had expensive rooms in the right wing, with real wooden doors.

The allocated chamber was windowless and exuded sticky wheat moon heat, and had not been cleaned or tidied since its previous occupation. Merida told herself she could not expect Riverian standards here. At least she had a room to herself, with a heavy curtain over the entrance, which was better than sharing roof-space with strange men.

She gulped down half the water. She stirred the greasy goo in search of non-animal matter and contemplated scraping the meat juice off a carrot slice, but put it down uneaten.

After piling the earned copper rings next to the sleeping mat, she cheered. Thirty-two tanni would buy the provisions she needed for the journey into Zigazia. She pulled off the sweat-heavy tunic. Since the water was too sparse for a proper wash, she rubbed it over her body. Tomorrow, she would buy a new dress, and then she would never again put on clothes someone else had worn.

"Fine, fine," said a man's voice from the door curtain. "I be comin' to you now."

Merida snatched up the yellow scarf and held it before her naked front. "Get out!"

Black Dog's drooping cheeks quivered with excitement. "Titties-wobblin' for me now."

His arms opened to embrace her.

"Get out!" she yelled again, backing towards the wall.

When his hands grabbed her shoulders, her body locked rigid. This could not be happening. Not to her.

His tongue slid across his lips like a fat pink slug. His fingers worked under the fabric and cupped her breast. Merida snapped out of her trance.

She stomped down hard on his foot, rammed a knee into his groin and punched the Woodpecker sequence into his face. She followed it with The Boar's Tusk and an extra-fast Thunder Cloud.

When he sagged to the ground, she applied The Toad's Vengeance. For good measure, she smashed the jug over his skull and slammed the food bowl, upside down, into his face. His grunts turned to groans. Since he lay curled with his hands guarding the crotch, she stomped him into the kidneys. This was a forbidden move that would get her expelled from the Disciplined Path class, but nobody would find out. She kicked once more. Symmetry mattered.

She fled from the room, seeking safety. But where? Not in the streets of the night, nor among the rabble on the roof.

The nice tradeswomen had rooms in the other wing. Tying the scarf around her torso, Merida raced down the dark corridor.

She banged at the first wooden door. It opened at once.

A male chest. Unclothed. Further down... She gulped. He was not wearing any garment at all.

Footsteps pounded the corridor. "I be getting' you, you bitch!" Black Dog panted. "You be payin' for this." She had not hit her assailant hard enough, and now he was after her. Panic threatened to throttle her.

Black Dog was a proven danger. The man at the door might be safe.

"Please, good sir, help me! I need your protection."

"Come in."

Once in the room, the door snapped shut behind her, and a bolt slammed.

To avoid seeing her rescuer's unclothed body in the sparse light of the oil-lamp, she looked at his face.

The greenbelt.

CHAPTER 25

Zaina

Dahoud stared. The woman in his bedroom wore a big turban, a scarf clutched to her chest, and nothing else. She was tall, fair-skinned, flushed and frightened. Her eyes darted as if looking for an escape route.

He cleared his throat.

Someone else pounded at the door with the ferocity of a battering ram. "Open up!"

Dahoud could not hope this surprise visitor would be as delightful as the one already in his room. He pulled the door open. "What do you want?"

The landlord's face glowered, caked with blood and blooming with bruises. A swollen lump rose under his eye. "I be wantin' that dancer."

"Too late. I be wantin' her myself." Dahoud slammed the door shut and bolted it. "Did you do that to his face?"

"In self-defence. If you lay a finger on me, I'll do the same to you."

A woman who could fight! His body pulsed with excitement. It would be delicious to measure her strength.

Her fingers pulled at the scarf, as if trying to make the fabric stretch it to cover more skin. She was as skittish as a frightened horse.

He picked up his under-tunic from the floor and tossed it to her. "Wear this."

When she held it to her nose and sniffed at it, he was glad it was clean. He had only worn it four days.

He turned to the window to let her dress. Since his own nudity might make her nervous, he slipped the green tunic on and fastened the plaited belt around it.

In the meantime, she had draped the shawl over the under-tunic, hiding every hint of breast. "Thank you, kind sir." She tiptoed towards the door. "I'll return the garment as soon as I have the means."

A wave of warmth washed through him and pounded him with urgency. "Wait! Do you have somewhere to go? Stay here. I'll pay your fee for a night."

"I'm no whore!" Her words lashed across his face.

His face fired. He had said the wrong thing. "I just... I want you to be safe for tonight. You take the mat. I'll sleep on the floor." For once in his life, he had the chance to redeem himself. He would shelter this woman chastely from harm. Yearning need twisted through his chest. "I won't touch you, I promise."

Hesitation flickered over her face, and her glance darted between the window and the door.

He unsheathed his sword and held it out to her, hilt first. The curved blade was the only item he kept from his legion days. "Will this make you feel better?"

She did not touch the weapon, but the tension dripped from her shoulders. "I'll be glad to stay the night. Thank you, sir."

Like a traveller who sees the oasis after a long desert journey, Dahoud thanked the Mighty Ones for their gift. Tonight he would complete his defeat of the djinn.

He pushed the sword back into its sheath. "I'm Dahoud. What's your name?"

"M... My name is Zaina." She blushed as she spoke.

A Darrian name. "Sleep well, Zaina," he said in her native tongue. "Tomorrow we'll plan how to keep you safe."

"Yes, sir. Thank you, sir."

Joy sang like wine in his blood. He savoured the precious, poignant pleasure of the moment.

As she curled into a tight ball on the mat, his thoughts circled around her like a hawk above prey. Other bellydancers floated in the music and shared their joy with the audience, but Zaina's dance had had the dogged determination of a legion drill. Was she new to her art? Why did a grown woman take up tavern dancing as a new career? What had she done before, and what fate had forced her on this new path? Why did she keep her turban on to sleep? Other dancers liked to toss their hair, but she kept hers hidden. Had she shaved her skull to rid it of lice, or had it been cropped to punish a prostitute? How good a fighter was she? How long would she last against Dahoud?

He pushed the wrestling out of his mind before it could kindle and set his fantasies on fire, and planned how he would capture the fake whiteseer.

When the morning sun poured through the window, golden and clear, Dahoud woke with a light heart. He had not touched the dancer. Faced with temptation, he had stayed strong. His control of the djinn was complete.

"Good morning, Zaina. Will you join me for breakfast?"

She stretched, yawned, and adjusted her sleep-dislodged turban. As she fumbled with the cloth, a thick mane of copper hair spilled over her shoulders. Bronze! Recall shot through him like a dart: the Riverian magician had tossed such hair.

Zaina was the rain dancer, the fake seer, the runaway concubine.

He acted at once. He grabbed her from behind, locked his hands under her ribcage and forced the air from her lungs.

"Don't hurt me," she whimpered. As soon as he relaxed his grip, her elbow rammed into his stomach. Fists rained into his face and slammed on his skull.

A heartbeat later, she unbolted the door and vanished. He fastened his dagger belt and vaulted out of the window.

She was racing out of the courtyard into the road, glancing over her shoulder, bumping through market stalls. She knocked over a display of copper pots. The vessels clattered onto the road and forced him to slow.

"Rapist! Rapist!" she yelled, running.

How dare she! He would get her.

"Stop the mangy greenbelt!" a dozen voices screeched. "Save the girl!"

People crowded in on him. A black-clad giant blocked his path. Something slammed on his head. The world turned orange, then black.

⁓

A hot hand clamped around Merida's arm, pulling her into a shaded alley. She screamed.

"Hush, dear," a female voice soothed. "We're all friends." The woman had green hair and the biggest bosom Merida had ever seen.

"Who are you? What do you want from me?"

"Up that ladder, dear."

Merida climbed up the ladder which ended on a second storey rooftop shaded with woven palm fronds and strewn with rags. Two figures rose, one a slight female with pink plaits, the other a man with the pointed face of a rat.

"I bring a friend," the green woman wheezed. "Nearly got herself raped, the poor dear."

"Where's the assailant?" Rat Face demanded.

"Dogal got him."

Rat Face bowed to Merida. "Who do I have the honour of meeting?"

Merida saw no reason to reveal the truth to these weird strangers. "I'm Zaina, a bellydancer from Darria. Last night I performed at the Black Dog Inn. That's where the greenbelt molested me." In recounting the events of the night, she tweaked them so that Dahoud, not the landlord, featured as the attacker.

The woman's bosom swayed from side to side. Small eyes peered through strands of green hair. "I'm Shibshib, the woman with two heads. Men are such beasts." She squatted between Rat Face and Pink Plaits, sifting through piles of garish garments.

The sun drove broad golden spokes through the awning of plaited palm fronds. From neighbouring roofs came the cackling of chickens and the *tap-tap-tap* of a copper engraver's hammer.

Rat Face rose and spun around so that his rainbow-shimmering cape twirled. Then he bowed. "It is a source of amazement how certain men do not consider the distinction between a dancing artist and a female engaged in prostitution. May I enquire if, in his insolence, he caused you much harm?"

Merida gaped. This speech sounded like that of the most pompous palace courtier, yet he looked dirtier than the poorest beggar she had ever seen. Pink Plaits gazed at him with dreamy eyes.

'I barely managed to defend myself," she said. "This morning, he almost overpowered me, and would have had his vile way with me. Fortunately, members of the public intervened."

'Dogal heard his cue," Shibshib of the green hair said.

Rat Face explained, "In every play we put on, Dogal acts the same two roles: professional torturer, and rescuer of females in distress. He doesn't have a surfeit of brains, but he can act on cue. Whenever a woman screams 'Rapist, rapist!', he jumps on the villain." He twirled his cape again. "Know, esteemed Zaina, that we perform the most marvellous play, 'Escape from the Harem'."

Merida almost gagged, but recovered. Joining a troupe would be the perfect cover. "This sounds fascinating. In which town will you be performing the play next?"

"Tonight is our final show. My personal presence is requested by His Most Lustrous Brilliance, the Emperor of Darria. That's why we're sorting what costumes we can sell." He waved over the mound of garish rags.

The news snuffed her glimmer of hope, but perhaps she could get a new disguise. She pulled an ash-grey item out of the pile.

"You don't want that, dear," Shibshib said. "It's a Riverian thing called trousers, very uncomfortable. The people in Riverland hide their legs. Crazy, isn't it?"

A dark giant heaved himself from the ladder onto the roof. "The greenbelt's body is in the courtyard. Took these off him." He dropped a bundle at Yann's feet.

"He's dead?" Merida asked, aghast.

Rat Face fished the money pouch from the green garments and weighed it in his hand. "You wish to see your assailant dead?"

"No, no! Just unable to pursue me."

Shibshib of the Green Hair made sympathetic clucking noises. "Let me take care of that, dear. As soon as he comes to, I'll gather him to my bosom like a mother, and make him drink my very special juice. It'll make him sleep for a long time, and when he comes to..." She giggled. "He won't feel like having breakfast, and he surely won't think of molesting a dancer again."

Rat Face spilled the contents of the pouch and counted the money rings, whistling. "A good catch, this one. Real silver. The authentic greenbelt uniform should get us a good price, too. These daggers are such masterpieces of craftsmanship, I may keep one as a souvenir." He flipped a piece of silver at Merida. "Here's your share, Zaina."

"Thanks, but I don't want it." Having deceived the greenbelt and gotten him beaten up, she did not want to profit by her deed.

Rat Face's eyes narrowed. He said something in rapid Darrian, so fast she could not follow it. When she struggled to compose an answer in that language, he cut her off. "You're no Darrian. Who are you, and why was the greenbelt really after you?"

Merida thought rapidly. Whatever lie she made up, he would not believe her. She might as well speak the truth. "I'm a crazy Riverian. I've just escaped from the harem of the Consort, who sent the greenbelt to catch me."

Shibshib gurgled with laughter at this unlikely tale.

Rat Face chuckled. "I'm Yann, the authorised spy of the Darrian Emperor."

"I am honoured to make your acquaintance, oh illustrious spy." Since the troupe was disbanding, she could not hope to travel with them, so she revived her previous plan. "Is there a way I can get into Zigazia without a travel pass?"

Yann clicked his tongue. "I wouldn't recommend Zigazia. The country is still in ruins from the wars, with little employment for respectable dancers, and the climate is uncomfortable."

"It doesn't matter. I must get there."

He pursed his lips and pulled at his ear. "There's a nomad track with a river ford an afternoon's ride south from here. Nobody bothers nomads for passes or permissions."

Shibshib was already rummaging through the discarded costumes. "Wear this." She tossed a brown tunic and scarves at Merida. They had patches of dark stains which looked like dried blood, and smelled faintly of urine and vinegar.

A disguise was a disguise. Merida slipped the new costume over the green under-tunic. Now she was wearing two people's used clothes on her body.

Yann applauded. "If you had goats with you, I'd swear you were a nomad. Since you don't want silver, we'll give you provisions for the journey. Oranges, dates, a goatskin which you must refill at every waterhole. Now you need a camel or a horse. Can you ride?"

"A little, but I have no money for a mount."

Yann exchanged a glance with Shibshib. "I presume there's a horse currently stabled at the Black Dog, whose owner won't claim it soon."

Before the sun reached mid-sky, Merida had added horse-theft to her growing list of sins.

✐

When Dahoud opened his eyes to the fierce sun, his muscles felt shredded and his bones crushed, like after a bad battle. His groping fingers met gritty slime that reeked like the soured piss in a barracks latrine. He was lying in a rubbish ditch, naked and drenched in his own puke, and above him towered the yellow walls of Djildit Town. The woman had used him and discarded him, and he would make her pay.

With pain pounding his skull, he limped to the road to appeal to a crone carrying produce baskets into town. "Excuse me, Mother, would you..."

Shrieking, she bolted into the safety of the walls.

He rubbed the worst of the gore from his skin and hid behind a thorny shrub until a trader came by with a laden donkey.

"Please, help me. I need clothes."

The man whipped his animal to the other side of the track.

The guards at the gatehouse barred Dahoud's entrance with their spears. "Only clean beggars allowed in Djildit Town."

"I'm not a beggar." Dahoud's tongue, still heavy and laden, sounded drunk. "I'm the Lord of Koskara."

"Sure, and I'm the Emperor of Darria. My mate here is the Queen of Quislak." A spear-tip pointed at Dahoud's belly. "And now that we know each other, you filthy swine, get out!"

At last, he found a crippled beggar who didn't recoil at the sight and smell of him. "Listen, good man. Will you take a message into town for me? There'll be a reward for you at the other end. Five dinar."

The man's grey face pulled into frowning disbelief. "Who be havin' so much money for givin' away?"

"The lord-satrap of Djildit will, I promise. He knows me. I'm Dahoud of..." He checked himself. "I'm his son's friend. My name's Dahoud. I've been attacked by... robbers." Dahoud's brain almost creaked with the effort of thinking out a message. "On a mission for ... for my boss. Tell Lord Adil where you found me, and how. You know where the residency is, don't you? Speak to the satrap in person. He'll give you the money."

The beggar eyed him as if he still did not believe in either the connection or the money. "Right. I be goin' to the residency and tellin' the lord-satrap there be a crazy beggar by the south gate, naked, rantin', howlin' like a djinn, and stinkin' latrine-like, claimin' to be friends-like with the satrap's son, and I be askin' five dinars for such-like message."

"I'll be much obliged," Dahoud said firmly.

When the beggar limped off on his crutches, Dahoud hid as best he could in the shade of the walls, and rubbed himself down with a handful of grass.

An eternity later, scented servants lowered an elegant covered litter at the roadside.

"That be him!" the beggar shouted. "That be the madman that promised me five dinar!"

⁓

A little later, cleaned up, dressed in borrowed green garments, Dahoud joined Lord Adil for a meal, and treated him to a heavily edited version of the events in which he had been mugged by robbers.

In every feature and every movement, Adil was Tarkan's father. The lines around his eyes crinkled deeper, and silver streaked his dark hair, but he had the same tall, slender build, the same elegance, the same courteous charm.

He held out his hands with the palms up. "My dear Dahoud, why didn't you spend the night here? You know you're always welcome in my home."

Dahoud had avoided staying in residencies because he wanted nobody to probe about his mission for the Consort. He was not going to reveal it now. "I wanted to see the bellydancer at the Black Dog."

'A dancer? Don't you have any of those in Koskara?" Adil stroked a manicured finger along the rim of his wine beaker. "Three moons ago, I received a letter from the Lady Esha. Naturally, I did not believe a word of it I know you, my friend. You wouldn't hurt a woman. I simply forwarded the letter to Kirral."

A headache pounded Dahoud's skull. He said nothing.

A servant shuffled towards their table, with his head lowered as if he expected it to be chopped off. "Begging your forgiveness, my Lord. This humble servant has visited the Black Dog hostelry, as specified, to obtain your belongings and your steed, as instructed, and..."

'Get on with it," Dahoud snapped.

'It's with deepest regrets, and humble apologies, my Lord Dahoud, that I'm obliged to report that my errand hasn't met with full success. The landlord won't release your bag or your sword until your bill is paid in full."

"I'll take care of that," Adil said.

"I beseech your forgiveness for my thwarted efforts, Lord Dahoud. Your horse has vanished."

The theft of his horse heated Dahoud's anger to boiling point. He would make the bitch pay.

CHAPTER 26

Pursuit

The rhythmic *shush* and *crunch* of the horse's hooves were the only sounds under the searing sun. The sun stood nor more than four-finger-breaths above the horizon, but already Merida was cooking in her own sweat. Sharp sand crept into every skin fold and crevice, even between her legs. Her dry lips stung, and her arms, no longer protected by clay, burned red. She could almost smell her flesh roasting.

A plain of grey gravel and sand stretched before her, dotted with dusty acacia shrubs under a sky of monotonous blue. Her buttocks hurt from the strange saddle, and her throat scratched with sand and thirst, but she rode on. If nomads could make this journey, so could she.

Hollows in the earth, surrounded by stunted trees, might have been the water-holes mentioned by Yann. If so, they were depleted by years of drought. Since crossing the river at dawn, Merida had not found a single source of water to replenish the goatskin and let the horse drink. Already, the horse's gait dragged.

In the cruel sunlight, she fantasised about the pattering rains and the shadow-giving clouds back home. To coax the horse onwards, she gave it her last orange. The mountain clump to the left of the track had cracks and erosion-carved outcrops which would offer shade.

The horse baulked at the snaking path, tossed its head and rolled its eyes. Froth dripped from its mouth, and when it finally moved, it was with jerky, sweating steps.

Half way up the hill, she halted. The green plantations where she had slept the night before were out of sight. The gravel plain below shimmered like a glistening lake. A silhouette formed, grew, and coloured. A moving figure. Merida shook her head to clear her vision. Mirages were supposed to show lush palms and pink palaces. Instead, there was a rider on a horse. The rider wore green.

She sucked in breath so sharply it singed the back of her throat. Kirral's greenbelt would not dare to ride into the desert, nor would he know where to seek her. Besides, they had taken his green tunic and his horse. It had to a stranger in a faraway place, projected into this desert by a trick of the light. It had to be.

But her stomach felt as if she had swallowed several handfuls of gravel. She remembered his callused hands: not those of a pampered courtier. He might have borrowed a green tunic and a horse for his pursuit. What if it was him?

Below in the plain, her tired horse's hooves had left a clear trail in the dusty gravel, revealing that she had left the track and come to this mountain. She needed a breeze to wipe out the treacherous line.

Fatigue knotted her limbs. Tired, unprepared, in clothes of the wrong colour and without supporting musicians, could she call a wind strong enough to make gravel roll? This was magic in adverse circumstances again. She would add this experience to her treatise on the subject.

Fortunately, the ground here was rich in magical energy which she could harness, and she still had the power of shaking her long hair. In the absence of fire or water, she could use earth. Picking up two handfuls of gravel and raising her arms heaven-wards, she chanted to the Virtues, and then sang the rhythm: *doum-tek doumtek.*

Already dizzy with heat, getting into a trance was easy. The mountain's magical energy propelled into the higher levels so fast, it was like taking wing and lifting off into the sky. But even in the fifth level, no wind was close enough in space or time to call into the present. She had to go higher. This was an emergency in which restraining rules did not apply. Sixth level, seventh. At last, she sensed a distant breeze. She summoned it with all her might, but received no reply. She had to go further. Eighth level. Had any magician ever gone that high? She channelled every ounce of the earth's power into her summons. She wanted a wind strong enough not only to hide her tracks, but to drive the greenbelt back to where he came from.

Just as she sensed a reply from the distant wind, her strength seeped away. Would the breeze hide the hoof-prints before her pursuer found them? She ought to do the grounding ritual, ought to plan her next steps, ought to rest in the shade, but the place offered only hot rock and blazing sun.

"Come, horse, we must find shelter."

The horse, damp with sweat, and with foam dripping from its mouth, refused to let Merida mount.

Her vision blurred into a glaring haze.

She pulled the horse behind her up the steep, narrowing path. The stirrup scraped against the rock.

Her own feet stumbled. The flimsy sandals were not meant for walking on detritus and sharp rock. Stones, loosened by their steps, clattered into ravines.

The reins jerked from her hand. A high-pitched scream sawed her bones. Legs thrashing, the horse slid down the rocky slope, and came to a halt on a boulder where it lay on its side, groaning. One foreleg was bent, and naked bone stuck from the other one.

Merida clambered after it but could do nothing to help. Even if it were possible to heal broken bones with magic, she had no energy left. She could not even work a spell to soothe animal's pain. Dazed, she struggled on up the mountain to find shelter.

Without horse, she was trapped, imprisoned in the desert as surely as she had been in the harem. Before long, she would perish from thirst. Now she wished the greenbelt would find her: he was her only hope.

She would have to disable him, take his horse and flee. Once she had reached distant safety, she would send someone to his rescue. This plan was thinner than a river reed, but the best her power-drained brain could conjure up.

She could barely form sensible thoughts, let alone refine her strategy. With every heartbeat, tiredness clawed deeper into her. At last, she crept under a cooling rock and collapsed.

Dahoud pressed his fingertips into the hard muscles at the back of his neck. The single set of hoof-prints was fresh, but led straight into the hellish heat of the Zigazian desert. The woman was crazy: She had crossed the border at the old nomad ford and was heading for the distant caravan road.

Dahoud knew the track. When he was a child, his clan had trekked here regularly, driving flocks on annual migration. It had been a greener land then, before drought had sucked most waterholes dry, and before war razed the settlements and burned the plantations. Only the hardiest nomads still clung to tradition of this route, and only in winter when faint rainfall sent grasses shooting from the baked soil, not in the summer furnace when everything was dead.

Under the blasting wheat moon sun, with no waterhole for three days, the runaway and the horse would drop like overripe figs and, unless picked up, shrivel and rot.

The brown gravel-dotted rug of the desert stretched before him, with mountains scattered here and there like cushions. A moth-eaten rug it was, bleached by the harsh light. As a general, Dahoud had mutilated this land into submission. Not a tree would grow on the soil he had salted, and not a lizard could find shelter in what was left of the places he had razed. The mountains still rang with the death cries of the rebels hiding in caves until he had smoked them out.

At the foot of Sentinel Mountain, Dahoud hobbled the gelding, watered it from his hands, and went in search of the fugitive. The hoof trail showed she had forced the horse up the steep goat path. His gentle mare, always spooked by mountain terrain, would suffer greatly. He would punish the woman for this cruelty. He strode up fast.

Suddenly, the air crackled with magic. When he stretched out his arm, the little hairs stood up, tingling. Faint swirls of rainbow colours clung to his skin. Magic had been worked here, he was certain. Had she tried to call rain to the desert or to send the sun to an early sleep?

When the path tightened into a crumbling track, a groan alerted him to his mare's fate. Twenty feet below, Peace lay dropped on her side, two legs misshapen with fracture, a broken cannon bone piercing the hide. Dahoud slithered down the slope to get to her. The blood vessel in her neck pulsated. She groaned as if begging him to save her, her big eyes trusting.

"Farewell, Peace." He stabbed the borrowed dagger into the centre of that pulsing vessel and wiped the blade on her coat.

Were the culprit a man, he would thrash him until every bone in his body was broken. Since she was a woman, what could he do?

Still, the djinn stayed silent.

He straightened. The western horizon, which a moment ago had shimmered in silver heat, glowed yellow under a purple line, the way it had fourteen years ago, the day of the djinn. This kind of storm was supposed to come only once in a generation, but even as he strained his eyes, the violet band on the horizon grew. The air smelled purple, too. The marrow in his bones vibrated in anticipation of the disaster.

He raced down the mountain, slashed through the gelding's hobbles and stripped off the tack. With luck, the horse would find shelter by instinct, and rejoin him after the storm. Grabbing the water-skin, he hurried up the slope. He he had to reach the cave where nomads had once shut out the unwanted boy, and where Zigazian rebels had once tried to defy the Black Besieger.

What about the woman? The familiar voice was back. *Shall we let her smash against rock, every bone in her body broken?*

Of course not! But the djinn persisted, sending images of violent ferocity: The storm's hand gripping her and whirling high above the ground. Her body twisted on the rock, legs smashed, while she screamed in pain. Her corpse at Dahoud's feet, bronze hair matted with blood, brains spilling from the crushed skull.

Shall we get ourselves to safety, and when the storm is over, inspect her punished remains?

Even with the fury roaring inside him, Dahoud would not let that happen. He would save the woman from the storm.

Already, the sky darkened and the air smelled of storm, the first thunder roared, and flameballs sped across the plain. At last he found her cowering under a rock, her lips cracked, her arms sun-blistered and insect-bitten, her palms chafed and bleeding.

Clouds of churning sand piled up higher than the mountain, rolling closer, swallowing the land. He pulled her up and forced her to face towards the purple menace. "Come. Unless we shelter fast, that storm will kill us."

When he dragged her towards the rebel cave, the wind picked up and slammed hard sand into their faces, forcing them flat on the ground.

He groped his way with eyes almost shut, with the water-skin over his shoulder and one hand clasped around his captive's wrist. Desert sand ground into his nostrils. Flying debris slammed into his back.

At last, they reached the cave. In its deepest womb waited a shelter of stillness. He could still smell a trace of the smoke with which he had killed rebels, lingering in the cool and musky air, and hear the victims' curses as if the rock clung to the memory.

Silently, he thanked the Mighty Ones and the Great Mare the gift of safe shelter.

In the dark, he sensed rather than saw the presence of his captive.

'We're safe now," he said. "Here's water. Drink." Although his dry throat scratched, she needed it more than he did.

He heard a couple of thirsty gulps, but she returned the goatskin without drinking much.

The storm was running against walls, crashing, falling, renewing its attack like a besieging army. It howled and whined in fury, an untamed force demanding control.

As Dahoud's eyes adjusted to the dark, he saw the outline of the woman's body beside him: head, arms, shoulders, breasts.

Locked in this cave, she could not resort to trickery. Their combat would be an honest measuring of body against body, strength against strength, will against will. His groin fired and his blood boiled with need. She would strain beneath him. She would struggle and fight and scratch and bite. He would win.

Whose under-tunic is she wearing on her skin?

He could see it in the darkness, the fine fabric lying sleekly over her breasts, brushed by her nipples. The very thought made him half mad with desire. He wanted to place his hands on those mounds and squeeze them. He wanted to get close enough to smell her sweat and to suck the salt off her skin. He wanted to hear her pant with fiery resistance, her breath mingling with the storm's howls. He wanted her.

Won't we take her?

The djinn had tricked him.

For over three years, Dahoud had resisted the djinn's urgings. Suddenly it had switched strategies, suggesting the opposite of what it wanted. By refusing to let the woman perish in the storm, Dahoud had fallen into its trap. He had danced like a blind man who did not recognise the old drummer when he heard the new rhythm. Now he was locked into this cave with the woman and his raging desires until the storm ceased.

Dahoud sat with his arms clasped around his knees. Outside, the gale made music, like a bad orchestra in which flutes, straighthorns and drums all competed for dominance without achieving a moment's harmony. Puffs of air sneaked into the cave, carrying gritty, abrasive sand that scratched and itched on his skin.

"This storm is so frightening," she whispered.

"We're safe here," he soothed.

"How long will it last? What if the fire comes in?"

He heard her shift. A moment later, she was leaning against him. "I'm so afraid."

He put an arm around her. She snuggled into his side. His heart raced in surprise, his body responded, his mind melted. His need for love, denied for so long, burst awake.

A faint movement brushed at his waist.

His hand shot down and found hers on his dagger hilt. He clamped his fingers around her wrist, squeezing hard to hurt her.

He hurled her on the ground, threw himself on her, pinned her shoulders. This woman had tricked him, humiliated him over and over again. She had faked a white reading, pretended to be a dancer, presumed his protection, abused all that was good and honourable in him, stretched his self-control to tearing point, and in return, had gotten him beaten up, drugged and dumped in a ditch. Devious bitch. Just like Esha. Just like all women. How much abuse did a man have to take?

Her body slackened. "Don't take me back to the harem," she pleaded. "Kirral was keeping me as a captive concubine against my will. He's cruel and crazy—"

Lies, lies, yet more lies. He pressed her mouth shut. She deserved to be subdued, to be taught the lesson that Dahoud the Black Besieger was not to be trifled with.

His other hand found her breast. Warm, soft, pulsing.

The thrill of desire roared through him like a hot storm. His control melted in the familiar flames of lust. These moments preceding a rape were exciting, much better than the act itself, the fighting, the woman's resistance, the measuring of their strengths, her fury matched against his need.

She whimpered. When he took his hand from her mouth, she whispered, "Please don't. Please don't do that to me." Her voice sounded choked.

For a moment, the fire of lust fought against the water of pity. He had never ravished a woman who pleaded with him, only the fighters. Yet this woman might fight if he kindled the fire of her fury. He could force her to defend herself, could enjoy her struggles, squeeze her resistance out of her drop by drop.

With the last splinter of willpower he let go. He would not dance to the djinn's drum again.

Not trusting her meek mood one bit, he rolled her on her belly, pressed a foot into her back and tied her hands with his belt so tightly the leather cut into flesh. With the scarves, he bound the legs into a painful position favoured by Darrian torturers. Then he gagged her with her own head-cloth so she could not beguile him with further lies. "If you try one more trick, I'll break every bone in your body."

Keeping her uncomfortably trussed up for hours was not as fun as raping her, but she would suffer while the storm lasted, and he savoured the satisfaction.

As soon as it was safe to leave the cave, he would drag her back to the pampered safety of the palace. He would serve out the remainder of his court service in the palace on mindless peacock-feeding duty until time came to return to Koskara. He would never need to see this troublesome bitch again.

CHAPTER 27

Fools

Highness." Tarkan kept his voice patient and tried not to drum his foot on the carpet."You were going to brief me about the political plans for Tajlit."

"Tajlit, Tajlit, Tajlit. Every day you pester me about Tajlit." Kirral glowered through the cloud of incense smoke. "Don't I have more important matters to think about? Look at this. Look at it!" He adjusted the tower of quivering greenstone disks on the table before him.

Tarkan chose his comment with care. "This is very high, and it balances beautifully. What does it signify?"

"Research." Kirral steadied the construction with his fingers to stop a tremble, and scrutinised it with his turbaned head tilted and his eyes narrowed to slits. Today, the henna-tinted moustache hovered horizontally. Beads strung along its lower edge gave it the semblance of a serrated knife. "Last night, I permitted thirty men too choose: They could have their large toe nail pulled out without anaesthetic, or be drowsy with poppy juice while their toe was amputated. All thirty opted for the nail." He ran a caressing fingertip down the stacked tokens. "This morning, after they witnessed the torturer do his job on the first man, all the others offered to give their toes in return for the poppy juice. What made them change their minds? The blood, or the screaming, or something else entirely?"

"Perhaps a combination of factors." Tarkan glanced at the scrolls in the spider-webbed shelf, and the desk overspilling with documents and dust. The Consort had not touched real work for some time. "We will never know."

"I must know." Kirral slammed his palm on the table. The token tower trembled and broke. "The sample was too small. Thirty prisoners can't reveal what the average Queendom subject wants. I will repeat the research with a larger segment of the population. A randomly selected village should give a good cross-section of age, gender and occupation. What do you say?"

"Possibly." Tarkan's throat tightened, but he tried once more. "Tajlit has been without a satrap for two moons."

"I told you, Tarkan." Kirral's voice was swift and sharp like the crack of the whip. "Do not bother me with politics."

"Allow me to assume the burden of politics for Tajlit, to free more of your time for vital research."

"You have my permission to depart Tajlit. Go, go, go!"

Tarkan let out a breath he had not known he was holding.

He had reached the door when Kirral called him back. "No, wait! You can not leave yet. Tomorrow is Fool's Plea!"

"Yes, Highness." Tarkan's throat was constricting again.

"A satrap needs wisdom, and Fool's Plea is the best time to learn. A few fools will win wonderful rewards, while most get punished severely. For the merest chance of a prize, they will endure public humiliation, risking their reputations and their lives." Kirral's purple-slippered feet bounced with excitement. "Watch the fun, witness the pleas, grow wise."

"I will, Highness." Tarkan bowed once more. "Thank you for the opportunity to learn from you."

The Consort's madness was increasing by the hour. Tarkan pitied the people who were staking their lives tomorrow.

✑

Neatly shelved scrolls and orderly desks in Teruma's study suggested a focused mind at work. The window lattices allowed circulating air and daylight. The yellow linen drapes were the finest a weaver's loom could produce, and matched the hue of the divans. Priceless knotted rugs, each one the work of a lifetime, and delicately embroidered cushions showed refined taste as well as wealth.

Teruma put down her stylus. "Lord Tarkan. What may I do for you?"

She was the most elegant woman Tarkan had ever seen. The asymmetrical dress shimmered in two tones of turquoise silk. Her necklace, earrings and bracelets all stemmed from the same silversmith's design.

"I wonder if I may presume on some of your precious time, my Lady."

"Please sit." She gestured to the divan closest to her. "When will you leave for Tajlit?"

"The day after tomorrow. I've delayed my departure until the Lord Consort could apprise me of the political situation."

"I assume he is occupied with other matters. Will you have some mint tea?" She poured from a painted pot into slipware beakers which were the work of a master craftsman. Then she rose with the fluid grace of a gazelle, and selected six scrolls from a shelf. "These are copies of your predecessor's reports over the past year. Trade, budget, infrastructure, climate, religion, taxes. You'll find them thorough and reliable. The councillors you inherit from him are competent, too."

"What about his chief councillor? If he acted as regent during the satrap's sickness, will he resent me for getting the post?"

"He'll soon be the satrap elsewhere." Teruma sipped tea. "Succeeding Govan."

"Lord Govan is dead?"

"As good as. Govan spent two hours in private consultation with a general, and nobody knows what they talked about, which proves they plotted treason."

Tarkan put his beaker down. "Please say this again."

"A satrap and a general had a long chat without witnesses." Her voice was as bland as if she was talking about the results of local camel show, but her eyes flamed with meaning. "This is proof they planned to kill the Consort. Kirral finds evidence of intended treason in many places. He has devised a form of trial which proves the guilt of the accused beyond doubt."

Even in the face of paranoid madness, this woman kept cool control.

"Given the Consort's current preoccupation," he said carefully. "Will you be safe?"

"In my position," Teruma said, "safety has ceased to exist." She picked up a pile of wax tablets. "Fool's Plea Festival will be a gruesome affair. The twenty cases I've selected are so bizarre, they'll keep Kirral amused all day long, devising cruel punishments. The victims are all volunteers."

"I'm surprised anyone volunteered this year."

She shuffled the tablets. "A selected Fool may change his mind until the eve of the festival. Then I substitute his plea with one from a waiting list. Judging by the number of withdrawals this year, rumours are leaking."

Tarkan felt sorry for those who had not heard the rumours or with no sense to opt out. In two days, he would be on his way to Tajlit. Until then, he would avoid rousing Kirral's ire.

'Drought is the core problem in Tajlit," Teruma said. "It has caused seven failed harvests, parched pastures, and widespread poverty. The rural regions are depopulated, the towns overcrowded with unemployed. This has led to spreading sickness and social unrest."

For an hour, they talked. Teruma knew every single person of importance, every holder of public office, every facet of social and religious life, and she suggested solutions for everything.

"I have fond memories of growing up in Tajlit Town where my father was satrap before your predecessor. Many beautiful pre-conquest buildings still stand, with arches and alcoves, with murals and mosaics. I've heard that before the conquest, Tajlit was famed worldwide for its artists and craftspeople. Under your government, will it become again become the artistic centre it once was?"

"I would like to make it so, but feeding the people will have priority. Irrigation and anti-erosion projects will use up most of the budget." Tarkan gestured at the previous year's financial report. "I doubt there'll be much left over for sponsoring the arts."

"Perhaps not." Teruma studied him like collector assessing a work of art. Then her lips curved into a smile. "Or perhaps there will be. Who can tell?" She tapped a bundle of tablets. "These are reports I commissioned on the geology in Tajlit. I used a dozen experts, so no single person knows the whole picture. If I had the time to assess them, I might realise that Tajlit is not as poor in natural resources as is generally assumed."

Tarkan looked up. "What might you have discovered—if you had made an assessment?"

"Read for yourself." She swivelled on her chair and dropped the tablets into his lap. "Naturally, if you learn that Tajlit has, for instance, rich deposits of silver, you will report it properly to Kirral, who will exploit the wealth as he sees fit."

Tarkan tried not to tremble as he understood the nature of Teruma's gift and the risk they were both taking. "Naturally I shall do the right thing. Thank you, my Lady."

"Now you had better leave," Teruma said. "If you stay any longer, palace spies will suspect a conspiracy."

❧

Tired from the long journey, Dahoud hurried up the palace stairs for a rest in his allocated room.

He nearly bumped into Tarkan coming down the stairs.

He clasped elbows with his friend. "I see you're wearing the purple fringe. My congratulations, Lord-Satrap Tarkan."

"We need to talk—in a public place." Tarkan sounded as grave as an officer reporting defeat on the battlefield.

"How about a drink to celebrate your appointment?"

"No. Let's go to the palace temple to pray."

❧

They left their sandals by the temple entrance, rinsed their feet, and descended the steps into the cool, carpeted darkness. The air smelled of olive oil and myrrh. A thousand tiny flames glimmered on wall shelves.

Tarkan led the way past statues of the Mighty Ones and their prostrate worshippers, toward an isolated niche which harboured a less popular deity. "Here we're in the public eye, yet nobody will find it odd if we keep our voices low."

A bald wooden head grinned serenely: They were paying homage to the Goddess Danila, who protected from head-lice, piles, and the action of mad-men. He scratched his scalp and touched his forehead to the statue's gilded toes. "Now tell me what the problem is."

"Kirral has become as dangerous as a mad dog," Tarkan said.

"He's always had a cruel streak."

"He's turned worse. The past moon has been an orgy of malice. Even the Lady Teruma's influence is on the wane."

'I've carried out his mission." Dahoud said. "He won't punish me for failure."

'He punishes anyone, with or without cause: foreign ambassadors, satraps, his wives. Yesterday he had his youngest concubine boiled alive, and invited the others to either eat her flesh or become the next dinner. Keep away from him until you can return to Koskara, and don't provoke him."

Insight settled as a hollow ache in Dahoud's chest: Merida had spoken the truth in the cave. Her desperation had been real. "I've hunted down a harem woman who had escaped. I returned her to Kirral."

'Dahoud! How could you?"

'I didn't know what she was running from." The excuse sounded weak to his own ears. Only desperate woman would flee into the desert alone. Why had he not listened to her plea? Instead of protecting her, he had delivered her into the arms of evil. The spear of shame twisted in the pit of his stomach. "Is there a way to free her? A legal means? She's a Riverian national."

"Ah, the magician. Merida. I heard about her." Tarkan scratched his ear. "Kirral no longer cares about international relations, nor about the law, and no judge dares displease him."

There had to be a chance, a solution, a way out. "What if she appeals on Fool's Plea Day?"

"Imagine what would happen if a woman publicly announced that she no longer liked being Kirral's concubine." Tarkan shook his head. "She would be safer stepping into a cage of leopards."

"Then I'll be the Fool pleading for her freedom," Dahoud decided. "If the crowd asks for Merida's release, Kirral has to let her go."

"Kirral doesn't listen to the masses, not if it means losing an opportunity to torment. If you get between him and his pleasure, he'll roast you alive. He'll probably ask you whether you wish to be served with peppers or with sprouts."

A priest shuffled past, gathering spent oil-lamps into a bucket. Dahoud raised his palms to the goddess, as if beseeching her earnestly for freedom from head-lice. Her gold-painted eyes squinted down at him.

He kissed her feet once more, wishing he could kneel before Merida and kiss her feet instead. "I'll have to try. Can you think of anything that would help?"

Tarkan rubbed his lips. "First, your plea must be selected. Officially, there's a selection committee, but in practice, Teruma picks the programme. Next, it must appeal to the masses. Finally, it needs to please Kirral."

"I'll do what it takes," Dahoud promised. He had to undo the harm before it was too late. "Anything."

"Anything? I wonder." Tarkan cleared his throat. "There may be a small chance. Does this Merida like you?"

"Like me?" Dahoud laughed. "To her, I'm the enemy. She didn't talk to me all the way back. I had to guard my dagger, or she'd have carved me up."

"Then it may work. We know Kirral seeks to punish her. We'll have to offer him something more enjoyable, a more exquisite form of cruelty than physical torture." He cleared his throat again. "Life in a land she considers unbearably uncivilised, and marriage to a man she hates."

"Marriage to a...? To me? Are you mad?"

"Technically, Merida is Kirral's wife, but he can repudiate her," Tarkan pointed out. "Since her mother is the Riverian equivalent of a satrap, she qualifies as a Ladysdaughter. You, as a widower, are free to marry. In Koskara, she'll be nearly safe from Kirral's wrath. Wait a few years until Kirral has forgotten the affair, apply for an annulment, and let her go."

"It would make her Lady of Koskara." He had already inflicted one unsuitable Lady on the Koskarans. Merida would be worse.

Tarkan held up his palms. "The alternative is to leave her to whatever fate Kirral devises."

Dahoud stared at the statue's gilded toes. "I'll do it."

"It may not work," Tarkan warned. "Even if your plea gets selected, even if Kirral doesn't simply have you both executed, even if he grants your wish. Annulments are rarely granted to Ladies and Lords. The only precedents are based on non-consummation. You must never consummate the marriage. Do you understand? Never. Under any circumstances. You must never even be alone with her. Can you settle her in the residency with a chaperone, and avoid her unless there are witnesses present?"

"Yes."

"As the next step, we must persuade Teruma."

"Teruma will approve," Dahoud speculated. "She wants to aid the Samil, and Merida will bring much-needed rain. How can we reach Merida to prepare her for our plan?"

"Don't tell her. Let her natural disgust speak. Give Kirral the joy of seeing her spit into your face. Now consider the audience. What appeals to a rabble? Romance and humiliation. They'll be thrilled to witness a satrap eating dust, and adore the story of hopeless love. Can you act the passionate lover, devoted to a woman beyond your reach? Practice now with me. What is she like, this woman to whom you have lost your heart?" When Dahoud volunteered no description, Tarkan suggested, "Your beloved has hair the colour of a desert sunset, eyes like polished amber, breasts like two peach halves."

"Nobody knows that."

"The day we drummed, the wet dress clung tightly. Her nipples were as pink as—"

Dahoud's fists clenched. "You're disgusting!"

Tarkan laughed. "Wonderful. This jealousy sounds convincing. Tell them that in Kirral's beautiful garden full of roses, Merida is just one more bloom, but to you, who live in the desert satrapy where roses are a rare sight, she is a precious flower."

All Dahoud could think of was the rose plantations in Ain-Elnour, and the revenue from rose oil. "I can't make a romantic speech. Will you write one for me to recite?"

Tarkan paced along the temple wall. "You need more help. I'll come into the arena as your goodspeaker."

"You'd risk your life!"

"Isn't that what friends are for?"

"Tarkan, you're a shady tree in the heat of the desert. I'm honoured to have you as a friend."

"Spare your romantic descriptions for Merida," Tarkan said brusquely. "Now let's go. I'll put our plea before the Lady Teruma."

"If I can ever return the favour in any way, count on me."

"Assuming we live to return favours."

Dahoud tried to joke. "If you ever want my help in stealing a woman from Kirral's harem..."

"That gaggle of brainless birds? Not my taste. Now let's go. You get some sleep, and I'll have a word with the Lady Teruma."

Vine wreaths with dark grape clusters smothered the banner poles. The air smelled of the charred flesh from the morning's burned offering.

Dahoud sat on the low bench at the arena edge, along with the day's other Fools, guarded like condemned prisoners. Tension knotted the muscles across his shoulders so tightly that they hurt.

As case after case was heard and each Fool and his good-speaker were punished for their pleas, the remaining men kneaded their hands. When a pair tried to sneak away, guards forced them back with the bronze-blades of their spears.

Trumpets blared musical support for the whipping of the eleventh fool. Another dance troupe spilled into the arena, whirling gaily coloured cloths.

Teruma strode to the Fool's bench, trailed by servants bearing baskets. "I trust you are enjoying yourselves." Her voice sounded almost sincere. "I've brought citron water and fruit for your refreshment."

A small man dropped on his knees, clutching her tunic hem to his cheek. "Lady Teruma, I've changed my mind. I beg you, tell these men to let me go."

Teruma ran the tip of her stylus down a waxed wooden tablet. "You're the weaver whose shoes got stolen, aren't you? Didn't I warn you of the risk when you applied?"

"I thought it would be like other years! This year, everyone gets condemned, whether they've done wrong or not. It's not fair!"

"Who said Fool's Plea Day was fair?" She tapped her stylus on the tablet. "Number twelve. Your plea comes up next, after the dance." She replaced the tablet into her basket. "Dahoud. You're new and didn't get the official warning. Your plea may get rejected as well as granted, and you may get punished. Do you want to go ahead?"

"Why does he get to leave?" the small weaver wailed. "It's not fair."

Dahoud's hand was gripping the beaker with citron water so tightly he feared it might break. "Yes."

"You're number thirteen." For a heartbeat, she laid a hand on his arm. "May the gods protect you."

When she had left, Dahoud plucked a handful of fruit from the basket. The grapes tasted bitter, with more pips than flesh.

A greenbelt pushed the weaver into the arena below the royal grandstand.

The master of ceremonies, imposing in a green tunic and a large staff with ribbons and bells, introduced his case. "Applause, please, for Amad the weaver and his good-speaker."

Feet stomped and tongues trilled.

"My friend is a loyal subject of the Queen," the good-speaker began with his arms raised as if in prayer, "a lifelong citizen of Quislabat, an honourable practitioner of his trade. Members of the royal guard frequently borrow items from his home—most recently a pair of fine sandals—and refuse to give them back."

Bending forward, Kirral instructed a greenbelt to deliver his judgement.

"Since Amad mourns the loss of his sandals," the greenbelt's voice droned, "It is the Royal Consort's will that he shall never want for sandals again. Cut off his feet." He paused for a roar of approval from the blood-drunk spectators. "Also cut off one leg. Either from Amad, or from his good-speaker. Amad, the choice is yours."

During the screeches of panic and pain, Dahoud stared at his own black-sandalled feet.

The master of ceremonies shook his beribboned staff. "Next, we have, for the first time ever in the history of Fool's Plea Celebrations, a satrap! Please welcome Lord Dahoud, the satrap of Koskara!"

Five thousand voices, drunk with blood-lust, cheered. Ten thousand feet stamped. Dahoud strode into the arena with large, steady steps, waving his arms to display the purple fringe on his wrists. Cold sweat glued the tunic to his skin. Had Kirral already decided the outcome and devised a penalty?

On the blood-soaked patch of grass before the royal grandstand, Tarkan slapped him on the shoulder. "Aren't we're fortunate? After twelve condemnations, Kirral must be looking for a case where he can be generous, don't you think?" The cheer in his voice did not sound convincing.

The master of ceremonies poured sand into the urn that limited the time for every plea. "Fool Dahoud, your time starts now!" He pulled the plug from the spout, and a pale stream arched into the painted bowl.

"Your Fragrant Luminancy, Ma'am. Your Supreme Highness, Sir. People of Quislak." Tarkan's voice was deep and resonant, practised by years of legal work. "Last year, my friend lost his beloved wife in a tragic accident. Before his own eyes, a leopard ripped her flesh and stole the living light out of her. His grief has been a pain for his friends to contemplate. Can he eat? He cannot. Can he sleep? He cannot. Witness his pallor. Behold how haggard he has become." Tarkan opened an arm towards Dahoud, as if the far-away spectators could judge the state of his musculature or the hue of his skin. "Satrap Dahoud suffered in heart-tearing solitude. He is inconsolable, and no woman has been able to rouse him from his grief."

Dahoud hung his head to feign suffering.

"Ma'am, you advised him to wed again, for his own sake, for the sake of his people, for the sake of the Queendom. Today, he willingly bows to your wisdom. Only this moon, the Mighty Ones have granted him a miracle. When a guest vanished from the palace, you, Highness, had the foresight to send Dahoud to rescue her. He searched the Queendom, he braved thugs and thirst, he stood in sandstorms and violence, all to save the woman from certain death. His barren heart opened, and bloomed with the wonder of love. The woman is not only a Ladysdaughter—child of a Riverian Administrator in charge of province—but a magician." Tarkan opened his arms wide, palms turned up. "People of Quislak, she is the magician who brought rain to our parched land! You will remember her spectacular success here in this arena last year. My friend wants to invite her to Koskara to practice her art. Moreover, she is resourceful and resilient, trained in statecraft and in trade, the perfect Lady to rule Koskara at Lord Dahoud's side."

Tarkan bowed and whispered, "Now you speak. Drench them in the wine of romance."

Dahoud cleared his throat. "Since meeting Merida, I have thought of nothing but her hair which is the colour of a desert sunset, and her eyes, which are like polished amber..."

Kirral waved a hand to shut him up. "Merida is here. Let us hear what she has to say."

Guards pushed her to the front of the royal grandstand. She stood stiffly, her hands probably tied out of sight behind her back.

"My dear Merida," Kirral said. "You have met Lord Dahoud. Do you wish to wed him?"

"No!" The shout whipped through the arena. A dozen greenbelts throughout the arena repeated the word to ensure every spectator heard it. "No—no—no—no!"

"You do not find him attractive?"

"His manners are appalling, he did not wash for a whole moon, and his breath stinks of garlic and onion."

"...stinks of garlic and onion—and onion—and onion... And onion," the greenbelts repeated.

Tarkan rubbed his hands. "This is great."

"He claims to have fallen in love," Kirral went on. "How did he treat you?"

"He gagged me and threw me across his horse, face down."

"Unusual courtship behaviour," Kirral commented, and the audience roared.

Tarkan raised an arm, requesting permission to speak. "Since she is nominally your wife, Highness, naturally my friend refrained from expressing his affections. With your gracious leave, he wishes to do so now."

Kirral played with the bead on one side of his moustache. "By all means, but remember, the sand clock is running and will soon be spent."

Greenbelts dragged Merida into the arena. They slashed her bonds, but stood close behind her, with their spear tips touching the grey dress.

Dahoud dropped on his knees to kiss her hand. She slapped it across his face.

The audience stamped to show their approval. But the sand shooting from the urn's spout was already thinning.

"I know you hate me," Dahoud spoke in a low voice so the greenbelts would not hear. "I return your feelings, but please listen: Kirral will punish you for running away. He'll let you choose between marriage to me, and death."

Merida stared haughtily. "I prefer death."

"You don't mean that."

"Oh yes, I do. For a Riverian, death holds no threat. Even if I'm destined to perish slowly, I'll die as a martyr to the Virtues. The Virtue of Discipline, above all others."

The sand flow thinned to a trickle. Dahoud had no time to listen to lectures.

"We'll go through the rituals, get a priest's blessing, that's all. Once we're in Koskara, you're safe. The marriage will be annulled and you go home."

Her eyes narrowed, as if assessing the truth of his word. "A marriage in name only? You will never force yourself on me?"

"I promise."

Bells jingled. The master of ceremonies shook his staff. "Time's up!"

"Then I accept your offer," Merida said as if granting a boon. She held a hand so Dahoud could kiss her fingertips, and crinkled her nose in disgust when he did.

"Rejoice!" Tarkan called. "Applaud the future Lady of Koskara!"

Throughout the spectator ranks, coloured scarves fluttered in approval.

From the royal grandstand, Kirral waved. "Since the bride is nominally my wife, we will get an annulment at once. The happy couple shall wed this very day, and depart tomorrow."

Applause roared like thunder. Dahoud clasped elbows with Tarkan. The ordeal was over and they were safe.

Kirral tugged at both ends of his moustache as if to increase its size. "The ceremony before the people of Quislak will make a fitting conclusion for the day's entertainments. We shall revive the ancient Quislaki rites to see these two wed in the style of Ladies and Lords of the past."

The blood drained from Dahoud's face. "Highness! Not the ancient rites. This is madness!"

"Be silent," Tarkan hissed. Aloud, he said, "You may wish to reconsider, Highness. A traditional Samili wedding in Koskara would be appropriate."

"The Koskarans had the pleasure of his previous wedding, less than one year ago," Kirral said. "The good people who witnessed Dahoud's plea for his love in this arena today deserve to see share his joy. The first enactment of the ancient rites in two hundred years will be entertaining."

Dahoud tried again. "I beg you!"

Merida said, "I don't care what ritual is used. Let's just get this over with."

Dahoud stared. He thought she would shake worse than a goat before slaughter. Instead she looked impatient.

"Form is unimportant," she informed him. "Except in the visual sense, when symmetry creates balance. In a ritual, it is the intent that counts. Everything else, pleasure or suffering, is to be endured, and welcomed as a chance to practice Discipline."

Kirral rubbed his hands. "A compliant bride. Is she not lovely? She will return to the palace forthwith to prepare."

At his signal, the greenbelts marched her out of the arena.

While the flutes chirped for the next dance, Kirral waved Dahoud to climb up to the royal grandstand.

"Congratulations on your betrothal, my dear Dahoud."

"Highness, I beg you. Not those rites!"

Kirral pulled at the ends of his moustache. "You are a loyal subject, are you not? Good. To help you stay loyal, I want you to see something." He called for a tablet and stylus, and told two men from his personal bodyguard: "Dahoud is going to visit the dungeon. Give this to the warden on duty." He snapped the tablet shut and pressed the hilt of his dagger into the seal spot. "You look pale, Dahoud. Wedding nerves? Do not spend long in the dungeon. We need you back here in time for your performance."

CHAPTER 28

Rites

Merida braced herself to enter the harem dormitory one last time, while her wardens waited at the door. Odours of over-ripe fruit and old urine battled with those of unwashed clothes and personal perfumes.

Most inmates were at the festival, parading their finery, but Haur-vatat sat slumped on her bed. Merida greeted her friend with joy.

Instead of showing pleasure, the girl's eyes grew wide. "Go away."

"I'm getting wed today." Merida infused her voice with cheer as if she was a genuine bride.

"Go away. Please, please, go away!"

"I'm sorry I took the sandals without your permission. I'll leave most of my clothes here, and you can have everything."

"Keep the sandals! I don't want anything. Just go away!"

Startled, Merida checked the girl's aura. Its usual red physical ener-gy was depleted, replaced by a murky mix of grey and blue. Merida swallowed. The blue was faint, but unmistakeable. "You're with child!" Pregnancy explained the odd behaviour. Yet the blue was tinged with the grey of sickness. Small wonder, given the appalling hygiene in the harem. The grimy wash-water and stale air could make anyone ill.

Clutching a wooden bowl to her chest, Haurvatat spooned its con-tents into her mouth. The blackish flakes looked like fungus scraped from a damp cellar wall.

'Eating that vile stuff may harm your child," Merida warned.

'Go away!" Haurvatat howled.

Since Haurvatat would not see reason, Merida decided to give her the privacy she seemed to want, and started packing. She would take a single change of clothes and leave everything else behind, even the set of scrolls. A treatise about architectural symmetry would be useless in a place where people lived in round tents, and she would definitely not worry about djinns.

Tiredness encroached her mind. After a night spent on the bare stone floor of a prison cell, she longed to snatch some sleep in her former bed, but resisted the temptation. Instead, she prayed for a long time thanking the Virtues for her deliverance.

'Merida."

At the intrusion of Teruma's voice, Merida jerked out of her meditations.

'I only have a moment before I must return to the festival," Teruma said briskly. "Do you want something to help you through the ritual? A herb wine to dull the senses, or joy-flowers?"

Merida frowned in distaste. "I prefer to keep a clear head."

'Are you sure? It can't be pleasant, especially in public, and if you don't even like the man..."

Haurvatat's scream ripped through the air. She lay curled on her side, writhing. Teruma and Merida ran to her bed.

'Stay with her," Teruma commanded. "I'll fetch the healer."

'Not Merida!" Haurvatat wailed. "Take her away. Don't let her touch me."

'I won't be long," Teruma soothed. "The healer will make everything right."

Merida sat on the edge of Haurvatat's bed.

The girl's face was ashen, her aura now grey and green. "Take the spell off me," she moaned.

'This is no spell," Merida told her firmly. "The nasty fungi have given you stomach cramps."

'Your spell!" Haurvatat cried. "You cursed me. Danced around the lamps. Made evil signs in the air."

Merida laughed. "That was no spell, just a joke. I would never, ever curse anyone. Least of all you, Haurvatat."

"You hate me. The rat… the cockroach spell…" Haurvatat whispered, then writhed and groaned as fresh pain sliced at her. A cloud of odour rose from her, like smells from latrine shafts and rotting food. The fungus had obviously upset her digestion.

Merida gagged, but disciplined herself to stay seated. "I don't hate you, Haurvatat. I know you told Kadiffe about my fear of rodents, and she put the dead rat into my bed, but I don't blame you for that. That dance around the lamp wasn't real magic, it was just to frighten the person who tried to harm me with the cockroach spell, and it had nothing to do with—"

"Stand aside." A spindle-thin man with clinking amulets on his chest shoved Merida away. His knees creaked as he knelt beside Haurvatat's bed.

Merida rose. "She was eating those fungi by the fistful."

"I told her to. They're medicine."

Merida shuddered. "Medicine? Eating mould can make a healthy person ill. For a pregnant woman, it can be poison!"

"The mould has helped the Queen and the Consort," Teruma said. "We have every hope it will protect Haurvatat and the first royal child to be born in this generation."

Ignoring Merida's outburst, the physician laid a hand on Haurvatat's forehead, nodding gravely. "Cold fever." He checked the pulse on her neck, and finally pushed his hands under the blanket to examine her belly. Haurvatat screamed, and kept screaming even after the physician withdrew his hands. The stink increased.

He spread a bundle of coloured scarves around the patient, held up a black carved idol, and sang an incantation.

"I'll find a fresh blanket and open the windows," Merida said.

"This patient is under my protection." His thin hands clawed into her arm. "You will not open a window, or kill her in any other way."

Haurvatat's face was the colour of old ashes, beaded with sweat. "Stop this… Take the spell off me… The cockroach spell… forgive me… pleeeeeease."

Merida gasped. "You? You put the cockroach into my bed? Why, Haurvatat, why?"

"Magic to make you like me," Haurvatat whispered. "The rat … to frighten you, make you sleep in my bed."

The silly woman! All the time, Merida had suspected malice, when it was just another of Haurvatat's ploys to force affection.

"My finger cymbals, Merida," Haurvatat croaked. "You coveted them. Take them."

"I don't want them, Haurvatat. They're heirlooms. You must give them to your daughter."

"I want to live. I want my daughter born. Take the curse off me. Take the cymbals. Take them. Take them." Her pleas shrilled. "Take them!"

'I didn't..." Merida tried to explain again.

Teruma's hands dug into her shoulders. "If you're half as intelligent as you claim to be, you know what to do. Take the spell off her."

Merida understood. If superstitious Haurvatat thought she was cursed by sorcery, she would not get better until she believed herself freed.

She loosened her hair, and chanted a general-purpose healing spell, translating it into Quislaki so everyone would understand. "Virtues, draw your clouds over this painful day..."

"Take the spell off!" Haurvatat cried again.

Merida tossed her hair and waved her arms while she made up an invocation. "I call upon the Four Virtues to Witness that I accept the finger cymbals from this woman here. I revoke the evil spell I cast on her."

She hoped it sounded convincing enough to give Haurvatat some relief. The groaning had stopped. For good measure, she fanned Haurvatat's face with the treatise on architectural symmetry. "Bless this woman, bless this child. Give them peace, give them sleep, remove all pain from them forever. Thus it shall come, in the name of the Virtues."

The physician stood up, kneecaps creaking.

"She's dead," he said. "You killed her, sorceress."

Merida stared at the bed, at the body, unable to believe that sweet, stupid Haurvatat had betrayed her and was now dead.

The guards closed in, weapons clanking, and grabbed her arms.

"To the dungeon?" one asked with a flint-hard voice. "We heard the killing spell."

"I didn't kill her." Merida struggled to keep her voice as cool, although her mind was a whirlpool of panic, confusion and grief. A moment ago, the door to freedom had stood wide open. Now it had slammed shut. Would she be punished for a murder she had not committed?

"To the arena," Teruma said. "The spectators are waiting. I take responsibility for her, and I assure you, she won't escape."

Relief washed through Merida. The fake wedding was still on. She would join in a primitive ritual, say the required words, and depart from this accursed place forever. "Thank you, Teruma."

✢

The paunch-bellied guard shoved the scroll into his belt and beamed at Dahoud. "The Consort, he writes you'll inspect the private prison, where the special guests are housed. An honour, it is, my Lord. You'll find everything in very fine order, even today, when most staff are at the festival. Me, I'll guide you personally."

Dahoud strode with his back straight, refusing to reveal the apprehension he felt. The dungeon guard would not see a trace of fear in the satrap of Koskara.

The Consort's private prison stood like a pleasure pavilion in the centre of the rose garden, plastered with playful ornaments and pink pilasters, surrounded by rose pergolas and strutting white peacocks.

"The prisoners, they scream, my Lord," the guard explained. "Some sensitive folk don't like that. A peacock cry, it sounds just like a mad person with pain. So the prisoners, they scream, everyone thinks it's the animals."

The guard led him up the steep cedar steps to the upper storey. The door had neither lock nor bolt, and squealed under the guard's push. "Your feet, mind that you wipe them. Sorry about the smell."

Light speared through narrow slit windows and painted pale stripes on the carpets. Piles of cushions and pretty brass-top tables suggested this was a place of sumptuous pleasure. The air was thick enough to slice with a sword. Smells of frankincense and vinegar fought with the prison reeks of piss, puke and shit. Beneath them lay the odour of rotting flesh.

"Someone died here," Dahoud said.

"Normally, the corpses, I get them cleared away at once, but this one, the Consort wants to keep, so he can watch it rot." The guard waved an arm at the big incense burners and braziers with bowls of simmering vinegar. "These, I brought in to purify the air, but after four days, the carcass, it gets bad. Please, my Lord, if you get sick, step outside. Puke, it ruins the carpets."

Dahoud knew death stink, but familiarity did not make it easier to bear. When taking charge of a conquered town, his first command had always been to burn the corpses.

The guard offered him a phial. "Mint oil, it helps, my Lord. Dab a drop on your upper lip. Now, the living guests, they're in cells one to four.' Instant wails rose, begging for attention, mercy and release. "Ignore them. They always howl when they hear someone talk up here."

Dahoud lowered his voice. "Who are the prisoners, and how long are they here for?"

"The Consort's permanent guests."

"Starved to death?"

"Oh no, my Lord!" The guard looked shocked at the suggestion. "I feed them daily at dawn. The freshest bread and the finest dates they get. Our guests, we treat them well."

Dahoud glanced at the naked man huddled in a bed of shit. "Indeed."

"The guests, they don't treat themselves well. When they see they won': get out alive, they smear their dung first on the walls, then on themselves. Next, they try to starve themselves, but with fresh-smelling bread and water, they can't resist. The Consort, he likes it when they get creative, bite their wrists open and such."

"The corpse is in cell five?"

"That hole, I wouldn't stick my nose down, my Lord. Clever, this one was, though. Cheated the Consort. Stayed calm, exercised, kept himself neat, prayed, this one did. Real dignity, that one had, until one day, very sudden, he got mad."

Dahoud knelt by the edge, bracing himself for the sight. A sliver of light fell into the cell. The view slammed him in the gut.

Black blood caked Paniour's silver hair, and the face lay in a dried puddle of puke. A head wound. "How did he do it?"

"Slammed his skull against the wall, full force. Takes will and strength, that. Others, they tried the same and didn't hit hard enough. This one, he knew what he was doing. Took him only a few tries. He passed out before we could get the Consort, and then he was dead. The Consort, he was angry."

"So he comes to watch the body rot." Dahoud refused to let the guard guess how shaken he was. "It'll be a tough job to get the corpse out of there."

"We won't have to do that. Tomorrow, the Consort, he will release rats, so he can watch them have a feast."

Dahoud pictured Kirral sitting on silk, inhaling the foul air as if it was perfume, stroking his moustache, while the rodents gnawed at his former friend's flesh.

He said a silent prayer for his mentor's soul.

"That will be all." He rose with the dignity that befitted the satrap of Koskara. "I'll return to the arena now."

~

A pair of greenbelts led Dahoud into the centre of the arena. Five thousand people roared, excited like dogs at the sight of raw meat. His stomach tightened. He had to consummate the marriage before this crowd. For once, the woman's role was the easy one. She only had to lie back and grit her teeth until it was over.

The high platform was the size of a tavern table, covered in black cloth, and flanked by benches from which selected spectators could get a close view. There was no chance of faking.

He strode forward with a tightening stomach and cold sweat dripping down his neck.

Drums pounded to announce Merida's arrival. She marched as resolutely as a soldier into battle, her face composed but pale. When Dahoud squeezed her cold hand, she granted no response.

He listened to the bow-legged priest's wedding chants, and answered all questions in the affirmative. Yes, he wished to take this woman Merida as his wife and make her Lady of Koskara. Yes, he knew she was once-widowed, once-divorced. Yes, he accepted that she was presumed barren. Yes, he would cherish her forever. Yes, he would ensure she did not leave Koskara without the Consort's permission.

He avoided looking at her pasty face, at the scraped-back hair, at her stiff figure in drab clothes. Nothing about her roused his desire, but he had gotten her into danger, and he had to get her out of it.

The Consort's selected guests shuffled to the benches, competing for the seats closest to the promised action. The men stared at Merida in thirsty expectation, their tunic fronts bulging. The jewel-bedecked women twittered and jostled for the best vantage points around the table. Kirral, with pink roses pinned to his turban, licked his moustache.

'You'll have to help me do this," Dahoud said quietly to Merida.

She dropped his hand and stared, eyes and mouth wide with terror. "This... they... we... They can't mean this. No. No!"

She had not known. Her compliance had been ignorance. Understanding of what the old rites involved was only just sinking in.

His heart pulsed with pity. He had to take charge. Grasping her hand, he soothed, "It won't take long, and it won't hurt much."

She shoved his hand away. "You promised we would never do this. You promised!"

A million ants crawled over his skin. "I don't want to do this either, but we have no choice. Lie face down and try to relax, then it will hardly hurt at all."

"Most entertaining." Kirral clapped his hands. "Let the sand-clock be filled."

The master of ceremonies poured a big bowl of black sand into the painted jar. Then he rammed his staff on the ground. The bells clinked and chimed. "Lord Dahoud, your time starts now."

Merida stood stiff like a stone tower. "I won't participate in this barbaric ritual."

Cold sweat washed over Dahoud. If she refused to cooperate, it would be rape, and that must never happen again.

"Just this once," he urged in a low voice. "In Koskara, you'll be safe, and then we never need to do it again. Trust me."

"The sand is running," Kirral said. "Get rutting before the jar runs out, or the bride dies."

Merida wrapped her arms around her chest. "I choose death."

The men on the benches guffawed. One roared with laughter and slapped his thighs so hard the amulets on his chest bounced. The women giggled.

"She'll die anyway," one of them chirped. "Like the last wife he killed."

"Dear Merida, you do not get to choose between life and death. The choice is Dahoud's." Kirral's pink tongue flicked over his moustache.

"Dahoud, either you perform now, and take your new wife to Koskara." He smoothed the creases in the table's black drapes. "Or Merida takes up residence in the cell currently occupied by the late Paniour, next to his corpse. You, dear Dahoud, will spend the remaining twenty-eight days of your court service watching her die." His tongue flicked again. "To make it entertaining, we shall give her the company of flesh-hungry rats."

Merida's composure cracked. Her hand shot to the front of her neck, and the last drop of colour drained from her face. "Rats?"

Dahoud tried again. "Please, Highness -" But asking Kirral for mercy was like battering a stone wall with a spear-tip.

"Hurry up, man, show us some action," demanded the man with the amulets.

"Take off your tunic," a girl chirped, "so we can see the size of your passion."

Kirral's fingers tapped on the black table, and his voice was as hard as bronze. "Much as I enjoy your dilemma, do not take too long. Or the sand-clock will decide."

Whichever way Dahoud turned, he would fall into an abyss.

The only way to save Merida's life was rape. For almost four years, he had fought with every fibre against the demon inside him, had resisted torments and temptations. Now the evil was finally weakened, almost asleep, only sometimes troubling him with demands. He could hope to live out the rest of his days in a semblance of peace, as long as he did not wake the djinn, did not feed it. Four years of hard-fought abstinence would be wasted. The hard-won partial victory over the evil inside him would be lost. Everything that was good and noble in him would be ground to dust. The djinn would triumph, growing again to unbearable power.

But if he walked away, a helpless woman would suffer a slow death, enduring unspeakable pain and descending into madness, gnawed alive by hungry rats and by fear, because at the crucial moment, Dahoud had failed.

"Rape or rats?" Kirral sang. The glass beads in his moustache glinted.

Dahoud girded his resolve and reached for her shoulder. "Merida, I promise..."

"I'd rather have a thousand rats," Merida snarled with the insolence of an enemy refusing surrender. "Don't touch me, you stinking swine!"

Anger lanced him like a sharp spear. Clasping a hand around her arm, he dragged her to the table. She struggled like a goat pulling away from a leopard's teeth. How dare she treat him like this! In his legion days, he had ravaged women who had fought like this. It had been fun. His blood simmered, pulsing with the heat of fermented fury.

He held her face between his hands to force her to look at him. "Listen, Merida."

She spit on his cheek. The furnace inside him churned. He flung her on the table and pinned her down. Five thousand voices roared their approval.

She twisted, bit his arm, drew blood. His body responded with fierce intensity. Swirls of lust and fury swept through him like blue fire. His blood pumped, hot and thick and fast. His need, denied for so long, burst awake. He had to cool his burning palms on this woman's skin.

He held out his hand. "Highness. Your knife."

Kirral's dagger slid from its sheath. Dahoud tested the blade and found its point and serrated edge sharp. Perfect.

"Careful now," he said. "I have a knife and I don't want to hurt you. Try to relax. If you lie still, it won't hurt much."

She slammed a fist into his jaw.

He grabbed her tunic at the neck, sawed into the fabric and ripped, baring her breasts. They lay, pink-tipped and defiant, waiting to be conquered.

Dahoud pinned her arms behind her head, and slammed his mouth on her breast. She fought to refuse him, like every woman always had. Scratching and biting like an enraged leopard, she was still no match for his furious strength. The breast was his by right of conquest, for him to do with what he pleased. He clamped his teeth around it, singing the cool flesh in the furnace of his mouth.

"The Virtues will punish you for this." Even panting with the effort of defence, her voice had the sharp hum of a deadly arrow. "Your genitals will fry. Your skin will be peeled off you with a thousand knives."

He had heard such curses from many women before her. Laughing, he sawed through the waistband and ripped the seam between the legs.

Applause roared like a desert storm. Battle fire swept through him and his body turned into a battering ram. Her muscles strained in a final effort to defy him. He forced entry, savouring the soft, moist sweetness he had denied himself for so long. The crowds cheered. The priest chanted an ancient blessing and poured a pitcher of cow's milk over the couple.

In a moment, Dahoud's heat was spent, the fire of passion collapsed into grey ashes. He stood, straightening his milk-drenched tunic, all hope drained from his heart. Where his inner strength had been, a hollow gaped.

Merida pulled her garments into place, her face a stiff white mask. At least, she was safe now. But Dahoud stood once more enslaved to the djinn.

"This," Kirral said, "was most entertaining. You have earned your prize, Dahoud. Take your bride to Koskara. I wish you joy of her."

At his signal, drums pounded, flutes wailed, and trumpets roared.

"Just one more little matter." Kirral leaned forward so only Dahoud could hear him through the din. "You will not forget your promise to keep her in Koskara, will you? Your wife has been caught killing through sorcery. We have suspended the death penalty for as long as she is under your guard. Should she ever leave Koskara..." Kirral clapped Dahoud on the shoulder. "Happy marriage."

CHAPTER 29

Husband and Wife

After two moons of tediously slow travel on horseback, reaching the residency in Djildit was a relief. Jasmine and honeysuckle clung to local-style mudbrick walls, from the kitchen came the inviting scents of sage and spiced beef. Dahoud's stomach rumbled in response.

"Lord Adil is an old friend from childhood days," he explained to his sullen bride. "We'll be more comfortable here than in an inn."

Merida lifted her brows and nose as if surprised by a speaking dog before following him up the steps to the reception hall.

Lord Adil, elegant in his plain tunic of white wool, clasped his elbows in a warm welcome. "Good to see you, Dahoud. Have you eaten? I'll get a room readied for you at once."

"Two rooms," Dahoud said. "I have the honour to present my Lady Merida."

"You really have wed her? I took it for a malicious rumour." He handed Dahoud a beaker, fragrant with citron and cool grape. "I appreciate that you were forced into this marriage. But do you have to bring her into my home?"

When Adil lifted the second beaker to his own lips without offering Merida a drink, Dahoud put his beaker back on the tray. "Are you refusing hospitality to my wife?"

"This is a respectable home. I cannot have it soiled by a sorceress."

For a moment, the air seemed thick with honeysuckle, so similar to the sickly-sweet smell of a town under siege. He had never imagined he would have to use the formula of warning against a fellow satrap, let alone a friend. He pronounced it word for word. "Watch the Words that Burn Your Tongue."

Adil's face softened to a genial smile. "My dear Dahoud, there's no need to get heated about this. Naturally, I take back what I said if you find it unacceptable. I spoke in haste, in concern over my home." His smile now extended to Merida, but it did not reach his eyes. "I'm sure your bride is quite harmless, and perfectly charming, in her way. Of course she may stay at the residency. The stables, or even the servants' quarters. I can easily have those purified afterwards."

Dahoud upended the beaker. The citron water splashed on the stone tiles. "I wish you a pleasant evening."

In the courtyard, he grabbed the horses' reins from the groom.

Merida sulked. "I'm hungry, and thirsty, and tired. I've ridden all day, and you make me ride even more?"

Dahoud's throat screamed with thirst and his heart with fury. Protecting Merida had cost him a valued friendship, and she bickered instead of showing gratitude.

She mounted her horse. "Hurry up and load that luggage. Get us to a decent hostelry, with proper beds."

This woman deserved to sleep on the dung heap. Or in his bed, underneath him, so she would feel his fury, would learn to respect him.

How about the Black Dog Inn, where we gave her shelter, and in the morning she ran through the street, yelling about rape? Shall we take the same room, pin her on that same mat, let her feel what we can do?

Dahoud tasted the fantasy, liked its flavour. Oh, how she would fight! How she would bite and buck and strain, how she would curse and cry, how he would savour her resistance. He would punish her, force her to take him, again and again, until at dawn her cries subsided to a defeated whimper.

No! No, no, no! No to the Black Dog, no to the shared chamber, no to the rape! He drove his horse into a fast trot to out-ride temptation. Instead, he would punish Merida by taking her to a hamlet three hours south of town, to sleep in the seediest tavern he knew.

⤸

Dahoud savoured Merida's discomfort, the way she struggled not to look at the cockroaches scuttling across the floor, at the drunken snorers, or the whores and their men rutting in the corner. She picked at her food and drank water with her eyes squeezed shut.

'Is this where we sleep tonight?" she croaked. "With these... people?"

The revulsion in her face was priceless. Up to now, he had gone out of his way to make her comfortable, which had earned him nothing but disdain. Tormenting her was more enjoyable.

"Don't worry, honey-cake. We'll have privacy. I've paid the landlord to let us sleep in the stables. If you've finished eating, let's go." He waited for her shoulders to relax with relief, and added, "You don't mind stable rats, do you?"

✂

The stables smelled of dung that should have been mucked out long ago. He could almost hear Merida's shudders.

"You take that section at the end," he told her. "I'll sleep here. This way I'll hear if you try to escape, or if you get attacked by rats."

Through the wooden partition, he listened to the rustling straw, knowing that she was readying herself to fight off his advances. He could go there now, measure his strength and will against hers, feel her strain and buck and rear. He squeezed the thoughts from his mind, forging chains to fetter his budding fantasies before they could burst into bloom.

What harm would there be in it? Isn't a husband supposed to mate with his wife?

He had not held a woman in his arms for a long time. It felt like two lifetimes ago. Even more time had passed since he had last measured his strength against a woman.

She'll enjoy it. Why do we keep her waiting?

Dahoud's heart thudded, and his palms grew hot with the need to touch her body, to pin her arms to the ground, to bite her flesh. She could fight and would like the wrestling part. Lust singed the edges of his self-control. He had fucked her before, what difference did one more time make?

Doesn't she owe it to us?

Horses huffed, tails swished, molars ground.

"Be careful, Merida," he said loudly. "Samili stable rats are big, with three-foot bodies. Teeth as long as human thumbs. They always gnaw the toes first."

Frantic rustling of straw told him she was putting on her boots. "They also like noses. Some folks wake up in the morning to find their toes and noses gone."

He was sure she would sleep poorly tonight, if at all. But the sliver of malicious pleasure did not distract him for long. He lay awake long into the night, throbbing with the pain of his dark desires.

✆

The landscape was rugged, broken and harsh, golden grassland with bands of thickets and scattered trees, under a wide sky of brilliant blue. Merida breathed deeply of the free, clean air.

"In an hour, we reach Koskara Town. From now on, you'll behave as befits the Lady of Koskara." Dahoud sounded like a parent giving a wayward child one last chance. "I've had rooms in the residency cleared for you. You won't leave the town without my permission or without an approved escort."

Letting his speech wash over her like pattering rain, she surveyed the sweep of ochre savannah, and the distant yellow hills, plotting her escape.

"I've asked my councillors to hire a woman chaperone. She'll advise you, guide you, watch you."

Merida pictured a grim-faced hag. She would outwit that one, too.

She could smell the animals and manure even before the town came in sight, a jumble of low yellow houses surrounded by a crumbling outer wall and a thorny hedge, with livestock roaming around black tents.

As they road through the crumbling brick gate into Koskara Town, inhabitants flocked like a cluster of brightly coloured butterflies. Some welcomed Dahoud with warmth, others stood with arms locked across their chests, and they all devoured Merida with undisguised curiosity. Clearly, the courtesy of introductions was as unknown here as in Quislabat.

Dahoud jumped off his horse to clasp elbows with a brown-skinned man who looked like the bandit in the mural of Mother's parlour.

A young girl pushed to the front of the crowds, her tunic a faded red, copper bangles jingling on her arms, a mane of beaded plaits chinking around her head, her pretty cheeks marred with cross-shaped scars. She halted before Merida, walked around her horse once, and declared: "You look exotic."

Merida plastered her face with charm. "I am pleased to meet you. My name's Merida, and you are...?"

"I'm Yora, your protector. You needn't be afraid of anything." The girl tapped her dagger-studded belt and grabbed the reins. "Get off your horse. I'll show you where we'll live."

Merida laughed silently. With a fifteen-year old jailer, escape would be easy.

"To the residency!" Dahoud called. The crowd surged onwards, bare feet thudded on the dusty dirt road between sacks of produce and market stalls. Shacks roofed with palm-mats alternated with mudbrick houses whose wooden balconies jutted over the road blocking out the searing sun. Goats peered from roofs and doors, and knobbly-kneed camels gargled and spat. Whiffs of olive oil, blood and spices punctuated the smell of manure.

Not the slightest tingle of earth energy tingled through Merida's soles: The Koskarans had built their capital in a site devoid of magic.

The procession halted at a two-storey building outside the town walls. The curving greenstone façade, the glazed animal tiles, and the bronze-studded door fronted by fake pillars gleamed with menace.

The palace from which she had escaped was waiting to devour her again. Only this time, she would be Dahoud's captive instead of Kirral's, and Dahoud was many times worse.

"No!" She crossed her arms and braced her legs, ready to fight. Dahoud strode forward, his face grim. Something hot and dangerous came and went in his eyes.

She chose a new strategy. Holding up her palms beseechingly, she addressed the natives. "Please, may I live in a townhouse like everyone else? Or even better: in a tent?"

Mutters and foot-stomping gathered volume until they roared like thunder. Merida thought her request had caused anger, but when her guard beamed, she understood they were cheering her choice.

Dahoud stared at her through narrow eyes as if she had just grown a second head. "Yora, take her to your yurt," he snapped. "Get her some sensible clothes, don't let her out of your sight."

While he uttered further instructions to Yora, Merida beamed her gratitude to the assembled folks. She had just won a victory over Dahoud. It would be the first of many.

∝

Yora linked an arm through hers and dragged her back into town, chattering, pointing out the temples of this deity and of that, the bathhouse, the olive press, the building where the oil jars and the fleeces were stored.

Merida studied everything intently: the graceful movements of the emaciated bodies, the plain tunics in bright colours, the piles of oranges and intricately woven rugs on the market stalls. Her hasty flight from the palace had failed because she had not known enough about whiteseers to impersonate one for long, and had lacked understanding of geography and climate. This time, she would be prepared. She would learn about Koskara and copy the natives until she could pass as one.

Skinned animal carcasses hung above doorways, some still dripping with blood, others shiny with masses of blue-winged flies. Chickens scratched the baking soil.

Wherever an alley led off the main road there was a shrine with carved idols, smeared with paint and mashed food. Strings of woollen tassels, wilted blooms and dead poultry were draped around them.

One day she would write a treatise, *Primitive Cultures and Their Hazards to Health and Sanity*.

"Can we please go to the bathhouse?" Merida pleaded. "I need a wash."

"Yes, the bathhouse will be open tonight. Now we buy clothes. Dahoud pays."

A cluster of curious natives followed them to the vendor's booth.

"Uncle, the Lady Merida needs new clothes," Yora said.

The fabric vendor flicked his tongue over a fat lower lip and pulled out bolt after bolt of shimmering fabric. "Finest Darrian silks, from the old days, before trade was forbidden."

"Wool, please. Something thin, and practical." Merida smiled at the women clustering around the stall. She would wear what they did, to blend in. "I like the local style."

'The last Lady always wore silk."

'Wool will do for me. Something ready-made. I'm sure that one will fit, and that scarf to go with it." She pointed at a vomit-coloured tunic hanging from the palm-frond awning, and a headcloth in the hue of a cowpad. The colours would blend into the local landscape.

"You'll look like a camel," Yora complained. "At least get something pretty for the festival tonight."

The trader pulled out his pink silks again. "The last Lady wore..."

Yora waved at his offerings the way a cow's tail flaps away flies. "Uncle, this Lady likes the local style. She'll wear a Koskaran dress to the feast." The watching women cheered. "She'll buy that tunic over there. It's like a well-ripened pepper. That sash, like a carrot. Those scarves in cucumber green."

Merida resigned herself to looking like a bowl of vegetables.

The vendor showed tasselled shawls, ruffled sashes, translucent scarves. "The Lord Dahoud will expect you to take more than two outfits. The last Lady always bought at least five."

"The last Lady had as many gowns as the year had days," Yora confirmed. "Dahoud says we can spend a lot of money. It helps the economy."

"Very well. One more outfit." Merida lowered her voice. "This one is for you, Yora. Choose something pretty for the festival."

Yora's eyes danced with excited pleasure, as if she had never owned a new garment before. Merida brushed the spots of guilt from her conscience. If Dahoud wanted to spend money on clothes, his generosity should benefit someone who appreciated it. Merida had what she wanted: a native outfit in which to escape.

Once again, Dahoud was standing by the altar, awaiting the ritual of symbolic sacrifice. This year, the grass in the arena was so sparse the bare baked soil showed. The sun was a fiery ball against the descending curtain of twilight. The air smelled of smouldering charcoal and summer dust.

Dahoud stood in his new costume, with a short scarlet tunic over a longer maroon one, with sash and headcloths in the same colours, projecting confidence. Merida had set aside her foreign garb in favour of a layered native dress which emphasised her height and athletic figure. Zun wore a ring-trimmed red robe so long it trailed on the ground with the snake curling like a collar, and stroked the knife's long bronze blade.

When Mansour led in the stallion, hemp-drugged and garland-hung, to clapping hands and stamping feet, Zun brought the knife to his lips to kiss the blade, and held it out to Merida. "My Lady."

She leant away. "I can't."

"It's easy," Naima assured her. "I've drawn a blue line on its neck. Just slit along there and blood will come. This is an important ritual. Either the horse or the Lord has to die."

"The horse has done me no harm."

Dahoud's blood started to boil. How dare she!

Two thousand eyes watched the scene at the altar, waiting. Even the birds ceased their twitters. Only a child cried. Tension rose like a bowstring that tightened and tightened. Unless the arrow was let loose soon, the bow would break.

Merida had declared war. He would not take this lying down.

How shall we teach her to obey?

"My Lady." Keera stepped forward. "Would you like me to do it on your behalf?"

She held out her hand for the knife, but Mansour was faster. He snatched the weapon and slit the stallion's throat. Blood spurted in a high arc. He bowed, grim, triumphant, and dripping with blood.

Dahoud lifted the ceramic bowl and swallowed the bitter blood. Keera and Mansour had smoothed a tense situation, but their decisive actions suggested different agendas. What was going on? And more importantly: how could he keep Merida controlled?

CHAPTER 30

Lady of Koskara

The next morning, the familiar smells of frankincense, mint, wool and leather swirled in the black yurt. After three moons absence, Dahoud had to assert himself anew as the leader and take the reins firmly into his hands. The councillors would have grown used to Mansour's leadership. He checked their postures to read their intent. Some bodies were angled towards Mansour, some to Keera – what did this mean? Most, however, were studying Merida with undisguised curiosity.

The new Lady of Koskara sat with her legs modestly tucked under, spinning wool like a native. After Esha's arrogance, this should have offered him relief, but he did not trust her meekness one bit.

How will she undermine your authority today?

Dahoud fed granules to incense burner to invoke the gods. "It's good to be back in Koskara. How have things been going?"

"Before we start." Naima raised a tea beaker towards Merida. "Shall we make our new Lady welcome with the Riverian custom of introducing people?"

"By all means." It was important to give the impression of mutual liking and respect. "The Lady Merida came to Quislak as an ambassador for her nation. She has made me the happiest man by consenting to be my wife." When Mansour's brows rose a fraction, Dahoud added, "She finds many of our local customs bewildering, and needs a little time to adjust. Yora is helping her to settle in."

"I hope to be a quick learner," Merida said.

The native tunic left most of her arms bare. He remembered how much strength she had in them. Fighting her had been a pleasure, although the circumstances had not allowed him to savour it.

Keera handed her a tea beaker. "Welcome to Koskara, my Lady. I'm Keera, councillor of law. This is Naima, councillor of health, who has achieved miracles with limited resources. She knows your country and speaks your language. This is..." She introduced other councillors, praising each, then finished with "Wurran, councillor of trade. Mansour, chief councillor. Zun, the high priest."

Was this coincidence, or was Keera emphasising the importance of some and downplaying that of others?

"I'm pleased to meet you all. Keera. Naima. Wurran...." Merida repeated each name, and bestowed the same amount of smile on everyone, except Dahoud.

The earth-yellow tunic made her pale skin look sallow. Dahoud remembered her radiant in last night's jewel colours, and better still, without clothes. Skin as white as milk, breasts as softly rounded as a pair of hills in the landscape....

He must focus on the meeting. What was Keera doing?

"If there's anything I can do to help you feel at home," Keera said. "I'll be happy to assist. Naima, too. You can count on us."

"When the women are done chatting," Mansour said, "Can we get started?" He reported about events of the past three moons, from the men-lovers he had rounded up and killed, to the results of the eighth year of drought—waterholes drying up, flocks perishing, over-grazed pastures, sand dunes swallowing hamlets, poverty.

He had barely completed his summary when Naima took over. When she described the suffering, the starvation, the sickness that came from lack of water, Merida's face softened with compassion.

Compassion is worth a donkey's spit. Why doesn't she offer to dance for rain?

"The new town of Oubar will bring relief," Dahoud declared. "Displaced farmers can cultivate crops on terraces, and nomads can shelter their flocks during the dry season. Can we speed up the building? How far has it progressed?"

For five heartbeats, silence ruled. Then Keera said, "Mansour halted the project."

'Indeed I did," Mansour said. "You promised there would be plenty of water on the site. There's none."

'There will be," Dahoud said. The water should already be flowing. Criton, the former mining engineer, should have linked the old mine shafts and tunnels. What had gone wrong?

"Work on the citadel will resume at new moon," he decided. "Keera, get every available labourer there, skilled or unskilled."

Mansour raised his spindle. "What about water?"

"There's a water pocket in the karst nearby. We'll drill into that." In fact, the water would come from almost three thousand feet away, through an ingenious linkup of old mines, but this had to stay a secret. No enemy must ever guess the true source of the citadel's water. "Until then, workers can use the mountain brooks, and we'll get additional water from Ain-Elnour."

"From Ain-Elnour?" Mansour laughed. "The camels drink almost as much water as they carry across the desert. Show us the wonder water, and we'll start work."

"I'll travel to the site and supervise the work. You'll see water soon," Dahoud promised, but the councillors' faces remained closed, with narrow eyes and pinched lips. Their enthusiasm for the new town had waned fast.

"You know how superstitious nomads are," Keera said. "The gatehouse opens to the west, the direction of death."

Merida bent over the plan, forcing herself into Dahoud's view. Strong shoulders, inward-curving waist, round hips. Her body was practically begging to be clasped.

"The gatehouse facing west is essential for the defence," Dahoud said. "Zun, from a religious perspective, is the direction of the gatehouse a problem?"

'Not yet." The high priest contemplated his snake. "But Koskara needs a school of healing."

'The school will be the first public building we complete." Dahoud picked the plans for the new citadel from the rug and showed the location. "Right here between the temple and the tavern."

Keera leant forward. "Naima has developed a curriculum, and I have a plan how to recruit teachers, unofficially of course. You can count on us."

"Excellent," Dahoud said. "Five years from now, the citadel will be a living town, and in ten years, it will be a flourishing centre and an invincible fortress." This was what mattered: He would give Koskara the safest citadel that had ever existed. It would guard the Eastern border and keep danger out of Koskara, and should the need arise, a thousand people could find refuge there.

"Invincible?" Mansour asked.

"Invincible," Dahoud insisted. "The walls will be thicker and higher than any in the known world. An attacker would have to climb up a track which is too steep for siege engines, and pass below the curtain wall exposed to our missiles, and breach three gates with doors of solid cedar. To get to them he has to walk between the walls, so he'll be shot at from both sides."

"So much passion." Mansour swung his spindle, caught it expertly in the other hand. "Why focus on defence and not a peaceful activity like trade?"

"Or agriculture?" Merida said. Her lips were fuller than he remembered. Like fruit, waiting to be bitten and bruised.

"There'll be terraced fields, and a caravansary below. But if we want peace, we must prepare for war. Oubar was Koskara's only remaining defensible town."

"So you don't trust the Quislak legions to defend us after all."

"Not entirely," Dahoud said.

Do we trust Merida? What plot is she hatching now?

Wurran said, "This is a civilian's vision of a citadel. Impractical."

"Naturally, I bow to your expertise," Dahoud said. "I'll welcome suggestions for improvement from everyone who has fought in a real war. I know Mansour was a unit commander. What was your role, Wurran?"

"I led the civilian resistance against the Black Besieger," Wurran said. "Someone had to."

"Of course." The Black Besieger had squashed the resistance. What a conquest that had been! So satisfying, so sweet.

"I made sure he didn't get the supplies he needed, and I suffered for it. He stole all my horses, ruining decades of breeding-"

"All of them?" Dahoud had left him half a dozen dams in foal.

"All my good stock. He burnt down my stables. He killed my sons. He—"

'I'm sure Mansour will advise me on the design of the citadel," Dahoud said, "to turn the civilian's vision into a workable fortress."

Before the meeting drew to a close, Merida asked, "How may I make myself useful? I can write, translate, keep accounts. I'm trained in statecraft and in trade. Or perhaps in New Oubar..."

'The council can do with someone who understands trade and accounts," Keera said. "Naima and I will show you what to do. Perhaps you could check the trade balances."

When the councillors had left, Dahoud blocked Merida's way out. "If you really want to help, you know what we need."

'I won't dance for rain."

'Another year of drought, and the water-holes will dry up, the pastures will parch, the flocks will die, crops will fail, women won't be able to feed their children. Do you want that?"

Does she care?

For two heartbeats, she gazed at the floor rug, her lips tight. Then she jutted her chin up. "I told you: If you bring me here, I won't make magic, not for wealth and not for water. Do I have to tell you why? Then I'll explain it point by point – at the next council." Her voice had the deadly hum of an arrow in flight. "Everyone will know. How will you like that?"

How do we like that?

He wanted to punish her, hurt her, to subdue her to his will. Controlling his anger, he tried one more appeal. "Don't you see it was the only way to save you?"

'Save me? Is that what you call it?" Her eyes glinted like spear points. "No, Dahoud, I won't dance for rain here. Ever. Give me a task which local women perform, and I'll do it without complaint."

Dahoud wished there was a job involving rats by the legion. Fortunately, Koskara Town had a lot of work suitable for shocking the fastidious Riverian. "The dyers need a helper in their workshop, to stir the pots of boiling piss. How will you like that?"

'Show me the way."

Without ado, she followed him to the dyers' workshop downwind from the town. Even when they neared the shacks and the stench hit, she merely clenched her nostrils and lips and marched on.

The pair of dyers in their stained tunics bowed and fussed over their arrival.

"My Lord, what honour!" the man enthused. "You bring glory to our humble site."

The woman knelt in a puddle under the line of dripping yarn. "How may we serve you, my Lord?"

"The Lady Merida wants to learn your trade. Treat her as an apprentice."

The woman struggled with this information. "The Lady wants to..." she repeated, chewing every word.

The man simply stood, mouth gaping.

"I'm so grateful for the opportunity," Merida said. "I promise to work hard. Where do you want me to start?"

He waited for her to gag and beg to be released, but she took the proffered stirring staff and applied herself with vigour. When she smirked at him, oozing triumph, he wanted to shove her head-first into the boiling piss. He consoled himself with the knowledge that few people could cope with this labour. Very soon, she would beg to be released from the labour and the stink.

While the man babbled on about what an honour it was, Dahoud fixed his wife with a commander's stare. "The Lady Merida will come here every day, and work from dawn to dusk, except when engaged in council matters. You and your husband will guard her. You will not let her out of your sight, not for one heartbeat, until either I, or Yora, or a member of the council pick her up at night." To forestall questions, he added, "I'm concerned for her safety. I hold you responsible."

The couple were bowing and babbling again. Dahoud took his leave.

On his way out, he heard Merida ask, "Why are the strands on this rack changing from yellow to blue? Will that be the final colour? What plants do you use for the dye?"

She was not suffering nearly as much as he had hoped, and the punishment was not giving him nearly as much satisfaction as he needed.

He wanted to wipe that smirk off her face, to punish her insolence. He wanted to rip that tunic, to bite her breast and suck the salty sweat off her skin. He wanted to hear her pant in defence against his pleasure. He wanted to hurt her. Really, really hurt her. The thrill slithered through his bloodstream like strong wine, awakening every fibre, until even his fingertips pulsed with anticipation.

He shook off the fantasies before they swept away his self-control. Merida was constantly rousing the djinn. To get peace, he needed to keep her away from him, yet he also had to prevent her escape. Setting her to work for the dyers and to sleep under Yora's watchful eye was not enough. The Koskarans would expect their Lady to attend council meetings, but even being in the same tent with her was a strain.

He had to find a face-saving pretext to remove her from the capital, while keeping her in the satrapy under close guard. There was only one solution: he would send her on a spiritual retreat.

❧

The air in the arena still smelled of cold smoke from the cooking fire, and bits of bone littered the grass. Zun, bare-chested and oiled, was lifting stones.

Dahoud picked up the largest pair of stones, took up position next to Zun, and started lateral raises. "When you return to your mountain temple, will you please invite the Lady Merida to stay with you for a few moons?"

"Did she ask you to ask me?"

"I'm sure she'll be glad to join a spiritual retreat, but the idea needs to come from you."

Zun performed a series of slow bicep curls. "You just got married, and want to separate already?"

To make an animal bite, the bait had to be right. "Will you invite her if I make the school of healing a priority, and find instructors for it?"

Zun peered over his bent arm. "Is this a bribe?"

"Of course not. Merida could become a teacher at the school."

"Does she know healing?"

No, but that would not stop her from lecturing. "She's a natural teacher."

"I see." Zun switched to overhead presses, counting. "...Twenty. Twenty-one. Twenty-two. You mean, Merida needs to get away from you. You worry what you'll do to her if she doesn't."

Dahoud lowered his stones. "Can you read thoughts?"

"When they're as graphic as yours. No, I won't invite Merida, regardless of what you think of doing to her."

"It's not me who wants to harm her. It's..." Dahoud swallowed. A priest might comprehend. He would be shocked to learn the truth, horrified even, but he would understand the need to remove Merida.

Dahoud pushed the truth out. "I have a djinn. It makes me do things. Terrible things which my conscience would never allow." He braced himself for Zun's reaction.

"How convenient to have a djinn."

"Convenient? To be possessed by a djinn is convenient?"

"How else can you outmanoeuvre your own conscience? Fifty-nine, sixty. If you've finished with the large stones, may I borrow them for the upright row?"

"You don't understand!" Dahoud snapped. "I'm forced to do things my conscience abhors. Djinn possession is like burning alive from the inside out. I've sacrificed my career, I've sacrificed my friendships, I've sacrificed everything I've ever held dear, all to protect women from the djinn inside me. You have no idea what it's like."

Zun raised his shoulders and elbows, bringing the stones to the front of his neck. "Twelve. Thirteen."

"I didn't choose to have a djinn," Dahoud insisted. Furiously, he worked on lateral raises, lifting stones far heavier than what he normally used for this exercise. His muscles quivered under the weight.

"You didn't choose to have a djinn," Zun repeated. "Who would you be if you didn't have it?"

"Who would you be without your snake?" he shot back.

Zun laughed. "Exactly."

"Will you please invite Merida?" Dahoud tried again. "Surely that's not asking much? She'll enjoy studying with you. She'll be glad to get away from me. She'll be safe."

"You have remarkably strong arms. Have they always been like this?"

Dahoud flexed his biceps. "They're the result of tough training."

"Why don't you train your resistance to the djinn? Wouldn't life with Merida be tough training?"

Annoyance churned. Dahoud needed to avoid triggering the djinn, not to invite it.

"Will you invite Merida?" he tried once more.

"No. You need the exercise more than I do."

Dahoud tossed his stones on the grass. "I've finished. When you're done, put the weights away over there. Have a safe journey home."

He picked up his jug, gulped down the water, and walked off in anger. For Zun, self-control was nothing more than a muscle to exercise, and a djinn was merely an unruly pet. Zun had no idea of the price Dahoud had paid for his one mistake in that stormy night. Dahoud regretted his naivete, regretted his compliance, regretted the violence, and the rapes and the ever spiralling needs resulting from that one moment of weakness.

He would never have harmed a woman from choice. Why could Zun not understand that? Memories knocked, demanded admission. Dahoud blocked their entry.

A responsible high priest would have hurried to help, would have removed the woman from the danger and afforded Dahoud some peace. Zun, however, was more a showman than a spiritual leader, understanding neither the nature of djinns nor the dark corners of the human soul.

Dahoud had to put a safe distance between himself and Merida before the djinn made him do something terrible.

The wet heat of the steam bath unknotted Merida's tension. Under Yora's watchful eyes, she lathered herself in olive oil and scraped the dirt-mixed grease off with a strigil. Since the bathhouse allowed each customer only two jugs of water, she budgeted how to use hers. Above all, she needed to rinse the day's stink out of her hair. Yora recommended conditioning the hair with fresh camel urine, which would kill most lice and ensure a natural gloss, but Merida stuck to the fresh-scented soapberries and water.

After carrying buckets, stirring textiles in huge vats, and hanging strands of wool on overhead lines all day, her shoulders ached if she had performed every drill of the Disciplined Path a thousand times. The hot water cascading over her head soothed the muscles.

'... were so beautiful, but the trader wanted two fleeces for them...' Yora prattled.

'How often do trading caravans come here? Where do they go next?"

Merida had to escape. In Koskara, she was as much Dahoud's prisoner as she had been Kirral's in Quislabat. Now that the chance of an annulment had been squashed, death was the only way to end the accursed bond. Dahoud had already murdered one wife. Her ignorance of whiteseer customs had undone that disguise. This time, under the pretext of wanting to adapt, she would learn everything she could: geography, climate, local life. Fortunately, Yora bubbled words like a spring threw out water.

When another woman plunked her jug on the floor, Merida threw on her tunic rather than be seen naked by a stranger. But it was Naima, the councillor of health, wearing a floaty dress the colour of forest moss, and smelling of oranges. "I think you here," she said in broken Riverian. "Hygiene important for health, yes?"

"Very important," Merida agreed, remembering the maggot-crawling, fly-wrapped carcasses hanging from the butcher's stalls. In the council meeting, Naima had reported the results of hygiene measures, such as moving the sheep pens away from the river. Since people no longer drank dung-mixed water, illnesses had dropped drastically. "I think you're doing a great job, Naima."

"You think so, yes? Then you help me make hygiene in Koskara, yes?" Naima slipped off her tunic and lathered soapberry paste under her arms. "Clean homes, clean bodies, clean foods. You make Dahoud listen."

"My influence on Dahoud is limited. Can I help in some other way? Perhaps you can show me on a map where the water sources are, which of them are contaminated, and where epidemics have occurred." A map would be useful in plotting her escape.

"In residency. We go there now?" Switching to the native language, she said, "Merida and I are going to do council work in the residency."

"But I'm not allowed in the residency," Yora protested. "And Dahoud says Merida must always be watched."

"I won't let her out of my sight. You can go home."

"Dahoud always checks on us at nightfall."

"That's not for two hours. I'll deliver Merida back to your yurt before then."

When Yora yielded to Naima's authority, Merida wanted to sing with triumph. Now four different people were guarding her at different times, which would make it easy to confuse them.

On the way to the residency, Naima placed a covered bowl before an idol shrine splashed with red paint and mashed food. "Meats and maggots." She lifted the lid to reveal crawling flesh. "If placed at the shrine during a full-moon night, these animals can draw poison from wounds."

Merida shuddered at the thought of touching maggots, let alone exposing an injury to these creepy worms. Naima might have learnt much in Riverland, but she still adhered to primitive ways.

≺

The satrap's study was cobwebbed from disuse and stank of horses.

Naima struck a spark to light an oil lamp. Its sparse shine did little to illuminate the room.

Besides a single shelf holding tablets and scrolls, the room was bare. Naima brushed a film of powdery dirt from the scrolls before untying them. "These are the statistics of epidemics, blindness from eye infections and deaths in childbed, woefully inadequate, of course. Nowhere as thorough and efficient as in Riverland." She was speaking in the local language again. "Perhaps you'll help?"

"I'll try. You mentioned a map?"

The map was fanciful and not to scale, but it showed what Merida needed to know. The capital, Koskara Town, was in the satrapy's north, and the quickest way to get away from Dahoud would be to retrace the route they had come, to get into Tajlit and Djildit.

To disguise her interest, she asked about water sources, pollution and infections. "What about Dahoud's new town? Where is it?" When Naima pointed to the mountains in the south-east, she said, "I see no water source marked on the map."

"That's the problem," Naima said. "Dahoud believes he can get water there, from mountain streams or an underground lake, but so far this hasn't happened."

The new town's location was interesting, too, just three or four days from the Darrian border.

"Why is the school of healing to be built down there and not in the capital?" Merida asked.

Naima shrugged. "Teaching healing arts is illegal. The more remote the location, the less likely it will be found out. But it won't help. Even if we had teachers, which we have not, it takes years to train a good healer. Whereas cleanliness can be improved in a single moon."

"A worthy cause," Merida agreed. "Can I see the trade balances?"

Naima waved a hand across the cluttered shelves. "Somewhere in there. Help yourself."

Merida checked scroll after scroll of accounts and reports, most written in scarcely literate hands—presumably Dahoud's and Wurran's. Here and there, Keera's neat lettering stood out, and some documents were written in the graceful hand of the ill-fated Esha.

Many documents were missing, while some had been scribbled on wax tablets and shoved into the shelves without transcribing.

Merida puzzled over the accounts. The Koskarans did not use money rings. Instead, certain items had the function of currency: a large amphora of olive oil equalled three fleeces. The nearest equivalent to money was the rings paid for community work. The previous Lady of Koskara had received some, so she would as well, but those weren't spendable. They had to be paid back, as a form of tax to ensure everyone contributed to society.

Koskara was mired in debt to Quislak, and ninety percent of the olive oil and fleeces were earmarked to pay outstanding taxes. This left little for the natives' own use, and nothing for export.

Merida applauded Wurran's initiative in trying to export spun wool, but the revenue barely covered the cost of transport. The only lucrative trade goods were the perfume oils from roses grown in the oasis of Ain-Elnour, and those profits were eaten up by the purchase of raw metals from Copperland. Every moon, Koskara was sliding deeper into poverty and debt.

"It's getting dark," Naima said. "We have to leave soon."

Merida fished random parchments from a pile: a letter from Teruma offering to sponsor a temple, a couple from Kirral refusing to allow a healing school and praising the execution of men-lovers, a foreign trader asking about taking a caravan to Ain-Elnour. Merida absorbed every morsel of information, but Naima was already tapping impatient fingers on her knee.

Merida placed the documents back on their shelves. "I can sort the files, to make them easier to access, and I'll read them at the same time.

Then we'll make plans how to improve the hygiene in Koskara. I've promised to work for the dyer every day for the next moon. Shall we come here early in the morning, late at night, whenever it suits you?"

'I'll have to squeeze it into my schedule, and I don't have much time." Naima said. "But I can snatch an hour tomorrow at sundown, and at dawn the day after."

An irregular schedule was perfect. People would see her now with Yora then with Naima; now at the dyer's workshop, then in the residency. Nobody would be able to predict her movements, or grow suspicious if she was not in an accustomed place.

On each visit to the residency, she would bring provisions. Then she would purloin one of Dahoud's horses from the residency stables, and ride north-east to Djildit Town where she would slip into a new disguise.

She had to act before Dahoud did. He probably planned an accident: a collapsing riverbank, a misguided arrow, a runaway horse, a mauling leopard. Poor Esha had left her escape too late. Merida would not make that mistake.

By the time they reached the yurt site, darkness was hugging the town.

The anger from Dahoud's eyes prickled on her skin like a cold fire. "Merida must be guarded at all times."

"I guarded her," Naima said pleasantly, unruffled by his gruff voice. "The new Lady needs to be familiar with the council records, don't you think? Besides, what mischief could she do in the residency?"

"It's for her protection."

"For her protection." Naima rubbed her eyes. "Of course it is. Merida offered to keep the accounts for us. Isn't this nice of her?"

"Very nice." He sounded like a dinner guest complimenting his hostess on a poorly cooked meal. "Will you go with her to the residency while she works there?"

"Why not you, Dahoud?"

"I don't have the time."

"You think I have? With an overflowing healing practice, with my work for the council, with all the extra tasks you've given me?"

Dahoud's brow furrowed, and Merida saw her chances slip away, but Naima said, "I'll take her whenever I can steal a moment. Either at dawn or at dusk. I'll pick her up and hand her back to Yora. Is that good enough?"

"Perfect," Dahoud said.

~

In the small yurt, Yora heated water. "To make Samil tea, we drop the dry leaves in here and let it stew. Then we add the fresh mint leaves, and pour it out, and in again, and out, and in..."

Merida's mind brimmed over with the bright, blinding impressions from the day, and whirling plans for escape. Dahoud probably plotted to stage an accident. The previous Lady had been dragged against her will on a hunt where she was attacked by a leopard. Even if Merida did not go on a hunt, dangers lurked everywhere. A horse might bolt, a riverbank collapse, a ceiling cave in, a poison snake lurk in her bedding. The sooner she got away, the better.

"... so the aphids sink to the bottom of the bowl," Yora concluded.

"Aphids?" Merida choked. "Greenfly?"

"Greenfly, whitefly, blackfly. They sit on the stem of the mint when you put it in. They're quite dead now because they've drowned."

Merida sipped through clenched teeth.

"The exercise you did outside the yurt," Yora asked, "is it Riverian fighting?"

"It's derived from martial art—boxing, kicking, swinging a staff— but I don't fight."

"I like fighting," Yora declared. "We'll fight, you and I. You show me how to kick and fight with a staff, and I teach you how to fight with knives."

"I don't fight," Merida repeated.

Her arm was jerked on her back and a cold edge pressed against her throat.

"What will you do now?" Yora asked close to her ear. "Fight?"

Merida held her breath. One false move, and the knife would slit her throat. There was nothing she could do. Nothing. The Disciplined Path held no way out.

"All right," she said with more calm than she felt. "Put the knife away. We'll practice another time, and then you can teach me how to defend myself against a knife, so I don't need to be afraid of men."

'You're afraid of men?" Yora asked with the same tone of disbelief Haurvatat had employed to ask 'You're afraid of mice?'

'Let's talk about it tomorrow," Merida said with a firmness that should have made it clear the subject was closed.

"You married Dahoud. You're not afraid of him, are you?"

Merida unfolded and refolded her new clothes.

"Men like Dahoud are very easy to handle," Yora assured her. "He always does what I want. Almost always, anyway. Sometimes he wants to protect me, as if I was a child. He won't even wrestle me."

"You asked Dahoud to wrestle you and he refused?" Perhaps Dahoud had some scruples after all.

"Yes. It's unfair, isn't it? Just because I'm a girl. But I'm grown up and I want to wrestle."

Yora might have a woman's courage, but she did not yet have a woman's sense. "Wrestling between men and women can lead to… problems. If you really want to grapple, practice with a woman. Why don't you and I have a go?" The proximity of another body held no appeal, but it would help keep Yora safe.

'Yes! I learnt all Dahoud's tricks from watching him and Mansour, and I'll show you. Is he your first husband or were you married before?"

Kirral did not count. "I had a husband in Riverland." Merida meant to keep the details to herself, but they poured like water from a broken dam. "A drunkard who beat me. He killed the child in my womb. Believe me, women have reason to fear men."

'Is he dead?"

'He fell from the roof into the river and drowned."

'You killed him with magic!" Yora clapped her hands. "Wonderful."

"I did not. Now I need to sleep, in case Naima comes for me at dawn." Merida knew Naima would not come tomorrow, but the girl swallowed the excuse and ceased prattling.

But there was no silence. A lamb was mewing, a light call of 'meh', immediately followed by a deeper 'baah'. More sheep joined in, each with its individual voice.

Merida imagined their conversation. 'Be quiet.'—'Be quiet yourself.'—'Hush, it's time to sleep.'—'Shut up all three of you.'—'She started it.'— 'Now will you be quiet?'—'You're the one who keeps talking.'

"Merida? Merida, do you hear me?" Yora's voice was as persistent as a dog's bark. "Don't kill Dahoud with your magic. He's my friend, and Mansour says we need him alive still."

Merida feigned sleep.

That night, lightning tortured the sky with searing bites. Through the yurt's smoke hole, Merida watched the ragged white gashes. The sky writhed and groaned with thunder, yearning for the release that rain would bring. But no rain came.

In the morning, Merida woke to a cacophony of bleating sheep and yapping dogs. Light crept through the gaps of the entrance flap. The thunderstorm had passed without granting the relief of rain.

"Good morning, Yora."

Grunting, the girl shoved her face into the fleece.

Merida stretched. Her shoulders had stiffened overnight, and the arm muscles complained about yesterday's work.

She tested her guardian's alertness. "Maybe Naima will fetch me this morning to go to the residency."

"Naima?" Yora's voice was sleepy.

"Didn't you hear her agree to this with Dahoud?"

Yora grunted. Early morning was obviously not the girl's best time. Merida resolved to plan her escape for morning sometime soon. She invented a strategy on the spot, and tried it out.

"Yes, Naima," she said loudly. "Just a moment."

Yora half-rose on her elbows. "You're going to the residency?"

"Yes. Naima is waiting." When the girl did not question this, Merida added, "She'll take me straight to the dyer. You'll pick me up from there at dusk, won't you?" Hastily, she shoved oranges, dates and a filled waterskin into her reed basket. "I'm coming, Naima."

She could have used a spell of inattention, but that would have drained her own alertness. Sleep-drunk Yora did not need it anyway.

On her way, Merida cheerfully greeted the traders who set up their stalls for the day, as if she was meant to walk here without a guard.

In the residency, her head swum with how easy this rehearsal had been. She would study records, do some actual work, and then walk downriver to labour at the dyer's vats until Yora picked her up.

From small high windows light fell in dusty beams and painted rectangles on the floor. She rifled through a basket of travel permits and picked out one for a female trader which might fool the border guards.

She sneaked into the stables at the rear of the residency. Five horses huffed, shifted on their hooves, craned their necks and pricked their ears.

What if she simply rode away now?

Yora expected her to be with Naima, and then with the dyer. The dyer would assume she was on council business or had lost her enthusiasm for stirring stinking cauldrons. Naima would be too busy to think about her at all. Hours would pass before she was missed, an opportunity too good to let pass.

Everything she needed was here: horses, fodder, tack. She spoke softly to a docile-looking silver horse, stroking its neck. A few heartbeats later she was on her way to liberty.

The sun was already rising for another hot, dry day. She rode downslope through the desiccated fields. Endless olive-trees, their silver leaves curled in the drought, their unripe fruit already falling, and vast expanses of the stiff-stalked straighthorn grass that was good only for kindling.

If she travelled through the day's heat, she might be out of Koskara before nightfall, and a few days later reach Djildit Town, that bustling trading place which felt almost familiar in her memory. There, she would assume a new disguise.

After an hour, the track petered out, and the gaping emptiness around her gave no clue which direction to take.

Only one hill, bare rock shaped like a crescent, relieved the plain. Merida coaxed the horse up to the top, and gazed around. To the south west lay Koskara Town. Those buildings on another rock in the north east had to be the military place. That faint line leading towards the horizon seemed to be the track leading north to Tajlit.

The northern horizon glimmered, as if a burning thread was stretched along it, a thread that thickened even as she squinted to see it more clearly. She blinked and looked again. If this was a wildfire, it would travel fast, feeding on oil-rich olive trees and expanses of straighthorn grass.

Her heart thudded, and her thoughts raced. As long as she stayed on this stony hillock, she was safe. The fire would flow around her like river around an island. Then she could ride across the burned land, and the town's residents would be too focused on saving their own lives to notice her absence and ride in pursuit.

Many would die from fire biting into their limbs, from smoke searing their lungs: Yora, Naima, the dyer, all the women in Koskara Town who had shown her such kindness. Merida's heart clenched: Their fate was in her hands, and she had to choose between freedom for herself and safety for the people.

Merida drove the horse back south. Every heartbeat counted.

CHAPTER 31

Facing the Fire

The parched landscape flew by as Merida raced the horse back to the town, past the stretches of straighthorn grass, past the olive groves, past the residency, into the main street.

'Fire!" she yelled. "Wildfire from the north!"

Figures spun, staring, but their shoulders shrugged and they resumed their haggling at the vending stalls.

'Fire on the horizon. Hurry!" Merida urged. "It's coming here. Save yourself!"

'What's she saying?" one woman asked another while examining a ceramic pot, studying its glaze, pinging it to check for invisible cracks.

'She says there's a fire."

'Well, she's a foreigner, poor dear."

An old man called from his rooftop, "I see no fire."

'You can't see it yet because it's still far off downslope, but fire moves fast!" Merida jumped off the horse, her bloodstream pumping. Time was seeping away like oil from a leaking jar. She ran up to Yora's uncle behind his clothes stall. "Won't you believe me? I've seen a fire in the north."

"Of course you've seen a fire," he soothed, shaking out a dress, smoothing its ruffles, hanging it up, picking a piece of lint from its hem. "Nomads cook over flames."

"A large fire, all along the horizon!"

"The sun in Koskara can get very bright," he said. "I've brewed nice fresh mint tea. Do you take it with honey or with cardamom?"

She tore down the street, dodging donkeys, searching for someone with sense, someone who would believe her, someone who would know what action to take.

Dahoud and two councillors came striding up the road.

She ran up to him. "Dahoud. There's a wildfire from the north. You can't see it yet, because it's downslope, but it's all along the horizon."

He drilled his stare into her. "Where did you see it?"

"From the crescent-shaped hill. I rode back as fast as I could."

For a heartbeat, his brows rose. He wet a finger and held it up. "We have an hour. Less if the wind rises. Evacuate."

"Evacuate?" The barrel-bodied councillor with the triple chin objected. "For a fire that can't be seen?"

"Better act on a thousand false alarms, than miss one that's real," Dahoud said. "We'll protect Koskara. Release all animals, Wurran. Open the pens, the stables, let them run."

"Do you have any idea how long it will take to get them back?" Wurran demurred. "There hasn't been a wildfire in Koskara for generations."

"Nor has there been an eight-year drought, a thunderstorm and a steady wind. Do it. We're counting on you."

He turned to the other man. "Mansour, the river is a natural firebreak. Use it. Widen it. Cut down the olive trees, burn the grass. A swathe two men-heights wide, along the northern side, as far as you can along the river, to protect the land south."

While the two men dashed to do their duty, Dahoud roused the reluctant townsfolk. "Get the other councillors to me. You, stay on the roof, watch when the fire comes. Send riders to the villages and nomads, tell them to go behind the river and start firebreaks. Get tools, get water, get yurts. Behind the river, everyone." To Merida, he said curtly, "Help the vendors pack their wares. Food especially."

Glad Dahoud had heeded her warning, Merida hurried to pour the fruit seller's oranges into baskets. Behind her back, people muttered about hysterical foreigners and overreacting satraps.

Had she gotten it wrong? Could the glimmer thread have been a trick of the morning sun? Could she have needlessly thrown the town into havoc, caused the sacrifice of precious trees, and ruined her own chance of escape?

'Fire!" a voice shrilled from above. "Fire. Fire. Fiiire!" The scream soon echoed from a dozen rooftops.

The lethargy vanished as people panicked, and the pace picked up. They fluttered and flustered, and dropped what they were doing to dash for precious possessions and safety. In the alleyways, bodies swarmed like wasps around a threatened hive, aimless and angry. Bodies pushed towards the bridge.

"My donkey!" a crone cried. "If there's a fire, I must find my donkey.'

The caravansary landlord dragged two clattering copper vessels into the alley. "Who cares about your donkey!" he yelled. "Help me move my kettles!"

Horses whinnied, dogs barked, goats strained at their ropes.

Naima and another female councillor were herding everyone into an almost ordered evacuation.

"But my donkey!" the crone protested, looking small and lost. "I won't go without Donkey-Darling."

Naima grabbed her by the shoulders to turn her south. "Your donkey is already on the other side, waiting for you." She shoved her stumbling towards the bridge.

Merida was swept along with the stampeding crowd.

In the safety of the opposite bank, she helped drag cut-down trees across the river. Her eyes stayed transfixed on the horizon, where the glimmering thread was fast thickening into a rope that stretched as far as the eye could see.

Wind rose, lashed the air and drove the inferno forward towards the deserted town.

The growing swathe of scorched earth, added to the river's wide bed, made a broad firebreak behind which they would be safe, but it covered only a short stretch. Somewhere else, the wind would whip sparks across the river, setting the parched pasture aflame, inviting the fire to devour all vegetation in its path until it reached the sandy desert dunes. Koskara, already crippled by drought, would have nothing left but ashes.

Nothing could stop the disaster but rain, lots of rain, but she had sworn not to bring rain to this land.

A pair of hands gripped the rope she was pulling. Dahoud knelt next to her. "Merida, will you dance for rain?" He held up his palms, beseeching. "Please?"

She nearly let go of the rope in surprise. Dahoud was asking, not commanding, not forcing, sounding almost humble.

"I don't think I can," she stalled while she dragged the tree out of the water. Firewood, precious in Koskara, would soon be even rarer. "I'm not prepared, haven't kept the right diet, I've even eaten flesh at the festival. There's no earth power here and the planets aren't aligned. Without a platform, without a square of fire, without music, there's nothing for me to work with."

"Please—Will you try?"

"Dahoud!" Naima called. "We need you over here."

Dahoud rose and followed the councillor.

To work rain magic, Merida had to surround herself with a square of fire, and while this was not possible, there was the space between two walls flame, between the defensive fires and the approaching inferno. She might visualise the rest. Instead of a platform, she could use a high building—if she returned into the town she had just fled, back into the inferno's path.

She had to act fast.

At the stone bridge, burly men blocked people from returning to their homes.

"Just let me get my loom," a woman urged. "It'll be back in a heartbeat."

"The bow was my father's, and my grandfather's before him," a man pleaded.

"I have to get Donkey-Darling," the crone wailed. "Donkey-Darling doesn't like being alone."

Nobody got through the chain of bodies.

Putting on an 'I'm-the-Lady-how-dare-you-stop-me' look, Merida strode right past them.

Among toppled booths in the main street lay broken jars and squashed fruit. The place reeked of oranges, wine and olive oil. She hastened to the highest house. Her steps thudded on the wooden ladder.

On the rooftop, the air sang, already tense from the faraway heat. The glimmering thread had grown into a white band with a canopy of smoke. The wind drove it towards the town.

Standing alone above the silent town, she ripped off her headwrap and unravelled her plaits. She prayed to the Virtues, invoking their support, and pleaded with the spirit of water to send succour. In her mind, she pictured the wildfire and the glowing beads of the firebreak linking into a circle. She tried to hear musicians drumming the zarri, but fear drove the imaginary sounds away. She swung her arms, her torso, her head, willing the magic to take hold.

Her belly cauldron remained empty. All she felt was the cold hand of fear squeezing her guts. If the fire engulfed her, she would die without ever again breathing the cool air of a fir forest, without ever again cupping the rain-beaded mounds of moss, without ever seeing her home again.

Wind wafted heat into her face. Cold sweat glued the tunic to her chest.

This might be the last thing she ever did, and she would not fail. The Koskarans would remember her as the great magician who gave her life to bring rain. She would not be forgotten. But what if no rain came?

Terrified wild goats and gazelles darted south, all seeking by instinct to cross the river. The wall of brown smoke rolled towards her. Fingers of fire zinged out. She heard the fire whisper, felt the hairs rising on her arms.

Shrubs crackled and burst, shooting flaming leaves into the air, and billowy clouds of black smoke wafted skyward. Birds fled before the fire, crying with fright. The air was orange tinged purple, tilting within a heartbeat into yellow and white.

As the menace rolled closer, it devoured the outlying yurts with a stink of smouldering wool. The increasing wind whipped Merida's hair around her neck.

The first of the palm trees that fringed the northern town wall exploded, each burst quickening the pace of Merida's heart, spoiling the pattern of rhythm she tried to keep in her mind. Black leaves with glowing edges rained down.

Then Dahoud came up the ladder, a clay drum under his arm, and their eyes locked. For once, they were united, joined by the intent to save Koskara. With the drum across his thigh, Dahoud tapped the rhythm, steady and loud over the din, improvising over the basic pattern, the way he had drummed in Quislabat for her rain dance, a lifetime ago. *Doumtek, doumdoumtek.*

Shocked by his cooperation, she sank into his rhythm, and their energies linked. Eyes closed, she danced, danced, danced until her mind found a rain cloud, and held it fast. The prickling ran through her fingers, zinged through her flesh.

When she squinted at the sky hoping for relief, no rain cloud was in sight, only clouds of smoke.

The whooshing wind halted, changed direction, attacked again. The air smelled white with heat. A bird dropped at Merida's feet, its wings singed and smoking. Fire sheets jumped the city walls, fell onto stables, ignited the hay store, and sent billows of black from the wool warehouse.

Houses filled with fire and the air thickened with acrid, hot, wool-stinking smoke.

Columns of grey smoke rose from the house, wrapping around Merida's legs. Charred leaves, ashes and sparks rained down. With an ear-splitting roar, a palm tree split halfway down its trunk. Flames shot out of the oil-storage windows. Koskara Town was aflame, and they were in the centre of it.

The fire roared like an angry beast. Wooden balconies broke, crashing into the alleys below.

Heat seared her lungs with every breath, but she must hold out. She touched the faraway rain, she held it, but she needed to bring it to Koskara. She put all her strength into pulling the rain close.

The roof cracked. Smoke and brick dust bit her nostrils and robbed her sight. When she could see again, half the roof was gone, and the ladder with it.

Dahoud gestured, shouting something she could not hear above the fire's roar, pointing to another roof. Weakened as always after magic, with no time for a grounding ritual, she ran after him. They jumped to a lower roof and raced along a crumbling wall, barely outracing the pursuing inferno.

When her feet hit the firm ground of an alley at last, her legs buckled. Dizzy, disoriented, and blinded by smoke, she struggled to right herself, but her hand touched hot brick.

Beams crushed down, blocked her way, preventing her from going forward or back. She grabbed smoking timber, tried to shift it, pushed at panels and kicked the wood, but the barriers did not budge. Each kick brought further debris down in sparking showers. With her strength depleted and her escape barred, this burning cage held her trapped. Biting sparks singed her skin and gnawed her flesh. Her hair burned, her fingers, her thigh.

So this was how she would die, convenient for Dahoud who did not even have to murder her. Hundreds had seen her go back into the town, against dire warnings. Dahoud would embellish her tragic death, how a collapsing building had killed her. Another wife lost shortly after the wedding, he could say, so sad.

Hot, dense, biting smoke forced its way into her lungs, leaving only the hope that inhaling smoke would be less painful than roasting alive.

All around, thick acrid grey. Blistering heat. Part of her wanted to live, yelled at her hands to act. But her eyes saw nothing, and her fingers no longer knew what they grasped. Smoke that seared through the nostrils into the brain.

"Get down." A voice. Someone's. Someone she knew? "There's less heat on the ground. Less smoke."

Low on will, she ducked and clawed at the stones that pebbled the road. Timbers creaked, crashed. Flames whined.

"Quick now!" Dahoud's voice? Was the way free? Where was it?

No matter: her legs would not rise.

She was dragged, lifted, tossed. Then she passed out.

⁊

Merida came to on the other side of the river. When the numbness of shock wore off, pain stung her cheek, and tore at her arm. A crone wrapped her into a wet blanket. Although Merida shivered in its cold embrace, it relieved her burning skin. Naima slapped wine and honey on her wounds.

Still the wall of fire marched towards them. High flames and black columns of smoke rose in Koskara Town. Trees cracked, split, roared and fell. Sparks dropped on the shaven land, into the water. Animals cried. The people grew silent, terse. Would their fire defences hold?

Pain clawed deeper into Merida's flesh. Her cheek, ear, arm, calves and heels shrieked with agony. The burn wounds heated the blanket until it offered no more relief. She wanted to lie in cold water, but the river surface floated with glowing debris. Half her tunic had burnt away. Her hair was so brittle it crumbled in her fingers.

The sky was a mass of seething fire with flames that coiled upward with a roar. Then a flash of lightning tore the sky open. For a moment, all was purple stillness.

Thunder rolled like horses galloping across the sky, and then the rain came, a downpour so thick that it blocked the vision, so rapid that it raced across the ground, and so hard that it hurt.

"Rain!" hundreds of voices cried. "Rain!"

The scene dampened down at last. Merida allowed the falling water to soothe her burns, the hard pounding of the drops more than offset by their cooling effect.

Yora danced, women ululated, a man lifted Merida on his shoulders.

For hours, rain pelted down, and with the rain came clarity of mind. Dahoud had not let her die. Therefore, he had not planned her death, nor had he probably murdered his first wife. She had misunderstood everything. She had to thank him and apologise, but how did one take back an unspoken suspicion, and how did one thank a ruthless rapist for saving one's life?

After hours of pounding downpour, the river was a swirling broth of yellow earth and black ashes, swollen with animal carcasses, sluggishly pushing south. Of the town only a few stone walls remained as blackened stumps, while the brick and wood structures had crumbled away. The workshops had gone, the food stores, the wool.

Merida found Dahoud with the other councillors, kneeling in the ash, scouring the charred remains for stone tools and lumps of molten copper. His bare back was broad and browned, and streaked with sweat and ash. A life of physical work had built up hard, curving muscles on his arms. He did not notice her.

"It will take years to rebuild," Naima said.

Dahoud rose. "We won't rebuild this town."

"Are you sure? The nomads can take to the savannah, but we haven't salvaged enough yurts for everyone. Ain-Elnour can only take so many refugees."

"We won't rebuild," Dahoud repeated, kicking at the debris. "We have another town, already half finished. Oubar will be our new capital. If we all help with the building work, it will soon be habitable. The water is almost connected, and until then we'll drink from the mountain brooks." He dipped his head. A hint of a smile ghosted across his face. "My Lady Merida?"

'Dahoud...' she started. Although her heart overflowed with gratitude and guilt, she still hated him for what he had done to her, hated those hands that had pinned her in public. Now they were blistered, oozing, red and raw.

He had hurt her, yet he had born hurt to save her. She swallowed, hot with confusion and shame.

'These wounds must be treated at once," she told him.

His smile vanished faster than it had appeared. "Must they?" The cold anger in his tone pushed her away.

'Yes. Bandaged with honey and wine. Naima, you're a healer, how can you leave Dahoud's hands untreated?"

'How much wine do you think we have? How much honey?" Naima asked with vinegar in her voice. "The little we had went to treat your wounds, Merida. Dahoud insisted. Is there any more lecturing you want to do?"

Dahoud had sustained those burns while freeing her, and now he was foregoing treatment? "Please, do something. At least, bandage his hands. Dirt can kill if it gets into burnt flesh."

Dahoud turned his back on her. "Come, Naima. Let's organise the trek to Oubar."

CHAPTER 32

Dahoud's Citadel

When most workers fled the torrid midday heat for a rest in the shade of half-built walls, Dahoud laboured on, lugging trays of bricks under the flint-hard sun. Clouds of shifting dust filled the site and dried his throat. Two moons after the fire, the New Oubar was still a building site, with few houses complete, and the gatehouse no more than chest-high foundations. Much work needed to be done to complete the citadel, and not enough people had heeded his call to help build it. The displaced residents of Koskara Town preferred the comfort of the wealthy oasis of Ain-Elnour, and nomads stayed away because there was not enough water for their flocks.

From the scaffolding of the outer curtain wall, he watched as Merida unloaded a stone-carrying donkey, her arms now tanned, her calves streaked with dust, her movements decisive and strong.

The way she lugged the basket proved she had gained strength in recent moons. She was also practising wrestling with Yora, and although the girls were secretive about it, he could imagine their bodies entwined. It would be fun to let her try to wrestle him, to feel her muscle and fire, to measure strength against strength. With her increased skill, she was sure to put up a good fight.

He sensed someone's glare on his back, he spun. Zun stood on the ladder, his snake like a green collar around his neck, an arm raised in greeting. Remembering the priest's ability to read graphic thoughts,

Dahoud tried to wipe his mind, but instead of blurring, the fantasy picture of rape sharpened.

Zun laughed. "Don't bother."

How dare Zun spy on his thoughts! It had been a mistake to admit to the djinn. Dahoud slammed a brick on the wall so hard that it cracked. Had Dahoud kept his secret to himself, the priest would not now be curious, would not watch his thoughts, would not draw false conclusions. He camouflaged his resentment with courtesy. "It's good to see you in Oubar, Zun. We need more labourers."

Zun unwound the snake from his neck and dropped it into a linen bag. "I'll gladly lend muscle. But mostly I'm here to learn what progress you've made with your problem. From what I see, not much."

"If you want to make yourself useful, bring up stones from that pile down there." Dahoud pushed a reed basket at Zun. "A djinn isn't convenient."

Zun paused on the ladder. "Isn't it?"

"A man doesn't choose a djinn any more than head lice, or runny guts."

"Given the choice, would you rather be without the djinn?"

The question was an insult, best ignored. Without a djinn, Dahoud would have peace, a clear conscience, the strength to resist forbidden desires. He would not even think about forcing a woman. Not in times of peace, anyway. War was different, and Dahoud would have done his share of the soldiers' duty, but he would not have brought opportunities about. It was the djinn who had engineered the circumstances with increasing cunning. Dahoud was not responsible for the djinn.

The walls of conviction were holding up, but he could feel doubt hammering against them. He did not want them to collapse under the onslaught.

On his knees, Dahoud kept working. This outer wall had to be five man-heights high and two man-heights thick, strong enough to keep the most persistent enemy out.

The ladder creaked, and the basket thudded on the scaffolding planks. Zun slapped dust from his kilt. "There's no problem that can't be made worse by closing our eyes."

"My eyes aren't closed. Every waking moment, I'm fighting the djinn."

Zun's brows rose. "I thought you were fighting women."

Dahoud slammed stones into the cavity. "I'm fighting women because I have a djinn."

"What if you had the djinn because you're fighting women?"

Dahoud hammered to pack the stones into a solid mass that no weapon would penetrate. "Can we postpone the wordplay until the work is done?"

"Would you rather talk about water?" Zun shot back. "The water you promised we would have a moon ago?"

By now, the distant waters should be gushing through the old tunnels into the new town. The nearest stretch was long complete, with an open channel running from the mountains across the ridge to the rocky outcrop and into the citadel. The middle sections were also finished, dug by workers who believed they were searching for copper ore. Only the furthest part, which Criton had promised would take him less than a moon, was unfinished, and the old miner met one obstacle after another. Dahoud could not send extra workers there, because the citadel's water source had to remain secret.

Nomads came, looking for a town where they could water their flocks for the summer and do temporary work, the way they used to in the old Oubar and in Koskara Town. When they found that water was scarce, they left. With every day that the water did not materialise, Dahoud's credibility shrank.

In the meantime, they had to gather what water they could from nearby mountain brooks. Camels brought waterskins from the oasis of Ain-Elnour, but the journey there and back took five days, during which the beasts consumed a large portion of the water they carried.

"I would rather you kept your mouth shut and did some work," Dahoud said. "We'll talk about water when we have it, which will be soon."

Zun said nothing. Instead, he dragged up another basket of stones.

"Dahoud!" Keera's head peeked up the ladder. "There's a whiteseer in the forum, advising everyone to get out of the citadel. The last nomads are getting ready to leave."

Oubar could not afford to lose more workers until the defences were complete. "Get witnesses. Zun, come with me."

From the cover of a half-built wall, they listened to the seer's voice. Female and shrill, she urged people to visit faraway relatives, to go on a

pilgrimage, to emigrate abroad, and to take their families and possessions with them.

Is this woman undoing all your work?

"Use your influence, Zun," Dahoud said quietly. "Tell them that the
seer is mistaken, that Oubar is blessed."

The high priest studied him as if he were a strange specimen of
snake. "You would have me lie, Lord Dahoud?"

Dahoud had to halt the panic-spreading before it resulted in a mass
exodus, but arresting the whiteseer would only ensure that rumours
about the citadel's doom spread faster.

As soon as she had finished with a client, he peeled from the shadow
and pressed a tanni into her palm, "Tell me, seer." He spoke loudly, so
the four dozen people Keera had mobilised would hear it. "What must I
do to make this town safe and prosperous for all who live in it?"

While she scratched his hands with her long nails he caught a whiff
of damp wool, an odour many seers seemed to carry even in this dry
heat. She was slight and fragile, with ten black rings painted on her clay-
whitened arms.

She obliged with a practical reply. "Inaugurate it on the right day
with the right ritual."

"The town will be safe and prosper if we inaugurate it on the right
day with the right rituals," he repeated aloud to make it sink into
bystanders' minds. "What is the day, what is the ritual?"

"The ninth day of Flax Moon. The high priest must bless the new
water at noon. At dusk, offer a sacrifice to the Mare Mother: an adult
man of perfect form in good health who welcomes death with joy in his
heart. His blood must soak the soil under the gatehouse arch."

Dahoud repeated the conditions to the growing crowd. "It will be
done."

However difficult, he would meet the conditions to reassure the
people and protect the citadel from harm. Finding a volunteer for the
sacrifice would be a challenge. A disease-ridden cripple might be glad to
escape a life of pain, but the seer had specified good health. This was a
case for Keera who excelled at problem solving.

Two moons did not leave enough time to complete the town as he
had envisaged it. He would scale down the plans so the citadel looked
presentable on the day. The bathhouse, the school of healing, the

caravansary and the glorious sports arena at the foot of the mountain would wait. Even the second and third curtain wall and half the watchtowers had to be left out for now. Once the town was open and safe, he would expand and improve it. But could the old mining tunnels be linked in time to channel water into the cistern?

≈

Criton's voice boomed through the underground tunnels. "Come, come, my Lord. There's something you must see."

Dahoud squeezed through the narrow passage from where the sound had come. The darkness was thick with the smells of olive-oil and dank smoke. "Are you making good progress? Everyone's excited about the coming water."

"You won't believe your eyes, my Lord. Look at this beauty." Criton held a thumb-sized lump of rock to the oil lamp's flame. It shimmered green.

"That's copper, isn't it? Not surprising in an old copper mine." Dahoud leant against the damp wall. "We must bring the date for the flooding forward, to give the citadel water by Flax Moon. How many more workers do you need?"

"This is malachite." Criton held up the lump between his thumb and forefinger. "Rich in copper."

"The channel from the hillside into the citadel is complete, and the masons are putting the finishing touches to the cistern house. All that remains is connecting the old mining tunnels and shafts and tapping into the underground lake. I'll give you what you need."

"Here." Criton tapped his flint hammer against the wall. The chinks echoed through the corridor. "I reckon behind this layer lies a real vein. My ancestors mined this mountain for sixteen generations. Today is a proud day, the start of new life for our glorious mine."

"Criton, we can't drink copper. We need the water, and we need it fast. How soon can you flood the mines?"

"This mine was the lifeblood of Koskara. Sixteen generations of my ancestors have given their lives for it." Criton clutched the copper pendant on his chest like a protective amulet. "You can't let our mine drown."

"You promised to connect the old tunnels to lead water from the underground lake into the citadel, and I'm paying you well. Do it by Flax Moon, and I'll double your fee."

"Sixteen generations!"

"Supplying water will crown your family's achievements. Your ancestors will be proud of you."

Criton locked his arms across his chest. "I won't destroy this mine."

"Then get out. Someone else will finish the job. You can work on the walls, like everyone else." They were already behind schedule and could not afford to loose a single hour more. Dahoud picked up the bag of malachite nuggets. "These will be an offering to the Mare Mother."

Dahoud placed the open reed basket on the stone step before the altar. Dusty shafts of light fell into the temple's dim interior. The spiky lumps shimmered silky-green.

The limestone statue of the Mare Mother from the arena of Koskara Town had survived the fire unharmed.

"Great Mother," he prayed, "Please accept this humble offering. Permit me to protect my people. Help me complete this town, and shelter it from all dangers that might besiege it. Send me a suitable sacrifice whose blood will do you honour on the chosen day. Allow water to flow through the ancient tunnels to fill our cistern and nurture the land."

The crone face gazed down at him, unmoved.

Dahoud found the whiteseer in the tavern courtyard and requested a private reading, hoping for advice on how to stop Merida from triggering the djinn.

After a big yawn, she went once more through her palm-ticking routine "Get stronger arms."

Dahoud laughed. "Is this the standard reply among seers? One of your colleagues said the same thing two years ago. Guess what: I took her advice. My arms are so strong now, you won't find many stronger in all of Koskara." He flexed his biceps to demonstrate muscle.

She wrinkled her nose. "Anyone else?"

Merida pushed into the courtyard, accompanied by Zun, holding out her hand. "Yes, please. I've had white readings before and know what to expect."

"Private readings only. I've said what I have to say about this town."

"I want advice about..." Merida glanced at Dahoud, then away. "Advice for the near future." Her tanned arm looked dark against the seer's pale clay.

After the rubbing and sniffing, the seer delivered a single sentence: "Give up your scruples."

"What scruples?" Merida's chuckle tinkled like a dancer's cymbals. "I don't think I have any."

Dahoud laughed. Merida was hampered by more scruples than anyone else.

Zun slid onto the bench next to him. "Sometimes," he said quietly, "people don't see the whole picture of themselves."

"Is this one of your generalities, or are you stabbing a spear at me?"

"Do you feel a stab, or are you wearing your armour?"

"Seer, I know you!" Merida cried. "Weren't you in the palace at Quislabat? You told me how to escape."

To Dahoud, all clay-plastered whiteseers looked identical. But the pointed face, grudging manner and smell of damp wool were familiar. What if...?

He jumped up. "I know you, too! Two years ago, in Idjlara, you told me to get stronger arms. This advice saved my life more than once. You also told me I would find Merida in Djildit Town. I did."

The whiteseer shrugged. "I look into the future, not the past."

Dahoud did not believe her disdain. She had saved his life, she had steered him and Merida together, she had seen into his past and future. She had come here for a purpose. "We need to talk."

"I've given my advice."

He persisted. "Let me buy you a meal."

"I've eaten."

"Let me give you a council post."

"Whiteseers travel. You've had your advice. Now let me go." She rose, followed by Merida who still tried to get details.

Dahoud turned to Zun. "If you can see futures..."

'If, my Lord?" Zun's mouth curved. "Many futures wait, and I cannot foretell which of them will happen. I rarely read the futures. Watching a dozen versions of a single hour takes all day, and I still don't know which of them to expect."

'Why don't you tell me what you've seen?"

Zun laced his fingers before him. "Would you listen to something you don't want to hear?"

'Will there be war?"

'In most futures: yes."

Then Dahoud needed to press ahead with the building of the second and third curtain walls, create additional strongholds, fortify towns, lay in stocks, raise an army. "When? Against which enemy?"

'Take your pick." Zun counted off his fingers. "In a moon or a year or five years. Against Darria, Riverland, Quislak, Copperland, Koskaran rebels, a mysterious Kingdom..."

'What must I do to keep our people safe?"

Zun tugged his earlobe. "Remember what it means to be Lord of Koskara."

'I'll prepare for war, then. Yet, it won't happen if I dedicate the town on the right day with the right ritual, will it?"

'You're right." Zun blew breath out of his nostrils. "It won't happen. If."

Teruma rode through the tassel-hung gatehouse into the newly-built town, ahead of Lord-Satrap Tarkan of Tajlit and a string of pack mules. She waved at the onlookers who spilled from houses and alleyways to stare at the visitors. Her simple Samil-style tunic was sure to find favour.

Afternoon sun gilded the citadel. The air was full of yellow dust and smelled of latrines and animal sweat. The whole town was still a building site. Yells and curses rang above clanking hammers and creaking pulleys.

When Teruma and Tarkan stepped from the searing noon heat into the delicious cool of a newly built tavern, a dozen people crowded in after them. Before someone could offer her a seat on the single bench, she sat on the floor.

She surveyed the allies she had placed in Koskara: Dahoud, the military genius. Merida, the magician who could bring rain. Ambitious

Keera, who knew a solution to every trouble.

A muscular man with a scarred face and artificial nodes above his eyebrows had the air of a leader. The others allowed him space and treated him with deference. So this was Mansour, the former rebel. The revolt was recent and smouldering, and a pot did not stop boiling as soon as the fire was doused. As soon as the Queen died and the Queendom was embroiled in fights over her succession, this Mansour might lead a useful new rebellion.

When the meal arrived—plain bread, yoghurt, water—she spoke the traditional Samili prayer before tearing a piece off the loaf, several fingers thick, with a chunky golden brown crust and a fluffy inside of yellow barley.

"I've missed the Samil so much. So I offered to bring the gifts personally." With a shy, low-lidded look at Tarkan, she added, "I grew up in Tajlit, you know."

A fat man in a purple tunic shifted his bottom closer to her. "Is it true you're descended from a Samili Lady?"

So the storytellers had done their job and the rumour had taken hold. Teruma knew better than to confirm it. Questions always took on the greatest significance if they remained unanswered. She tasted the creamy, sour yoghurt. "This is so refreshing after a long journey."

"Was your ancestress a Samili lady?" the big man asked again.

"How could she be? The Quislakis were thorough in their conquest, killing all Ladies and their female offspring." She leant towards him to whisper. "I was never allowed to learn the truth about my ancestress. There was some terrible secret about my past." People were always ready to believe any secret. With a dramatic sigh, she tinkled the bead hangings in her ear. "These earrings are all I have to go by, an heirloom from my great-grandmother. They look Samili, don't they?"

They were the oldest-looking ones her agent had been able to find in the market of Djildit, garnets and blue ceramic with cracked glaze.

She straightened as if bracing herself for a difficult duty. "I come as a messenger. The Lord Kirral, Consort to the Great Queen, has heard of the drought and the fire and wishes to helps Koskara. He sends..." She swallowed as if embarrassed. "He sends a pot of pickled locusts."

Mocking snorts mixed with angry mutters. Teruma went on with the determined face of someone who was pained to say what she had to but was bravely speaking anyway. "Further, to beautify Koskara, he gifts you two rose plants from his personal garden, which must be watered four times every day."

By now, the resentment was stirring. Mansour's nostrils flared.

"I've also brought a few little gifts of my own." She flipped the lids of her reed baskets, revealing hundreds of tools of real bronze and the finest flint, and many bars of precious salt, paid with funds appropriated from the Queendom's treasury. "Tell me what else I can do for Koskara."

People gasped. The fat man whistled.

"We need healers, masons, engineers," Dahoud said.

"Storehouses and caravansaries," the fat man said.

Since Keera was touching the top of her ear, signalling 'important person', Teruma put on a thoughtful look. "Storehouses and caravansaries. So important for developing the economy. I can help with those."

Another man pushed his way in. He wore a priest's leopard kilt and a snake curled around his bare waist. "Koskara needs a school of healing."

Teruma did not need Keera's sign to guess this was the high priest. "Koskara will get a school of healing," she promised. "I'll use my influence to get the anti-healing law repealed. It's a cruel law that should have been repealed long ago. I'll find teachers to staff the school." If local sensitivities permitted, the institution might even be named The Empress Teruma School of Healing. "Will you allow me to award prizes to the best bards at tomorrow's celebrations? Some trifles I brought with me may make suitable rewards." She intended to establish herself as a generous patron of the arts. It always paid to court the goodwill of artists and storytellers.

~

The sun was sliding towards the horizon, and the buildings were still far from complete. Dahoud drove everyone back to work. Pulleys squealed, donkeys brayed, and workmen yelled. Even Merida was working, leading a donkey to carry stones from the downhill quarry into the citadel. Hosting the important visitors had taken precious time, but by labouring into the night, they might finish the houses surrounding the forum, achieving a semblance of a real town for tomorrow's dedication.

But they still did not have a willing able-bodied male to sacrifice. Would a volunteer come forward in time? For the past two moons, Keera had sent messengers all over Koskara to search for men tired of life, offering generous compensations for the families, and Mansour had promised an easy death to the men-lover who turned himself in – to no avail.

The third problem was the water. Would it flow? Dahoud had put workers to the final stretch of the tunnel, making the connections based on Criton's plan. But Criton had refused to oversee the progress. Supposedly, the gradient was just enough for a steady flow from the underground lake into the cistern, but they would not know until they tried tomorrow.

"Dahoud, come to the temple," Keera said. "The priests have caught a thief filching gifts from the altar."

He wiped sweat from his forehead. "Can't the priests deal with it?"

"Theft from the gods," Keera said. "Punishable by death."

"I'm coming."

✧

A red robed priest jerked the fettered captive up. "We caught him in the act, stealing the basket of copper from the altar."

"Criton!" Dahoud cried out. "Why did you do this?"

Criton stared in sullen silence.

"Answer, scum." The priest slammed him in the back.

"My family worked this mine for sixteen generations!"

More priests clustered around, and Naima arrived as well.

"Why did you steal from the gods?" Dahoud could guess. Excluded from his beloved mine, Criton had worked on the curtain wall, smouldering with silent resentment. Hearing Teruma's promise to provide whatever Koskara needed, Criton had seen one last chance to stop the flooding. He had taken the ingots as evidence that the mine contained copper.

Dahoud yawned. "How sad that a family line of sixteen generations will end with the hanging of a thief. You'll dangle from a gallows, jerking like a clown, your bowels open, and the crowd will laugh. Your ancestor's spirits will howl with shame." He paced on the tiled temple floor, and then looked at the prisoner again. "You can choose a death of honour instead. 'Noble Criton,' people will say. 'He gave his life to protect us and please the gods.' Your ancestors will be proud of the man who saved Koskara. The choice is yours."

"You want me to sacrifice myself for this accursed town? You think I care a donkey's spit about its fate? Let it be cursed, let it suffer, let it die! First you destroy the mine, and now you want my blood? Piss off."

"Shall I take care of this?" The tip of Naima's tongue danced across her lips. "I'll make him willing. When the time comes, he'll be grateful for the option of a quick death."

"Remember he must be in perfect shape and good health."

"His limbs will stay fully functioning. They just won't feel good."

"Do it." Dahoud turned to the half dozen priests standing by. "Do you have a secure room where his cries won't disturb?"

"We can use a cell in the cellar, my Lord, and put guards on the door."

"Good. Don't let anyone near him whom you don't know."

The air was cool, but without chill, and night hung over the town like a star-threaded veil. Teruma sat in the tavern's courtyard, savouring the quiet.

Tarkan came in, bearing two beakers and a jug of yellow wine. "May I join you, or do you prefer solitude?"

She gestured to the space on the bench beside her. For a long time, they sat in companionable silence.

"Teruma, these earrings of yours are remarkable," Tarkan said at last. "Beads of garnets and glazed clay, the style the local women wear. An heirloom from your great-grandmother, you say?"

She inclined her head in assent. "Why do you ask?"

"That lovely blue glaze was developed only a generation ago."

Teruma's heart galloped. Was he threatening to expose her? She kept her voice pleasant and her face under tight control. "I didn't know you were interested in jewellery, Tarkan."

"Very interested. In jewellery— as well as other things. And, if I may say so, I admire these particular beads greatly, their blend of boldness and subtlety. They suit the Samil. I've been looking for something like them."

Teruma heard the message beneath the words. He was proposing an alliance. She thought fast.

She liked Tarkan's style, his quick intelligence, his discretion. As a secret men-lover among people who killed his kind, he needed a complicit wife. As Empress, Teruma would a consort, preferably one who did not bother her with marital matters. Tarkan was a skilled administrator, a gifted diplomat, of noble birth, blessed with connections. Possibilities glinted like silver sparkles in the light.

"Would you care to join me for a pre-breakfast stroll tomorrow?" she asked. "Sunrise in these mountains is said to be spectacular. Shall we walk up to the ridge and share the view? You and I have much to discuss – about jewellery, and other areas of interest."

"I'll be honoured." He rose with courteous grace and bowed from the waist without lowering his gaze. "Welcome to the Samil, my Lady."

CHAPTER 33

The Day of the Sacrifice

The day of the inauguration dawned, and freedom beckoned. Merida could already taste her liberty, fresh and sweet. The disguise was ready, and a donkey was waiting with provisions in the woods. All she had to do was act normal, and then pick a moment when everyone's attention was diverted.

The festival, with hundreds of strangers streaming in and out of the gate, gave the perfect opportunity to sneak away. She had researched her daring plan well. She would ride to the Darrian border and get herself arrested. Citing her Riverian nationality, she would demand to speak to a person of authority. Since Darria was the most bureaucratic nation in the known world, they would investigate, and bring her matter to the Riverian ambassador in the Darrian capital. Eventually she would be sent home to lush, rain-filled, civilised Riverland.

The morning sun sprung into a clear sky and brushed the walls with gold. On the trading stalls, scarves dangled their bright colours in the slight mountain breeze. In the nearby pine forest, hundreds of birds twittered and chirped. Koskara was beautiful—why had she not realised this before?

The smell of frying onions and rosemary wafted. Merida chatted with poets, joked with jugglers, and joined Yora to haggle for cheap jewellery. She examined bold-striped rugs, djinn bowls and chunky ceramic beads.

"Try this one, my Lady. Finest rose otto from Ain-Elnour." The buxom perfume trader dabbed oil on the back of Merida's hand, releasing a delicate scent. "I've already sold more in one hour today than in the last two moons, and two Quislak traders have asked about buying in bulk."

"I'm not surprised," Merida said. "Your perfumes are superb."

"We owe the success to your planning, my Lady. You have a nose for trading."

"I'm glad I could help," she said modestly, startled by the praise.

"I love your dress, the way it sparkles in the light. I've never seen something like it."

"I bought it this morning." The green tunic was covered in blue fringe with copper beads which swayed with every move and glinted in the light like the surface of a deep river, bound to attract notice. When she had vanished, people would look for the river dress, not for a trader in Samili garb with a coned straw hat.

Wurran joined, huffing with importance. "This is the start of a new era for Koskara. Your planning has made all the difference."

People really appreciated her work. The weight of resentment slipped off Merida's mind. Her limbs felt lighter than before, and her heart wanted to leap in a crazy dance. Back home, she would remember Koskara with fondness: the colours, the scents, the people who worked cheerfully in harsh conditions.

Dahoud was checking bridles at a leather goods stall. In the morning sun, his muscled arms gleamed with health and strength.

"A great day for Koskara," she said, not intending to stop.

"A successful day, and the beginning of a new era, I hope." His eyes were olive-dark, and the sunlight danced in them.

"This new town will make a difference to Koskara," she said. "In a short time, it will become a centre for trade, for culture, for learning, for safety. You've created something special."

"I'm hoping to make this market a regular event, attracting traders from far away. They'll come once we've built a caravansary for their comfort, and if we have the goods to sell. Dried dates, rose oil, fleeces, spun wool... these may find buyers all over the Queendom." A smile lit his features. She had never seen such warmth in his face.

Since she was leaving, he had no more power over her, and she could relax in his presence. "Why only the Queendom? Koskara can trade all over the world. Think of the wealthy nations: Copperland, the Mountain States, Riverland."

'The transport costs would drive the prices sky high."

Merida thought back to the year she had spent with her father, the trader. "Could you export finished products? Riverians would pay a fortune for Koskaran textiles."

'Show me which."

At the rug trader's stall, Merida stroked over the finely woven wool. "Rugs and wall-hangings to keep out the chill. The geometrical patterns will appeal most, maybe with the colours toned down."

He watched her with his lips pursed and his brows raised. For two heartbeats, their eyes connected, then she broke the gaze. He was standing so close to her she could smell his scent: soapberries and leather.

'Textiles transport well. They don't spoil or break." Eagerness filled his voice.

When he picked up the corner of a rug to check its edge, she recalled the first time she had seen these hands: brown and strong, not the soft fingers of a courtier, but the calloused hands of one used to labour. Four moons ago, those hands had singed and blistered to save her from the fire trap.

She swallowed and gazed away. "Riverian traders are looking for exotic goods. Not too exotic—not mere adornment, but practical use. If a Riverian trader saw these..."

She checked herself: talk of her home country might make him suspicious of her plans, and mentions of traders might give her chosen disguise away. "This afternoon, there'll be a poets' contest, won't there?" she asked brightly.

"Yes, and storytelling and dances. The sports contests have to wait until we've built an arena, but everything else is perfect. And the sacrifice will ensure the gods protect this town forever."

At the mention of the human sacrifice, Merida's golden mood evaporated, and her stomach soured.

He must have seen her flinch, because he added, "And we don't even need to kill an innocent. Criton is a traitor who deserves to die. This way, he'll redeem himself."

A man was being killed for the sake of superstition, and Dahoud was rejoicing. She had to get away before she spit her true feelings at him. "If you will excuse me. Yora is waving. I promised to help her choose a new bangle."

She rushed across the forum, glad that after today, she would never again need to witness Dahoud's atrocities.

The victim was less lucky. Roped in a dungeon under the temple, he was even now suffering torture until he volunteered for a death. If only she could set the poor man free!

However, she had provisions for only one person, only one set of traders' garments, and only one donkey for her own getaway. Who needed freedom more—Criton or Merida?

⚮

Although far from completing Dahoud's vision of an invincible citadel, the town looked complete, and tassels and banners distracted the eye from unfinished façades and heaps of rubble. The celebrations were going well, with brisk business at the vending stalls, important people giving speeches, bards competing for prizes. The air held the warm odours of honey and earth, of pine resin and goat sweat, mingled with the scents of frying oil and spice. Birds chirped, adults chattered, children squealed.

He watched Merida walk between stalls, chatting with traders, sampling wares, her bronze hair gleaming in the light. The copper-streaked fringe around her hips swayed with every step, bathing her buttocks in shimmers, like a caress of liquid sun on naked skin.

He liked her ideas for exporting finished goods. He liked how she had planned the market, how she was talking with traders now, how she understood the importance of the citadel, how she insisted on living as simply as everyone else. There was lot to like about her. She was the perfect Lady for Koskara, although nobody could have foretold this. The gods had led her here by strange paths.

She might never be his wife in more than name, and she might never forgive what lay between them, but they could be allies, jointly ruling Koskara.

The shadows shortened. Soon, the workers would break through the rock connecting the final stretch, more than three thousand feet away. Dahoud gave the signal for Zun to lead the procession to the wellhouse, a monument of golden limestone adorned with rose garlands and bunches of blue-blooming flax.

Cool earthy air embraced him as he descended the spiralling stair to the cistern. Torchlight glinted off glazed tiles. Women and men thronged on the stairs, crowding into the narrow space. Others leaned over from above, their heads craned, waiting to witness the miracle.

The tunnelling had been completed according to Criton's plans, leading water from an overall gradient just enough to ensure a steady stream to keep the cistern filled.

Few people knew how far the water had to travel, how many turns it wound through tunnels and shafts. They just wanted water. Feet shuffled, throats cleared. Would the water come? All depended on it: The fate of this town, the nourishment of the fields, the green of the pastures, Dahoud's standing as Lord of Koskara. The silence stretched.

Then a distant gurgle glugged, turned into a roar. Water gushed into the cistern. People gasped in wonder as the water swelled to the rim of the basin.

Priests slaughtered cockerels, splashing the sacrificial blood on the limestone steps and the glistening tiles. Zun chanted in his deep voice, praising all the known gods for their gift. His snake slithered around his body in a strange dance.

Dahoud held the garlanded bucket, his heart swelled with happiness. He wanted to share this moment of triumph with Merida. He scanned the crowd for bronze hair, for a river-blue dress.

With swift grace, Teruma stepped forward. "It is my pleasure to distribute the gods' gift." She splashed the bucket into the water, pulled the rope, and filled beaker after beaker with life-giving water.

Even as people cheered and clapped Dahoud on the shoulder, praising his success, he longed to have Merida at his side. Where was she, and why had she stayed away?

≈

The airless cell stank of soiled straw and blood. In the dark, Merida could barely see the prisoner, half sitting, half hanging, head lolling on his chest.

"Criton," Merida whispered. "Criton, can you hear me?"

She dropped the reed basket and prodded him with a quick finger stab into the arm. "I've come to save you. You have to get away before the cistern blessing ends." She knelt in the damp straw, shutting out the stink of urine and curdled blood, and sawed the fetters with her flint. "Can you walk? Ride?"

"Curse Dahoud," Criton groaned.

"Put on these clothes, so you'll look like a trader."

Criton's eyes rolled in his head. "He'll drown the mine in water."

"Yes, yes." Tiredness clawed at Merida's brain. She had cast a spell of inattention on the watching priest, and it was throwing a haze over her own mind. "The gatehouse guards didn't check passes, they just entered names into the book. When a trader steps out for a stroll, they don't even ask the name but scratch a mark on a tablet. So you pretend you're a trader taking a break. Do you understand?"

"Sixteen generations of my family worked in this mine."

"Get out of Oubar, or die." Tiredness numbed her thought. She reached out to the wall for support and wiped her forehead. "Your donkey waits in the wood on the third plateau. Saddlebags. Food. Water. Hurry."

Now that she had given away her best chance of escape, what would become of her? She longed to curl up into a tight ball and sleep, but her long absence would rouse suspicion. She had to buy time for Criton to get far, far away.

⁓

When Dahoud found Merida, slumped on a cushion under the canopy, like a flower wilted in the heat, his heart clenched. She had worked so hard, labouring on the building site for longer hours than almost anyone else, in an unaccustomed, harsh climate. Organising the market and the festival programme on top of that, she had clearly exhausted herself.

He wanted to wrap her with his protection, to shelter her with his care. "Take a rest," he said gently. "Lie down in your room for a while."

She pulled herself straight and managed a small smile, but her pupils were glazed like those of a joy-flower smoker. "I'll do my duty."

"That's brave of you, but you've worked so much, and you're not yet used to our climate. We'll manage without you."

"Yes, go," Teruma urged. "I'll take over your duties."

"If you're sure, then..." She stood, swayed, leant against a pole, gave them a wobbly smile. "Thank you."

Dahoud watched her walk into the shade. He missed her already, but there would be other days when they could be together.

For today, all that remained to do was to bleed the sacrifice under the gatehouse arch. While bare feet stamped, bell-bands around ankles rattled, and tasselled skirts swirled to the beat of the drum, Dahoud asked Naima, "Is he willing?"

"He wasn't this morning. Obstinate."

"Dusk falls in six hours. Do what it takes to make him crave a quick death before then, but keep his limbs intact."

Naima nodded. "My torture teacher in Darria taught me a burning technique. It hurts beyond what a person can bear, but it keeps the bones and muscles intact. All the time I'll tempt him with cooling water as a reward for volunteering."

"Perfect," Dahoud said.

In the centre of the arena, bards told of the heroic deeds of Samili people in days past, their voices loud, their arms sweeping. Teruma, energetic and regal in a yellow tunic of local style, draped the winners with garlands of jasmine flowers and presented them with rich strands of copper rings.

Then she sat in the chair vacated by Merida, picked a dried date from the tray, and glanced at Tarkan.

Tarkan put down his fan and rose. "Dahoud, I wonder if you will grant us a favour."

"Anything," Dahoud said at once. Now that his town was dedicated and his position secure, he could be generous. Tarkan had done so much for him, he would gladly repay the favour.

"Tomorrow, I return to Tajlit. The Lady Teruma wishes to stay in Oubar a little longer." Tarkan bowed to her. "May I entrust her to your care?"

"Having you as a guest will be a pleasure, my Lady," Dahoud said at once.

"According to the ancient Samil hospitality law?"

At Dahoud's side, Mansour tensed, leaning forward as if he wanted to leap out of the seat.

"Why so formal?" Dahoud asked.

Teruma tilted her head. "I may need to call on you for protection."

Tarkan pressed her hand against his chest. "Teruma has agreed to be my wife."

Dahoud put his beaker down. Water sloshed over the rim. "Teruma is Kirral's head-wife."

"I'll ask Kirral for a divorce," Teruma said. "He'll rejoice to replace me with someone more amenable to his games, and pretend that divorcing me was his idea. But his pride will be pricked at first, and I fear his wrath."

"That's why she needs your protection." Tarkan explained, "Staying with me would be inappropriate until she's divorced. In Koskara, she'll be both chaperoned and safe."

Dahoud had failed to protect one woman fleeing from Kirral's cruelties. Here was a second, and this time he could do what was right. "I'll think it through."

"We need a quick decision," Teruma said. "Getting the message to Quislak will take a moon or two, more if we don't get a fast messenger. There's a courier leaving in an hour."

Mansour rose. "We must talk, Dahoud. Alone."

Naima came striding, her green tunic fluttering. "Dahoud, I need a word with you, at once."

"Not now, Naima."

"It's urgent."

"Does the Lady Teruma have your hospitality or not?" Tarkan pressed. "You may remember our conversation in the temple, before Fool's Plea Day..."

Dahoud had promised to help his friend, should he ever wish to steal a woman from Kirral's harem.

With a small, sharp shake of his head, Mansour beckoned Dahoud.

Dahoud followed him to the entrance of a shaded alley. "What is it? Be quick."

"Why do those two want to wed?"

"Love?"

"Donkey crap. He's a men-lover."

"Then aren't you pleased he's leaving behind his vice and getting wed? And Teruma is the perfect Lady for Tajlit. She grew up there, you know, and she loves the Samil."

"She's a schemer. Those two come trailing trouble as surely as a wounded antelope draws hyenas."

"What kind of trouble? Kirral won't come to Koskara besieging our citadel and demanding his runaway head-wife back. He'll save face by repudiating her."

"He'll punish us for abetting her desertion."

"Assume we don't know her intent," Dahoud said. "If we extend hospitality to Kirral's emissary, how can he object?"

"Dahoud." Naima pulled at his arm. "Please come. It's urgent."

"I'm coming. Mansour, tell Teruma she's a welcome guest in Koskara."

Dahoud hurried after Naima through jostling crowds and the temple's black-pillared entrance. "What is it?"

"Criton has vanished," Naima said.

Dahoud shone a torch into the stark cell: silent stone walls, straw, cowhide straps which had been slashed with a flint knife. While everyone's attention was on the new water, an accomplice had cut the captive free.

"How did this happen?" he demanded of the priests. "You were supposed to guard him and let nobody near."

The older one pulled off his skullcap and twisted it between his fingers. "We watched that door every heartbeat, the Mare Mother is our witness. Only authorised persons went in."

"Who?"

He glanced at the healer. "Naima."

"And...?"

"We can't rightly say." He his skullcap back on. "Nobody can have been, somebody must have been, and maybe someone has been, but maybe no one, and if there was someone it was an authorised person."

The garbled reply and unfocused eyes prompted Dahoud to sniff the priest's breath for wine or joy-flowers. Nothing. "What did you eat before you came on duty? Drink?"

"I can't recall."

His colleague yawned.

Criton and his accomplice had tricked the priests and sneaked away at the only time the forum was almost empty, during the well dedication. Three hours had passed since noon. By now, the fugitives would be far from Oubar, too far to catch in time to sacrifice at sundown.

Dahoud had to act at once. "Naima, we must pretend the sacrifice has already taken place. Get blood from an animal and spill it under the gatehouse arch." This would not avert the citadel's doom, but it would prevent immediate panic.

In the light of the wall torch, Dahoud probed ever finger-breath of the cell for a clue. The straw was soaked with the sweat of suffering and fear. Caught in it was a thread. He held it close to the flame. Blue-green, streaked with copper, tipped with a glinting bead.

Merida! She had sneaked in here during the cistern blessing and bespelled the guards' alertness. Unable to bear the knowledge that the man was being tortured, she had set him free. By her own values, this was a daring, noble deed, and he cherished her for it. But she did not understand how the Samil gods reigned, nor realise that her act called doom down this town.

A torrent of thoughts and emotions flashed through him: admiration, annoyance, worry, anger, hurt. A Lady betraying her own people, exposing them to the wrath of the gods! If the Koskarans learnt who had deceived them, they would turn against her. He must protect her from this.

But he knew she was not the ally he had imagined her to be. The moment he had opened to her, she had betrayed his trust.

Even as his fist closed around the thread, the djinn sent an image of Merida's white throat.

CHAPTER 34

Threat

In the moon following the town's dedication, dozens of nomad families came to the citadel, seeking employment, and water for their flocks. Dahoud set them to work on the outer gatehouse and the second curtain wall.

Although nothing suggested imminent danger, situations could change, and a spark was enough to escalate into a fire. A handful of Koskaran dissenters still clamoured for independence. The Queendom's ongoing war with Darria might spread south. The whiteseer had warned of danger, and the gods had not been appeased. A good commander prepared for battle before the enemy was in sight.

From whatever source the threat emerged, however many years from now, Koskara needed the protection of the citadel. In a crisis, Dahoud would shelter a thousand people inside its strong walls.

Dahoud directed the workforce, most of them nomad women, hardy and strong. He saw the sheen of sweat on their arms, the dust on their muscled legs, the breasts curving under clinging cloth. He heard the breaths panting with the effort of lugging baskets, and grunts of relief when they dumped a load.

In their midst, Merida laboured, her body moving with a dancer's grace even when carrying the heaviest loads.

Our wife, Dahoud. Delicious.

She straightened and stretched, arching her back. Her breasts pushed forward.

How long since we touched her? Isn't a husband supposed to mate with his wife?

The sun was dying in streaks of gold and purple, and the sky bruising into night when a royal herald arrived. Dahoud broke the seal, expecting one of Kirral's usual instructions for the care of his rose plants.

"The High Lord Kirral, Consort to the Great Luminous Queen, greets Lord Dahoud, Satrap of Koskara: From the nineteenth day of Flax Moon, the satrapy of Koskara is part of the Darrian Empire. A representative of my good friend, his Lustrous Brilliance the Emperor..."

Dahoud read the sentences twice. Kirral's good friend the Darrian Emperor? Koskara part of the Darrian Empire?

"... will relieve you on the fifth day of Barley Moon. Prepare to hand over the satrapy on that day. Report to Quislabat where you and the Lady Merida will assume new duties. For both of you, I have a choice of jobs..."

The K of the signature sprawled obscenely across half the parchment.

Dahoud called an emergency council.

≁

The charcoal of the incense burner glowed in the stone chamber's near darkness.

Dahoud lowered the letter he had just read. "What do we do now?"

Faces paled, and lips parted, and fists balled in tense silence.

Mansour was the first to speak. "You have sworn fealty to the Queendom, and loyalty to Koskara. Which oath will you keep?" He pointed his spindle to the door. "If you side with Quislak, leave with your life and your honour intact – but leave."

"I'm Lord of Koskara," Dahoud said."We're in this together. All of us."

Even Merida? Do we trust her?

Dahoud glanced at Merida, who was sitting as rigid and tight-lipped as always, who had defied his orders and set the prisoner free. Could he trust her? He pushed the dilemma from his mind: Merida was the Lady of Koskara and belonged.

'Darria wanting Koskara makes sense." With the point of his dagger, Dahoud drew an outline map into the sand tray before him. "Here at the Queendom's southernmost tip, Koskara digs like a tooth into Darrian flesh. Darria wants to pull the tooth to smooth the border. But why the Queendom's sudden change? Why does Kirral call his arch enemy his dear friend and gives Koskara away?"

"Punishment for aiding Teruma?" Wurran speculated.

"Hardly. If he wanted to punish us, he'd keep us in his power. And when he wrote this letter, he cannot yet have heard."

"The Queen is dying," Merida said. "The government was in turmoil because she was ill and had no daughters to succeed. Her alleged recovery was celebrated with a big event—which she did not attend. What if she never got well? On her death, Kirral will be at the mercy of the next Consort, and I doubt his successor will let him live."

"Makes sense." Dahoud nodded. "Kirral is buying sanctuary in Darria."

"Never mind the court intrigues of Quislak," Mansour said. "What does this mean for Koskara?"

Dahoud looked into his councillors' eyes, one after the other. "When the Darrians conquer territory, they send the able-bodied to slave in the salt mines and slaughter the rest. Then they parcel out the vacant land to their aristocrats."

"The average survival in the salt mines," Naima said, "is under four years."

"We'll die fighting before we submit to slavery," Mansour said.

Keera chewed her lips and rubbed an ear. "Koskara against the might of the world's most powerful empire? Untrained nomads against professional soldiers? I don't like it."

"We can win." Dahoud put confidence into his voice, making the slight chance sound like a certainty. "The Darrians will march against Koskara to take by force what they think is theirs. But they expect an easy victory. If we put up strong resistance, they'll realise it's not worth it. If the cost of war is greater than the potential gain, they'll go away." He raised his eyebrows at Mansour, who gave a barely perceptible nod. "Mansour and I will ready Koskara for war. We'll keep you safe."

"Six years ago, we nearly shook off the Quislaki yoke," Wurran said. "Until the Black Besieger came and ruined it all. Two years ago, we had another chance, and were winning. Until Dahoud came and ruined it all."

"Dahoud is one of us," Keera said. "You can't compare him to the Black Besieger."

"Without Dahoud, Koskara would be free, and the Quislaki Consort wouldn't sell us to the enemy."

"You're right," Dahoud said. "I meant to bring peace. I was mistaken."

Mansour put his spindle down. "We didn't claim our liberty then. We're claiming it now."

How dare Mansour declare a momentous decision like this! Independence was the only way forward, and the time was right, but it was for Dahoud to announce it.

He rose. "From this moment, Koskara will be an independent nation. We meet again at dawn and draw up a strategy, which we will announce. Until then, keep this quiet and don't alarm anyone. Now get some sleep. Tomorrow we'll need clear heads. Mansour, I need you to stay."

When the door curtain fell behind the last councillor, he turned to his second-in-command. "We have ten days. Three for the Emperor to learn of our refusal and declare war, seven for an army to get here across the desert. What weapons do we have—that I don't know of?"

"None," Mansour said. "If you refer to the cache of weapons captured in the war against Quislak, that went down the sinkhole."

"Training and weapons crafting are priorities," Dahoud decided. "I want every man, woman and child armed and trained. Get the bronze smiths to force blades, the tanners to make leather armour. Get people to knap arrowheads from flint. I'll ready Oubar so we can shelter refuges."

Mansour stroked the tip of his thumb along his jaw. "The sacrifice was faked, wasn't it?"

"Zun says I can avert the doom if I remember that I'm Lord of Koskara."

"Do you remember what that means?"

"I'll be the Lord Koskara needs, and protect the people from harm. I know what it takes." Dahoud squeezed the fingers of one hand in the other. "Mansour, I'm not entirely without experience of war. I've fought Darrians, and defeated them."

"I know." Mansour locked his hands behind his neck. "At the sight of the carnage at the garrison, you asked the questions an officer would.

355

Your idea of the perfect town was a military fortress with civil amenities added. Why the secrecy?"

"I didn't only fight Darrians. I fought Koskarans—six years ago."

"Under the Black Besieger?" Mansour let out a low whistle. "You were one of the monsters who ravished our land. If that comes out, your life won't be worth a fig."

"Will it come out?"

Mansour studied him gravely. "Not from me: you're too useful. Tell me about fighting a Darrian army."

Dahoud and Mansour stayed up until almost dawn, planning the strategy to protect Koskara from the inevitable attack.

When he left the council chamber, fatigue knotted the muscles at the back of his neck, his eyes burned with tiredness, and his brain felt as if squashed in an olive press.

Outside, Merida uncoiled from the corner where she had huddled against the night cold. "A word, please, Dahoud."

He needed to go to his room, to snatch an hour of sleep. But she had waited all night for him and deserved his attention.

"Yes?"

She looked frail in dark, frightened. Her gaze focused somewhere behind his left shoulder. "Kirral can no longer interfere with us, can he? I'm sorry to be so blunt, but..." Her voice trailed off.

Dahoud thought he saw a ghost of a blush on her cheeks. Without Kirral's meddling, they could put their relationship on fresh foundations and be friends. An oasis of hope glimmered on the horizon. Perhaps they would even have a true marriage.

She straightened and met his eyes at last. "Now that Kirral has no more power over us, will you let me go?"

"Let you go?" he repeated, rubbing the ache at the back of his neck and groping for understanding. Fatigue made his voice deep and raspy.

"I want to go home to Riverland. Will you give me a divorce?"

He stared in disbelief.

"Please, Dahoud. I know you have other things on your mind, but this is important for me. I need to know."

His chest was ripped open and his heart yanked out. She meant it.

He had been a fool to hope otherwise. Her loyalty lay with her own family, her own country, her own values. Koskara, far from civilisation she she knew it, offered nothing to hold her. He was not a man to whom she would ever bind herself. She had never wanted their marriage, and she had never forgiven what he had done to her. Nor would she ever be safe from his djinn. His hope that they would be friends and rule Koskara together had been a fool's fantasy.

As she stood before him—dusty, sleep-bedraggled, cold—he realised he did not want to let her go. He wanted her at his side, as his friend, his ally, his lover. His palms burned with the need to hold her, his throat with the urge to beg her to stay.

"Please, Dahoud. Don't keep me prisoner: let me go."

It was too late for hope: an eternity too late.

With perfect clarity, he understood that there was one way how he might redeem himself at least in part: by giving her the gift she craved. He grasped at the chance like a thirsting man at a water-jug, even if the water was bitter to drink.

"Of course. As soon as it is safe for you to travel, we will divorce."

The light of relief in her eyes snuffed the last glimmer of his hope.

∽

Teruma stood among the assembled population in the forum and listened as Dahoud broke the news, painting a picture of the fate awaiting them in Darrian hands, and announcing Koskara's independence. Surrounded by his councillors, he spoke with the calm assurance of a leader, the dignified enthusiasm of a young Paniour, and a confidence that could not be real but sounded sincere.

Behind him, the Koskaran banner seemed to grow in size, a yellow horse on scarlet felt, flanked by silver-grey horse tails, topped with an oversized spearhead of shiny flint.

He concluded, "Koskarans will never be slaves!"

Still stunned by the news, most people stood rooted to the spot, although some took up his final sentence and chanted it like a battle cry. Now was the time to act.

Teruma strode forward and climbed the speaker's stone. "People of Koskara! I'm honoured to be here in Koskara's finest hour, proud to be part of this historic day." Even though Kirral's decision had unleashed events earlier than Teruma had planned, she was ready to put her strategy in place. She knew that staying in Koskara on the brink of war was dangerous, but great schemes always carried great risks. "Challenges lie ahead, hardships and trials. But Koskarans are famed for their bravery. Koskarans fear nothing, and no one! With a leader like Dahoud..."

She extolled his capabilities, and went on to praise his council, then laid the foundation for her plan. "During her trials, Koskara will not be alone. All the world will be watching. All the lands which once were the Samil will recall how once they were one with Koskara. A hundred years ago, the Samil was united, mighty and free, until envious nations clawed it apart. Today, Samil lands lie in bondage to Quislak, Zigazia, Darria, suppressed, exploited and ignored. But the Samili spirit is alive, and the Samili blood pumps in all our veins."

She paused, allowing them to remember the rumours that she was a Ladysdaughter from Tajlit. "Political borders mean nothing. The claims of the conquerors are vain. What counts are the Samili tradition and the Samili blood. Before long, all Samilis will shake off their shackles, and join together to make our nation great again." The opening postures and raising chins showed that the listeners were warming to her words and vision. Frightened by the suddenness of the upheaval, they needed to hear that all would be well, needed someone to paint the picture of a bright future. "Let Koskara lead the path to greatness! Let us blaze the torch of freedom for the Samil!"

⚮

When the Darrians swept in from the south, the first panicked reports talked about millions of soldiers overrunning the land. More reliable scouts suggested between two and four thousand.

Next came rumours of moving mountains, immortal monsters with teeth the size of a man's arms, and legs as big as cedar trunks, trampling everything in their way.

Dahoud called an assembly in the arena. "The Darrians try to scare us with their rattling weapons and shiny armour. Their equipment is fine, but their stomachs are not. Do you know why they are moving so slowly? It's all the equipment they carry, the supplies, the luxuries. When the Darrians make war, they take everything with them: silk and silver, pastry and perfumes, artisans and astrologers, musicians and masseurs. Imagine how those delicate dandies will run when they meet their first Koskaran warriors!"

The smiles told him that people liked this vision. He pushed to strengthen it. "When I was an officer in the Quislak army," he said, stating it as if it was a known fact, "I fought many battles against Darrian armies, and I won every time. Do you see this fine sword?" He unsheathed the weapon, baring the blade of glinting bronze. "I took this from a Darrian officer. I've given the Darrians more than one good beating. I look forward to giving them another – this time, one they won't forget!"

Naima was the only person whose brows rose at this mention of his military background. Everyone else was too absorbed in the current situation. He spoke in a loud voice, his chin raised, kindling confidence. "I've met Darrian elephants, too. Get an arrow into an eye or slash a trunk, and they just give up the fight. Show them a fire, make a noise, and they'll flee. A squealing piglet is enough to fill an elephant with terror. We'll drive them out of Koskara, the Darrians and the beasts!"

He smiled into the enthusiastic applause, hiding his concern. He had expected a couple of cohorts, not a huge army overrunning the land like an unhaltable sand dune. Koskara's nomads with their flint knives and bone-headed spears were no match against the professionally trained, superbly equipped infantry and chariots.

≂

With his second-in-command, he could be frank. When Mansour joined him on the parapet of the inner wall, he pointed at the vast plain below, where heat waves shimmered across stubbles of desert growth. "The flat terrain favours chariots and large armies. We must not give the Darrians a pitched battle."

"We'll avoid pitched battles," Mansour agreed. "Koskarans are skirmishers. We'll strike the Darrians so fast they won't know what hit them, and withdraw into the mountains where they can't follow. That's how we hassled the Black Besieger."

"Winning a lot of skirmishes won't win a war. You didn't drive the Besieger out, did you?"

"You have a better plan?"

Dahoud gazed at the plain which unfurled below, the earth baked bone-dry by the heat, cracked and pallid, the sparse pasture burnt thin. "An army that size needs a lot of water, a lot of food. Provisioning all the way from Darria isn't practical. They count on feeding off the land."

"They'll sweep the land like a plague of locusts and it eat it bare."

"We'll give them nothing to devour." Dahoud's plan was brutal. "We'll deprive them of food, of fodder, of water, of everything they expect to find. Fell the fruit trees, burn the pasture, poison the wells."

"You want to destroy our own land?" Mansour's face set in a rigid mask. "Koskara has scarcely recovered from the Black Besieger."

"Nor from the drought or the fire. By destroying what little is left, we deprive the Darrians of sustenance and force them to withdraw."

For a long time, Mansour stared out at the ochre plain on whose sparse growth the nomads depended. At last, he said, "It must be done."

≈

In the council, the decision produced first silence, then outrage. "Has the sun addled your brain?" Wurran demanded, both hands on dagger hilts. These days, he was clanking with weapons and importance as if he was a great warrior expecting to battle the enemy inside the fortress. He turned to Mansour. "Tell him we need the pastures. We need the waterholes. Above all, we need Ain-Elnour. The oasis is Koskara's economic hub, our orchard, our granary, the seed for our future."

"Either we destroy it, or the Darrians will," Mansour said. "Do you want us to survive, or the Darrians?"

"What about our livelihoods?"

"Grass will grow again," Mansour said. "People who die in slavery stay dead."

"Every waterhole we poison, every tree we fell, every house we torch will be a step towards our victory," Dahoud explained. "We must do it before the enemy gets there. I count on you to ride tonight and give the orders."

"He wants us to order the people of Ain-Elnour to destroy all they have." Wurran was still addressing Mansour.

"Breaking it to Ain-Elnour will be hardest," Dahoud acknowledged.

"It takes a special kind of man to do that, a hero without fear." Wurran, thirsting for glory, always boasted of his single act of courage four years ago, when had refused to trade with the invaders. "The kind of man who was not afraid to defy the Black Besieger. Will you do it, Wurran?"

Wurran sat straighter. "I'll do it."

"Good," Dahoud said. "Mansour, get sheep carcasses dropped into waterholes. Keera, send riders to the settlements...." He glanced at Merida, took in the worried frown on her face, the tense way she was gnawing her lips. Once again, her bid for freedom had been thwarted, and she was forced to stay until the end of the war. He passed her over and allocated tasks to everyone else.

The massive enemy army must find nothing but scorched earth, ruins and foul water. Within days, they would turn to capture the flourishing citadel, the centre of Koskara's resistance.

After the meeting, Merida stayed behind, her posture straight, her chin raised. "It looks like I'll have to stay in Koskara for a while longer. There's much to do, and little time to do it. How can I help?" Resigned to the delay, facing the inevitable. Brisk, efficient, unflappable. "Shall I take charge of the food cellars?"

"Yes." He studied the bright courage in her face. "And something else. If you're willing. If you can."

"Try me."

"The people," he said. "The people of Koskara, the people here in this citadel. In times of crisis, people need a figurehead. Someone to look up to, to draw courage from. In the Samil, people worship the Lady. It would help if..." He did not meet her eyes, but gazed at her feet. Small feet in simple sandals. "Allow them to believe that you really are the Lady of Koskara. They need this belief more than anything else. Will you give them this gift?"

Merida's eyes narrowed, and she gnawed her lip. At last, she rose. "For as long as I'm here, I'm the Lady of Koskara. You can count on me: I will do my duty." She brushed dust from her tunic. "On one condition: in private, you keep away from me."

"Thank you, my Lady." He rose and bowed, unsure whether he had won a victory or suffered defeat.

With the sword strapped on, he marched everywhere, inspected everything, dispersed clipped orders, and was obeyed. The role of commander fit like a familiar old tunic. It felt good to be in charge, preparing for war. Once he had been famed for squashing every resistance. Now he was using the same skills to protect.

Almost eight hundred people crowded into a half-built town ready to hold only a hundred. Teruma allocated accommodations, squeezing families into unfinished houses. Goats, chickens, donkeys, horses, sheep jostled for room, and Mansour had to enforce drilling space on the forum.

Dahoud's councillors worked tirelessly. Keera vetted the nomads flooding in to identify Darrian infiltrators. Naima confiscated everything edible the new arrivals brought, and Merida controlled the food stocks.

"We can't feed eight hundred people for long," she reported. "We have one hundred and forty sacks of dried dates. Thirty sacks of barley. Eighty-two sacks of wheat. Eight barrels of salt meat. One barrel of pickled locusts."

Her voice was even, matter-of-fact, without a trace of panic, like an officer reporting before a battle. He wanted to praise her efficiency, but decided not to: anything he said might be misread, fracturing the fragile truce.

"We have meat." He swept his arm across the penned flocks. "We'll slaughter the lot."

As word of his command spread, the *chink-chink-chink* of the flint-knappers ceased, and wails rose. "We've brought our sheep here to keep them safe!"

"Would you rather feed Koskarans, or the enemy?" Dahoud asked. "Wurran will select the best animals to set aside for breeding."

Based on scouts' reports, the Darrians were already marching on Oubar: time for a final check of the outer defences.

Dahoud and Mansour assessed the citadel from the outside. Neither catapult nor battering would ram get up the steep slope or squeeze through the narrow gouged track. Instead of leading straight to the gate, the path zigzagged three times the full length of the western wall, exposed to arrows and stones. At intervals, stacked boulders waited to be released to smash the hapless attackers' legs.

Approach from the back would require abseiling a stark cliff, then climbing along a long narrow ridge to the outcrop where the citadel sat, all under a barrage of arrows.

Should the enemy reach the citadel despite all, they would meet the thickest, highest curtain wall the world had ever seen, too high for siege ladders, too thick for battering rams. Behind that, a second curtain wall, and a third, each secured by a heavily defended gatehouse with bronze-studded cedar doors. To get from one gate to the next, the incomer had to run the gauntlet between curtain walls from the north to the south, and then again from the south to the north. Crenellations and archery slits picked out in red emphasised the daunting prospect while painted skulls and curses threatened anyone coming close.

Mansour nodded in approval. "They'd have to breach a hundred defences to even come near."

"They won't try," Dahoud said. "This will be a passive siege, where they cut us off from supplies until we surrender out of hunger and thirst. But our food will last longer than theirs, and our water supply is endless. - What's Sirria doing out here?"

While Mansour slipped behind the stacked boulders, Dahoud blocked her way. "Go back inside. The Darrians will be here soon."

She touched the bow slung across her back. "Good. I'm going to kill Darrians."

"Sirria, these are armed soldiers."

She laughed. "You think I don't know I'm going to die? A woman my age, they won't bother sticking me in a harem or sending me to the mines. But when I die, I'll take Darrians with me. That's a promise."

"They'll torture you to learn about the citadel." That was what the Black Besieger had done. "Darrian torturers are famous. They'll burn you, cut you, peel the skin from your limbs... We need you in Oubar. With your siege experience, you can teach others."

"Cooped up in the citadel I couldn't avenge my children's fates. Now let me go."

"I won't let you."

"Won't you?" She crossed her arms and raised her chin. The scarred cheek glowed in angry purple. "You asked the price for my silence. This is it: Let me go. If you lay one hand on me, I'll reveal your secret."

Should the Darrians discover about the food shortage, they would prolong the siege. Should the Koskarans discover he was the Black Besieger, they would turn against him.

"Sirria, please be sensible."

"Dahoud won't touch you. But I will." Mansour uncoiled from the shadow of the boulder stack. "Will you go back, or do I have to make you?"

She snatched up her bow and tried to push past him.

Without ado, he turned her arm onto her back and squeezed her neck with his elbow until she went limp. "Problem solved." He tossed the slight body across his shoulders. "We can't have talk under torture, nor word spreading on whose side Lord Dahoud once fought."

From the watchtower, Dahoud observed the Darrian approach, a glistening flood sweeping from the west across the sand, like a shimmering trick of heated air. As they came closer, armour and helmets dazzled in the sun. Infantry was followed by horsemen and chariots, camels and finally elephants, all in well-ordered formations. Hundreds of hooves pounded against the earth and stirred up clouds of ochre dust.

Within sight of the Koskarans, but far out of bowshot, the Darrians set up blue-topped tents, dug trenches, erected palisades, cleared the trees, and there was nothing he could do to stop them. With the only way out blocked at the bottom of the slope, the Koskarans could only wait until Dahoud's strategy proved right, until the enemy ran out of supplies and withdrew. Until then, they were stuck in the citadel like leopards in a cage.

Mansour leant forward on the parapet. "How many men?"

"Judging by the number of tents, almost nine hundred."

"That's a lot, for a passive siege."

Dahoud concurred. Bringing so many soldiers was costly as well as pointless. A fraction of the number would suffice to block the exit. Keeping so many would cause a logistic nightmare, especially without a water source nearby. Even crazier was the presence of two dozen elephants, each of whom needed as much fodder as fifteen camels. Those beasts could trample an enemy in a pitched battle, and they could batter down walls, but in a passive siege they served no purpose. This tactical mistake would soon bring the siege to an end.

"I bet the general is a clueless aristocrat," Dahoud judged. "Princes get appointed and promoted to ranks they have not earned. They strive to extend their troops so they can lay claim to fancy titles: Master of Nine Hundred, Lord of The Elephants, Light of the Charioteers. Soon, he'll regret having brought so many mouths to feed."

"Unless he knows something that we don't," Mansour said.

One by one, the three giant gatehouse doors slammed shut and bolts creaked into place. Oubar was under siege.

At sunrise, Dahoud walked down into the enemy camp, carrying no weapon but the spiral staff of an envoy.

Four men in leather breastplates and plumed helmets closed around him. "Greetings, envoy. We've been expecting you. Who may we tell the general is speaking for the citadel?"

"I'm Dahoud, Lord of Koskara. Who's commanding you?"

"His Highness, Ray of the Silver Sun, Banner Carrier to the Divine Peacock, High General of the Imperial Legions, Master of Elephants, General Baryush."

Not someone Dahoud knew from his legion days, then. The name 'Baryush' was as common among Darrian aristocrats as 'Dahoud' was among Samili nomads, and told him little. Baryush might be distantly related to the imperial family: Princelings often got promoted fast to high military office.

Impaled corpses flanked the camp entrance, fly-covered and limp. These were the people who had refused to take refuge in Oubar, whom the Darrians did not bother to deport to the mines because they were too old.

The soldiers walked Dahoud past the training ground where the heavy infantry drilled, their short swords clanking, while an officer with feathers in his helmet called out orders. To Dahoud's assessing eye, they looked well trained, well equipped, well led. No doubt the display was intended not just to keep the soldiers in shape, but to awe the enemy envoy.

The morning sun glinted off the bronze peacock standard before the command tent.

Inside, General Baryush rose and bowed. "The gods' greetings, Lord Dahoud of Koskara. You honour me by your visit. Some rulers would send an underling for their negotiations. I'm delighted to talk to an equal. Please, be seated. I trust you will find the chair comfortable." His Quislaki speech was heavily accented but clear. He had the face of a typical Darrian: black-bearded, curly-haired, with a face as white as if it had never seen the sun. He wore a tiered tunic, trimmed with silk, and broad jewelled armbands. An ornate dagger sat sheathed on his belt, and the curving sword on the table was almost identical to Dahoud's own. "May I offer you refreshment?"

Dahoud sat on the broad, thickly cushioned chair. On the low table beside him, silver-rimmed trays were piled with fruit, succulent dates and honey-dripping pastry. He picked and peeled an orange while Baryush poured cinnamon-scented tea for both. Bare-chested slaves waved huge palm-frond fans.

Only a Darrian would furnish his command tent with carpets, ivory-inlaid tables, incense burners and hangings of embroidered silk.

"I hope you find the tea sweet enough, Lord Dahoud. The honey comes from my own estate." Baryush gave Dahoud a beaker of thin brown ceramic. "It is my pleasure to lay before you the terms for your surrender. All residents of the citadel, and of the whole of Koskara, shall be under my protection, unharmed. As citizens of the Darrian Empire, they keep their lives, their freedom, their possessions. They will pay tribute and worship His Divine Brilliance The Peacock Emperor. You, Lord Dahoud, will naturally be relieved of the burdensome duties of a satrap. I will accept your submission now."

Dahoud sipped the tea, a brew so thick with honey that its sweetness threatened to make him sick. Baryush's conditions were startlingly lenient. He had expected the initial terms to be deportation to the mines for the population, and beheading for himself. "I appreciate the generous offer, and I decline."

"Then this citadel is under siege. Surrender today, and my generous offer stands. If you tarry..." Baryush's smile revealed glistening teeth. "We'll drive your people out with only what they can carry on their backs. Since you are not familiar with siege warfare, let me spell out the rules for you: every new moon, you will come here at dawn, and every time you will find the terms less to your liking."

"I understand, General." Besiegers always offered easy terms initially to inspire quick surrender. With every passing moon, the conditions were harsher, until the victims desperately regretted not having accepted the early terms. This method often brought about early victory without the need to fight. "Here's my counter offer. You withdraw from Koskara today, and none of your soldiers will be harmed."

The smile on Baryush's lips did not reach his eyes. "Many men have thought themselves safe in their citadels."

"Our cisterns brim with water and our cellars burst with food, whereas you're without supplies. Tell me, General: How will you water the men, the horses, the camels, the elephants?"

Baryush inspected his fingernails. "A Darrian prince's title takes priority over his military rank. The proper address is 'Highness'."

"We'll sip sweet chilled water and wallow in our bathhouse while your troops count the drops from mountain rivulets."

"If you try to stick it out, I will starve you until you eat your sandals and the rats in your street, until mothers begrudge their newborn's milk, until you slaughter your sick for their flesh. When I conquer I will have every woman raped, every child tossed over the ramparts, every man impaled."

Dahoud switched to the Darrian language. "You're hardly in a position to make threats."

Baryush's eyes widened, narrowed, widened again. He clanked his beaker down. "I know you."

Recognition punched Dahoud in the guts. That white face. Those obsidian-black eyes burning with hatred. He had seen them before – in a woman. A Darrian siege captive, a noblewoman, a young officer's sister...

"You're the Black Besieger," said the man whose sister he had raped.

Dark chills chased down Dahoud's spine. He sat very still, assessing the new situation.

"I swore you would pay for what you did to her." Baryush drew his chair forward. He leant so close that Dahoud could smell the cedarwood oil of his beard. "I lived for the day when I would rip the skin from your flesh, Black Besieger. Fate deprived me of that pleasure when I was told of your death." He swirled the tea in his beaker. "I thank the Great Peacock you're alive. My sister will be avenged, and my life has purpose again."

Dahoud thought of offering single combat, but squashed the idea. The chance of a quick death would not satisfy this enemy, and the Empire wanted conquest. He sipped more tea. The cloying taste clogged his throat.

'Once I get you into my hands, you will regret you are alive. I will prolong your pain for many moons. With every heartbeat, you will wish you had really died. I will pierce your tongue with needles, tear out your nails strip off your skin. If you were not protected by the envoy staff, I would start now."

Dahoud tightened his grip around the spiral staff.

"Fan my guest harder," Baryush told the slave. "He is getting hot. I see sweat streaming on his cheek."

The fan's chill sent shivers across Dahoud's skin.

"By fortune, the torturer I have brought with me is one of Darria's finest. She is the most skilled, the most experienced, the best. Would you care to meet her while you are still able to converse without screaming?"

"You make her sound charming, Highness. Alas, I'm too busy today to indulge in social chat."

"I will brand you, impale you with hot bronze spears, peel the skin off your genitals, squeeze your eggs like olives in a press." Baryush squeezed his fingers into his palms. "...again and again, for three moons, never allowing you to lose consciousness. Ah, how I shall make you pay."

Dahoud stretched out his legs, laced his fingers behind his head, and forced a yawn. "First you have to get me."

"Do you have a sister, Lord Dahoud? No? How sad. I would dearly have made the acquaintance of a sister of yours. You have, I believe, a wife, don't you?" Baryush's voice was as cold and cutting as a sword. "I shall use her, and so will every man in this camp. You shall watch."

On the incense burner, granules melted with a hiss.

"First you have to get her. Now, Highness, much as I enjoyed our chat, I have work to do."

Dahoud rose for a formal bow, tensing his leg muscles so his knees would not quaver.

In the council chamber, he reported. "A very polite person. He plied me with cakes, had an attendant fan me to keep me cool, and would have introduced me to a female follower had I permitted it. He knows he doesn't stand a chance of defeating us, so he offers generous terms if we surrender without fight."

"Can we hold the citadel?" Mansour asked.

"We will sweat and we will suffer, but we can hold Oubar forever."

"Let there be sweat. Let there be suffering," Mansour said. "But let there be no surrender."

On the way back to his quarters, Dahoud met the high priest.

"Tell me the truth, Zun. Is there still a curse on this town?"

"There never has been," Zun said.

"Then all those seers and soothsayers were mistaken?"

"Had that miner bled out his life as sacrifice to the gods, suffering would have been averted."

"You've seen the future?"

"Several possible futures." Zun sounded sad.

"What do you recommend?"

Zun glanced at the abandoned building project that would have become the school of healing.

Dahoud said, "As soon as this war is over, we'll build a magnificent school of healing and staff it with the best teachers. For now, we need to fortify the defences and build houses." He wondered if Zun was foreseeing sickness and death, and would be adamant about the healing school.

But Zun only nodded. "Of course."

"What else can I do?"

Zun looked into the distance, then at Dahoud, then into the distance again. "Remember what it means to be Lord of Koskara."

∽

Dahoud drew his bournous tight against the chill, and peered down at orange dots of torches in the enemy camp. Beside him, Wurran and two other men chuckled over jokes. They were squatting in the curve of the narrow track outside the citadel, awaiting the first attack.

Sand whispered from the clock spout as the night's fifth hour approached, and with it the time Darrians thought auspicious. This,

Dahoud was certain, was the hour General Baryush would choose to advance his machines and men under cover of darkness. Dahoud would prove that his citadel's defences worked.

Night hung like a star-threaded veil, fragrant with pine resin and rosemary, pulsing with the excited impatience of men wanting to fight.

"Looks like they're not coming after all," Wurran said, his legs locked around the first boulder, ready to release it at the first sign of approach. "They want the honey but they fear the sting of the bee."

Dahoud raised his hand. "Quiet now."

He listened to the noises of the night: the faint rustling of pine needles, the gurgles of the irrigation channel, the incessant burr of cicadas, a night-bird's chirp, the call of a distant owl. Then, from far below, a series of squeaks so faint they would be inaudible to the untrained ear: The squeaks of wood against wood, of wheels labouring under their load, of battering rams crawling up a steep slope.

Another squeal, and then a screech as the siege engine pulled around the first bend in the zigzagging path.

"Now, Wurran."

Wurran shoved the first missile forward, a round-hewn stone the diameter of a man's handspan. It bumped on the deep-gouged track, ricocheted from the flanking walls, gathered speed, and roared downwards into the darkness. Forty heartbeats later, Darrians screamed.

From the citadel came a chorus of triumphant yells.

"Next." Another ball rolled to smash the attackers' machines and legs, and another, and another. Wood splintered, metal clanked, men howled in agony. Injured and stuck in the darkness between the track's flanking walls, their machine and rolling boulders, they could not escape the trap. The screams of panicked pain from below mingled with the victory chants from the citadel.

Wurran rubbed his hands. "This will teach them."

"Well done," Dahoud said. Now Wurran could feel a hero at last, and would be a loyal supporter. The taste of victory would boost morale and silence the doubters. Dahoud's citadel was invincible: the enemy had not even passed the first line of defence.

But the real siege had only begun.

CHAPTER 35

Under Siege

Throat-scratching smoke curled from the many fires where strips of salted meat hung on racks to dry.

Sirria hammered black flint shards into arrowheads, shiny and sharp. She longed to see them in flight, longed for them to hit Darrian flesh, longed to hear Darrians scream. Next to her on the battlement, Merida was smoothing the edges of her first piece.

"That will do," Sirria urged. "We want to kill Darrians, not adorn them!"

"It's not symmetrical yet."

Sirria grabbed the arrowhead from Merida's fingers and tossed it into the basket. "Just make them sharp. Start with the next."

Chack-chack-chack-chack. Dark splinters flew. "Do you think the Darrians will come within bowshot?"

"They tried last night, didn't they? Of course we won't let them." Sirria glanced across the merlons at the outer walls, the watchtowers, the solid gates.

"You've been in sieges before. Did you win them all?"

"We lost, but then we didn't have..." *We didn't have the Black Besieger on our side,* Sirria almost said. "We didn't have such a good citadel. Just look at these walls. And think of all the defences Dahoud put on the slopes, the sharp bends, the boulders, the narrow half-way gate. It will be a miracle if the Darrians ever get to taste our arrows. But I hope they do." Sirria rubbed the satisfying sharpness of her latest arrowhead. "I want to kill Darrians before this war is past."

Drums summoned everyone to the forum. On the speaker's platform, Dahoud stood in his scarlet tunic, the curved sword at his side.

"Last night, we beat a lesson into the Darrians, a lesson they won't forget." People chanted in triumph. Wurran inflated his chest. "If they try again, we'll beat them again. I doubt they'll dare." He laughed, and others laughed with him. Dahoud held his hands and arms high, projecting confidence. "They will sit out there, waiting for us to surrender. But they cannot get food or water from anywhere in Koskara. They will not last an hour longer than thirty days. Can we hold out for thirty days?"

A hearty chorus of "Yes!" resounded.

"We have food for thirty days, and they have not. As a precaution, we'll ration our food to last for fifty."

Sirria nodded to herself. The Black Besieger knew what he was doing, and he would be ruthless.

≈

On the first morning of Wheat Moon, Baryush declared his new terms: Unless Dahoud surrendered before nightfall, Koskara's leaders would be executed, the rest enslaved. Dahoud laughed in his face: The Black Besieger never surrendered.

Back in the citadel, he relayed the terms to the councillors, adding, "They need enormous supplies and can't get them from nearby. Before Wheat Moon is out, they'll be gone."

But the heady rush of the first victory was wearing off, and since the Darrians had not attacked again, everyone's nerves were tauter than bowstrings

In the forum, people talked louder than before, and walked with wide-swinging arms and clenched fists. Dahoud reminded everyone that the war would be over in twenty-eight days, and set them to work with flint-knapping and archery drills so they had no time for fearful thoughts.

As the sun descended on the final day of Wheat Moon, hundreds of Koskarans stood on the walls, staring at the plain below, at the enemy's blue-peaked tents and the palisade of spiky bunched beams which surrounded them like a thorn hedge.

Merida pressed her hands on the rough stone of the merlons. The Darrians were supposed to be gone, but their camp still squatted at the foot of the mountain, their foot soldiers drilled in the plain, their cavalry rode in formations.

All along the wall, angry growls cut through the sobs of despair, and fists bunched. "He promised it would be over by the end of this moon!"

Dahoud's miscalculation had cost him the people's trust. Unless she acted fast, morale would sink, and she must not let that happen.

Whatever had happened between her and Dahoud, and whatever choices she had made for the future, her loyalty of the moment belonged to Koskara.

She climbed on the battlement, her legs splayed for balance, and addressed the crowd. "Listen." Speaking loudly, and applying the large, confident gestures she had seen Dahoud use, she improvised a speech. "The Darrians think they scare us with their display. Are we going to let them?" She paused to allow thought and mutters. "We have defied them for more than a moon. Shall we now let them strike fear into our hearts, or shall we laugh and defy them for a few days more?"

This, she trusted, would inspire hope, if not confidence.

Dahoud pushed his way onto the curtain wall, his hand on the sword hilt, the muscles around his mouth tight, and climbed onto the rampart where Merida had stood.

"You've heard the Lady." His voice was loud, resonant, oozing confidence. "Why are the Darrians still here? Because not everyone had as much sense as you, not everyone brought their flocks into the citadel. Those who didn't heed our call had their animals captured. This has given the Darrians meat for a few days more. But it won't last. Do you see all those men, those horses, those elephants? How much food do they devour? More than a few captured goats can provide, and then there'll be nothing, because we had the foresight to destroy every food source in sight."

Knowing that people were watching her as much as Dahoud, Merida nodded with pointed conviction. However hateful he was to her personally, he was a good leader, and in this crisis, the Koskarans would do well to follow him.

He was wearing a scarlet turban and cloak, which made him look taller and broader, and a leather-sheathed sword strapped to his side.

His gestures were larger than normal, his voice deeper, louder. He was acting a role, and he was good at it.

"At the most, they have food to last them ten more days," Dahoud declared. "We, however, have enough for twenty!"

"Dahoud is right," Merida said loudly. "I've personally checked the food stores in our cellars. Because of Dahoud's foresight, we rationed our food not for thirty days, but for fifty!"

"As a precaution," Dahoud said, "We'll now ration the food so it lasts until the end of Grape Moon."

Merida stifled a cry of surprise. The end of Grape Moon was fifty-five days away. The rations were already sparse. Now they were to be stretched over fifty-five days instead of twenty?

"The Darrians will be gone long before then," Dahoud promised. "Very soon, Koskara will be free."

As he climbed off the battlement, a woman muttered, "If he's so sure the Darrians will leave in ten days, why can't we have food now?"

Dahoud stood close to Merida, so this scarlet cloak almost brushed against her arm. "Thanks for your support. I need it. Stay at my side. Walk slowly. Smile at everyone."

Merida complied, falling in with him, sharing the rhythm of his steps, by unspoken agreement keeping a knife's edge of space between them.

She beamed assurance at the people, even as worry wormed into her mind. "Fifty-five days?"

"A precaution," he said. "In war, it pays to be prepared for the worst."

That night, hunger bit. Merida's body had coped with thirty days of reduced rations, expecting a definite end. Knowing that the rationing would go on for longer, with even less food, her stomach rebelled. She tightened the leather belt around her waist to reduce its growling, but found little sleep at night. How could she endure more days of hunger? And how long would it last? Dahoud thought it was a matter of days before the Darrians left, but he had miscalculated before. What if he was wrong?

She woke with air bubbling in her stomach, and a dull pain creeping from the back of her neck across her skull.

At the meeting, councillors drew up plans for guarding the food cellars, and talked about how they would normally harvest the first figs by now, their once-bright auras almost invisible, their voices raw with resentment and longing. Dahoud was in the Darrian camp for the ritual exchange with the enemy leader. She missed his reassuring presence.

When Dahoud arrived, his aura was strong and his posture straight, but his eyes and voice were grave. He conveyed the latest terms: Unless they surrendered by nightfall, the Koskaran leaders would be impaled, the adults dragged into slavery, the children and elderly tossed from the battlements. The councillors agreed to resist, but their voices wavered.

~

Two moons into the siege, Teruma assessed her situation:

The Darrian camp still sprawled below, receiving caravans of laden camels, their line of supply better organised than Dahoud had predicted. The Koskarans might starve before the enemy left. By allying herself with Koskara during a crisis, she had risked much. She might lose all, or she might win all. She would play to win.

On Dahoud's orders, daily rations shrank to a small bowl of couscous with slivers of meat. Naima warned that unless the stomach received more food, it would start devouring the body from the inside. They had no choice. Even the animals set aside for breeding were devoured, and so were the beloved pets and the high priest's snake. The only beast alive was the silver horse, consort to the Goddess, who would die at the Feast of the Stallion.

Silence lay over Oubar, as oppressive as a thundercloud. People talked in muffled tones about the succulent grapes they should be harvesting now, about how they used to roast mutton, about the sweet oranges which once grew in Ain-Elnour. The trader begged in a low, toneless voice for someone to buy her now useless knick-knacks. Birds croaked and twittered louder than ever before, as if they could not bear the quiet.

Teruma walked among the people, offered encouragement and inspiration, planted much-needed hope into people's hearts. She gave rousing speeches, praising Dahoud's leadership, Koskaran courage, Samili defiance. The starving people sucked up her words as if they were food If they lived through this, they would remember her with admiration and gratitude, and she could count on them to support her rule.

≍

When Date Moon arrived with the summer's full heat, ninety-two days into the siege, Merida had learnt to ease the pain in her stomach by filling it with water, and by lying on her front. Her dreams were filled with mounds of steaming cabbage, and crusty cumin bread.

The daily ration for adults now consisted of four dried dates. The customary shared evening meal now consisted of hot water in which leather scraps were boiled to softening chews. Pine needles and a small measure of grain turned the brown water into a soup of sorts. Once Merida had refused to eat flesh; now she was grateful when the broth included crushed grasshoppers or morsels of rat.

With her belt tight against the hunger pangs, she knelt between the curtain walls, scratching for grubs and grass roots in the stony soil. How much longer could the Koskarans stand this suffering? Dahoud kept promising that the Darrians would soon be gone. Merida wished she could believe it, but he had said that twice before. What if the Darrians never left? Hunger gnawed at her guts and fear at her heart.

Some thirty feet away, a woman was sobbing in soft despair, huddled against the wall, hugging her baby close. Merida wanted to collapse next to her and join her sobs, overwhelmed by hunger and hopelessness.

Then she saw Dahoud, and squeezed into the shadows to avoid him. If he was going to dish out further platitudes, she did not want to hear him.

She did not hear what he said to the woman, but he saw what he was doing: he was giving her his four dates. Then he placed a finger on her lips to urge her silence.

≍

Grape Moon gave way to Fig Moon and the siege was still alive. Wherever Dahoud walked, he felt accusing stares in his back.

No more birdsong graced the air of Oubar. Tempers fermented in the sun. People talked louder again, in hard, grating voices, bellowing laughter with a bitter edge to it. Marching four abreast, men pushed solitary walkers out of the way. Women's faces lay in wrinkled folds like dried dates, their arms skeletal, their bellies flattened so much that hipbones and ribs stuck out under skin and clothes. However many beakers of water they swallowed, they could not fill the holes of hunger, nor gain the needed nourishment. The first people died from sickness and exhaustion.

He had misjudged the Darrians' ability to get supplies from their motherland. However, the expense would be enormous. Before long, the emperor would count up the cost and decide that Koskara was not worth it. It was a matter of holding out until then. He ordered the rations tightened further.

This time, his announcement met cries of protest. "Food, food! We want food now!"

"The Darrians will leave soon," he announced.

"That's what you said before. Food! Give us food!"

He had to do something drastic to regain their trust, to make a statement that would convince them. There was one animal left alive in the citadel, a beast whose flesh would sustain everyone for several days: The sacred silver stallion.

"Slaughter the stallion," he said.

Cries ceased and mouths gaped. Shock, astonishment, and wonder chased across the emaciated faces. They had protected and fattened the stallion to sacrifice him at the most sacred of festivals, when either the horse or the Lord must die.

"Slaughter the stallion," he repeated. "When the festival comes, we will choose a new animal for the sacrifice. When the festival comes, the Darrians will be gone. When the festival comes, Koskara will be free!"

The townspeople ran to tear the big beast to pieces. Rationed, the meat would bring respite for four days, but as a statement of confidence, the decision would last longer.

Mansour laid a hand on his shoulder. "A brave choice—Lord Dahcud."

On the first day of Olive Moon, dawn crept up behind the mountains in hues of violet and pink, and Dahoud laboured down the slope again, envoy staff in hand. The tunic could not hide his emaciated limbs, but the fleece wrapped around his middle pretended bulk. Perhaps it would fool his adversary. It had to.

The air in the command tent was lush with the smell of cooked spices and roasted meat. Dahoud squeezed his stomach muscles to squash the betraying rumble.

'Your visit gilds my day with pleasure, Lord Dahoud." Baryush bowed with immaculate courtesy. "Will you honour me by sharing my modest meal?" He gestured to a table laden with cinnamon-sprinkled bread, freshly fried aubergine slices and baskets of succulent fruit. A whole lamb, dripping with juices, rested on a bed of steaming couscous. He carved the meat with the tenderness of a lover. "This lamb is stuffed with pine nuts and comes with a rich coriander cream sauce. I trust it meets your approval."

Dahoud waved the offer away. "Not for me, Highness, thanks. I've just had breakfast." His ration for the day: two small dates and half the tail of a rat.

For the fifth time, he sank into the seat opposite his enemy. He restrained his eyes from devouring the food, but his nostrils could not escape the assault. Water pooled in his mouth, and his stomach cramped with desire.

Baryush held the fruit basket before him. "Surely you will take some fruit, Lord Dahoud?"

Golden oranges and fragrant dark dates tempted. Succulent melon slices almost seduced Dahoud's self-control with their pink tenderness and sweet scent.

"Thanks." He selected an orange and peeled it with the disinterested expression of someone who eats only because he does not wish to offend his host.

As soon as he swallowed the first bite, his stomach clenched at the unfamiliar acid, but soon demanded more, more, more. He suppressed the urge to gulp down the ball of sweet flesh. Instead, he ate slowly, savouring every bite.

"Why do you persist in this siege, Highness?" he asked. "You know you can't win. We have food for a long, long time, and endless water, whereas you're without." He chewed another juicy slice. "All those soldiers need provisioning. So do the horses and the elephants. They would drink a river dry. You have no river, have you? Merely a few measly mountain streams. You need to get supplies from Darria, from nine days away. A logistic nightmare. I pity you for it."

Silence drew out while Baryush speared pieces of meat and chewed. Dahoud gazed at the remaining two fruit segments in his palm. He had to make them last.

"When my army advanced, the Koskarans withdrew, leaving a wasteland behind. A remarkable move, Lord Dahoud. May I compliment you on your strategy?" Baryush carved another section of the lamb. "Will you not try a morsel of this meat? It will melt in your mouth. Enlighten me how you persuaded your people to leave their land and to destroy what they owned, to ruin the pastures, to poison the waterholes, to cut down fruit-bearing trees, to torch the towns. Did everyone applaud your plan?"

Dahoud bit into the second-last piece. "This orange tastes nice, considering it has travelled all the way from Darria."

"I am delighted to assure you that from tree to table, it has travelled only two days. The oranges of Ain-Elnour are said to be the best in the world. Now I've sampled them myself, I agree they deserve their reputation. Incidentally, the town's architectural artistry holds my particular admiration."

A cold fist squeezed around Dahoud's chest. "Ain-Elnour?"

"Did your men not tell you they spared the green jewel? Did they report the town's destruction? Did they say they had burnt the buildings and poisoned the water and chopped down the orange trees? I'm glad to say the houses still stand in their ancient glory, the horses perform well in my cavalry, and the fresh water is just two days' ride away. My men appreciate the oranges, and soon they'll harvest the summer figs." Baryush leant back in his chair, with the hands laced behind his head. "Are you not eating the rest of your fruit? Does its taste no longer please?"

"I don't believe you."

"Of course you don't believe me. Why should you?" Baryush popped a golden date into his mouth and spat the stone discreetly into his palm. "Your subjects are so loyal, they would never defy your orders. They love you so much that at the Feast of the Stallion, when they have to choose between killing an incompetent Lord or substituting a horse, they will know what to do. When is the event—fourteen days from now? Thirteen?"

Dahoud glanced at the remaining orange segment in his hand.

"If you no longer like the orange, try the melon, Lord Dahoud. Or I can send for horse meat. The beast was slaughtered only yesterday and has not had time to hang, however I assure you its flesh has been thoroughly bled."

"I didn't come here to eat or exchange pleasantries. Can we get down to business?"

"As you wish, Lord Dahoud. As you may expect, my offer is less lenient now than if you had handed over the citadel five moons ago. However, I will not be ungenerous. I have the pleasure to offer a quick death to everyone under six or over thirty, and also to all adult males. The other lives will be spared for the brothels and the mines. Naturally, these terms only apply if you surrender before you leave this tent." Baryash ate more meat and smacked his lips. "If you waste more of my time by attempting to hold out, the terms change. We'll take the youngest women only and kill the rest, after torture, of course. I have an excellent torturer with me. So, Lord Dahoud, what do you choose?"

"I won't surrender."

"Of course you won't surrender. Why should you? With your wealth of food, with your subjects' absolute loyalty, with your water—that vast supply of wonderful water from the secret source."

He summoned a soldier to escort Dahoud out of the camp, and bowed. "Your visit has gilded my day."

Dahoud walked out of the tent. The sun slammed him hard. Dizzied with hunger and light, he had to lean on his envoy staff. He managed to walk straight until he was out of sight of the Darrian camp. Then he dragged himself up the rest of the way.

He made it to the council chamber. He was about to open the meeting, and to tell his emaciated councillors about Ain-Elnour, when Naima grabbed his arm.

"Dahoud, the wellhouse." Her face was tense with a furrowed forehead and knitted brows. "The level is getting low."

"Show me." Already, his guts crawled with the certainty of disaster, but as leader, he had to see the site of every crisis with his own eyes.

The councillors' steps echoed hollowly down the stairs of the well-house.

Kneeling, he held his head above the basin to listen. No splash, no gurgle, no sound of life. He plucked a rose from the vase at the shrine and dropped its bloom. It floated on the surface without moving.

"This is a temporary lull, isn't it? It has to be," Naima beseeched him, as if he could make it true. "The source is irregular and the water will come back?"

"No." Dahoud faced his councillors. "Once this water is gone, we'll die."

He knew only too well what would happen: painful convulsions, sluggish brains, loss of consciousness. Eventually the Darrians could just walk in, the way he had walked into citadels he had forced into submission. People could survive hunger, but thirst left them too weak to resist.

"Close the bathhouse," he instructed. "No more washing. Naima, what's the minimum an adult needs to drink each day?"

She rubbed her palms on her thigh and flicked a nod at the clay jugs in the corner. "One jar this size. The body functions, but the thirst still bites."

"Ration it. Post armed guards outside the wellhouse."

"Even rationed, the water will last five days." Merida kneaded her neck. "No more."

"Then we have five more days to live and fight," Dahoud said. For the sake of his people, he had to drive the fear from his heart, or at least from his face. But he knew the truth: the citadel had become a tomb.

❧

"How could the Darrians capture the water?" Keera asked. "Our archers watched the mountainside day and night."

"The water came from an underground lake a mile away, through the old mining shafts," Dahoud said. "The Darrians shouldn't have known that." Who had told Baryush? Few were aware where the water came from. Even fewer knew along which paths it ran. "Criton oversaw the connection of the tunnels."

"The man you sacrificed under the gatehouse arch?" Mansour asked.

"An accomplice helped him escape. He must have sold the secret to the enemy."

An accomplice we know well, don't we?

Merida's head hung, and her lower lip disappeared, as if she was biting it to draw blood. The pain of guilt radiated from her face. She was realising what she had done. She had as good as condemned them all to death.

Mansour balled a fist. "When I find that accomplice, I'll strangle him with my own hands."

Nobody knew it was Merida—and nobody must guess. Dahoud averted his gaze to avoid drawing attention to her. The trust the people had in their Lady was all that stood between them and certain defeat.

Merida raised her head. "I'll dance for rain." Her voice was loud and clear, without inflection. Only Dahoud could see the torture in her eyes.

He could not hate her. She had freed Criton because her faith demanded it, and she was a woman of principles. Now she was accepting responsibility for her deed, even though nobody knew she was the one to blame. She who had sworn never to dance for rain again, was setting her principles aside to undo some of the harm. A lesser person might have consoled her conscience by thinking it was not her fault Criton had turned traitor. Merida was admitting her guilt to herself. This took courage.

He followed her up the stairs and into the glaring sun.

"Merida!" he called.

She stopped, arms locked across her chest.

How could he explain that he knew her guilt and forgave her, that he would keep her secret to protect both her and the people? He reached for words, but they would not come.

He fumbled in his belt pouch, and drew out the shimmering thread from her river dress. On his palm, the copper bead at the thread's end stabbed a sharp glint at her. He watched recognition ghost across her face only she owned a dress with fringe like this, and she had worn it only once.

"I found it in Criton's cell." Words were coming at last.

Her face whitened. In her widening eyes, he read shock, fear, horror, and finally, puzzlement. "You knew? All the time you knew it was me, and you didn't tell?"

382

He tried to explain, but the his word flow had dried up again. Their gazes met, passing on stories which their tongues could not tell: stories of guilt and regret, of secrets and of blame, his and hers, and questions about the future.

"Thank you," she said at last. "I'll try to dance for rain."

Still unable to summon more words, he watched her go. She had doomed them, but he could not hate her.

CHAPTER 36

Pressure

The borrowed white dress clung to Merida's body, already drenched in sweat. Everything depended on her success this afternoon. Unless she could lure clouds to pour their water over the citadel, eight hundred people would perish from thirst.

Sirria pressed four dates into her palms. "Eat. You need your strength for the dance. We've been pooling our rations for you."

Merida wanted to decline, but her stomach screamed to accept the gift. "Please give my sincere thanks to everyone." She could not look Sirria in the eye. If they knew the truth about who had released the sacrifice, they would not be so generous.

"We'll beat those bastards," Sirria said. "They think they can take away our water, but we'll show them."

Teruma said, "We have fifty flutes, eight straighthorns, and two hundred drums. We would have had more, but some have boiled the goatskins on their drums. Everyone wants to watch, so you won't have privacy, but I've cleared a space around the fire, and kept the spectators at a distance."

"Thank you, Teruma. This is the biggest orchestra I've ever worked with, and the highest fire."

Merida watched labourers drag the last of the precious building beams and firewood to the stack. With so much music, a strong fire, and energy from a large audience, Merida would succeed. She had to.

"Every bowl and bucket stands ready to receive the rain," Teruma said.

When Merida climbed on the platform, the sky was an even, desiccated blue, with no wisp of cloud in sight.

Dahoud sat at her feet, the clay-drum under his bare arm. His fingers danced on the drumskin, feeding her the energy of his rhythm. Around them, two dozen drums picked up the pattern, pounding and roiling: *Doumtek doumdoum tek. Doumtek doumdoumtek.*

Smoky flames crackled through the wood. She felt the fire's heat on her skin and in her throat. Bitter wood smoke scratched her nostrils.

Eight hundred pairs of eyes stared at her with a hope she might not fulfil, and a trust she did not deserve. Still light-headed from prolonged fasting, she entered into a trance with ease by swinging her head. The energy of the music and the yearnings of the people pulsed through her, but no magic took hold. Not the faintest tingle reached her skin, let alone the cauldron inside her soul. She danced and danced. The day the wildfire threatened Koskara Town, rain had arrived eventually. It had to happen today, too. But in Koskara Town, she had made a connection with water-bearing clouds. Today, she sensed nothing. Nothing at all.

She did not meet Dahoud's imploring glance. He was giving all had, and so was she, and everyone else. It was not enough.

Impaired by hunger, her stamina slackened. Her moves grew slower, smaller, struggled to keep pace with the drums. She pushed herself further, dancing under the merciless beat of the burning sun. Nothing.

By the time the sun had sunk to finger-breadths above the horizon, exhaustion claimed its toll. Merida shuffled off the podium, past Dahoud, past rows of expectant buckets, not daring to look at the disappointed faces. "Sometimes it takes a while," she said, but she knew she had failed.

Trying again another day would be pointless: Too many sins stained her soul. A magician must be virtuous at all times, but Merida had cheated again and again. Her stubbornness and deceptions had led to the people's despair and wiped out her magic.

She curled up on the hard floor of her tower room. When Sirria offered a jug of honey water, she waved it away: she did not deserve sustenance. How could she redeem herself?

Thirst hurt far more than the hunger had. After just one day on the restricted ration, Dahoud felt his mouth drying and his throat screamed for relief. On his way to the council, he saw pinched faces, and knew he was not alone: Everywhere in the citadel, people's nerves were as frayed as old bowstrings, their hearts brittle like waterskins left out in the sun, and their thickening blood was boiling with heat.

Last night, crones had attacked the cistern guards, demanding water. "Shit on the council's orders!" one of them had screeched. "They've rationed the food, they've rationed the firewood, they've rationed the water. Are they going to ration the air next?"

Opening the meeting, Dahoud sprinkled more incense on the burner. Perhaps the amount would make the gods take notice. He invoked the Great Mare, the Mighty Ones, and every minor deity he could think of, even the peacock god of Darria.

"The Darrians are here for good," Wurran said. "Dahoud promised they would soon leave."

"They would have left," Dahoud pointed out, "had you kept your promise to get Ain-Elnour destroyed. By sparing the oasis, you presented them with endless water and food and every comfort they can want."

Wurran bristled. "Is he blaming me now? I passed the orders to the townspeople. Is it my fault if they didn't obey?"

Dahoud glared at him. If Wurran had stayed to see his orders carried out, the war would be over.

But if a leader's composure cracked, everyone else's courage crumbled, so Dahoud forced confidence into his voice. "We haven't lost yet. The gods may send rain."

"After eight years of drought?" Wurran countered. "If the gods took an interest, they would have intervened long ago."

Fear had sunk bone-deep into his councillors, and that could be deadly. 'Victory is an exclusive mistress,' Paniour had always said. 'She doesn't favour the man who in his thoughts embraces defeat.'

"Tarkan may raise an army in Tajlit." Dahoud tried to sound as if he believed in the possibility. "Or Kirral may change his mind and demand Koskara back. The Emperor may recall the army to cut costs or to deploy them elsewhere. Plague may break out among the besiegers. A bolt of lightning may strike their general."

"What good would that do?" Naima demanded.

"A lot. Darrians look to the top man for commands to filter down. They have few officers, and those are seldom part of the strategy. Take out the general, and their whole army is lost."

"What if no miracle happens?" Naima asked. "You promised you could hold Oubar forever. You promised the water supply was safe. We believed you, and now we'll die."

"We won't die," Dahoud lied, needing it to be true.

The granules on the incense burner melted with a hiss.

Naima licked her lips and ran the back of her hand across her jaw. "What if we surrender?"

"Impalement is no more pleasant than starvation," Dahoud said.

"Hasn't Baryush promised we could leave with our clothes and be resettled?"

"That was an earlier condition. Long past."

"Why did you reject it?"

"Surrender," a chorus of councillors beseeched him. "Tell the Darrians we've changed our mind, we want to live."

Tension knotted the muscles across his shoulders so tightly that they hurt. "Siege terms always get harsher. There's no going back." A commander had to set an example and treat the resisting citadels with the harshness they deserved, harsher for every moon they resisted. Leniency would only encourage other towns to hold out. If he showed enough brutality, future cities surrendered without bloodshed. Dahoud had used this method often enough.

"It's too late to surrender," Dahoud repeated. His scalp itched. He did not want to spell out the gruesome details of what would happen if they surrendered now. It would drive more fear into their hearts.

"The Darrians wouldn't be so cruel," a woman councillor said. "They really want peace. They offered to let us live in Koskara, just paying tribute to the Emperor. That's what they wanted, only Dahoud rejected it."

"Dahoud promised he could hold Oubar forever," Keera said. "I said he was wrong. Now he says surrender is impossible. I say he's wrong."

The councillors' eyes were narrow, their jaws set, their postures tense. They blamed him for everything: the war, the hunger, the thirst, the hot weather, the lack of rain. Pain gnawed at his guts as if he had a rat trapped in his stomach.

He raised his arms, palms up. "Listen. If you surrender now, your wives will be raped, your children thrown over the wall—and that will be the last sight before your eyes are gouged out."

"You're wrong." Keera sat very straight. She looked taller and stronger than Dahoud remembered her. "None of this will happen if we negotiate again—with Lord Mansour as our leader."

Dahoud drew in a sharp breath, but Keera spoke with confidence, and she had everyone's attention. "There is one chance that they will let us surrender on the original terms. One chance only." She placed the tips of her fingers together. "If we tell their general that Dahoud didn't speak for us, that his choices were not ours, he may allow a new leader to negotiate afresh."

Eyes widened, swivelled from Keera to Mansour. Nobody looked at Dahoud.

In silent concentration, Mansour twirled his spindle.

Dahoud's head throbbed. Keera, whom he had protected and promoted, was rebelling against him, siding with Mansour whom she had always opposed. Since the highest rank a female commoner could achieve was chief councillor, Keera had first schemed to discredit Mansour who held that post. Now she had changed tactics, aiming to depose Dahoud. If he was deposed and Mansour became Lord, the chief councillor post would fall to her. It made horrid sense. He should have seen it before.

"We won't surrender," Dahoud said. "The meeting is closed."

As he walked out, he felt the flaming arrows of hatred and blame in his back, and knew the councillors were scheming.

⚮

When Dahoud walked through the crowds to the battlements, mothers held out the limp bodies of children and spat curses. He kept his head high.

He sat on the outer wall that separated the world inside the citadel from that of the enemy camp. The sky bruised from yellow to purple, anticipating one of the dry thunderstorms which tormented the land during the summer. The first thunder crackled from the far south. The remaining pine trees stood against the merciless sky, stiff and still as spears. The birds had stopped singing, even the cicadas were dumb.

Pain pounded his skull, his neck crackled with every move. Keera had used him from the start. Now that she had no further use for him, she dropped him like a camel dropped shit.

Did we expect differently from a woman?

Lightning scratched the sky in single, heart-beat long flicks, and thunder came closer, like a legion's rolling drums. The southern horizon looked yellow and sick, tinged with splotches of grey.

Koskara was dying because of Wurran's carelessness. He had dumped the order in Ain-Elnour and left without checking that it was carried out. If Dahoud had learnt before the siege that the oasis was not destroyed, there would still have been time to shape a new plan.

'With civilians, never assume anything,' Paniour used to say.

Dahoud heard his mentor's voice, and flushed at the rebuke. He should have interrogated Wurran on his return, pressured and probed until he knew for sure. He had not done it. He, too, had assumed that his orders would be carried out. It was not Wurran's mistake, but Dahoud's own.

Thunder rumbled like battering rams in action, like brickwalls crashing down, like warfare in the sky.

By loading the blame on Wurran, he had denied his own responsibility. What else was he denying where the fault was his?

Voices below the battlements jolted him out of his thoughts. Voices he knew. Low, secretive. Merida and Mansour stood together, clasping elbows, exchanging confidential whispers and deep looks. He drew back against the watchtower so they would not see him. Although he could not hear their words, he had seen enough. They, too, were plotting to depose him. Were they allies, or lovers, or both? Bitterness bloomed in his chest. The people loved Merida, and saw Mansour as their leader. Married, the pair would have everyone's support. All they needed was Dahoud's death.

Anger churned with the ferocity of a desert storm, joining the thundering turmoil above. He would not take it lying down. He did not have to. He would teach that bitch Merida what he could do. She hated him because he raped her? She did not know what rape was. He would make her beg and cry and scream, and he would not show mercy. She would learn what kind of man she had dared to betray.

He could taste his need, hungry, bitter and hot. With his heart racing, he hurried to his room to strap on his dagger belt and get his sheathed bronze sword. His death was close, the time had come to once more savour the glory of victory, the pleasures of rape, the power he deserved.

To his surprise, the djinn stayed silent. But this was between Dahoud and Merida alone.

He climbed the steep steps to her room. In her arrogance, she had chosen the highest finished building for her abode, and even when refugees crowded the town, she had insisted on keeping a whole room to herself.

When she tried to slam the door in his face, he would force entry. He would pin her, force her, defeat her. He would claw her breasts and bite them and when he was done with her, he would slice her with his sword, see the blood well and stream, and chop her into pieces, the treacherous bitch. Dahoud the Black Besieger would live again.

CHAPTER 37

Merida's Plan

Roaring with anger, Dahoud charged up the stairs and banged the door.

It creaked open a slit. "Dahoud? Please come in." Merida flung it wide open and stepped back. She looked fragile, her once-smart blue tunic hanging limply from her gaunt frame, her waist so thin he could snap it between his hands, her breasts small.

He stomped into the sparsely furnished cell. A mat, a rug, a chest, a cooking pot. The window framed flicks of lightning, sharp and fast.

"Dahoud, I'm glad you're here. I need to ask you something. Please sit."

He remained standing, legs braced, a conqueror in command. He could hear his own breathing, laboured and harsh. Even thinned by hunger, Merida was full of life, bursting with a vitality that promised resistance, that thrilled him more than her curves or her smile. She would soon stop smiling when he seized a handful of her hair and dragged her, screaming, across the floor.

"I never thanked you," she said. "You saved me in the desert, in the arena, in the fire, and again, when Mansour would have killed me because of the water. You sacrificed much to protect me. I'm sorry I thought so low of you for so long. Can you forgive me?"

His heart thudded in his throat, in rhythm with the roaring thunder. The sword in his hand weighed as much as a pile of bricks.

"I should have danced for rain when I arrived in Koskara, and I should have let Criton die. If I'd trusted your judgement, and if I'd not been so wrapped up in my pride and principles, the land would not have dried out, the fire would never have happened, the cistern would still be filled. I know it's late, and we may not live through this, but I trust you now. With my life, and everything."

Dahoud stared at the woman he had come to rape and kill. He let her words wash over him, while his guilt throbbed like a wound.

Insight slammed him in the face and sliced his heart. Zun was right: he was the monster. The djinn was only the manifestation of his own dark desires.

Above, thunder tore the sky apart. He needed the walls of denial to hold him up and hide him, but they were crumbling. He cursed the war, he cursed Kirral, he cursed himself for being so weak and deluded that he had succumbed to evil and blamed it on a djinn. Guilt gnawed at his soul. Had he, who always took charge of every situation, failed to take charge of his own dark side? Had he protected the evil inside him by denying it?

"It's my responsibility to get us out of this," Merida said. "I have a plan that may save us yet: I'll take out the Darrian top man."

"How would you do that?" There was no way she could get near Baryush.

"I'll infiltrate the Darrian camp." She spoke with confidence, as if she was talking about nothing more difficult than visiting a neighbour. "I'll pose as a travelling entertainer, a bellydancer. I'll get the leader alone and kill him."

The plan had more holes than a piece of wormed wood. Not only did emaciated Merida have all the seductive allure of a shrivelled fig, but Darrians abstained from women until the war was won. "Even if they believe your story, they'll disarm you before they let you into the camp."

"I can box and kick, and I'll grab anything at hand to use as a weapon. Whether you help me or not: I'm going."

He took in her defiant posture, the squared shoulders, the raised chin, the fists pushed into her sides, and nodded.

"Take his sword. He'll keep it within reach. It's not your common kind of sword, though. Look here." He unsheathed his own gleaming blade, softly curved and almost three feet long. "This is similar to

Baryush's sword. You don't thrust with it; you slash." He sliced the air with two rapid strokes. "Try."

She hesitated to grip the wooden hilt.

"You've never wielded any sword?" Dahoud sank the blade back into its sheath. "Then a palm tree will grow eggs before you kill the general."

"Teach me," Merida said. "Teach me to kill."

"Swordcraft takes years to learn."

"We have two hours before it gets dark."

Even knowing that the plan was almost doomed to fail, she had the courage to go through with it. What a Lady she would make for Koskara – if they lived.

Her stubborn bravery sparked a corresponding hope in him. The plan was crazy, but the gods favoured the mad. "Have you ever handled a weapon at all?"

"The staff. Not for real fighting, or sparring even, but the drills are supposed to be derived from martial arts." She picked up a stick, five foot long, square rather than round, and as thick as a wrist. "It trains strength, balance and concentration."

She performed a strange dance with the staff on her head, bending and pirouetting beneath it, an impressive balancing feat, but useless for combat. Spinning with both hands clasped around the stick had potential only for the battlefield. Then she performed single-handed thrusts and twirls, their pace excruciatingly slow, hypnotic to watch but pointless in a fight, and far too sweeping for the confines of a tent.

Still, she had the balance, she had the stance, she had the agility, and he could work with that.

"That sequence where you thrust on the forward lunge and then draw the staff across. Show me that again."

The way she lunged forward and leaned her whole body into the move would allow her to injure Baryush from five feet away, before he could reach her with his dagger.

"Try this. When you lunge forward, stab not straight forward, but down. Imagine him sitting on a chair. Aim for his stomach, not his ribs. You don't need to run the blade through him, just pierce. He'll bring his hands down in protection, which leaves his neck free. Pull the blade back with the backward lunge, same leg, just the way you did it, but very

very fast. Like this." He demonstrated several times and then put the weapon back into her hand, careful not to touch. "Now, before you lunge forward again, twist your upper body. Hold the sword arm across your chest as before, but rest the blunt edge against the inside of your lower left arm, like this. Then push both arms forward. The blade near the hilt will be at his neck."

He wanted to stand behind her, to lock his fingers around hers to guide her movement, and then clasp an arm around her chest to caress her, control her, claim her. He held on to the edges of his self control. "Now pull it across, so the whole length of the blade slices across his neck."

Merida shuddered. "Will there be blood?"

"Plenty."

Her lips tightened.

She practised until she had mastered the basics. But Baryush would not sit still while she snatched his sword and attacked him with it. By the time she had unsheathed the blade, he would have his dagger at her throat.

"You need to be quick," he said. "His surprise will give you about five heartbeats. Eight if he has drunk wine. Step between him and the sword, grab it with your left. Get out of his reach while you draw the sword from the sheath. Then do the stab and the slash."

He made her rehearse: Grab, step back, unsheathe, lunge, stab, slash. Even when she had mastered the sequence, she was far too slow to stand a chance.

"Can you use magic to distract him?"

She rubbed her wrist to ease the strain from holding the heavy sword. "A spell of inattention would slow my reaction even more than his."

To give her a break, he took the sword from her hand. "This is a masterpiece of Darrian manufacture. Only Darrian bronze smiths can make swords this shape that don't break, and they're so expensive only aristocratic officers can afford them. Common soldiers in the Darrian army have leaf-bladed swords, while in the Quislak legions, everyone fights with straight short swords." He placed the blunt inner edge on the back of his left hand. "See how it balances on the edge? The weight is perfectly distributed, even with the hilt. You won't find many of these outside Darria; they're not available for trade. I killed its owner."

He watched her face: If the mere mention of death still made her squirm, she would not stand a chance.

Her lips tightened for a moment, but she did not recoil.

"Let me try something." She placed the blade on her head, balancing it on the narrow inner edge the way he had done, and rotated her hips in spirals. Her face shone in triumph. "How's this? I'll get him to give me his sword, so that I can dance with it on my head. Now it's in my possession, ready to slash. No more time lost grabbing and unsheathing it."

"If you can fool him into giving you his weapon to play with, you'll defeat him easily." He forced sincerity into his voice.

He drilled her until she could perform the sequence at high speed. She rubbed her wrist but did not complain.

"Enough for now," he said. Without lamp oil, nightfall put an end to most activities. He walked to the window. Behind the Darrian palisade, the blue-topped tents became grey silhouettes, and camp-fires lit up as fiery beads.

She joined him, her hands next to his on the sill. They were standing so close together he could smell her sweat. He hungered like a dog for her forgiveness, but he did not deserve it. He did not ask.

Her wrist, so close to his, looked small. He wanted to circle his fingers around it to give it strength, to run his fingers along her arm, to brush her skin with his thumb, but he dared not.

There was barely enough space between their arms for air to pass. She made no movement, neither to get closer, nor to increase the distance. Surely it was not normal for someone to be standing motionless for so long?

The djinn stirred streams of heat in his blood.

Dahoud drank in her closeness without glancing at her. His heart beat high up in his throat, fast, an excitement which did not come from the threat of enemy camp-fires in the dark.

He shifted his weight, as if to make himself more comfortable, in the process brought his wrist even closer. The shock of her skin on his shot through him. A spike of pain, a streak of lightning, a sting of a thousand nettles.

They remained nailed to the spot, wrists touching. Blood whirled in his head like a sandstorm.

Nothing moved, except his racing heart. No woman had ever sought his touch. There had been women who feared him and fought him. Women who wanted the benefits that came from sleeping with the commander. Women who sought the thrill of coupling with a ruthless brute. Merida was different. She knew what he was capable of, and disapproved, and yet...With every pulse, the touch sent flashes of heat through him, awakening feelings he had thought dead. Feelings more disturbing than destructive desire. Respect. Affection. Tenderness. With them came needs he had suppressed for so long. What would it be like to be loved?

He directed his thoughts to practical matters. "We must talk to Mansour about this."

"No," she whispered. "Not tonight. It's getting dark, and-"

"Why don't you want him to know about this plan?"

"He already knows." She did not meet his eyes. "He didn't want... He said not to involve you. Only, when you came here tonight, I-"

So Mansour and Merida had plotted not just against the Darrians, but against him. They had deposed him already. Anger soured his stomach. Merida's warmth had been nothing but pity.

Was it even pity? Or did she use us? Squeeze knowledge from us like juice from a citron, and then drop the unwanted fruit?

Dahoud broke the touch and pulled away. "We must see to Mansour. Now."

✂

Mansour raised his brows and gestured to the fleeces on the floor. The sparse light from the window shone on spears in the corner and animal skins on the walls. He measured water from a lidded jar into two beakers, drop by drop, and passed them to his visitors.

Sitting on the sheepskin, Dahoud gazed at the beaker in his hand. The water was Mansour's daily ration: He was adhering to nomad hospitality and giving away all he had.

The cool scent of water teased Dahoud's nostrils. He controlled the urge to drink it in one gulp.

Instead, he permitted a single drop to roll across his lips onto his tongue.

"So?" Mansour asked.

"So you've deposed me." Dahoud set the cup down. "When were you going to tell me?"

"Tomorrow morning."

"How did you plan to do it?" Dahoud demanded. "Honourable combat, or simply slash my throat?"

"Drink," Mansour said.

Dahoud took another drop. Could he risk trusting Mansour?

"What do you know about Darrians, Mansour? You're leading half-dead untrained people with poor weapons against a professional army. I've fought Darrians. I understand their tactics, their strengths, their weak spots. For Koskara's sake, use what I know."

Mansour fished his spindle from the pouch and fed it with wool.

Dahoud tried to sort his thoughts into ordered rows like soldiers, but thirst had made them sluggish and they would not obey. Every further hour of dehydration would slow his thoughts more, and Mansour's and Merida's, too. "Take the battle into their camp," he started. "In the confines of their palisades, they can't deploy their cavalry or their chariots. Use surprise: Darrians plan everything long in advance, and aren't flexible about the unexpected. Disrupt their command structure: They depend totally on direct orders from their general."

"You said so before, and I believe you," Mansour said. "That's why I back Merida's plan."

"Yes. Normally, before a battle, the general outlines the strategy to his senior officers, who pass it down to their centurions and the sergeants, who then give orders in the heat of battle. The senior officers also know the overall strategies with alternatives for every eventuality. That's how I led my troops, and how you did, too. But not the Darrians. Also, if we died, our next-in-command would take over at once, continuing the strategy. Among Darrians, a general's death leads to a panicked delay while they successor gets to grips with the situation and establishes authority. The new man may have no battle experience, no leadership skills. Therefore, when Merida has taken out their general..." —He made a point of saying *when* rather than *if* — "their command structure breaks down. Eventually, they'll rally, but if you attack in that confused moment, you'll have the advantage."

"How attentive are their guards?" Mansour asked.

"They'll be prepared for a break-out from the fortress, so they'll react to the smallest movement on the slope and raise the alarm. Create a distraction inside the camp."

"Fire," Merida said. "As soon as their general is dead, I'll set a tent on fire, to signal it's time to attack. This will also distract the guards."

"Burn several tents," Mansour said. "Stampede the horses."

"And the cattle, and the elephants," Dahoud added. "With the roar of the flames, pounding hooves, and panicked screams, the guards won't hear the Koskarans approach. Make the fire spread through the camp, so the Darrians will flee through the main gate."

Mansour nodded. "As soon as we get the signal, we'll creep quietly down the track, taking out any guards on the way. Then we wait until the fire drives the Darrians out, without weapons or armour. Perfect ambush. Our archers and stone-slingers pick them off from a safe distance as they come running." He laughed. "All those arrows we made are coming handy after all."

"Night time will be best. By the time they realise it's a battle, and their general isn't alive to command them, you've already the advantage. They'll be confused, frightened, leaderless, without strategy."

"Problem solved," Mansour said. "Will you be my second-in-command?"

"Is the problem solved?" Dahoud blew air through his nostrils. "Only if they let Merida into their camp, if she kills the general, if she sets a large portion of the camp on fire, if the Koskarans get to the camp without being heard, if the fire spreads, if the elephants stampede, if the Darrians panic without leader, if they flee through the main gate. If the Koskarans are in a condition to fight. Are they?"

Mansour's eyes lowered. "No. Even if they still had the strength to walk that far and raise a bow, their vision is too weak to aim an arrow. It would work—if we had water."

Dahoud nodded grimly. "Yes. If we had water."

"I'm so sorry," Merida whispered.

Dahoud gave her a tight smile. She had let the secret of the water source escape, but she was not the only one who had misjudged. The greatest fault was Dahoud's. *Remember you're the Lord of Koskara,* Zun had said. *Remember what that means.* Dahoud had thought as a general when he should have been thinking as a Lord. A real Lord would not have been blinded by the potential of a perfect fortress. A real Lord would not have jeopardised his land. A real Lord would have put his people above his hubris.

Dahoud knew then what he had to do. The plan presented itself fully formed, with hard, heavy clarity. "Water is what we need. If the Koskarans can drink their fill, they can fight. Are we agreed?"

"We're not getting water, so there's no point thinking about it," Mansour said.

"Baryush will restore the water." Dahoud said. The steadiness of his voice surprised him.

"You're joking," Mansour said.

"He will. There's one thing Baryush wants, wants so much he'll give you water to get it: me. Alive." Dahoud cupped the beaker in both hands, looking at the precious water. "Baryush and I share a history."

He gave a brisk summary of the events in Zigazia. He told them of the djinn, of the rapes, of his darkest deeds, speaking quickly before his conscious mind could choose to hold him back.

"Tomorrow is the Feast of the Stallion: Koskara needs a sacrifice." His eyes locked with Mansour's. "Will you accept mine?"

Mansour raised his brows. "You want me to deliver you to Baryush, alive?"

"Yes. Betray me, depose me, sell me." When Mansour shook his head, Dahoud added, "You need to know one more truth."

"There's more?"

Dahoud's chest tightened, and his heart raced. "I wasn't a centurion in the army which devastated Koskara. I was a general."

Mansour's lids lowered, his eyes narrowing to slits. "There was only one general."

The back of Dahoud's tongue reared, blocking his throat. He fought to choke the word out. "Yes."

"The Black Besieger. The Lord of Koskara is the Black Besieger." Mansour's features hardened, and he rose, balling his hands into fists. "On behalf of Koskara, I accept your sacrifice."

"But Dahoud," Merida cried. "What if he tortures you before we come to your aid? You may have your legs broken or your eyes pierced or your tongue pulled out or -"

Dahoud cut her off before she could spell out more possibilities. "I'll risk it." He doubted she would be able to free him at all.

"Tomorrow morning, I'll take the envoy staff," Mansour said. "I'll tell Baryush I've locked up the old Lord and plan to kill him at the festival so I can marry the Lady and be Lord myself. When Baryush asks me to deliver you into his hands, I'll feign reluctance until he offers to pay with water."

Merida frowned. "Would Baryush pay anything? He could wait until we're too weak to offer resistance, conquer the town and capture you."

"He wants me alive." Dahoud shut his mind against what that would mean for him. "He doesn't want to give me the chance to kill myself."

"Will he keep his side of the bargain? What if he takes you without giving us water? What if he poisons it?"

"Darrian officers pride themselves in their honour in such matters. You'll have to wait a day before you carry out your plan, though. If you arrive on the same day as I, the Darrians will suspect a connection. Mansour, lock me into the cell now and tie me tightly so I can't change my mind."

CHAPTER 38

In The Hands Of The Enemy

The rope bit into Dahoud's wrists while Mansour stood exchanging courtesies with Baryush.

"I'm much obliged, Lord Mansour," Baryush spoke with the sonorous tone of a satisfied customer. "Do you wish to stay and watch the beginning of the torture?"

"I won't. Duty waits."

"Naturally. As the new Lord, you need to preside over doomed Koskara's final festival."

"I've delivered him." Mansour jerked his chin at Dahoud. "Now give us the water."

"With pleasure. We shall restore the supply before your festivities begin. Farewell, Lord Mansour. I look forward to our next meeting, when you will declare surrender."

Dahoud watched as his rival's broad back disappeared, leaving him alone in enemy hands.

Baryush raised the heavy curtain to open the tent. "This is where you'll be staying. I trust you'll find it uncomfortable. Come in."

Behind them, the curtain thudded shut, enclosing them in darkness. Only a sliver of sunlight reached through a roof slit. As Dahoud's eyes adjusted to the gloom, he saw straw spread across the floor, a chair, a brazier, and a long table.

A woman rose, smoothing her white tunic. She was small, padded like a comfortable divan with a girdle of fat around her middle, about the age Dahoud's mother would be. Coiled greying braids crowned her head.

"Meet your torturer, Dahoud." Baryush's voice brimmed with pleasure. "Laleika is a master tormentor. You'll be in good hands with her."

Dahoud's throat tightened. "I'm pleased to meet you," he croaked. The words were out before he could check their meaning.

Baryush laughed. "Laleika, this is your first client on this campaign. The most important client: Dahoud, former lord-satrap of Koskara. He's here for punishment, not interrogation. What do you think? Can you make him suffer for a really long time?"

She wrinkled her nose. "He stinks." She sounded as if Baryush was trying to sell her a lame horse. "He hasn't washed before coming here."

Baryush made himself comfortable in the chair. His silk garments rustled. "I apologise for the client's filth. He hasn't had much water recently."

Her face softened. "Not much water? Oh, the poor dear." She picked up a jug from the shelf. "Are we thirsty? Do we want something to drink?"

Neither Dahoud's throat nor his stomach had the strength to refuse.

Water splashed from the jug into an earthenware bowl. "Drink this, dear." She tilted the bowl against his lips. Precious moisture caressed his tongue. "That's all for now. More wouldn't be good for our stomach. Later we'll have more water. Red wine, too, to replenish the blood we'll be losing. Now be a good boy and take off your clothes, so we can have a look at you." She undid the knot that bound his wrists.

Blood prickled into his fingers. He undressed and stood naked, chilled, and vulnerable.

Laleika pointed at a water bucket. "Wash. We don't want dirt in our wounds."

Kneeling, he dipped his hands into the cool water, wanting to drink, but obeyed.

"Lie down here." She directed him to what he had taken to be a table, but was a sturdy lattice on four posts.

He wanted to bolt, but it would be pointless. With the drum of fear beating in his chest, he lay on the creaking surface.

"Drop your arms down the side. Are we quite comfortable? Good, because we're going to stay like this for three moons, or however long his Highness chooses to keep you alive." She slung strips of wet cowhide around his limbs, tying his limbs to the lattice. Her hair smelled of soapberries and jasmine blooms. "Now we would like a little more water, wouldn't we? Good. Swallow. Slowly. Isn't this nice?"

His tongue moistened with further relief, no longer glued to the roof of his mouth.

She scooped up his clothes and stuffed them into a sack. "They'll be burnt. Have we been tortured before or is it a new experience for us? Our first time? Then I better explain a few things. Everything falls through the lattice —urine, faeces, blood. The straw gets changed twice a day, so don't worry about a thing."

Baryush tapped impatient fingers on the armrests. "Please get started, Laleika."

"First let me assess him properly. Oh my, the poor dear isn't in good shape." She pulled a lamp stand close to the table, ran cool fingertips down Dahoud's side and pinched his thigh. "Much of the muscle has wasted away. Have we not been eating properly? We need a nourishing diet. Milk, with a little egg stirred in, and grated cheese in wine. Once the stomach is well again, we'll have some red meat to build up the muscle tone, so there's something to cut into." Her tender fingers probed his old battle scars. "Arrow, dagger, spear. Spear again. Sword. Did we use to be a warrior?"

"Yes." The past felt two lifetimes ago.

"He used to be a vile monster," Baryush said.

She bent to peer at Dahoud's abdomen. "Was this done professionally?"

He gathered that by 'professionally' she meant 'by a torturer'. "No. I met a leopard."

She clucked her tongue. "You're still alive? Astonishing. Few survive belly wounds. The healer who treated this had remarkable skill."

Dahoud hoped he would live to tell Naima about the compliment.

"Get started." Baryush's fingers drummed again. "I've waited five years to see him suffer. Make him beg. Make him bleed. Do something to his genitals."

She pinched the bridge of her nose. "Highness, this client is too weak for strong treatment. If I apply the egg squeezer, he'll pass out from pain. He'll perform better after a few days of nourishment."

An oasis of hope shimmered on the horizon. In two days, Merida and Mansour might be here.

'I'll give you one hour." Baryush stomped out, trailing his long robe behind him.

"His Highness is an impatient man, but he'll give us three days, you'll see." With skilled fingers, Laleika massaged Dahoud's shoulders and unknotted the pain at the base of his neck. "Leave it to me."

If the torture was delayed for three days, it might not happen at all. In three days, his friends might rescue him. Until then, he had Laleika's protection. Trusting her promise, he surrendered to her attentions.

For an hour, he submitted in helpless trust as she probed every joint and muscle, praised and scolded, and fed him sips of precious water.

When Baryush came back and splayed into his seat, she said, "The client will be ready in three days."

"I want to see him hurt. Now."

"Highness." Laleika folded her arms across her chest. "I'm a master tormentor, not a common bone-breaker!"

"A master tormentor who can't do her job?"

"In three days, he won't faint, and the flaying will produce a much richer blood flow."

Dahoud tried to look as if he was about to faint under her probing stare. It was not difficult.

"That may be so, but I want you to start now. Or have you no useful skill at all? What have I brought you for?"

She opened her mouth as if to hurl a retort, but closed it again. Professional pride and anxiety about her job fought all over her face. Then her lips puckered. "I'll burn him. Most clients stay conscious during that."

Her betrayal ripped like a blade into Dahoud's chest and combined with spiralling fear. He had counted on her promise of three days respite.

Has any woman deserved our trust?

Laleika's fingertips danced along Dahoud's thigh. "If you don't mind the smell, Highness. It makes some spectators sick."

"I'll love the stench of this man's burning flesh," Baryush said. "For what he did to my sister."

"Your sister, Highness?"

"I'll tell you another time. While you peel his genitals."

"Yes, Highness."

She bent over the instrument box. Metal chinked, and she came up with a wooden-handled copper rod. "It will take a while to heat this up." She stoked the charcoal with a poker, sending up yellow flames. When they subsided to an orange glow, she shoved the copper rod into the heat.

Then she held the bowl at Dahoud's mouth again. Pressing his lips together, he refused the traitor's gift.

"Better drink some more, dear. We don't want to be too dehydrated during the burning. It could give a shock." Like a loving mother, she stroked his cheek. "Trust me, it will be an experience. My family's been in the torture business for nine generations, and I've been doing this all my life. Burning is my speciality."

Then she showed him a piece of leather. "Bite down on this when the pain gets bad. It saves the tongue."

"No leather." Baryush leant back in the chair, with his legs stretched out and his hands folded behind his head. "Kindly grant me the pleasure of hearing the monster scream."

"Yes, Highness." She dropped the leather into her toolbox and pulled the rod from the fire to study its red-glowing tip. "That's nice and hot now. It'll make a good burn. I'll start on the thigh. Here." Her cool fingertip marked a spot. "And here, here, here. Are we ready?"

For an instant, the tool pressed his outer thigh, then eased. The pain was minimal, easy to bear. Then the sting zinged. Hot pain seared into his thigh, sung through his flesh, refused to cease. He bit his lips to stop himself from screaming. The rod struck again. And again. And again. His thigh was aflame with singeing grief. The air started to stink of burning meat.

While the instrument reheated in the brazier, Laleika wiped his face with a cool damp cloth. "There, there, now. We're a strong man, we can take this, can't we?" Once again she held the instrument in one hand while she stroked Dahoud's face with the other. "Just relax, dear. This is going to hurt."

The copper seared the length of his thigh. This time, Dahoud screamed. And screamed. And screamed.

⌒

Freshly washed, with her tunic laundered and her hair flowing and fluffy, Merida felt alive and strong. She could even see traces of auras again, although hunger still burrowed in her stomach, and worry churned in her heart.

Holding her arm, Mansour steered her through the crowd to the pedestal at the head of the forum. People cheered. They kissed the hem of Mansour's tunic and thanked him for the gift of water.

At the stone platform, Merida said in a low voice, "The water is Dahoud's gift."

"It's better if they don't know," Mansour said. "Climb up."

They stood side by side, waving, like a royal couple, his hand tight around her arm. She recalled how his aura used to shine with physical and mental energy, with willpower and spirituality. Starvation had dimmed it and overlaid the bright hues with the grey of suffering, but it was still the strongest in aura in Oubar.

Daylight slipped away, and the sky inked into night. By the sparse light of two torches, people drummed and sang, but lacked the strength to dance. Despite their new cleanliness and relief, they looked gaunt, their garments hanging loose on their thinned bodies. There was no wine, no food, no cooking fire.

"Today is the feast of the sacrifice," Mansour said. "We have celebrated it the proper way. In recent years, we killed a mere horse, but today, we killed the old Lord. In recent years, we drank bitter blood, but today, we drink sweet water."

"Water! Water! Water!" people chanted.

Mansour held a jar of water and tossed its contents into the crowd. "Today, we claimed our water back from the Darrians. Next, we'll claim our food! After that, our freedom! Are you ready to fight?"

Fists flew high.

"The Lady Merida will infiltrate their camp. With her cunning, she'll kill their evil general."

He made it sound a certain thing. Merida did not share this confidence in her success, but she understood that she had to look as if she believed it.

"Tomorrow morning she'll go," Mansour announced. "When she's killed that demon, she'll send us a signal. We'll take our arms and storm down. Bereft of their leader, they'll panic, won't know what to do. We'll simply mow them away."

That, too, sounded easier than it could possibly be.

But they lapped it up. They danced, cheered and chanted. They lauded her courage, her daring, her selflessness. A crone climbed onto the podium to pat her hand with spindly fingers. "Mansour is a good man, you'll see."

Nobody mentioned Dahoud. Merida raised her cup in silent salute to his sacrifice.

He might already be dead. She understood how deeply he had loved these people, and she resented how quickly they had forgotten him. To them, he was a sacrifice accepted by the gods.

Before the next nightfall, she might be dead, too. But she would try to free Dahoud, and she would try to save them all.

❧

Dahoud did not want to wake the next morning, but the stinging pain on his thighs and the torturer's voice woke him.

"How are we this morning?" She scooped up straw with both arms, bundled it into sacks, and spread fresh straw across the ground. The she washed her hands very thoroughly, and wiped her instruments. "We don't want an infection, do we? Burn wounds are so sensitive."

"May I have some water on my legs, please?" he begged.

"No, dear." She splashed her face. "Water would soothe the burns, and we can't have that, can we?"

He had to get through this day. By evening, if all went well, Merida would arrive. Tomorrow, if all went well, Mansour would fight to free him.

❧

As soon as the first light lanced through her window, Merida resumed her practice of stabbing the sword down and drawing the blade across.

Sirria came soon after sunrise, carrying a reed basket which she plunked on the rug. Her aura, too, was partially restored, turquoise and blue, and a surprising glimmer of emotional pink, although the grey haze of suffering surrounded her like everyone else. "You'll need these. I told the other women what you were going to do, and they worship your courage. Everyone wants to contribute to your plan." She pulled one item after the other, yellow, orange, and inferno red. "Costume. Sandals. Jewellery. Face-paint. Put them on."

The garish garments left Merida's belly bare and exposed much of her breasts.

"You need more curves. Fake them." Sirria shoved two bunched-up scarves down Merida's front and smeared a triangle of crimson grease in the centre of her chest. "Now show me how you dance."

With the sword balanced on her head, Merida blended Riverian steps with circling hips and shimmies and with the neck slides she had learnt from Haurvatat.

"You look as grim as if you wanted to kill someone," Sirria said. "Smile, Merida, Smile! A smile is a professional dancer's greatest skill. Anything you do will look good as long as you smile."

Merida worked to wipe the concentration from her face, and turned up the corners of her mouth.

"Not just the lips. Light pleasure lanterns in your eyes. Let your smile show how much you enjoy dancing, how much you enjoy the man watching you."

Merida grimaced. She would never enjoy a man's immodest stare raking over her body, although for once, she would suffer it to save lives.

"Believe me," Sirria said quietly, "I hated the man who owned me, but I still managed to smile. It saved my life."

Merida stopped dancing. "The man who owned you?"

"I told you I wasn't always a Koskaran nomad." Sirria's eyes clouded with pain. The pink and grey aura fields spread. "In my younger days, I lived in Zigazia, in a town like this. The Darrians laid siege, like they do now. They won. They killed the men and dragged the women off to slavery. They broke the women's legs—except mine, because I was a dancer. Darrians value dancers. That's why your plan will work." Her voice hardened. "Now practice. Step-ball-change to the left, step-ball-change to the right. Lean your shoulder into it. Shimmy the shoulders if you can. Nice."

"You were a slave? The Darrians took you to dance in a..." Merida could not bring herself to say 'brothel.'

"I was the prince's private concubine. Lighter on your feet." Sirria performed a few steps with a weightless grace that left Merida awed.

"Sirria, your dance is beautiful! You should go in my place. Baryush will be hypnotised."

"Trust me, he wouldn't. To Darrians, no woman is worth looking at once she's past thirty-five. That's when my master discarded me, although I still danced better than anyone else."

"So he set you free?"

"Set me free?" Sirria's laughter dripped with bitterness. "He sold me! I swore to avenge myself. Through you, I will accomplish it at last." From sadness, Sirria's face turned to eager anticipation, like that of a dog at the sight of bloody meat. "Once you've killed Baryush, I'll personally geld and kill every single Darrian down there."

Frightened by Sirria's blood-lust, Merida counted. "Step-ball-change, step-ball-change, smile, smile smile. Should I use finger cymbals?"

"Unless you want the general to summon musicians. You want to get him alone, don't you?"

The cymbals were among the view items rescued from Koskara Town, but Merida had not touched them because the memory of Haurvatat's betrayal and death still hurt. She dug them out of her trunk, tied them to her fingers, and proudly played the six-count rhythm. *Klickeklickeklicke klackecklackeklack.*

"Bravo!" Sirria shouted. "Death to the Darrians!"

Klickeklickeklicke klackecklackeklack.

"We'll geld them, we'll kill them, we'll slice them up."

"What do you think of my cymbal playing? Will it do?"

"Beautiful. Dip your knee deeper on the first step. Shimmy your shoulders on the second and the third if you can. Your cymbals have a wonderful bright sound. I haven't had the chance to play such good cymbals for a long time. May I look at them?"

When she received them, she drew in a sharp breath, as if burned by their touch. "They look Darrian."

"They are. A gift from a Darrian girl. Haurvatat was a concubine in Kirral's harem."

"Haurvatat! Is Haurvatat a friend of yours?" Sirria's voice sounded strangled.

Merida hesitated. She did not want to talk badly about someone who was dead, but Sirria's obvious hatred of all Darrians did not encourage praise. "For a Darrian, she was really quite nice."

"Where is Haurvatat now?" Sirria gripped her wrists. Her aura flared pink and the purple of her mutilated cheek swelled with pulsing anger. "Please, you must tell me."

Insight slammed into Merida's head. "Haurvatat was your...? Oh Virtues, you're Haurvatat's mother?"

"He sold his own daughter into a foreign harem, the bastard!" Sirria screeched. "Where do I find my girl? Is she still imprisoned in Quislabat?"

Merida held on to the wall. "Haurvatat is... I'm so sorry, Sirria..."

"Dead? Dead!" Sirria's face contorted into a mask of hatred. "Gods, I'll make those Darrians pay."

"She was pregnant, and there were complications." Merida groped for something truthful to say that would not add to Sirria's pain. "She was really happy to be in the harem. She had everything she wanted. She talked of you often, what a skilled dancer you were. Haurvatat enjoyed dancing, too, and she taught me the six-step and playing the finger cymbals. She was very religious, very kind to me." Superstitious, stupid, disloyal, and full of contempt for her mother. "I was there when she died. She had a skilled healer's care." Seeing Sirria stroke the finger cymbals, Merida said, "Please, take them."

Sirria's hands closed over the disks, then opened again. "No. You go into the Darrian camp with them and kill the general. Together, we'll avenge my fate and that of my children. Now go. May all the gods guide you and steady your hand."

With the basket clasped under her arm, Merida descended the stairs.

She missed a step and slipped. Her hands chafed against stone, and sharp pain shot into her ankle.

When she tried to stand, the hurt exploded. Leaning on Sirria, she limped back into her room.

How could she have been so careless! The stairs in this house were irregular, and Merida always counted the steps in the dark because the sixteenth was short and steep. But today, in the excitement of her plan, she had forgotten.

By the time Naima arrived, Merida's ankle was purple and hot, and a swelling like an orange sat under the skin.

Naima wrapped the limb tightly in wet bands. "That's all I can do. I have no poppy juice to ease the pain, nothing. One thing's sure: You won't dance any time soon."

"I must. Dahoud is getting tortured." Merida tried to stand, but pain pushed her back on the mat.

"Ah," Sirria said. "So you care about him?"

"Of course not!" Heat scorched Merida's chin and chest. "I mean, of course I do, but not in that way. I wouldn't want anyone to be tormented."

"Not long ago you wanted to see him suffer every pain in the world," Naima remarked. "You can't do anything about it anyway. Not with this foot."

"How long before it heals?"

"Can't tell with sprains. You may be able to walk again tomorrow. Or it may take two moons."

In two moons, they would all have perished from thirst, while Dahoud would be crippled to bloody pulp. She would rest the leg today, and try again tomorrow. She would pray to the Virtues, and even to the foreign idols. She would accept help from anyone.

⁂

Dahoud woke to his body yelling with pain, and his mind screaming with fear. The cold fever of despair gripped his soul. Merida had not come. The plan had failed. He was condemned to suffer this unbearable pain for the rest of his life, for as long as it pleased his tormentors.

Laleika patted his cheek. "We're not looking so good this morning. Have we not slept well?"

The citadel, as well as all the lives in it, were lost.

The torturer bent over him so close that her breasts teased with their smell of soapberries and jasmine. Studying the scars on his abdomen, she expressed surprise again. "It is rare that someone survives abdominal wounds, even if treated with high professional standards. I seldom cut clients' bellies until the final phase. Yours has mended well. The healer of yours was remarkable."

"She is," Dahoud said. "Naima trained in Darria. Healing, and torture."

"I knew a healer of that name once," Laleika said. "A student of mine, in the days when I taught at torture school. A Koskaran."

Perhaps he could save Naima's life. Laleika might have enough influence on Baryush to secure her former student's safety. "Naima often talks fondly of her time in Darria and your teaching. She's inside the citadel now."

"I never liked her," Laleika said. "Poor ethics. A proper professional stays detached, but she enjoyed hurting people. And she was always flaunting her female charms. Her morals would make a cat in heat blush. Disgusting." She scooped the straw into sacks, scrubbed her instruments, and scraped the black scale from the rod.

Dahoud focused his mind on the one good thing he could still achieve. In the three remaining moons of his life, he could weaken the djinn. Inactivity sapped its strength if Dahoud did not feed it with fantasies. However much he longed to hurt the torturer, he must not indulge in the wish, not even to distract himself from the pain. The new host might inherit a weakened djinn, and hopefully be able to resist.

Could Dahoud stay strong enough? Could any man suffer such malicious pain and not wish to hurt his torturer back?

Then Baryush took his seat in the tent, and the day descended into screaming agony.

Baryush said, "Now do you regret what you did to my sister?"

"I regretted that long ago." Dahoud panted with pain, but he summoned defiance. "What about you? Do you regret that you caused her fate? That you kept her presence secret instead of putting her under my protection?"

"Do something to his genitals," Baryush demanded. "Now."

She stroked Dahoud's cheek in the soothing way she always did when she had something particularly painful planned. "Yes, Highness. At once."

≈

When the healer bared Merida's ankle, Sirria's hope sank. Today, dark bruises blotched the swollen part, and reddish-purple stripes streaked from the foot to her calf. No way could Merida dance on this foot. No way could she save the Koskarans. No way could she avenge Sirria's suffering.

Despair carved deep furrows into Merida's face. "I tried to stand on it, I really did."

"The plan still stands," Naima soothed. "Someone else can go in your place. Sirria, are you willing to take the sword?"

"Willing to cut a Darrian prince into slices?" Sirria's scarred cheek pulsed with heat. She laughed grimly. "With the greatest pleasure, if I had a chance of getting him alone. But this task needs someone younger. You're an expert at seducing men, Naima. Why don't you go yourself?"

"I can't dance."

For several heartbeats, Sirria looked grimly at the two other women sitting on the carpet before her. Their cunningly crafted plan vanishing faster than incense smoke.

"What if—" Sirria started.

"The three of us together," Merida suggested at the same time.

"Yes," Naima said. "Between us we have what it takes."

A troupe was plausible: Female entertainers often travelled in groups. If Naima displayed her seductive charms, if Merida balanced the sword on her head, if Sirria danced with professional skill, they could keep the general distracted. But could they kill him? "We need Yora."

"She's only fifteen!" Merida protested.

"Fifteen is perfect for Darrians," Sirria said. "And she can kill."

"Very well," Merida agreed. "Let's pretend we're all from Riverland. Since you don't speak Riverian, leave the talking to Naima and me. If you're interrogated, watch my hands. Say 'yes' if I move my right and 'no' if I move my left."

"We'll be silent, too overwhelmed by his masculine presence to speak." Sirria rubbed her hands with glee. "Darrian men are vain."

CHAPTER 39

Merida and Baryush

Merida felt the general's gaze brush over her body, from her long bronze hair over the paint-enhanced cleavage and her bare belly to her sandalled toes.

"Tell me who you are and why you wish to serve me." His voice sounded dark and deep. The colours of his aura were so bright they almost blinded her. Intellectual. Physical. Spiritual. A strong man, and dangerous.

She repeated the reply she had already given to the guards on the slope, the guards at the camp entrance, the guards outside the tent. "We're entertainers from Riverland, fleeing Koskaran persecution."

Through clouds of incense smoke, she scanned the tent. Light falling through slits in the roof painted stripes on the thick rugs. Piles of embroidered cushions suggested a prince's leisure rather than a commander's work.

Wafts of jasmine and cedar mingled with the smell of boiled lentils. The stew bowls stood empty, but the remnants of the scent still twisted her stomach. Oranges heaped on trays cried out to be grabbed and eaten. Water pooled in her mouth.

Baryush sat in a large wooden chair with his legs stretched before him. Rosettes, peacocks and palm trees adorned his tunic, and his fingers glinted with rings. His beard looked like a mass of oiled black snails. His lips smiled. "Are you, indeed?"

Sirria fell before his feet, her face on the ground. "If you will permit this lowly woman at your feet to speak, your Fragrant Highness, oh Sparkling Ray of the Silver Sun, I humbly put forward that we are dancers, foreigners in this country. We were entertaining at Oubar, and the siege trapped us in that accursed fortress."

"Rise, old woman." Baryush kept looking at Merida. "If you are who you say, you shall live through this night, and many others. If you are not..." He let the sentence trail off, unfinished.

Merida's pulse beat so violently in her throat she could barely swallow. From the corner of her eye, she noted a curved sheathed sword on the table. It looked identical to Dahoud's.

A similarly dressed but younger man in the second chair said, "That ruse has been tried before."

Two slaves with expressionless faces waved woven fans up and down.

Baryush scrutinised Merida with pursed lips. "What is your name?"

"Zaina."

"A Riverian named Zaina. How unusual."

"It's the only name under which I've ever performed."

Baryush folded his hands in his lap. "In which country were you born?"

Merida kept her gaze steady. "In Riverland."

"All of you?"

"I can't remember," Yora said.

He pointed a jewelled finger at Naima. "Your skin is too dark for a Riverian."

Naima shrugged. "My mother is vague about who fathered me."

The man in the background tapped his fingers on the table. "These women talk too much."

Merida's skin turned cold at his words, but Baryush laughed. "What else would you expect from entertainers? They claim to be Riverian. I'll have this checked out soon enough." The dark blue of his mental aura thickened. He whispered an order, and the slave leant the fan against a tent pole and slid out of the tent.

A scream shuddered through the air, raw and piercing like the cries of the Queen's peacocks.

"Merely a captive being tortured," Baryush said. "How many persons are inside the citadel?"

"About seven hundred and fifty, but many are sick. Many have died." By revealing some truths, Merida hoped to gain his trust. "Food is terribly short."

"Go on."

"We haven't eaten properly for three moons. Rations are down to two dates per day. We're foreigners, so they begrudge us even that little. That's why they've thrown us out."

"You're lucky they didn't eat you. That's what usually happens to outsiders during a siege." He flicked a hand towards the tent entrance. "You may enter, Yannush."

A man in a silvery robe prostrated himself.

"You may rise. These women claim to be from Riverland. Talk to them in Riverian."

"Yes, your Fragrant Highness." The lamp shone on the alert pointed face of a rat.

"Yann!" Merida cried, and at once regretted her outburst.

Baryush fixed his eyes on her. "So you know each other? Convenient, most convenient. Tell me, Yannush: Who are these women?"

Merida's stomach fluttered. What had she revealed about herself that morning on the rooftop?

"I know only the tall one, Highness." Yann pointed at Merida. "I met her in Djildit Town last year, when she performed as a bellydancer at the Black Dog Inn. She speaks Riverian with the fluency of a native, and behaves like one. She called herself Zaina, though I doubt that's her real name. She was in trouble with Kirral's greenbelts."

"Thank you, Yannush, that will do. You have permission to leave." He turned to Merida again. "You shall eat tonight."

A series of screams ripped through the air again, so sharp she could feel the hurt slice into her bones.

"That's the former satrap of Koskara," Baryush said. "Did you meet him?"

Merida stiffened, uncertain how to reply.

Sirria spoke in her place. "Your Fragrant Highness, I beg you, do not torment our gentle Zaina with the memory of this monster!"

"Ah." Baryush's face softened. "So you have met the djinn of darkness, and suffered. You're lucky to be still alive. Rejoice, Zaina: this man will never hurt a woman again. Do you wish to watch his torture?"

"Thank you, Highness." Her voice quivered. "I'd rather not see the monster again." At least, she knew which direction the screams had come from and where to find Dahoud when the time came.

"What's the new Lord like?" Baryush asked.

"Mansour is a brute," Naima claimed. "A fanatic hater of foreigners. Yesterday, when we waited for food, he drove us out of the queue. Look what he did to Zaina." She whipped up Merida's skirt and ripped off the bandage, baring the swollen ankle.

"What kind of weapons do the defenders have?"

"Weapons?" Merida blinked as if confused by the word. "They have a lot of spears, I think. And arrows and knives, but I'm not sure about those. May we dance for you tonight, Highness? We have a very special dance." She gyrated her hips in a slow, sinuous circle.

"I shall enjoy your display once you have regained your strength. Tonight, and five days after, you shall be my guests. Eat, rest, allow your injuries to heal. Then you shall dance."

"Grant us the pleasure of dancing for you tonight," Merida pleaded.

Baryush smiled. "The wait will sweeten your pleasure."

Dahoud screamed again.

"How much will you pay for our performance?" Naima demanded suddenly.

A frown slashed down Baryush's forehead. "You come here seeking refuge, and demand to be paid?"

Merida's heart beat in her throat. Naima's greed put their safety at risk.

Yora locked her arms across her chest. "If you want us do dance for you, you must hire us. How much will you pay?"

Were they both mad?

Baryush glowered. "You get shelter, you get food, you get the honour of performing for me. That is payment enough."

"We accept the terms of hire," Naima said.

Yora grinned.

"You'll have a tent, and as much food as you want. Bread and yoghurt first; gentle food for starving stomachs. You may leave." Baryush waved as if shooing away chickens. He turned to the other man. "See to the food and the tent."

"At once. Guards outside the tent?"

"Naturally." Baryush covered a yawn with his manicured hand. "Never trust any civilian arriving in an army camp when a war is on."

⤨

Food! Bowls of yoghurt, platters of dates and piles of crisp golden bread, all fragrant and blessing the senses. Sirria's mouth ran with water, and her stomach growled at the sight of it.

"This food is our payment," Naima said. "You heard what he said. We're eating it not as guests; so the rules of hospitality don't apply. We're free to kill him. Eat slowly. Our stomachs aren't used to it. Chew well, or it will come up again."

Sirria dug into the bread, forcing herself to grind it with her teeth before sending it to her demanding stomach. It felt so good, so soothing, so sating.

Then she scanned the tent: Everything was in Darrian colours of dark blue, turquoise and pink, embroidered with twining palm trees, peacock tails and giant rosettes. Even the smell was Darrian, that mix of cedar and sandal oils, of leather and cruelty.

"I'll marry Mansour," Yora said, shovelling yoghurt into her mouth. "Then he'll have to wrestle me."

"Marry Mansour?" Merida sounded aghast. "He's almost forty!"

Yora stabbed a yoghurt-laden spoon forward. "Is that too old? When men get old, does their seed dry up and come out as powder?"

Merida coughed so violently that Sirria thought she was going to vomit up her food.

Naima licked yoghurt off her fingers. "Mansour is still working fine. You can have fun with him."

"Marriage isn't about fun," Merida stated with the earnestness of a lecturing priestess.

Arranging the cushions around her into a cosy nest, Sirria chuckled: she had had fun with both her husbands. "Mansour's a good man, Yora, and he's lucky to get you."

"Mansour may want a say in the matter," Merida said.

Yora tore off a chunk of bread and chewed. "I'll tell him when we've finished fighting."

"He'll be proud of you when you tell him how many Darrians you've killed," Sirria said. Yora would be lucky if she lived to tell

Mansour anything. This mission was almost certain suicide for all four of them. But they would kill the general, and Sirria planned to take several Darrians into death with her.

She scrunched a palm-embroidered cushion corner in her hand. "The Darrians got my first husband. Gouged out his eyes. Impaled him, alive. He hung there for three days. I was a dancer, so they didn't smash my legs as they did with others. Their commander claimed me as a concubine and tattooed me with his property mark." She touched the knotted scar on her cheek where she had gouged the tattoo out with a piece of sharp flint. "He got two children out of me, then he had no further use for me. I couldn't even hug my little ones farewell." She paused, letting that sink in. "That's how Darrians are. That's what they want to do to everyone in the citadel. We won't let them. Kill the Darrians! Kill them! Kill, kill kill!"

"Hush." Naima laid a finger on her lip glancing at the entrance. "The guards can hear."

The flap rustled as if in response. Sirria held her tongue.

"May I enter?" a female voice asked.

Yora fingered her belt as if searching for the daggers that were not there. Merida pulled the top of her costume higher before calling the visitor in.

The silver-haired woman carried a basket and a bucket of water. "I'm Laleika. I'm here to treat a sprained ankle."

Merida unwrapped the bandage. "Are you a healer?"

"A torturer. Put your foot in the bucket. The cold water will help. Didn't the healer in the citadel warn you not to walk?"

"The healer had no time for foreigners, and she was interested only in men." Merida glanced at Naima to see her reaction to this claim, but the healer sat facing the corner, with her head bent low over the food. "Besides, I had no choice: we were expelled from the citadel."

"Rest the foot overnight," the torturer said. "I'll send more cold water later."

"How soon will I be able to dance?"

"You'll know when you're ready. Now I must get to work. I have a client to torture."

⚮

Another morning. Pain flamed from Dahoud's singed limbs and flowed like poison through his body. He had bitten his lips to a bloody pulp. If he was being tortured to extract information, he would soon reveal anything. But for him, this choice did not exist. There would be no release.

He could almost hear the wings of death-birds circling above his head, ready to swoop down and carry his life into the realm of death. He wished they would hurry, but Baryush wanted to see him live and suffer for a long while yet.

While Laleika stoked the stove for another session, a slave carried in a second chair.

Dahoud heard Baryush's polite, deep voice. "After you, please, my honoured guest."

Straw rustled. Dahoud turned his head to look. The effort of moving sent agonising spikes through the burned skin of his neck. He saw Baryush's jewel-encrusted sandals in the straw. Beside them, a second pair of feet in pink slippers with purple pompoms. He forced his glance higher. Hairless calves. A yellow tunic. A large curving dagger. And still higher, a bruise-coloured turban and a waxed moustache.

"I believe you two are already acquainted?" Baryush asked. "Would you care for wine, Kirral? Red and fruity. It's from my personal estates. Perhaps a sip for Dahoud, too, to celebrate the pleasure of this meeting?"

Baryush instructed Laleika to proceed with her scheduled programme. "My guest wishes to compare Darrian torture methods with those from Quislak. He tells me he bricks up traitors alive, is this not interesting? Of course, Dahoud is a traitor only by Quislaki standards, because he has broken his oath to the Queen. For me, he is the man who violated my sister."

Dahoud swallowed as much wine as his swollen tongue allowed, but it did not dull the pain when Laleika rolled a glowing device across his chest. Nor when she flayed the insides of his thighs, cutting strips from his skin. He screamed.

"I knew you would come to a bad end," Kirral said. "It has been entertaining." He ran his fingernails down the dagger's bronze hilt. The scraping noise coincided with the work of Laleika's scalpel. "I came to Koskara to study the effects of a siege on the human soul, anticipating valuable insights in fallen Oubar." He pulled out the knife, studied the shiny blade, and rammed it back into its sheath. "How is the Lady Teruma?"

"Don't know." The swollen, bitten tongue could barely form the words. "Don't know... where.. Teruma is." Kirral might suspect that his disloyal head-wife was in the citadel, but he must not get confirmation. If he found out, he would do his utmost to get her into his hands alive for gruesome torture. By denying her presence, Dahoud might give her the chance of a fast death.

The rest of his own life stretched like an unrelenting nightmare, with pain beyond what he could endure, yet never enough to grant the oblivion of a faint.

≈

All night and all morning, the women were practically prisoners in their tent, plied with food and pampered with all they might desire – except the freedom to explore the camp and the chance to kill. Merida chafed from the inactivity.

At noon, they received a visit. The suspicious young officer from Baryush's command camp asked, "You're ready to dance today?"

"Yes!" Merida claimed, quickly reddening her lips with crimson grease.

"You'll dance on the practice ground where everyone can see. The army band will play."

"For the soldiers? We're artists," Merida protested. "We want to dance for his Highness."

"You're hired entertainers. You'll dance for whoever you're told. Hurry up."

"With pleasure," Sirria said. She wrapped her disfigured face in a flimsy shawl and daubed crimson on Merida's cleavage.

≈

Seven musicians blew straighthorn trumpets, clanked huge cymbals, and pounded kettledrums.

Hundreds of sex-hungry men leered. Merida shielded her bare belly with her tambourine. She picked up the cheerful Darrian six-count rhythm from the band's tune. With the weight on her good foot, she performed hipdrops on the other side, adding shoulder rolls, and otherwise leaving the dancing to her friends.

Sirria's dance was a mesmerising spectacle. The crone moved with the sinuous grace of an agile cat. Naima walked around the parameter, shimmying her shoulders so her spectacular breasts quivered. Yora hopped around, apparently unaware of any rhythm.

The men applauded, whistled and leered.

After an hour when the officer came to escort them back, Merida hobbled up to the chair where Baryush was sitting. "Highness, what you have just seen was not worthy of you. We have an amazing act which would be wasted on common men. We perform it only for men of noble birth. No band is required; we make our own music. The dance is..." She lowered her lids, inviting a blush to her cheeks. "It's very sophisticated, of a refined sensuality that crude minds cannot appreciate."

He stroked his beard. "You have permission to perform in my private tent tonight. Be ready by dusk."

Only six more hours. Merida wanted to yell with triumph.

CHAPTER 40

Sword Dance

Even after Laleika had scraped her tools, stowed her scalpels in the box, and bowed her way out of the tent, Dahoud's singed skin screamed with red heat.

"So, dear Dahoud," Kirral said. "We are alone at last. You were going to tell me where Teruma is." He pulled the brazier closer to the torture table and stoked the charcoal, reviving its heat. Even from a foot away, Dahoud's burns started to boil again.

"Are you wondering if my good friend Baryush approves of this conversation? Of course he does. He merely requests that I do not hasten your demise." Kirral blew into the charcoals. They flared glowing red. "What shall we talk about? The choice is entirely yours. Do you want me to cool your skin? Cool water on your skin will feel good." He picked up a wet sponge and squeezed it. "Shall we talk about Teruma?"

Dahoud had granted Teruma his protection. "I don't know where she is," he claimed.

Kirral shifted the brazier closer. Dahoud's nerves screamed from the pain.

Kirral returned to the chair, stretched out his legs, and laced his fingers behind his neck. "Think about it."

Silence stretched, every heartbeat an agonising eternity. Dahoud knew he could not hold out forever. Soon his skin would peel off in the fire, flesh bubbling and smoking, and he would scream until his throat burst.

Then the entrance swished, admitting Baryush. Relief hit Dahoud's nerves like rain splattering on a still-hot road.

Baryush smoothed the folds of his silken robe and glanced from Kirral to the brazier. "I hope you are both enjoying your conversation."

"Indeed," Kirral said. "I find it highly educational. The facial expressions are worth observing."

Baryush adjusted the fit of a jewel-glinting armband. "Perhaps you would like to take a break from your studies. Join me and my officers for a beaker of wine."

"Another time."

"We have a troupe of bellydancers to entertain us tonight."

Bellydancers? Dahoud's hope flared. Had Merida made it into the camp after all? Was she still alive? Would she put her plan into action, would he be saved?

Dropping the sponge into the bucket, Kirral rose.

Realisation pierced Dahoud like a spear. If Kirral saw Merida, her ruse would be ruined. Dahoud had to keep him here – and the only way was by offering himself up for more suffering.

"Teruma is in Koskara," he panted.

Kirral's smile set the corners of his moustache quivering. "Is she? Where?"

"I won't say another word until you take the brazier away."

"Will you not?" Kirral's green eyes sparkled with delight. He blew into the brazier to increase the heat. "Baryush, I shall not accept your invitation tonight. Neither wine nor dancers are as interesting as the entertainment I shall find here."

⊱

Lunge-stab-slash, lunge-stab-slash, lunge-stab-slash. Merida repeated the sequence in her mind over and over. *Smile. Smile, smile, smile, and lunge-stab-slash.* Everything depended on her wielding of Baryush's sword: their lives, Dahoud's rescue, the freedom of Koskara.

At last, the sun faded. Painted and ajingle with jewellery, the women filed into Baryush's private tent.

The air was thick with incense and perfume oil. "Ah, here are the charming dancers who will delight us tonight," Baryush said.

Merida's heart almost stopped. "You have guests, Highness?" She tried to speak casually as she glanced around, but her heart squeaked with fear. Instead of assassinating one man, they would have to fight four.

"Fear not, my enchanting Zaina." Baryush raised his cup. "My cousins are all officers of princely blood and discerning taste, well deserving of your special dance."

"We're honoured," she brought out. "Shall we begin?"

She drummed her fingers on the tambourine: *doumdakkadakdak, doumdakkadak. Doumdakkadakdak, doumdakkadak.* Sirria's cymbals joined: *clinkeclink, clinkeclink.*

Sirria launched into a pattern of steps so light-footed, she seemed to float in the air. Naima faced away from the men, then arched backwards to place her palms behind her feet, granting a spectacular view of her cleavage.

Auras flared like beacons.

The music, the movement and the heady incense gave Merida confidence while lulling the audience into a sensual trance.

Four dancers. Four men. Four swords. She resolved to risk it. "Each man may place his sword on the head of the dancer of his choice to claim her favour," she improvised. "We'll balance the swords to show our skill, and as a sign of our submission."

"We don't lie with women until the war is won," Baryush said.

"Lie with us later. Waiting will sweeten the pleasure." Merida gave him a dazzling smile. "But you may claim your choice now."

The officer who had escorted them earlier devoured Naima's cleavage with his eyes. "I'd rather pick a healthy woman now than pluck a sick one after a siege."

"I favour a woman who comes to me willingly." Baryush smiled at Merida.

"Do it, then," Merida lured. "Place your sword on the head of your dancer."

The door felt flapped, the bead curtain clanked, and a small man with a striped headscarf crept in. "Sorry I'm late, Highness, gentlemen. I was held up, but I wouldn't want to miss the show."

Merida's jaw fell. Five men, four women. What now?

Baryush must have seen her shock and misread its cause. "He's a commoner, but he won't claim a concubine. He deserves the honour of watching because he has helped us greatly. Joining us tonight is part of his reward." He waved at the cushions. "Please sit, Criton."

Criton? Could this be the thief, the sacrifice, the man she had set free? A lump of metal glinted on his chest. It was him. If he recognised her, all would be lost.

Averting her face from this man, Merida repeated, "Place your sword on the head of your choice."

The officers rose.

"Why can't I have a woman?" Criton demanded. "Didn't I tell you about the copper that will make you rich? Didn't I give you the citadel's water supply?"

"You'll get a woman when the citadel falls," Baryush said. He stood before Merida. His body smelled of leather and cedar oil. When he placed the sword on her head, he adjusted its balance with the tenderness of a lover.

"I don't want an old hag!" one man grumbled.

The entranced mood cracked, bristling with hostility. Shoulders squared, fists balled, elbows stuck out. The men seemed willing to fight over possession of Yora and Naima.

Then the youngest of the men, a slender youth, said, "Take this one. I'll have the crone." He kissed Sirria's hand. "I will honour you in place of the mother I've never known."

When Merida glided into her dance, all the stars of the night sky swayed in her hips. Baryush's eyes were those of a worshipper, submissive and devout. The man was her captive, hers to play with at will. Astonishing pleasure thrilled through her limbs. The web her dance spun around him was bodily as much as it was mental, and it felt good. A long-closed door opened, letting unimagined passion stream in. This could not be a sin: she was doing not for herself, but to save others. She let her scruples drop from her mind and her inhibitions melt. For once, being a woman did not restrict her, did not make her the victim of a man. Instead, it gave freedom, power, control over the man, sent a strange passion pulsing through her pelvis. She was the one in charge, and she liked it. Stunned by the ferocity of her pleasure, she rode on a wave of joy.

She held the tambourine under her left arm so she could tap it with a single hand—*doumdakkadakdak, doumdakkadak. Doumdakkadakdak,*

SWORD DANCE

doumdakkadak—and twisted her hips in soft snaky undulations, while slowly raising the free hand to the sword.

The hilt was on the wrong side. Baryush, in placing it with his right hand, had put the hilt out of Merida's easy reach.

She could not drum while she moved the sword to where she needed it to be. To hide what she was doing, she launched into a slow spin.

"That one's an impostor!" Criton yelled. "I know her. She's—"

Merida had to stop him. She lunged, stabbed, slashed. The blade sliced into his throat. Blood shot out in an arching spurt.

Baryush yelled a command. Furniture toppled. Weapons clanked.

The plan was foiled.

Sword in hand, Merida sprinted out of the tent. Pain shot through her sprained ankle.

She limped to where Dahoud's screams had come from. The air smelled of charred sweet flesh and agony.

She saw Dahoud's body tied flat on a table. Blood oozed between purple-blotched bruises and crimson burns.

Before she could move to cut him free, her arm was yanked behind her back. A cold edge scraped her throat. "My dear Merida," said a voice like treacly rubber. "What a surprise to meet you. Drop that weapon."

Shock curled over her in a cold wave, and her skin crawled. What now? Yora had warned her about actions which would not work in this hold: slipping out of the attacker's grip, prying his fingers from the weapon, headbutts, kicks - all useless.

"Drop the weapon," Kirral repeated. The knife pressed against her gullet. She let the sword fall.

"Please, don't hurt me," she whimpered.

The grip slackened a fraction. Kirral was no warrior.

She brought both hands up and clamped them over the one holding the knife to stop it from moving. Then she pulled it downwards, until the blade was a finger's breadth away from her throat.

Bless Yora and her fight drills. Merida twisted her upper body. The dagger point rammed against Kirral's chest - but it glanced off his ribs.

She chambered her good leg and slammed it into the back of Kirral's knee. She rammed a knee into his groin, and pounded a fist on his skull. The Woodpecker was so versatile.

With a groan, Kirral collapsed into the straw.

427

She hurried to touch her fingers to Dahoud's pulse. His eyes flew open. "Merida?"

'We have to fight." The water in the bucket smelled clean, so she sluiced it over his burns. Since the knots of his fetters were too tight to undo, she sawed through them with Kirral's dagger, careful not to cut him further. "Can you stand? Sit?"

Dahoud raised his shoulders from the table, but sank back, his mouth gaping as if he were about to vomit.

'Try again, slowly." She supported his back with her arm. "I'm counting on you for the fight."

Sitting, Dahoud tested his limbs. "You killed Baryush?" His voice sounded as if his mouth was crammed with sand.

"I couldn't. There were too many in the tent for us."

"Us? Who came with you?"

"Sirria. Naima. Yora. I don't know if they live." She grabbed his shoulders. "How bad are your injuries? Can you move? Can you fight? Everything depends on us now. I'll send the signal, and you must kill Baryush."

"Right." Dahoud swung his legs off the table.

A cold hand clasped Merida's ankle and jerked. Falling, she remembered to curl and roll. She landed on her back, just as Kirral bounced up, dagger in hand.

Merida snapped both feet up into his thighs. He stumbled backwards into the table, where Dahoud clamped his legs around him. Dahoud's hand snaked under Kirral's jaw.

With his neck caught in the crook of Dahoud's elbow, Kirral let go of the dagger. His fingers clawed without effect and Dahoud's arm. Then his hands dropped. The lips tightened, the eyes closed, and the face went white.

"Don't kill him," Merida whispered. "He hosts a djinn, and his death would set the djinn free. Better keep him imprisoned under close guard so he can do no harm." They could keep Kirral alive for decades, and if Helva Hein was right, the djinn would weaken during this time from inactivity. When Kirral finally died, the new host would have a weak djinn to combat, and might have a chance to resist.

Dahoud continued the chokehold. Then he nodded and dropped the Consort's slack body onto the torture table. "Quick now. We need to tie him up before he comes to."

Hurriedly, Merida gathered up the slashed leather straps. "Put on Kirral's clothes."

"Why?"

"Do you want to walk around nude? Wearing those, you'll pass for Kirral. Besides, anyone checking this tent must see a naked prisoner tied up."

While Dahoud donned the pink tunic and turban, Merida knotted the pieces of leather and tied Kirral to the lattice. As soon as he stirred into consciousness, she gagged him with a fistful of straw.

"Choose, Kirral. A quick death now -" She nodded to Dahoud, who laid the dagger blade at Kirral's throat. "Or a long life as a prisoner?"

"In an old mine shaft," Dahoud added. "Deep, dank, desperate. Endless time to remember Paniour."

Merida liked the symmetry. "Water and food provided, of course. You'll learn how it feels to slowly go mad."

Dahoud stroked the flat of the dagger blade across Kirral's white jaw. "So what is it to be? Blink left for the dungeon, right if you want your throat cut."

Merida knew that Kirral lacked the courage for an instant death, but it was good to see him torn, replicating the torment of his victims.

Kirral groaned through the gag. At last, he blinked left.

"Prison? What an interesting choice," Merida said. "You'll find it educational. We'll pelt you from above with food, and perhaps invite guests to taunt you. Mostly, there will be silence. No company - except rats. Big Koskaran rats, with teeth as long as human thumbs."

Outside, Baryush's voice rang. "Find the dancers. Kill them! - Peacock unit, search the supply tents. Lion unit, along the palisades..."

Merida fastened the wobbly tower of Dahoud's turban with a jewel pin. "Kill Baryush. I count on you."

"I will," he said. "My Lady, I will."

CHAPTER 41

Battle

Dahoud was stiff and dizzy from days on the rack. Flexing his back against the tent pole, he fought for balance. Tentative stretches opened his scabbed wounds, sending dribbles of blood down his legs.

An old soldier with a leather helmets peeked in. "Excuse me, Highness. I must search the tent."

"Of course. Please come in." The perfumed tunic chafed like fire on Dahoud's raw flesh. "What are you searching for?"

"Two women in dance costume. Have you seen them?"

Casually, as if adjusting a garment for style and fit, Dahoud pulled a section of the tunic away from his thighs to stop blood from seeping into the fabric. "Can't say I did. Are they important, those women?"

"The high general wants them." The soldier glanced at Kirral, naked and squirming. "Clearly they're not in here. Sorry to have bothered you, Highness."

"Where is Baryush? He promised to show me how he tortures that captive. When will he return?"

"I cannot foretell his Highness' movements," the old soldier said stiffly.

"Well, tell him I'm waiting." Dahoud tapped the dagger hilt with the impatience of a bored man not used to waiting for anyone. "Tell him also that I wish to reminisce about our first encounter five years ago, when I had the pleasure of meeting his sister. He will understand what I mean."

"When I see him, Highness." Despite his deferential bow, the man sounded exasperated with the visitor's lack of priorities.

As soon as the soldier had left, Dahoud picked up the sword Merida had dropped and tested it in his hand. The grip fit comfortably in his palm and the weight of the curved blade was familiar, a sister to his own sword.

He scanned the tent. With the anchored torture table in the centre, the big chair on one side and the brazier on the other, Baryush would have no room for elaborate manoeuvres.

He dropped the turban and dagger and kicked off Kirral's tight shoes. Bare soles gave a better hold on the slippery straw. With his sword in his right, and the bucket in place of a shield, he took position beside the tent entrance.

With luck, Baryush would take the message to mean his enemy was free and waiting. With luck, he would rush into the tent alone. With luck, he would take a moment to see the naked captive tied to the table was Kirral, giving Dahoud time to strike. With luck, Baryush was an unskilled swordsman. With luck, a single quick slash to the throat would suffice.

Dahoud would need a lot of luck.

Kirral, stretched flat on the table, strained against his bonds and groaned through the straw gag.

Dahoud ignored him. Bending his legs into a fighting stance, he listened for sounds from the outside. Horses whinnied, armour clanked, soldiers cursed.

Dahoud waited. And waited. The scabbed wounds itched, and more blood oozed.

~

Merida limped to the tent where she had danced. Stuffed with comforts, it would create a bigger blaze than any of the soldiers' tents. Her pulse pounded in her head, pumping a hundred thoughts at once. What had happened to her comrades? Could the injured Dahoud defeat the general in a fight?

Dahoud had accepted her orders. Was this because he was too weakened by torture to do anything else? Was he glad to submit to guidance and hand over the responsibility? Later, she would think more about this. If she was the one in charge, she did not need to fear Dahoud. If she did not have to fear him, she might even like him.

The tent was unguarded. Her knees quaked as she lifted the flap.

Inside, the air was soaked with the smells of wine, incense, excrement and blood. Bodies lay amidst broken beakers, tumbled tables and bloodied cushions. Criton lay where Merida had killed him, his dying hand clutched around the copper on his chest.

Naima had almost reached the exit. Her intestines spilled crimson across her white breasts. Her eyes were wide with horror, her beautiful face forever contorted with final agony. Behind her lay a Darrian, face down in faeces and congealing blood.

Sirria lay at the far end. She had managed to slit her opponent's throat even as he had rammed his dagger into her neck. They lay embraced in a pool of shared blood. To separate them, she pulled the dagger that locked the man's arm to Sirria's neck.

Three palm trees, entwined. Was this the emblem of the family that had held Sirria enslaved? If so, had she avenged herself and her children, or had she... Sudden insight sent sick bile into Merida's throat. The man had offered to honour the crone in place of the mother he had never known. It could not be. It must not!

Merida pried a cymbal from Sirria's fingertip, wiped off the thickening crimson, and compared it with the dagger hilt. The picture was the same. Refusing to believe, she took another cymbal off Sirria's stiffening fingers, then the third and the fourth. Still identical.

The man had killed his unknown mother, and Sirria had killed her lost son.

Merida jerked herself out of her horrified daze into action. At least, Yora had got away. She piled the cushions into a heap which she fed with lamp oil, and spilled burning charcoal on top. The flaming tent would call Mansour, cause a distraction in the camp, and serve as pyre for the two heroines.

On the way out, she snatched the striped headcloth from Criton, hid her hair under it, and hitched up her long skirt. It was not much of a disguise. Then she grabbed a torch and started to set fire to further tents.

Standing in fighting stance stretched the wounded flesh of Dahoud's thighs. Blood trickled down his legs.

At last, the entrance flap thudded and Baryush stormed in, his jewels flashing, the hem of his robe brushing the straw, his sword naked and ready to strike. Alone.

At the sight of the tied captive, he halted only for a heartbeat. Then he spun to block Dahoud's slash. Bronze clanked on bronze.

Dahoud struck again. Once more, his blow glanced off Baryush's blade. Baryush slashed downwards, past the bucket-shield, at Dahoud's leg. Dahoud jumped back just in time so the sword only grazed his skin.

Dahoud shoved the bucket against his opponent, sending him back in a stagger. For an instant, Baryush fought for balance, and his sandals slipped on the straw. Dahoud aimed for the throat, but Baryush evaded. The blade cut only his arm. Baryush swung his sword faster than Dahoud could anticipate. This time, the sword sliced deeper into the side of his thigh.

"Thank you for the invitation." Baryush spoke with effortless courtesy, as if the line of crimson beading on his arm was nothing, as if the fighting did not even speed his breath. His eyes glinted like obsidian flakes. "I trust Kirral will tell me how you got free. The chance to kill you gilds my day."

Weakened from deprivation and blood loss, Dahoud's limbs threatened to fold.

Baryush lunged, and blade crashed against blade. The Darrian was strong, fast, and fit. Even his long robe barely hampered his agility.

"Fire!" A scream went up outside. "Fire, fire fire!" more voices screeched. "Where's the general?"

Merida had succeeded in setting the fire, and the soldiers could not cope without their leader. Good.

Blood ran down Dahoud's cheeks, although he did not recall cuts to his face. More blood was seeping from his thigh, and his strength with it.

"Tired, Besieger?"

Dahoud tried every trick of swordcraft he knew, made every attempt the limited space permitted, threw every drop of skill into the fight, but could not match the blinding speed of Baryush's blade. He barely managed to block the attacks. The sword grip in his palm was slick with sweat and blood.

He must keep the sword moving, must maintain the fluid curves, must not halt the flow, or Baryush would break through. The Mare Mother be thanked, he still had strength in his sword arm, even as his knees started to buckle. On horseback, he had always swung his sword in a figure-eight. But there was no room for wide arcs in the tent.

"Were you hoping for a quick death? There will be nothing fast." Baryush promised. "Not for the Black Besieger." His blade hissed through the air. "I'll have the pleasure of slicing you limb by limb. Your life will bleed into the straw."

The air was thick with the smells of Baryush's cedarwood perfume, charcoal smoke and sweat. Dahoud's pulse pounded as if about to burst his chest, his bones jolted with every blow, and dizziness draped around him like a strangling mist.

His vision blurred. All he could still see clearly was the flames of the oil lamps reflected in Baryush's jewels, in his eyes, in his sword.

Blood dripped from his forehead into his eyes, blinding him. He backed away from the force of the general's fury until the edge of the torture table pressed into his back. A hard strike knocked the sword from his grip. It clattered to the ground. Now he held but a wooden bucket against the pelting blows.

Baryush would aim for Dahoud's knee, and the next stroke would cripple him. Had he lost his chance to kill Baryush and save Koskara? Merida was counting on him.

Get stronger arms.

The table was almost as high as a horse. No time or space for a run. He shoved the bucket in Baryush's face, threw his hands back to brace against the table edge, and took his body weight on both arms. He chambered both legs and snapped them forward, slamming them against Baryush's thighs. While Baryush stumbled, Dahoud raised himself up on his arms again. This time, he pushed himself forward, his legs wide.

He crashed against his opponent, landed on top of him.

The impact knocked the brazier. Sparks showered and charcoal scattered. Rustling flames rose and crept under the table, gnawing at the damp straw. The air stunk of Kirral's piss and smouldering felt. Scratchy smoke thickened the air.

Dahoud pinned Baryush and tried to prise the sword from his hand. He was the better wrestler, but his body was stiff and weakened from wounds. His thighs barely had the strength to hold Baryush underneath him.

Then the straw burst into orange. The heat bit into Dahoud's seared thighs.

Panting, they fought for possession of the weapon. Baryush tossed it to the tent flap, where Dahoud could not reach it without releasing his hold.

Kirral's curved dagger lay in the burning straw. Dahoud used all the strength of his right arm to keep Baryush's wrists pinned to the ground, and stretched towards the weapon. Flames gnawed at his hand as he snatched the dagger from the burning straw.

"One last time, Baryush: I'm sorry for what I did to your sister. But I'm not sorry for killing you."

He drew the blade across Baryush's throat. Blood shot up and showered him in its hot spurt.

Dahoud stood, knife in hand, and slammed a salute for his dead enemy.

On the table, Kirral's naked body bucked and twisted in his bonds. His eyes bulged, and big sweat beads grew on the fear-contorted face. Yellow flames rose from the straw, snaked around the table's legs, licked at the lattice. The straw gag swallowed his gurgle.

Trembling with fatigue, Dahoud kicked the smouldering straw away from the table. He had no time to move Kirral to another prison. He had to help Mansour's army to win the battle.

Dahoud brushed the worst of the blood from his tunic front with a handful of straw, wrapped the sword in Kirral's embroidered cloak, and ambled to the camp gate. The sky was bleeding into night, wrapping the camp in darkness.

Four guards, bare-chested with kilts and collars, were watching the mountain.

"Why aren't you helping to put out the fires?" Dahoud demanded.

"Our orders are to stay here, Highness." The speaker stared at the dark stains on Dahoud's chest, his eyes thinning to slits.

Dahoud could claim it was spilled wine, but an aristocrat would not explain himself to a common soldier. "Do your officers condone idleness?"

The guard clutched his spear in both fists and returned his attention to the dark slope. "We do as we're told."

"Very commendable." Soft wind whooshed against the pine tops on the mountain side. How close were Mansour's warriors? Since the guards would not be diverted, he had to stampede the animals.

When Merida came limping towards the gate like a bored woman out for an evening stroll, Dahoud snatched the chance. "That's one of dancers Baryush is seeking. She needs to be escorted to him immediately." He wrinkled his nose in aristocratic contempt. "Since you can't leave your post, I'll do it."

He wrapped his arm around Merida's waist and pulled her away.

"Baryush?" she whispered.

"Dead."

"Well done." She glanced backwards. "Sirria and Naima didn't make it. Yora got away."

By now, panic should have set in, sending the soldiers running in a directionless frenzy like bees around a disturbed hive. Instead, they were calmly tearing down the burning tents. Even the discovery of Baryush's corpse did not send them into panic.

Dahoud stopped one of them. "Soldier, I need your torch."

He steered Merida towards the elephant enclosure.

Dahoud lifted Merida over the five-foot pine fence. It was all separating the camp from the great elephants. Monstrous shapes loomed, three or four times her height. Faced with a forest of legs as big as a man's body, her muscles quaked. Should the beasts stampede in the wrong direction, their feet would trample her to mush.

"Set the awning on fire," Dahoud instructed. "Elephants fear flames. Start at the earthworks, so they'll stampede right into the camp. Fence and tethers won't stop them."

She reached the torch to the reed awning, but the flame did not catch. When she waved the torch, the elephants stayed calm, their trunks draped lazily across the teeth. One flapped its ears, glanced back at Merida, snorted, and went back to sleep.

Since fire did not work, she had to try noise. She fished the finger cymbals out of her blouse, tied them on, and vibrated one pair between the other, the way Haurvatat had done, filling the air with a shrill, high pitched *Riiiiiiiiing.*

Elephant feet shuffled. The beasts bunched together, surged forward, ears back, tails raised. The fence crashed.

The persistent ring shrilled in Dahoud's head. Giant bodies thundered past him. Screams and sparks shot into the dark sky. Fleeing from the maddened elephants, soldiers spilled out of the gate, few of them armoured or armed.

For a terse moment, there was silence. Were Mansour's warriors in place for the ambush? Then came the twang of arrows and hiss of slings, followed by screams and victory yells. Dahoud nodded grimly: Mansour had allowed the refugees to run into the plain before attacking them. This delayed the survivors' return into the camp in search of weapons.

He snatched up the throwing spears the guards had left at the gate, ready to kill as many Darrians as he could before they killed him.

"Dahoud, Dahoud!" Yora came running, carrying a shield, followed by Merida with a tent pole.

He took the hide-covered shield. "Thanks, Yora. This will help. You two wait in the elephant enclosure. You'll be safe there until..."

Laughing, Yora tapped the sash at her waist. "I found fourteen throwing knives."

Merida raised the pole in her hand. "This makes a good longstaff. What's the strategy, and where do you want us?"

A wave of Darrian soldiers spilled into the gate.

No time to argue. He hurled the first spear. "We stop as many as we can from getting weapons. To the tower, Yora. When your knives are gone, throw what you find at the top." The second spear. "Merida, on my right."

Spears gone, he shifted the sword from his shield hand into his right, and readied himself for the onslaught. His legs threatened to buckle, but he was still alive. The veil of fatigue tore from his mind and fighting fever flowed through his veins, drowning the pain. He would fight for Koskara, would save his people, would prove he was a worthy Lord.

It was good to die fighting. He swung the sword in an immense figure eight. At his side, Merida crushed spears and skulls with expert skill.
Enemies fell, wounded, but more came, dozens of them. They could not
stop all of them. Before long, some would reach their weapons and
return armed.

From outside the gate, he heard hails for Mansour. The Koskarans
were starved, weakened and poorly armed, but fury-driven and primed
for battle. And they fought under a leader they loved.

Fierce yells rang in the dark, shouts of triumph and screams of terror.

"The light of freedom lies in our fighting hands!" Mansour's voice
bellowed above the din.

"Our hearts for Koskara!" Dahoud shouted in answer. Mansour
needed to know that he was alive, that he was fighting the enemy from
the other side. With Mansour attacking from the mountain side and
Dahoud from the camp, they would crush the Darrians.

With the fire of battle singing in his veins, he kept the sword going.
Slash, cut, slice. Around him, limbs fell, wounds gaped, blood spurted.

Flames prattled, horses whinnied and elephants trumpeted.

Clanking metal from behind alerted him that the real menace was
now in his back. Darrian soldiers were returning from the camp, no
longer helpless, but fully armed. If they reached the Koskarans, the
battle would turn. He must not let it happen.

He spun, leaving Merida and Yora to fight off the thinning mass off
returners.

He ducked under a mace meant to kill. The blow grazed his skull.
Bless Kirral's fat turban. Another delay for his death. Shutting out the
pain, he wiped the blood from his eyes and fought on. He must stop
them from reaching the Koskarans. His starved friends would stand no
chance against armed Darrian professionals.

Bronze clanked against bronze. But many got past him. The whack-
ing of wood against bone told him Merida was still standing and stop-
ping at least a few.

But the howls of terror and pain outside the gate told him that
mauling metal was tearing into Koskaran flesh.

Dahoud fought off one swordsman after another. Then a spear
came flying faster than he could push his shield. Pain zinged into his
side. His fighting time was almost over. Time to meet death's embrace.

"Mansour!" Yora screamed. "No!"

"Mansour!" Koskaran howls. "Mansour is down!"

With grim certainty, Dahoud knew he was the only leader left. Dying was no longer good enough: He had to survive for Koskara.

"Dahoud, Dahoud!" Merida shouted.

"Our hearts for Koskara!" he yelled, slashing and slicing through flesh like had never before. Enemy after enemy fell under his sword's biting fury.

⬿

The battle was over. The ground was sodden and churned with blood. The air stank of smouldering felt, stomach gasses, shit and blood.

Mansour was lying on his back, his torso and thighs studded with broken spears, blood pumping where his sword hand had been.

"Mansour, don't die!" Yora pleaded. "We're going to marry and then you'll wrestle me, won't you?"

Red foam bubbled from between Mansour's teeth. "I look forward to it."

Dahoud knelt in the puddle of Mansour's gore. "We won." His own thigh started bleeding again, the red mixing with that of his dying rival and friend. "Koskara is free."

Mansour struggled for breath. Blood seeped from his lips, and ran in rivulets down his chin, but his voice was loud and clear. "Lord Dahoud. Take—"

Death cut him off. His breath stopped. The eyes glassed.

Loud wails rang into the night.

Standing straight, Dahoud raised his arm in a gesture of command. "Put the fires out. Save the food, livestock, medicines. The supply tents are the grey ones by the—" Then the world swayed faster and faster, and he collapsed into Mansour's blood.

CHAPTER 42

Merida's Revenge

Dahoud rose as the sun's pink fingers reached across the mountain top. The town lay in night-cooled silence, the smell of siege suffering now mingled with stale wood smoke and the stink of burning flesh from recent pyres. After a war was won, people wanted to feast, get drunk and sleep. After four days of poppy-doused rest, Dahoud needed to set an example and start working, even with the pain still pulsing in his thigh.

Forcing his spine straight and his chin up, he checked the pile of rubble that should have been the healing school, the huddle of trussed captives, the heaps of spoils.

Merida, still with a limp, was dragging a ladder and a reed basket to the gates.

"Let me carry this." He shouldered the ladder. "What's the plan?"

"Clean up the gatehouse façade, make it look more welcoming. I've sent messengers to friendly nations, asking for aid. When the first emissaries arrive, do we want them to be greeted by skulls and curses?"

He held the ladder while she climbed to the top of the arch, where a painted skull promised death to those who dared enter. With a large flint, she scraped until brick dust showered.

"I had the corpses burnt, the captured weapons counted, and the perishable booty stored. I commissioned a bard to celebrate Mansour's honour and glory."

"Well done." He shifted the ladder so she could access another skull.

"There's much to do," Merida said. "Keera and I have been doing our best but—"

"Keera?" He frowned. "You allowed the traitor to stay?"

"She's the only surviving member of our council," Merida pointed out. "She'll make a good chief councillor."

He shook his head. "Keera's a snake without a shred of loyalty."

"Wrong. She's loyal to her ambition: to be chief councillor. Why not use her?"

Perhaps Merida was right. He might harness Keera with a temporary appointment, until he found someone he trusted more. But there were other matters requiring action first. "Are the Darrians still at Ain-Elnour? Then we must—"

"Ain-Elnour is free. Idrahad led an attack. The Darrians weren't prepared. They were fooled by the Darrian horses and uniforms, and panicked when Baryush's head was catapulted into their midst. According to Yora, the battle was quick and fun." She twisted on the ladder, leaning towards the west. "The buildings at Ain-Elnour are unharmed, also the trees. But the food stores are gone, the flocks slaughtered, the people deported into slavery. As for the rest of Koskara— it looks bleak."

"It always does, after war."

"This may be worse than you imagine. Koskara has been ravaged by two wars, the ongoing drought, the fire. The flocks are slaughtered, the pastures are spoilt, the people enslaved in the Darrian mines. I sent riders to assess the land and rally the survivors. Whatever the final picture, it will be worse than we can bear."

"And we're alone, without support or resources."

"Not necessarily. Teruma plans a Samil Empire."

Dahoud absorbed the news. The time was right for Teruma's coup: while the Quislaki nobles squabbled over the succession, the Samil states could secede.

"Teruma seems to have a lot of silver, although she doesn't say where it comes from. She offers to spend it to rebuild Koskaran towns, revive the herds, and buy back captives from Darrian slavery—as long as Koskara bows to Empress Teruma."

"Koskara needs to join a larger nation, or it will get crushed like a grain between millstones," Dahoud said. "Teruma is an ambitious schemer. But she's capable, benevolent, and sane—a great improvement over Kirral."

Merida piled the pale skulls she had gathered into an orderly heap. "We didn't find Kirral's remains in the burned tent."

Dahoud recalled the slashed straps of hide, haphazardly knotted together. "He's probably fled to Darria. As a refugee, he'll have less power than as a Consort, and less opportunity for mental abuse. Of course, now that Kirral is no longer a threat, you're free to return home."

He would miss Merida. Her resourcefulness, her counsel, her courage. Even her opinionated, stubborn haughtiness. But most of all, her camaraderie. That glimmer of cooperation during the sword practice, and again when they disabled Kirral. And now.

She said nothing, just looked at him, her brows raised, her gaze steady. Had he really once described those eyes as 'yellow'? They were pure amber, deep and rich.

He cleared his throat. "I'll give you travel funds and an armed escort."

"Thank you, that's kind." She did not move away, but looked at the gatehouse, as if talking to the newly-cleaned wall. "It doesn't have to be at once. I'll wait until it's convenient to spare an escort. Until then, I'll work for my keep, of course. If you want me." She rummaged through her basket. "What do you think about hanging tassel garlands around the gate? That will be more welcoming to visitors than death heads. Koskaran colours, scarlet and yellow. I brought some tassels, but not enough, there really ought to be hundreds."

"If you could stay for a while, that would be good." He talked in the direction of the gatehouse, too. "I mean, with so much work to do, if you could help out until I appoint new councillors. You know the ropes and what needs doing, and I trust you..." He shouldn't have said that. "I mean, I know you'll be honest and work hard."

She put down her basket. "I trust you, too."

He spun and stared. Their eyes locked. Joy surged through him, then disbelief. Both gave way reality: She was talking of trust in order to remind him to respect boundaries.

He pulled himself together. "While you're here, you'll be treated as a visiting diplomat. Ambassador of Riverland."

"Thank you." She held a garland towards the gatehouse. "What do you think? Something like this, but with bigger tassels, to create welcoming cheer?"

Contemplating the effect of the garland, she took a step back. Now she was standing so close the space between their arms was barely enough for a fly to pass through. She did not seem to notice. "I'll ask the Riverian government to send aid workers. Irrigation engineers, masons, healers."

"I'll see to their comfort and safety," he promised.

If they touched, would the same searing heat flow through them as before? If he moved closer, accidentally brushing his arm against her shoulder, would she step away, or stay still? Blood throbbed in his throat, in his ears, in his temples. She said she trusted him. To touch her was to violate this trust.

He cleared his throat. "I'll—"

"Have a look at the captives, and decide what to do about them."

He rubbed his eyes. Was Merida telling him what to do? He bit back a retort. Clearly, someone had had to take the reigns while he was incapable. As Lady of Koskara, she was regent by default, and she seemed to have done a good job. "I'll see to them at once."

≫

In the forum, five dozen trussed prisoners lay coiled, beaten by the merciless sun. Their stares pierced him, some beseeching, some hostile.

"Dahoud!" Yora danced up to them, plaits flying, hair beads sparkling, hands on knife hilts. "Merida wouldn't let us kill them until you were back. Can we use them for dagger practice before they wilt away?"

"They're valuable" Dahoud said. "Keep them alive and get them some shade."

She pushed her fists into her waist. She was wearing Mansour's fringed dagger belt. "Mansour would have wanted revenge," she declared with the authority of a grieving betrothed.

"Mansour put Koskara's needs before his own desires." Dahoud glanced over the blood-stained tunics and fettered limbs. "These are trained soldiers, worth more than mine slaves. We can trade them to free many of our own people."

"That woman then." Yora flicked a bangled wrist at a slight figure. "She's no warrior and not worth much."

Laleika lay curled around the pole, shading her head with her arms. Dahoud's skin sang with recalled agony, and his muscles tensed with the memory of her betrayal.

"She's worth a lot. The highest-skilled torturer of Darria. But I won't give her in trade."

At his side, Merida drew in a hissing breath.

'I should have killed you when I had you in my hands, you monster.' Laleika's voice sounded as sharp as a scalpel, intended to cut. Only the loudness of her tone revealed her fear. "I should have opened your wrists to let you bleed to death."

"Laleika. It's a pleasure to see you alive," Dahoud said.

Yora clapped her hands. "If she's your torturer, we'll make her last all day. Many days. You and I will take turns, throwing first at the fingers, then the hands, then the arms."

"How does this sound to you, Laleika?" Dahoud said. "Yora is the best dagger thrower in Koskara."

"You were a wimp." Laleika spat. "Shitting like a babe, pissing with fear."

He laughed at the obvious ruse: she hoped to provoke him into killing her fast. "My friend Naima was a healer. She admired your skill, although you held her in contempt. Now she's dead. The new Naima School of Healing will train healers. Will you be its head teacher?"

Laleika's face changed from defiance to disbelief. She tilted her head and glanced at him sideways. "You won't kill me?"

"Your skill is too valuable." He cut her fetters and marched away before he could change his mind.

Merida hurried after him, laid a hand on his arm. Her fingers felt cool. 'Why did you spare the torturer?" she asked softly.

Without looking at her, he shrugged. "If I'm to make a traitor chief councillor, why not have a torturer for healing?"

The fingers around his elbow tightened. "She was in your power."

He snapped the gate to his soul shut should before she could enter and wreak devastation. "You mentioned Teruma's silver. If she purloined from the Queendom treasury while she was head-wife, it's ours by right. The Queendom got rich by robbing the Samil."

She did not let his arm go. "I'm glad you spared the torturer. Thank you."

Perhaps she meant it. Perhaps he could allow her closer. Perhaps it was safe to let her see some of his secret. "I wanted to tie her to a rack and give her a taste of torture and make her fear me."

"The djinn wanted it?"

"The part of me I called the djinn," he said.

Her eyes widened. "The part of you you called the djinn?"

"It's part of me." He waited for her to back away. When she did not, he said, "I'm stronger now than the djinn. The torture has changed me... the torture, and Koskara, and Zun, and Mansour. And you."

She tilted her head, assessing him. "I see." Then her mouth took on a hard curve. "And that's it? You think because you may be strong enough to resist most of the time, you're safe to stay free?" Her stern eyes fixed his until he dropped his gaze. "You think you won't be punished?"

"Punished by whom? How?"

Her eyes glinted. "Gelding comes to mind. Or dropping you into an old mining shaft, so you live out your life without the chance to do harm." She kept assessing him as if he were an animal for sale and she was probing for flaws. "As for 'by whom', I'll show you something outside the citadel. Come."

He obeyed. What harm could a woman do to him? She led him down the narrow sloping track, her posture erect, her thick braids swinging on her back.

The cool grey of dawn was changing into bright gold with clear colours and precise shapes. Morning birds gurgled and chirped in the pines.

He followed her, careful to produce an even gait that did not hint at his pain in his legs and the turmoil in his heart. "Where are you taking me?"

"Are your wounds healed? Are you strong again? If attacked, would you be able to defend yourself?"

"Adequately. Why?"

The air hung thick with the scents of rosemary and pine. Cicadas trilled in the day's rising heat.

"Over there." She veered off the track to a plateau where in peace time, goats had grazed among rocks and juniper shrubs. "On reflection. I'm not certain that gelding would be a solution. The djinn might find a different way to use you. Nor could you rule Koskara from the bottom of a mine shaft. Yet you must be punished." A smile curved around her lips. Her voice grew soft and dangerous. "For what you did to me, and for everything you did to every woman you abused."

Dahoud's heart pounded against his ribcage. "How would you—"

Her shin slammed into the back of his knee. He staggered. She jumped, snapped her legs around his waist, and pulled him to the ground. Her weight pressed on his back. His arms were jerked up onto her thighs, and her hands locked around his chin.

"Like this." She tightened the hold until his shoulders hurt. "Though this is only the beginning. Would you like to guess what else I'll do?"

His heart galloped. She loosened her grasp around his chin, giving him just enough freedom to ask "Revenge?" It came out as 'Rffffff.'

"Yes, revenge. But that's not all." She jerked his head sharply, squeezed her legs tighter, and increased the pull on his shoulders. Pain tore through his arms. "As a matter of symmetry, I'm going to right marital wrongs by enforcing marital rights. Do you understand what I mean?"

A flash of heat scorched his insides. His pulse pounded, his breath came pained and panting. Sharp rocks and bristly grasses poked into his back. Then she released his neck.

At once, his skill asserted itself. He reached back to grab her and break out of the familiar hold. She eased up her legs for long enough for him to turn, and at once straddled him, her thighs around his sides.

She laughed down at him. "If you resist, it will be much more fun for me."

The heat of understanding fired his face. She could not mean to ravish him. Could she? Was his wild dream about to come true?

"I'm going to do to you what you did to me. In every possible detail."

Do it, do it, he wanted to beg. Instead, his cautious, sane self prevailed. "Yes, but..."

Her bare arms, freckled and tanned, held him pinned. Her hot weight shifted closer to his groin. "But?"

"People can see us from the parapet. Let's go into the wood."

"What a lovely suggestion." Her amber eyes glinted with mischief. "For another time. For today, spectators are welcome. Five thousand can watch what I'm doing to you."

Dahoud threw himself into the fight, his skill and muscle more than a match for her boldness. Shivers of wanting ran through him as the djinn painted pictures of the pleasures of rape: He could hold her pinned under his weight, assert his dominance, teach her to fear and to weep. But for once, a greater joy might be his: the measuring of his strength and will against this woman.

For several long heartbeats, their eyes locked, and he knew she trusted him to honour her rules. The risk she took was immense. He relaxed his grip, allowed her to roll to the top.

The relief in her smile rewarded him. Her fingers brushed a caress across his cheek and sent his senses spinning. He smelled the scents of crushed young grass and fresh female sweat. His strength made her pant with effort of keeping him down. Desire shot through him with yellow hunger, and the feigned duress gave him permission to enjoy.

A sharp edge scratched the side of his neck.

"Careful now." The kind concern in her voice mingled with calm control. "I have a knife and I don't want to hurt you. Try to relax. If you lie still, it won't hurt much."

Symmetry. What he had done to her... But something more precious than punishment was at stake. It was about expiating his sins and purging his guilt and being wanted at last. If he gave her the power. If he dared to submit. If he trusted her not to abuse his gift.

Women always used him, then threw him away.

Rrratch. The front of his tunic tore.

She halted, her loins two finger-breadths above his. "Don't you need someone to help control the djinn? Someone to control you? Someone strong?" Her fingers danced tenderly across his skin, trailed down his chest, raising goosebumps despite the heat. "Don't you think that should be me?"

He lost himself in the intimacy, his head spinning, his heart thudding, his skin singing under Merida's touch. The djinn had no power because Merida cared.

For the first time in his life, Dahoud gave in. "I surrender."

[end]

Acknowledgements

Sincere thanks to my critique partners who have helped me shape Storm Dancer from its awkward beginnings into the finished book. You know who you are.

My gratitude also goes to the everyone who contributed their experiences and their expertise—on firefighting, horses, warfare, medical treatments and many other matters—to make this story authentic. You, too, know who you are.

The fabulous cover illustration is a collaboration between Paul Davies (*www.pdportraits.co.uk*) and Erica Syverson (*www.komicks.com*).

Dear Reader,

If you've enjoyed this novel, I'll be thrilled if you review it at Amazon.com, Amazon.co.uk, Barnes and Noble, Smashwords, Goodreads, or any other site. Let me know if you spot any typos or formatting oddities, so I can fix them.

You can contact me by email *rayne_hall_author@yahoo.com*. My website is *sites.google.com/site/raynehallsdarkfantasyfiction*. If you follow me on Twitter *@raynehall* and tweet me that you've read *Storm Dancer*, I'll follow you back.

Rayne Hall

Other Recent Books by Rayne Hall
(e-books)

The Colour of Dishonour - Stories from the Storm Dancer World
Six Scary Tales Vol 1
Six Scary Tales Vol 2
Six Scary Tales Vol 3
Six Quirky Tales Vol 1
Six Historical Tales Vol 1
Thirteen British Horror Stories (e-book and print)

Multi-Author Anthologies edited by Rayne Hall
(e-books)

Haunted: Ten Tales of Ghosts
Bites: Ten Tales of Vampires
Cutlass: Ten Tales of Pirates
Scared: Ten Tales of Horror
Beltane: Ten Tales of Witchcraft
Spells: Ten Tales of Magic
Undead: Ten Tales of Zombies

5296337R00253

Printed in Great Britain
by Amazon.co.uk, Ltd.,
Marston Gate.